1973 $1.

SO-ATM-433

Tomorrow
Will Be Monday

ELEANOR, Martha, and Penny King, though sisters, grow up in separate households, their lives linked yet completely individual. This intimate novel about them shows the three ways in which women can work out their own destinies in today's world.

Eleanor, charming and serene, becomes the successful wife of a successful businessman. Yet beneath the comfort and tranquillity of her outward life are frustration and incompleteness.

Penny, as greedy as she is breath-takingly beautiful, decides that she will take anything she wants from the world. In return she gives nothing, not even honest passion. Her reward is contempt and dislike from those she believes to be her friends.

Martha is a talented, common-sense girl who makes a reputation as a teacher and writer before she marries Bill Knight—and discovers that, once married, a woman's life is no longer her own.

How each of these sisters solves her own problem in her own way is the theme of this provocative novel by an author already successful in another field of fiction. Mrs. Marlett's story is a warm and human narrative of women in search of fulfillment in a world in which women's responsibilities have enlarged along with their opportunities.

Books by
MELBA MARLETT

Tomorrow Will Be Monday

Escape While I Can

Another Day Toward Dying

The Devil Builds a Chapel

Death Has a Thousand Doors

Tomorrow
Will Be Monday

MELBA MARLETT

WILDSIDE PRESS

Tomorrow Will Be Monday

Copyright © 1946, 1973 by Melba Marlett
All rights reserved.

Published by Wildside Press LLC
wildsidepress.com | bcmystery.com

For ALMA BALMAT GRIMES, my mother

Tomorrow
Will Be Monday

As Tommy Snooks and Bessie Brooks
Were walking out one Sunday,
Said Tommy Snooks to Bessie Brooks,
"Tomorrow will be Monday."

Mother Goose

1.

Old Mrs. Edwards—she was sixty-two, and her son's wife living in Cleveland a hundred miles away was Young Mrs. Edwards—slid the pie into the oven and went to stand behind the ecru curtains in the reception hall to watch her granddaughter come home from school. It wasn't a question of seeing that she got across the streets; Martha was twelve now. It was because she had suddenly realized that the youngster had no friends, that no other child had been in the Edwards house for more than two years now, that Martha had not gone to a party since heaven knew when. Oh, she saw her two sisters almost every day, and maybe that was enough for her, maybe she didn't want any more. Still, Mrs. Edwards had thought she would watch and find out for herself whether Martha was alone through the other children's choice or her own. Either way, it wasn't good for her.

It was worrisome, bringing up a child two generations away from you. Martha was a good girl, a wonderful girl, but she didn't behave like any child Mrs. Edwards had ever seen. Always had her nose in a book, always was making up little plays that she acted out herself, never seemed to miss the shouting and laughter of the other children. It wasn't that she was cold and unaffectionate either. Quite the contrary. The things, the people she loved, she cared for with a quiet intensity that was surprising. Martha's younger sister, now, nine-year-old Penelope, rushed about telling everyone how much she adored them and everyone was flattered and believing, not noticing that she never did a thing to prove it. The oldest sister, Eleanor, was turning into a snob and couldn't like anyone who wasn't Somebody. And here was Martha, the only honestly sympathetic one of the three, doing everything she could to be a good child, making her little sacrifices as a matter of course, content in return just to be tolerated. And, outside of her family and teachers, she seemed to be just that.

Perhaps the child shouldn't be living alone with an old woman. Perhaps she should be with her father and her sisters. There hadn't seemed to be much choice about it, though, four years ago, when

Norah Edwards King had died of a ruptured appendix, leaving her husband with three young daughters to raise. Jason was a good man—which, in Ashland, meant that he didn't drink or "run around"—but he was not equal to the job and he knew it.

He had come to see his mother-in-law two days after the funeral, and, though the day was sultry, they had sat in the parlor rather than on the airy front porch. Traditionally grief was supposed to shun light and air.

"Well, Mother," he had said heavily, "what am I going to do?"

"I've been trying to think of a good housekeeper for you. I know plenty who could do the work, but I don't know one I'd like to trust the girls to."

"Mrs. Saunders says she'll stay on, just coming in by the day, of course." Mrs. Saunders was a widow who "worked out," a respectable, homely woman who spoke bad English and laughed in a high cackle.

"That's well enough as far as it goes."

She had known this moment was coming and she had steeled herself against it. She was not going to take in three girls, aged twelve, eight, and five, to mother at her difficult time of life. She simply wasn't able, not any more.

But, looking at Jason, his rumpled suit, his shoulders grown round from bending over an accountant's desk, his pale sad eyes, she was sorry for him. That's why her Norah had married him in the first place, she guessed: she had been sorry for him too and had turned down beaux from three counties to take him. Well, Jason might be able to quote whole pages of Shakespeare, but he didn't have any getup or push to him. Old Mrs. Edwards had said that he would never get anywhere, and he hadn't. He'd die at that desk in the shop office.

"I'll tell you what, Jason, it looks as though you're going to have to split up your family for a while. Your aunt Ann might take Eleanor. She's crazy about her, and the girl's old enough not to be much trouble. I'd take Martha. She's more my style. And Penelope goes to school full days now. Maybe you could keep her at home with you, if Mrs. Saunders would keep an eye on her from the time school lets out until you get home. You'd be too lonesome if you didn't keep one of them."

So, simply, it had been arranged, and, now after four years, she could see the dangers of the order that necessity had wrought. Eleanor was becoming a mannerly mannequin, just like her great-aunt Ann; Penelope, having cozened Mrs. Saunders into submission, was running wild all over town; and Martha was turning into a little old woman. She's with me too much, thought Mrs. Edwards, and I love her too well to push her away. I must get over that. I must find some way to turn her outward to face the world. I must not use her fire to warm my old bones.

Through the lacy screen she saw the school children, the first wave of them, surging down the sidewalk from the top of the hill.

Martha King always walked down Linden Avenue to her grandmother's house by herself, moving with the crowd yet remote from it, a bluebird with a flock of robins. In truth she was a different breed. She had no childish attributes. She was not cruel, or vain, or ignorant, or afraid. Her twelve-year-old mind, fed by the hundreds of books she had already read and loved, was acute, sophisticated, cosmopolitan. Her ethical principles, modeled on her grandmother's, included dignity, reserve, good manners, and democratic behavior as matters of course.

Only her body was a child's. Her chief despair was that it remained so short and stocky, and never yet had she looked into a mirror long enough to see that she had a beautiful head. Yellow curls, a fine brow, vaulting eyebrows unexpectedly dark, expressive blue eyes, the straight classic nose so rarely found, a curved mouth, a round, firm chin with a slight cleft in it. The face had a thoughtful, a listening look. No sidewise glances, no little entrancements of curl and dimple, no head-tossings. Minerva rather than Venus. An adult imprisoned in a child's body, and her schoolmates had smelled it out and avoided her as they avoided other grownups.

She did not know the reason for her isolation, but she had long ago discovered that she did not know what to say to other children nor how to behave to please them. She had thought that being two grades ahead of her age group in school had something to do with it, that she had fallen down the canyon that lies between chronology and ability. Whatever the explanation, she accepted the fact and adjusted herself to it.

Ordinarily she was happy. She had the whole Carnegie Library to draw upon, and she had Grandmother. The two of them gardened together, wrinkled hands and smooth turning down the dark soil. As

3

the sun went down they often paced the yard, yellow curls and white pompadour, admiring their handiwork.

"The delphinium will be extra nice this year."

"The nasturtiums are so gay, Grandmother. I think I like them better."

"They're buggy things though."

Sometimes they sat on the porch swing in the twilight, watching the moon come up while the streetcars rumbled by on the half hour, and the honeysuckle spilled fragrance over them.

"Sing something, Grandmother."

"Heavenly days, child, I've sung those old songs a thousand times. You know them better than I do."

"Then tell about the time the cow went visiting." Or "Tell how this town was forty years ago." Or "Talk about you and Grandpa."

And Grandmother would fold her hands and swing gently and talk. Grandpa Edwards had been a lawyer, the best in town. It was his desk that was up in Martha's room now.

"My, I was impressed with him the first time I saw him," Grandmother would say. "Such a good-looking young man with such a fine horse and buggy. He'd been to college—that was rare in those days— and he was the best catch in town. I never thought he'd look at me, little homebody that I was."

"But you were awfully pretty."

"Well, I was far from ugly, and that was lucky, because my looks were all I had. I didn't know much, except how to read and write and cook and crochet. Schooling wasn't a usual thing for girls those days, and Father didn't see any sense in my going on to high school. Anyway, I had a lot of younger brothers and sisters and Mother needed all the help she could get from me. She didn't get too much at that, for I married when I was seventeen."

"Did Grandpa mind your not knowing anything? What did the two of you talk about?"

"There wasn't much time for talking, and that's a fact. The babies came along right away and I had my hands full with them. Two of them died young, but I raised the other two. Then his mother had a stroke and came to live with us. I had to wait on her hand and foot for seventeen years before she died, and it wasn't easy. She was the crankiest woman I ever met, and many's the time I nearly told her so! I'm glad now I didn't. It wouldn't have done any good."

4

"And didn't you have any fun, ever?"

"Women weren't supposed to have fun in those days. People didn't think that way then. A woman was supposed to find pleasure in doing her duty, and that was all there was to it. For years I couldn't find a minute to read a book, even. When I did sit down there was always mending and sewing and knitting to do. Hard work and sleep and hard work again. That was about all there was to it. And sometimes the sleep was hard to get. Mother Edwards slept most of the day so she was usually restless at night."

"I'd have made Grandpa get up and wait on her!"

"Oh no, you wouldn't! A man was supposed to get a good night's rest, no matter what. And unless his wife was awful sick she was expected to keep on her feet and keep going. That's why we were all old women at forty."

"You're not old. You'll never be old."

"Well, I've had a rest for the last fifteen years, since Grandpa's been gone."

"You do an awful lot. The house and the garden——"

"It's not a tenth of what I used to have to do. And there's no strain about it. I can take my time and sit down whenever I've a mind to. That suits me fine. I always was an independent one, too much so maybe. Yes, life's finer now than it ever was before. If I had known way back then what I know now I'd have done the whole thing differently."

"How would you?"

"I'd have run away from home if I had to and taken a job somewhere. Then, when I had enough money, I'd have gone to school, learned to be a teacher maybe."

"And would you have married Grandpa?"

"I don't know whether I'd have married or not. Keeping up a house and minding children isn't what it's cracked up to be. A woman's better off single, if she isn't the kind that'll get into a corner and cry the minute she finds out she's alone."

"But then you wouldn't have had me."

Grandmother would stroke the curls gently. "No, then I wouldn't have had you. And you'll have a much better life than I had, I'm going to see to that. You're going to the university when you're old enough. You're going to be able to stand on your own two feet and not have to take any back talk from anybody, man or devil."

5

Between Grandmother's reminiscing and the books from the Carnegie Library, Martha felt as though she were living in a story. In her mind she played with the words that could best describe the tale's continuity: "The moon was a white full-blown rose on the starry trellis when Martha King kissed her grandmother good night and climbed the golden-oak stairs to her room. She did not turn on a light immediately, because she liked to watch the shadows of the maple leaves outside work themselves into the floral pattern of the wallpaper. Anyway, it was not a night for going to bed sensibly. It was a night for white chargers and scaled battlements and a love song heard faintly in the distance." That expressed it pretty well. Perhaps the moon metaphor was a bit forced. She could tell better if it were written down. And "love song . . . in the distance" sounded as though she were hungry for romance instead of anxious for a little music.

The mental word game was her greatest diversion. It was best played alone, for it required concentration, and as the mind corrected itself into accuracy difficult backgrounds and characters could be etched briefly and vividly at a few seconds' notice. Right now she was telling herself the story of walking home from school: "The blue, the red, the green sweaters went on by, the navy-blue coats, the scuffed shoes, the coltish, springing legs; the shrill young voices died away, leaving a trembling in the air behind them, as a calliope does; the maples held their Gothic arch over the subsequent quiet of the sunlit street, empty now except for an afternoon caller hurrying home to put the steak into the frying pan before the shops let out. By five the town would be redolent with the smell of coffee brewed in granite coffeepots and meat turning brown in richly bubbling butter." She nodded to herself. The comparison with the calliope was good, and the cooking smells gave you the texture of Ashland, population twenty-five thousand, Kiwanis Club luncheon Wednesday noon, everybody welcome.

But now she had to stop the word game. Grandmother's house was only four doors away, and she had to act. By a hundred small signs she had known that Grandmother was worrying about her, wishing that she would like other girls her own age. She would have to show Grandmother that all was well.

She ran a few steps and caught up with three girls who were strolling ahead of her. She knew them, for they were in her grade, though she had never spoken to them outside of school before.

"Did one of you lose a blue handkerchief?" she asked.

6

She walked with them while they examined their belongings and discovered that they had not.

"Well, if you hear of anyone who has, I left it on Mrs. Barnes's desk. It was an awfully pretty one. I found it out on the playground."

They were momentarily diverted. When she stopped at her gate they paused too, while she described the handkerchief in detail. From the house it must look as though she were a member of a friendly and interested circle, she knew.

She waved them a warm good-by and turned in between the two white iron posts. Immediately her mind was back at the game: "The last they saw of her each day was when she turned off Linden Avenue between the iron posts that marked the Edwards place. Her dark blue skirt and middy moved up the sun-dappled walk and the screen door closed quietly behind her. That was the end of her as far as the grade-schoolers were concerned."

She knew she had succeeded in deceiving Grandmother the minute she saw the relieved smile on the pink, lined face.

"How did things go today, Martha?"

"Fine. I walked home with a bunch from my room. They wanted to come in, but I told them I was going to go down to the corner to meet Dad when he went by."

"You should have asked them in. You can go over to your father's any time."

"I wanted to talk to him about tomorrow. He's taking us all to the movie, but I get to choose it because it's my birthday."

"There's a pie for supper. Don't be late."

Old Mrs. Edwards felt better. Looking down into the lovely bright face, looking after the short, sturdy legs hurrying down the walk, she knew that she had been overanxious. Things would straighten themselves out all right. Martha was only a little girl after all.

Eleanor King smiled at her great-aunt over the tea service between them. "I'll have to run down and meet Daddy in ten minutes," she said. "Penny came over to say that he wants to see me, that he has something to tell me. It sounds awfully important, but you know how she exaggerates."

"Not 'awfully,' dear. 'Very.'"

"*Very* important. Thank you, Aunt Ann."

"I don't like to have you out on the street alone. However, since it's broad daylight and you're meeting your father, I dare say it will be all right. The dress you have on is suitable."

Eleanor sipped her tea daintily and thought how different a girl she had become in the last four years. At first she had resented Aunt Ann's constant correction and supervision of her every smallest activity, for she had had a healthy young temper and two younger sisters to order about. The whole first year she had been with Aunt Ann she had raged and stormed and wept, refusing to let herself be molded into her aunt's conception of Perfect Young Gentlewoman. Aunt Ann was ladylike but firm; the pressure was gentle but constant. Eleanor had responded at first unwillingly, and later, gladly. She found that it was convenient to know the proper thing to do and say on every occasion. It saved having to think and wonder and be awkward. By this time she reacted automatically to her aunt's smallest suggestion, and her temper was already buried beneath layers of conventional lacquer.

"Thank you for the tea," she said. "It was delicious."

"Don't be late for dinner, will you? After all, you're almost sixteen now. Not an age to dawdle in the streets."

"I'll come right back, dear."

She caught the flicker of satisfaction on her aunt's face at her polite response. She was progressing.

Martha was already at their usual corner, and Eleanor's clear gray eyes fastened on her with disapproval.

"You certainly don't get any taller, Martha, or any thinner either."

"I'm not short and fat because I want to be." Martha had found that it paid to be spirited with Eleanor these days. The chief defect with being a perfect lady was that you had to back away from strength of opinion and vehemence of expression, since they were undignified. It amused her to see Eleanor casting about to restore congeniality.

"You're not exactly fat. You'll probably grow out of it, if you ever grow. You're—let's see—twelve tomorrow. You'd better start soon."

Martha tugged at a sleeve with impatience. It was so seldom she had Eleanor alone and there was one fascinating topic on which Eleanor could speak with authority.

"Tell about high school, Eleanor."

"There's not much to tell. It's a deadly bore. When I'm eighteen, Aunt Ann says, I'm to go to finishing school. That'll be more like it."

8

"Oh, stop looking tired and tell!"

Eleanor told, and Martha's mind spun wonderful pictures. Eleanor in white lace with a corsage of roses at her waist, whirling and dipping at the Junior Prom. Eleanor walking down the hall with three boys to carry her books. Eleanor handing a perfect paper to the mathematics teacher with an airy gesture. High school must be wonderful, high school would be a haven except for, maybe, one small reef.

She attempted to gauge that reef now. "Do you think boys will ever ask me anywhere, Eleanor?"

The taller sister, pleased and warmed at having been so credible a heroine, was lenient. "Oh, I should think so. Not at first; you'll be there this fall, and you're only a baby! It's going to be a little embarrassing, being three and a half years older than you and only one year ahead of you in school."

"I can't help it. They keep promoting me. I'm glad, in a way, because grade school work is so easy that there's no fun in doing it. High school's a lot harder, isn't it?"

"It won't be hard for you. If I were you I'd stop reading so many books and get out and get some exercise. Boys don't like smart girls."

"Why don't they? I like smart boys."

"Well, it's all right to be smart. I am, myself, but I don't let it show when they're around. Boys like to feel big and clever and brave, and how can they unless somebody plays up to them and says, 'Oh, my goodness, did you really?'"

Martha's sense of fairness was outraged. "But *anybody* likes to feel big and clever and brave. Why couldn't a boy help *you* feel that way, instead of you always——"

"When you get older you'll understand."

"I bet I won't," said Martha. "I bet I never understand it. And, if I did, I wouldn't stand around and pretend to be feeble-minded when I wasn't. He can like me the way I am or he doesn't have to like me at all."

Eleanor sighed. It was so hard to explain things to Martha.

The five o'clock whistle blew and Jason King reached for his straw hat. He joined one of the long lines shuffling out the gates, his white collar and clean clothes making him conspicuous in the procession. Most of the shopmen wore serviceable dark clothes, their hands and faces were blackened, they swung their lunch buckets wearily in one hand and touched their hats to the people they knew with the other. Jason did not feel superior. Plenty of these men made more than he did and managed better with it too. The dirt and old clothes were necessities. These men would go home, wash and shave, put on clean clothes, eat their suppers and sit on their front porches, smoking their pipes and talking with their families. They owned property, they had bank accounts and insurance, their children could go to college if they wanted to and need never see the inside of a shop.

From a long way down the hill he could see his two daughters waiting for him. Brilliant, honest Martha. Gentle, courteous Eleanor. And at home there would be Penny, the loveliest child in the whole town. He was a lucky man to have three such daughters. Not a second-rater among them. All the best of their kind. But Norah had been a wonderful woman. It was not surprising that her daughters should be out of the ordinary.

This was the hour of the day when he had missed Norah most. For a long time after she died he could not lose the feeling that, somehow, when he opened the front door, she would be there, bustling and busy, but her smile always bright for him. It had taken him a long time to get over missing her. Her daughters were but fragments of her: Penny had her beauty, Eleanor her refinement, Martha her bright, flashing wit. But Norah had had all those things together. How fabulously lucky he had been to have such a wife!

But a man had to be practical. There was more to life than tender memories, unfortunately. A man needed, more than ever as he grew older, a companion, someone his own age to talk to, someone who would share his small successes, break the impact of his disappointments. By himself, he was no great hand at making friends, for he was a quiet man and shy. He needed someone to break the social ground for him, someone who could extend the hospitality of his house and accept invitations for the two of them. He had decided to marry again, and he did not know how to tell his two older girls.

His greeting was too hearty. "Two of you!" he exclaimed. "I'm unduly flattered this evening."

Something's on his mind, thought Martha instantly.

"I came to remind you about tomorrow afternoon," she said. "I've picked the movie I want to see. It's Thomas Meighan in *The Miracle Man*."

"Good. Fine. Lucky your birthday comes on a Saturday this year

10

and I can get off. After the show we'll go to the ice-cream parlor and you can have whatever you want."

"Grandmother's going to have dinner for us all. My cake is chocolate, three layers high."

"I'll come to the show," said Eleanor, "but I'm afraid I'll have to miss the dinner. I have an engagement. Sue Manning asked me to a party ages ago."

"Well, we can't blame you for going, can we, Martha?"

It's something awful, whatever it is, Martha told herself. He's being so gay and walking so fast. I can't stand not knowing. It makes me worry and my stomach gets all sick. Why doesn't he come out with it?

Penny rushed to meet them in the last block and threw herself at her father. "Have you told them, Daddy? Have you?"

He patted her copper ringlets and kept his head down. "You haven't given me time, sweet. It's not the sort of thing you discuss on the street."

"I can't come in, Dad. Aunt Ann expects me to be home by——"

"Well then." His eyes pleaded with them. His mouth tried to smile carelessly. "I'm going to marry Mrs. Saunders next month. I don't need to tell you that she won't take your mother's place in my feelings or yours. She doesn't expect to. But she's a good woman, and it'll be easier for Penny here."

Eleanor voiced the great question: "Does that mean that Martha and I will be coming home?"

"I hoped you would, but I won't insist. I know you're used to your new homes and you're happy where you are. We're within walking distance of each other. We'll see each other every day, just as usual. Won't we?"

Eleanor was standing off, but Martha grabbed her arm and pulled her into the hug she gave her father. She sounded happy and reassuring for the two of them. "Of course we will, Daddy. Oh, that's wonderful for you, isn't it? She's always been so very nice to all of us. Tell her to come along tomorrow and help eat my birthday cake. We might as well start breaking her into the family."

He was grateful and relieved. His shoulders, as he walked into his little house with Penny prancing beside him, were straighter than they had been for a long time.

"Well, I don't see that this makes any difference to us," said Eleanor. "We don't have to live with her."

Martha was trying to keep her mind on the sidewalk. Why did the cement kind always crack and the brick kind get so uneven? Somebody ought to invent a good sidewalk.

"No, it won't make much difference. Daddy's been kind of lonesome, I guess, and she does laugh a lot."

Eleanor shuddered. "I'll say she does!"

"The main thing is that he's happy." She stopped at the curb. "I'm going to slip over to the library, Eleanor, and get some books to read for this evening. You go on by yourself."

That revealed nothing to Eleanor. She didn't know that a book was the best poultice for sorrow that Martha could find.

Penny drew her napkin through the ring that had her name on it and asked to be excused.

"We're just going to play hide-and-seek around here, Daddy."

"Well, you be in at eight o'clock."

"Oh, Daddy, it isn't even dark at eight!"

Mrs. Saunders laughed, admiring the bronze curls, the antic mouth, the coaxing velvet eyes. "Let her go, Jason. I'll call her in when it's time."

Penny snuggled against the gaunt shoulders. "You're an angel! I'm going to love having you for a mother."

She rushed out of the room and the two middle-aged people smiled. "She's only young once, Jason. Let her have her head a little. She's going to be a beauty, anyone can see that. She'll show this town a thing or two. I was never pretty myself, and I've known what it was to miss it. But this one of yours, she'll make them sit up and take notice."

Beaming, they congratulated each other on Penny.

Across town, where the houses and lawns were larger, Aunt Ann sat stiffly in her chair and ate her small portions meticulously.

"Of course, what your father does is his own business. He needn't expect that I'm going to tolerate your seeing more of that woman than mere politeness demands, however. He can't force her down my throat, and I dare say he won't try. I haven't much of my money left, but I have enough to see that you get the background you need to marry well. And Mrs. Saunders will not be part of that background."

"I wish Daddy hadn't told us. I'm all upset, and John Kendrick is coming over tonight to help me with my geometry."

Aunt Ann's eyes made obeisance to the name. The Kendrick family owned one of the shops. "That's very nice. I'll sit in the library and you can have the parlor. Doors open, of course, so he'll know you're properly chaperoned. At ten I'll serve hot chocolate for all of us. Wear your gray and don't giggle."

"I'm much more apt to argue with him. He's so terribly bossy."

"A lady does not argue with a gentleman, my dear. She keeps her opinions to herself until they are asked for."

"Anyone's opinion would wait a long time before John asked for it."

"That's a very good sign in a young lad. It shows initiative and self-reliance. I've heard Mr. Kendrick say that, of all his children, he thinks John will be the most successful."

"Well, I'm not going to bow and scrape to him just because he's going to be a success!"

"There's no need for bowing and scraping, but I do expect you to be polite to him while he is a guest in your home. Don't combat his dominating traits; be aloof from them. Smile and keep quiet. That's not only good manners, it lends a touch of mystery besides. That's very desirable in a woman."

"You mean, keep him guessing?"

Aunt Ann shuddered at the phrase. "There was a saying when I was a girl, that, though vulgar, had a great deal of truth in it: 'Anger and pride are both unwise; vinegar never catches flies.' Brashly expressed opinions are not worth the friendships they might lose for you."

Eleanor sighed and put her napkin on the table. "I'll try. If only I can get over wanting to slap his face the minute I see him, I'll be all right."

At ten o'clock Martha put down her book and kissed her grandmother. "I'd better go to bed. I'll have so many things to do tomorrow."

She had not wept. She had given no sign that grief lay inside her like a stone. All evening her mind had skirted the emotion, examining, probing, gauging its extent, but the sorrow remained; there was no hauling it away in grains of cool reason. She told herself that she was silly, that nothing in her life would actually change with her father's new marriage. The only thing was that it made Mother seem so far away, so long dead, so definitely absent from the world. Crying won't help, she told herself fiercely; crying's no good at all. It'll just make Grandmother feel bad. I'm not going to cry.

Grandmother took off her glasses, polished them on her handkerchief. "You'll be glad of this one day, Martha. It's good for your father to have someone his own age to turn to. He'll have a companion for the rest of his life, and you girls won't have to feel that he's lonesome or neglected later on when you marry and move away. Mrs. Saunders is all right. She's not like your mother, but that's all right again. Your father's waited a long time."

Martha tried to make her smile convincing. "Oh, I don't mind at all. I think it will be fine. I asked him to bring her along to my birthday dinner tomorrow."

"That was right and proper. I'm glad you did. Once people have made up their minds to do a thing, might as well take it cheerfully."

For an hour after the girl was in bed old Mrs. Edwards sat in her rocker, hands folded in her lap. Give the child a chance to cry, if she has to, she thought. By tomorrow she'll have herself in hand again, and nobody, not even I who am closest to her, will be able to guess how she really feels about this. She's strong, stronger than I, stronger than her mother. She takes worry better than most grownups right now. The world will never get on top of Martha; she'll keep it under her feet, where it belongs. Amazing, the way she can discipline herself. With that one quality and that miraculous brain of hers, there isn't anything in the world beyond her reach. Because that's what genius is, isn't it? Superior native ability and the self-discipline to order and control it.

Her dead daughter smiled down at her from the far wall. Norah had been intelligent, too, and had an education and had been beautiful besides. And in one moment she had thrown away everything she could be, in order to live with a little accountant, doing his wash, mending his clothes, bearing his children. What a waste, when so fine a woman submerged herself in so mediocre a man! Yet it had not been a complete failure, for here was Martha. Out of all Norah's tragic futility had come a cool, firm answer that the world might someday hear. Martha.

2.

Eleanor King was graduated from high school in June 1923. The word *"laude"* appeared nowhere on her diploma, but the two girls who did achieve that distinction would have traded it for the special page in the high school annual on which Eleanor's picture looked out from under the caption: "Voted the Most Stylish Girl and Best Conversationalist in the Class, Eleanor King Also Ranks Fifth on the List of Class Beauties." Even the local photographer, with his penchant for thin-lipped, dead-eyed smiles, had been unable to disguise the smooth shine of her chestnut hair, the cool patrician lines of her face.

Nor could the dress she had chosen to wear change the essence of her appearance. It was her best street dress—Aunt Ann had said, "You don't want your bare shoulders in a picture *anyone* can look at by just paying fifty cents"—and it was the height of the currently ugly style. The top was a Paisley silk of reds and blues on light tan, and attached to it just above the widest circumference of the hips was a light tan accordion-pleated skirt that went down to a few inches above her ankles. The whole thing hung loosely from her shoulders, concealing her high firm bust, ignoring her slender waist. There was a braided leather belt in blue, but it marked nothing but the juncture of the skirt and top. Her slim ankles were covered with dark clocked silk, her shoes were Oxfords with raised heels. She looked tall and composed with no hint of sedateness. Her poise was rather that of the arrow at the bowstring, waiting the pull of the archer to speed her straight to her mark.

Aunt Ann, more frail these days than ever, was still the archer. For seven years now Eleanor had come home from school and gone directly into the sitting room where her great-aunt sat over a silver tea service. The ritual would begin.

"My dear," Aunt Ann's small, high voice would say, dropping each word into its exact niche of mental and emotional content, "you're a little late."

A kiss on the white, fragrant hair. The offer to pour. The sitting down, erect but not stiffly so, ankles crossed, hands pretty in the lap, in the chair across the tea table. "I know. I'm sorry. I stopped for a soda with John."

Aunt Ann smiled and handed her a cup. "That was nice. Not at McCaskey's?"

McCaskey's was the place where most of the high school crowd went. It was big and bare and noisy and smelled of fruit syrups and cream. There was a back room with a Victrola and Mr. McCaskey didn't mind if you played his records and danced to them, even if you spent only ten cents an hour. Aunt Ann said McCaskey's was common.

"No, we went to Kernson's."

Aunt Ann patted her mouth with her napkin, her diamond clusters in their old-fashioned gold settings flashing in the late afternoon sun. Those rings were to be Eleanor's when Aunt Ann was dead. The old woman prized them above her every other possession. At night, in her sleep, she sometimes hid them under the mattress or in the drawer of the bedside table, and there would be a tense search for them before breakfast. There had been times when those rings were all that had kept Aunt Ann's chin up in the face of her neighbors and misfortune and despair, and now that her arrantly unsuccessful marriage was long since over and her unhappy and turbulent husband dust in the Emmons cemetery plot for thirty years, the small twinkling stones were the only things that proved to her that she had not thrown away her life completely. Of their giver she thought not at all. It would have been a distasteful effort to her to recall the black-haired, warmhearted lover who had turned into an insurance man who drank too much. She had forgotten the feel of his arm about her waist and the tickling of his lips on the nape of her neck. Instead she evaluated her marriage thus: item, two diamond rings; item, a brief trip to Europe; item, a house, old-fashioned and too big, but bought and paid for; item, enough insurance money to last her the rest of her life if she were very careful; item, a moleskin jacket and muff.

She felt that she had been worth more than that. It was unfortunate that she had chosen a husband who could not give it to her. As a young man he had shown such great promise, too, and her own family had thought him such a suitable match for her. Who could have foreseen that he would flicker out in despondent inadequacy, in spite of all her efforts to make him hew to the line of concentrated work? The

16

world judged a woman's success by the valuables that her husband was able to give her, and by that standard, and through no fault of her own, she had been a failure.

But if the experience had brought her humiliation, it had also given her worldly wisdom, and that wisdom she was prepared to exercise to the full for Eleanor's benefit. Slowly, surely, she was grooming the girl for an excellent marriage, preparing her to submerge her mind and personality into a husband's and help him build a future that would be worth sharing. That was the only way in which a woman could triumph over the limitations of her sex: to push a promising man up the ladder before her and collect her reward when he reached the top. By that formula anything was possible: furs, jewels, travel, comfortable living, property, the envy of a whole community of women. Short of being an heiress, a woman could get these luxuries no other way.

And Eleanor was excellent material with which to work such an ambitious scheme. In the first place she was lovely. Not flashily pretty, as her younger sister Penelope was going to be, but that was a good thing. Beauty as pronounced as Penelope's would never inspire confidence in a prospective mother-in-law. Too beautiful women always made bad wives. But Eleanor, from her smoothly waving chestnut hair to her narrow, elegant feet, was the model of a young woman who would be a credit to her young man's family. Martha was smarter, maybe, but if Martha didn't come to the realization that her brains should be bounded by her sex she'd never get a husband at all. No man would be attracted by a woman who so obviously could outthink and outperform him. Eleanor was intelligent, but the intelligence was controlled by a respect for woman's conventional role in society. Her only fault, really, was a willful obstinacy that could be concealed but not quite drilled out of her. Yes, on the whole she was well pleased with Eleanor.

Aunt Ann had already decided whom Eleanor should marry. Young John Kendrick was definitely attracted to the girl, and she could not have a more promising squire. If he never did anything on his own he would still have his family and the Kendrick money to fall back on. There were obstacles in the way of the marriage, certainly. One was that he had four years of college to put in yet, and he would be away from town for most of that time. Another was that a good many other girls would be after him too. But if Eleanor played her cards skillfully there was no reason why John should not come back to her. His family would tell him that nowhere else would he find a more suitable match, and that would help. Sometimes, however, a young man was too emotional to be sensible about such things. Well, something would have to be left to luck.

Between the two of them the Kendricks were referred to casually, obliquely. Eleanor said with a careful avoidance of italics, "John says his mother will be calling you shortly. She wants to have us to dinner some evening before Commencement."

"That will be lovely. I'm sure we shall enjoy it."

"John says it will be the first time they've ever seemed interested in one of his—friends."

"Later—perhaps this fall just before John goes off to school—we'll have them for dinner here. Do they know that you're to have two years at St. Aubens?"

"I think they must; John says they want his younger sister to go there when she's ready."

"It's the only girls' school in the state worth mentioning. French from a real Parisienne, fencing, horseback riding, everything."

They laid their plans; their voices sank to murmurs as the daylight faded and the tinkling of the narrow glass strips hung on the porch light told of a rising evening breeze. Not once had it been suggested openly that Eleanor was to marry John. Aunt Ann would never be so crass. Their talk was all of clothes and possible invitations and the places Eleanor would go and the things she would or would not say, all the things that might add to her role of an eminently marriageable young woman in the eyes of anyone who might be looking.

There was something that Eleanor could not bring herself to tell her great-aunt. That was that John, while he could be dealt with nicely as a theory, was in actuality becoming something of a handful. The night of the Senior Prom was the worst.

She was proud of their elegance as they started out the door, she in her blue-and-silver changeable taffeta, he in his first dinner clothes. Most boys would have tried to give the impression that evening dress was an old habit with them, but John was frank and naïvely pleased.

"I sure waited long enough for this monkey suit," he said. "Dad said there was no use getting me one until I stopped growing a foot a day. I guess they figure this will see me through my first year at college, anyway. Some style, hey?"

"You've never looked better."

"Makes me look older too."

"You've always looked older than other boys your age."

That pleased him, she could tell. John could never be blasé or complacent. He might be selfish and sometimes bad-tempered, but he was honest. Suavity was beyond his reach, defeated by the excessive energy, the fury in him. He ran upstairs; he bounded into rooms; he was noisy and unaffected and, occasionally, lovable.

At the dance he was so consistently pleasant to her that she began to worry about his later intentions. He gave away her extra dances grudgingly. He wasted no undue politeness on the other girls with whom he danced, sweeping them off the floor at the final note, restoring them to their less brisk partners, and hurrying back to Eleanor. His gallantry was so conspicuous that Sue Manning commented on it in the dressing room.

"What in the world have you done to John, honey? He acts like the building would fall down if he stayed away from you for more than five minutes."

"I don't know what's gotten into him. It isn't like him."

"I'll say it isn't! Sure there isn't a secret engagement or anything in the wind?"

"Silly! Of course not."

Nevertheless she was the belle of the ball because of him. She had always been sufficiently popular, but now boys fought to dance with her. Any girl who could set John Kendrick running around like that must be some girl! And the other girls sought her in an effort to share the limelight that the masculine contingent had centered on her. She was bewildered and confused, but she smiled amiably and let the unexpected torrent of attention break over her, alternately hoping that the band would break into "Home, Sweet Home" and wishing that the drive home could be put off for another hour or two.

"Certainly wasn't another girl there tonight that could hold a candle to you," he said as he helped her into his father's car. "Gosh, I'm tired of these school affairs. Next time I take you out we'll go somewhere and have dinner and when the orchestra starts up there won't be any other guys pestering you to dance with 'em."

"Most of my dances were with you."

"You're darned right they were! I don't mind their wanting to dance with you—shows their good taste—but some of 'em made nuisances of themselves and I let 'em know it. If they can't bring a girl they can stand for a whole evening, they needn't expect to monopolize mine!"

He swung in to the curb in front of her house, keeping the foliage of a big tree between them and the street light. He turned sidewise to face her, stretching an arm along the back of the seat above her shoulders. In this uncertain light you could see what he would be like ten years hence. His hair was short and blond, crisping into tight little circles that resented the interference of comb and water; on either side of his forehead small triangles rose to mark the places where his hair would recede. The eyes were alert, but they were of the blue that faded. His mouth, not smiling, was sensuous. But his small ears lay back tightly against his skull, his strong neck rose out of powerful shoulders, his skin was ruddy and scrubbed, his hands fastidious but strong. From him there breathed a power that could not be reconciled with theory.

"Have a good time?" he asked.

"Wonderful."

"I didn't take a drink. Smell." He leaned forward and breathed.

"Maybe you couldn't find any."

The arm sank to her shoulders carelessly. "Don't kid yourself. It was flowing like water. Mickey Davis thought I was crazy."

"I doubt if Mickey Davis thinks."

He laughed. "That's what I like about you. You sit around looking so cool that butter wouldn't melt in your mouth, but every once in a while you come out with the old acid and pour it over somebody."

Now was the time to get into the house, while he was still in a good humor. She made a minute move toward the door and his arm tightened.

"Aw, Eleanor, don't."

"I have to go in. It's late."

He pulled her around and kissed her, something he had done only once before. His embrace was neither experienced nor awkward; it was simply wholehearted and affectionate. Through the stiff white shirt, through the fine black broadcloth, she felt his heart thudding against her side.

It might have been exciting, had she not been so distressed. This

20

was contrary to all her instructions: a girl was foolish to let this happen, a boy thought less of you for it. Though she was vague about the mechanism of sex, she knew that virginity, even in its minor aspects of kissing and hand holding, was a marketable commodity and the price of it should be marriage. John would be right in thinking her cheap if she permitted this, and somehow the news would get around among the other boys and her reputation would be gone and her chances of marrying anyone worth while would go with it.

In the back of her mind she envisioned Aunt Ann peering through an upstairs window, counting the minutes that the car remained, black and silent, at the curb. She pushed against his chest.

"Please, John."

"This isn't wrong. Why can't I kiss you if I want to? You like me, don't you?"

"Of course I like you. That hasn't anything to do with it."

"What has, then, I'd like to know? Gee, a kiss isn't much to ask. You act like I was going to kill you or something."

"I don't want to kiss anybody unless I'm engaged to him."

"Well, that's easy. Be engaged to me."

"We can't be engaged. We're too young."

"Listen, Eleanor, this isn't just—well, I'm crazy about you, and the family thinks I'm showing good sense for about the first time in my life. Gee, I have to go away to school this fall, and I won't be seeing you except for vacations. We could have such a swell summer if you'd just be a little friendlier."

His tone was coaxing, but he was getting a little angry too. He was not accustomed to being balked. There was always such a narrow line between his wishes and his temper. She didn't want to offend him. Her refusal must be definite enough to restrain him but so tactful that he would keep on liking her.

"Don't make it hard for me, John. It isn't a question of what I'd like. It's a question of what's right and what's wrong."

"For heaven's sake, this is the twentieth century! Don't be such an old-fashioned prude."

Her long-stilled temper flared. "And don't you dare speak to me like that! If you don't like me you can stay away. I'm not going to let you kiss me whenever you feel like it and that's all there is to it!"

He dropped his arms and moved away. "Well, let's not fight. How'd we ever get so stirred up about such a little thing?"

"That's just the trouble. To you a kiss is a little thing. To me it's a big thing."

He sulked, and now he seemed younger than his age and the dinner clothes were an incongruity. She remembered how he had danced attendance on her all evening and she leaned over to touch his arm.

"I'm sorry if I was rude. Please forgive me."

"I guess it doesn't matter too much to you whether I forgive you or not."

"Yes, it does. It matters a lot."

He pulled a cigarette from his pocket and lit it. "You're a funny girl. Some of 'em lead you on and then say, 'Why, how dare you? You must have misunderstood me!' That kind makes me mad. But you don't do any leading on, especially. You're just nice and pleasant and good company and easy to talk to. So I guess I can't be sore."

"Don't be."

He smiled at her. "It seems an awful waste of time, your fighting me off, when we're probably going to be married someday anyway."

Caution, here. "I'll apologize the day of the wedding."

They walked up to the porch arm in arm. "Good night could be a kiss too," he said.

"This kind." She stood on tiptoe and brushed his cheek with her lips.

He laughed. "At the rate you're warming up, you'll reach normal temperature in about ten years."

"My temperature may be higher than you think."

"I s'pose I'll have to stick around all that time to find out."

He whistled as he went back down the walk. He wasn't mad, everything was all right. Till the next time.

The summer was warm and beautiful and hasty. They went swimming, they ate hot dogs, they played tennis, they drank quarts of lemonade. Sometimes they took Martha, fifteen now and a junior in high school, along. John swam and Eleanor and Martha lay on the float in the sun.

Martha had opinions of her own. "I like John," she said, "but I don't know why he likes you. He's fire and you're ice. He's body and you're mind. Not that he's dumb. What I mean is he lets his emotions run him and I don't think you ever had an emotion in your life."

Eleanor took off her bathing cap and smiled tolerantly. "You talk like a book."

22

"Well, that's not so queer, considering. Anyway, books are right about people, a lot of times. Is pride an emotion?"

"I wouldn't know."

"If it is, that's one you've got. You're proud, and proud people are always stubborn, so you're that too."

"Thanks."

"Oh, you know what I mean. You're a lot of other things besides. I'm just trying to find the key to your character."

She's just a child, Eleanor thought, looking down at the short, stocky body sprawled beside her. A terribly clever one, a disconcerting one, but a child.

Martha's beautiful head turned to her abruptly. "I sound young, don't I? That's because I'm always trying to figure things out, and that's a childish trait. Grownups aren't supposed to have to figure things out. They're supposed to know. Only most of them don't, or they wouldn't be so surprised at the way things turn out."

"Do you know how you're going to turn out?"

"Sure. I'm never going to get married, because nobody's ever going to ask me. So I'll have to earn my own living, and the thing that pays a girl the best is teaching school. I'll be a schoolteacher and I'll be a good one, and I won't be dull and stodgy about it either. Maybe I'll wind up in a university somewhere, teaching literature."

John pulled himself up onto the float, as wet and glistening and lithe as a young seal. "Tell Eleanor's fortune, Martha. And mine."

"Eleanor's going to a finishing school and she'll learn all kinds of gup about how to shake hands and what to wear at tea. Then she'll marry a very correct gentleman and lead a very correct life. She's got a good head, but she'll never use it on anything more important than the right dress and the right table service. Just like Penny, who's smart as a whip but doesn't care about anything except that every kid in the neighborhood should like her best. Only Eleanor's ambitious and Penny isn't."

"I'm ambitious too," John said.

"The trouble is you're apt to change your mind as to what you're ambitious about. First you wanted to make the football team, and you did. Then you threw it over because you wanted to be in the class play. You made the debating team and never went to a meeting of it because you'd discovered that the glee club was going to get a trip to Washington that year, so you spent all your time at that."

23

"And I *did* get to go to Washington," said John, and pushed her off the float. "Your sister's an impudently honest piece," he told Eleanor. "Don't get it into your head that I'll ever change my mind about *you*."

The Kendricks gave their dinner, and Aunt Ann gave hers in return There was the last movie and the last dance, and in Eleanor's room was the chaos of preparation for going to St. Aubens. Suitcases sat on everything, filling to the top as the tide in the bureau drawers receded. The final days were stretched tight with the anxiety of change and the fear that never again would the world seem so golden and enchanted.

John came in ten minutes before he left for the train. Aunt Ann would have thought it bold of Eleanor to go to the station to see him off. They stood awkwardly in the hall and their silences were filled with the rasping of the locusts in the autumn afternoon.

"I'll probably make a frat," he said. "The first dance they have, I'll ask you up."

"I'll come if I can. It's pretty far, though, and it costs an awful lot."

"I'll pay your way. Gee, I'd be glad to."

"No. I'll come whenever I can afford it."

"And you'll write every day?"

"I'll write every day for the first two weeks, because we'll both be lonesome. But after that we'll probably taper off. Aunt Ann says once a week is plenty."

"That's all she knows about it."

"She says that if we try to write every day, pretty soon it'll be an obligation and not a pleasure at all. You know how you hate to write letters."

"Well, maybe." The hall clock chimed and he jumped. "Say, I'll have to run." He put his hands on her shoulders. "Going to kiss me good-by?"

"Yes." She didn't care what Aunt Ann thought; it was going to be a long time before she saw him again.

"That was very nice. Your temperature's improving."

"Thank you. Shall I work on it while you're away?"

"Don't bother. Wait till I come back. That is, if you don't forget all about me."

"I couldn't forget you." That might be bold, but it was honest. Watching his sturdy shoulders swing down the street, she realized that he had given her no like assurance, and that, if he had, it would not necessarily have been significant.

Martha went past her father's house to pick up Penny. "Eleanor might be feeling pretty bad," she said. "Let's go over and cheer her up."

"Why's she feeling bad?"

"John left for college this afternoon."

Penny skipped with the excitement of her sister's romance. "Do you think they'll ever get married, Martha? If she does we can go to live with her, because she'll have lots of money, and I'll have a new dress for every day in the week——"

"The Kendricks aren't millionaires. He'll have to work for a living. So will you, probably."

"I'm never going to work. I'm just going to have fun all the time and everybody will like me and people will say, 'Oh, have you met that charming Mrs. Whoever-I-Am?' That's the best way to live."

Martha looked at her and considered. Penny, at twelve, was taller than Martha at fifteen. Her auburn hair hung in shining natural waves, her teeth were white and perfect, her eyes so dark a blue that they seemed black.

"Well, maybe you won't ever have to work, because you're going to be so very pretty. Of course I've never seen a really good-looking person yet that was worth the powder to blow them up. They hardly ever amount to anything, because they don't have to. Nobody asks anything of them except just to look at them."

"That would be wonderful! I love to have people look at me. And I don't care if I ever amount to anything as long as I have fun."

Martha picked a locust shell from a branch. "Look. This is a perfect one."

The two heads, yellow and red, bent together.

"It's just like the real bug, but the bug isn't in it," marveled Penny. "And maybe he's a hundred miles away by now and has forgotten all about his old skin that he left way back here."

A train whistled at a far crossing and Martha listened until the ribbon of sound dragged itself over the horizon and was gone. John Kendrick was on that train. It might be a long time before he'd be back. Maybe, as far as his return concerned Eleanor, he would never come back.

25

Penny was still looking at the locust. "I wonder how often they change them, Martha?"

"Maybe he leaves a dozen or so behind him before he dies. I'll have to look it up."

They went in to cheer up Eleanor.

3.

In her senior year at high school Martha began to blossom into a sort of prominence among her classmates. For one thing, she had stopped looking like a child. She would never be tall, that was apparent, now that she was sixteen, but the squareness that came from having bones too large for her stature was beginning to be glossed over with roundness. There would be, until she reached full maturity, a touch of the ridiculous about her body. It was not absurd to be only an inch over five feet tall; it *was* absurd to be a six-foot person cut down eleven inches. Grandmother Edwards supervised the choosing of her clothes to obviate this shortcoming. Plain dark blue serge with accents of bright color at the sleeves and neck. Soft gray wool that was ambiguous at shoulder and hip but stern at the waistline, which fashion was now moving up to its natural, time-honored location. An evening frock of light blue crepe with heavy beaded trimming in a panel down the front. No ruffles, ever. No skirts and blouses. No suits. No sweaters. She had to be dressed older than her age. There was no help for it with that stubborn, vigorous body with its wide shoulders, its broad pelvic arch, its short, straight, muscular legs.

It was a miracle that she never in her life appeared awkward or ungainly. She had "classic dancing" and ballroom lessons and elocution lessons, chiefly because they were the only devices her grandmother could discover that would throw her into outside company on a non-school basis. She profited by them amazingly.

For "classic" you went to Mrs. Denny. Ashland knew Mrs. Denny as a woman from New York who had married a comparatively worthless Ashland man, had had two children, and, when they had grown to school age, had opened a dancing studio to augment the family income. She was a frail, dark woman with muscular calves and lovely movements of her head and hands. Many years afterward, when Martha saw the Russian Ballet, she knew that Mrs. Denny had studied long and well, somewhere, sometime.

The studio was the entire second floor above the florist's shop. It had a long shiny floor and many windows. Small dressing rooms, where the girls slipped into their brief panties and their light tunics and ballet slippers, lined one wall. Against the other was a long bar, skewered firmly into the plaster. You stood sideways to the bar and put one ankle up on it, keeping both knees straight. You bent your head forward until it touched the raised knee. You could do many astonishing things with that bar, and all of them tore you to pieces somewhere. In the many full-length mirrors that lined the walls you could see your face, passive and calm, above the torture in your legs.

It was in those mirrors that Martha made a great discovery. She had come so early that no one was there except Mrs. Denny, conferring with the pianist in the corner. She put on her tunic and slippers, idly thinking that her bobbed hair, the bangs straight and glossy, the rest a yellow blond frizz of marcel, certainly made her look more grown-up. With one arm curved up over her head and the other swept into an arc in front of her, she stopped dead, looking in the mirror at the upraised hand. It was horrible, with the fingers cupped like that, it made the arm look as though it ended in a stump. Straighten them a little, not stiffly. That was better. If the index finger were kept straighter than the rest it finished the line of the arm. There. That was it. The hand was long-fingered and lovely now. But it flopped at the wrist. Tighten the wrist, not too much, not rigidly. Just enough to get away from the impression of a break there. And the elbow—ugly things, elbows—made a bad angle, destroyed the sweep of the gesture. It was hard to curve an elbow, but it could be done, she discovered. There, now the arm was right!

She was so engrossed in the discoveries she had made that she was still at it when the class came in. The reason Mrs. Denny made you point your toes was that it made the whole leg look better. But if you pointed them with the foot turned straight ahead it drew your stomach along with it and made you bulge up above. Turn the foot a little and then point, and there it was. The curves of arch and instep were exposed, two pretty lines, the leg was longer, and the rest of the body was free to turn any way it wanted. If, along with that pointed toe, you wanted to bring your arms sideways and down and bend forward a little from the waist, you had a gracious pose, the beginnings of a polite genuflection.

From that moment on Martha watched the mirrors. You had to use discrimination. A pretty gesture was no good unless it could seem natural. The least impression that it was forced on the body instead of inspired by it made it laughable. She studied the other girls in the class. They didn't have the right idea. They went through the practice steps, through the dance routines, with their feet and legs. Or they did them with their hands and arms. They were not integers; they were an assortment of flailing parts, each geared to its own whim. They did not perceive that a split second's difference in the co-ordination of hand, foot, and head made an artificiality, a farce, out of something that could be beautiful and spontaneous. They didn't even see that, when you were on your knees in an attitude of supplication, you shouldn't have a broad grin on your face. And worse than that were the few girls who went too far the other way, who contorted their faces with anguish or horror or disgust, whichever grimace they felt the gestures called for. That was wrong too. In ballet it was the body that should primarily express an emotion; the face merely kept in line, looking vaguely pleasant or lightly serious.

Having discovered this truth, she worked at it, not only in class but at home, in school, everywhere. She became self-conscious in the best sense of the word. She knew what she looked like working at the table in the physics lab or paying the grocery bill. She had never heard the word "form" as applied to tennis or swimming, but she was working on it as a principle of behavior. Now when she gardened she knelt, eschewing the horrible posture of bent head, strained arms, and upflung hips that took the skirts with them and revealed much more than you would think of legs braced stiffly to maintain balance. She practiced even such a simple thing as sitting in a chair with her knees crossed. Where did your skirt get to when you did that? Was it straining tightly up your thigh where you couldn't see it, making someone embarrassed for you? How bad was the bulge of the calf?

Slowly she achieved a grace, a poise, an ease of motion that was never to leave her. It became so much a part of her that she didn't have to think about it any more. She made it seem so unstudied that no one ever suspected how hard she was working at it. The gym teacher said, "Martha, you have good muscular control. You'd make an athlete if you were interested." Penny said, "I never noticed before. Your hands are so pretty." Grandmother said, "My, the way you go up and down those stairs so light, anybody'd think you didn't weigh a hundred pounds even."

Mrs. Denny saw it too. The pained look of distaste that was usually on her face when she watched a dozen girls go gallumphing through a poem of motion lifted when she watched Martha.

"You're good, Martha," she said. "You're very good. It's a shame you're not lighter, smaller. You'd have made a dancer. A real one."

Shortly after that Mrs. Denny ran away from her husband, taking the two children with her. The lessons stopped, and even Martha did not realize that she had mastered, in her own way, one of the principles of great art, which is to make a carefully contrived artifice seem natural and honest.

Ballroom dancing she did not care about at all. The lessons were given by a genteel, decayed couple on the waxed floor of the basement of their big old house. There was always an equal number of boys and girls in a class, so that no one lacked a partner. Mrs. Sims, who had dyed hair and fluttery hands, would explain the step. Mr. Sims, thin and gallant, would step up to her, bow slightly, place his arm around her waist, hand turned politely outward, and they would demonstrate. Then the boys would step up to the girls, the piano would begin to jingle, and the couples, faces set and serious, would circle the floor.

To Penny, Martha admitted her defeat. "It's all right, I guess. I can do the steps; they're simple enough. But it's all so stiff and stilted, and somehow, when I dance with a boy, it's not a duet, it's two solos. I can't seem to learn to follow."

Penny couldn't understand that. There was a boy who went to high school and lived next door and he was teaching her. "It's so easy, Martha. You just go where they do, and it's a lot of fun seeing what steps you can do without getting tangled up in each other's feet. And when the boy's good-looking, it's kind of exciting."

"Well, that's the part I miss out on, then, and I guess that's the main point of ballroom dancing. Certainly if you just wanted to listen to the music you could do it better by sitting down. And if you wanted exercise you'd pick something lively that you could do outdoors instead of an old, dusty hall. So the main reason for ballroom dancing must be that people want to put their arms around each other and that's one way they can do it in public!"

Penny giggled. "I don't see anything wrong with that."

"There isn't anything wrong with it. Only it's not so good if you happen to be one of the people nobody wants to put their arms around. What do you suppose is the matter with me? I'm clean, my clothes are nice, my face wouldn't stop a clock, my figure'll pass in a big enough crowd. And not a boy has given me a second look since I was in third grade!"

Penny wrinkled her forehead. "Well, I don't know what it is, exactly. You're kind of independent. I mean, when you talk to a boy you talk to him the same as if he was another girl. I mean, he might as well be another girl; you don't treat him any different. Honest, Martha, aren't there any boys you like?"

Martha didn't tell Penny, but there had been quite a few she felt she could have liked, if she'd ever had a chance to know them. Hadn't she stayed hours after school, just to watch Alex Deane play tennis on the school courts? Hadn't she joined the glee club just to watch Worth Neilson and listen to his warm baritone? Didn't she do her darnedest to take the nearest seat to Hal Jones so she could overhear the funny things he said and watch his facile face? There were clever boys and athletic boys and picturesque boys, but they had one thing in common: they never noticed Martha.

There was no keeping her out of things, though. Her young contralto was good enough to keep her in the glee club and add her to the Methodist Church choir beside. She wrote better than anyone else on the school paper, and she worked on the annual staff. She was a member of the dramatic club and appeared at school assemblies to make speeches or give readings. All this, added to the lessons in dancing and elocution and her eternal library visits, filled up her days. Studying was not a problem with her. She had an enormous power of concentration, and her vast reading experience made high school books seem simple.

Grandmother Edwards was pleased. All her worries had been for nothing. Martha was acting just like any other girl, and, after all, she was a bit young for boys to come calling.

Winter left early that year. The bright splinters of crocus pierced the wet, green grass, the wind and sun drove the big white clouds so fast before them that the world turned giddy. Of all the people in Ashland, the high school pupils turned giddiest. The spring was rising in their veins; their last days of carefree irresponsibility were sifting through their fingers like gold coins from a spendthrift's hand and there was no way of stopping the clock. Time was running out, and the senior class at Ashland High School felt that it stood on the Threshold of the Future. Big Things lay ahead.

The first Big Thing was the election of the class officers who were "to guide, to guard, to serve" the ideals of the hundred and twenty pupils who were to be graduated. For president they chose the captain of last fall's football team, primarily because his name had become so familiar to them in their cheering. The two prettiest girls in the class were elected vice-president and secretary, and the president of the dramatics club, a youth who had stirred feminine hearts as they watched him play love scenes on the auditorium stage, was treasurer.

The second Big Thing was the class play, directed by Miss Woodhue, a history teacher. The play coach was chosen each year by the faculty, and the choice was not based on acting ability or on previous stage experience. The thunderbolt simply struck the member of the teaching staff who had the least ducking ability, and this usually meant that one of the newer, younger teachers drew the assignment. No one ever wanted it twice.

This year the play was, as usual, a comedy, but, unusually, one with the lead thrown to a mature-woman character who guided star-struck lovers on a difficult path and held everyone else at bay with a caustic tongue. Martha tried out for the title role, got it, and learned all her lines the first week.

Rehearsals were more fun than anything else she had done so far. It was exciting to see the auditorium empty, and heady to feel the footlights warm on your face. Miss Woodhue sat in the back of the house and called every five minutes, "I can't hear a word! Jimmy, if you don't learn this second act by tomorrow I'll annihilate you!"

Martha was glad she didn't have any of the love scenes to do. The minute a boy had to hold a girl's hand the cast went into hysterics. And the final kiss, of course, was faked in rehearsal. "The night we give it he's going to really kiss her!" It was all a lovely, stirring hodgepodge of props and furniture and clothes and grease paint and excited girls and nervous boys. Martha was the rock on which the play and Miss Woodhue leaned. She was the only one involved who was sure of what she was doing. And she was the only one who walked home alone from rehearsals, except sometimes for silly Minnie Sanger, who played the housemaid and had buck teeth.

As the last week of May drew near Minnie skipped faster and faster along the shadowy sidewalk going home. "Aren't you excited, Martha?" she would trill. "Couldn't you just die? Why, that auditorium has a thousand seats in it, and they say it's all sold out already. Sometimes I think I just can't go through with it!"

"You'll be all right."

"I don't see how you can be so calm about it! Just think if you should happen to forget to go across and open that window and——"

"I won't forget. And you needn't think I'm not nervous just because I don't look it. I wish the whole darned thing was over!"

She didn't though. She said that because it conformed, because it was expected of her. In reality she would be sorry. Secretly she was in love with Jimmy Riley, the leading man, who winked at her over the heroine's shoulder in the third-act hug. Of course Jimmy would have winked at anyone who had happened to be standing there, but at least he hadn't refrained when he saw who she was. And she turned cold as ice when the action demanded that he come up to her, kneel playfully at her feet, and say, "Please, Aunty—for me?" In her dreams she relived this scene over and over, except that instead of "Aunty" he said "Dearest."

The night of the performance came and Martha, lugging her suitcase full of costumes borrowed from her grandmother's friends and basted to fit, was at the side auditorium door a full hour too early. She felt foolish standing there in broad daylight, and she pounded on the door until deaf old Mr. Jenkins came to open it for her.

"In the play? A little early, ain't you? This is where the girls'll dress. I'll unlock the door for you."

The dressing room was only a classroom, converted for the evening by tacking white paper over the glass of the door and pulling down all the shades. Martha got into her costume and sat down. She watched the other girls straggle in, laughing and shrieking. When Elvira Kane had put on her first-act shimmery green evening dress, she was the *prettiest* thing, tossing her head, declaring that Lands, she'd forgotten every line of her part, what was she going to do! The rest chattered consolation like jay birds. There was much talk about a party at Jimmy Riley's afterward.

32

"I don't think I'll be alive after I get through this!"

"Yes, you will, Elvira, you'll be perfect. And you look simply scrumptious!"

The girls were all dressed now, waiting for Miss Woodhue to come in and put on their "stage make-up," but each time the door opened they shrieked and huddled together.

"Do you suppose those people out in the hall *saw* me!"

"Oh, girls, Jean says the auditorium is almost full. I'm going to die, I know I am!"

Gee, they're silly, Martha thought. What are they going to die for? They've been through this thing a million times and all this means is that they have to go through it once more. What's so awful about that?

Someone rushed out to get programs and they all soberly surveyed the magic of their names in print. Miss Woodhue, pale and important, came in with the make-up box and began to smooth grease paint over perspiring faces and draw long black lines around eyes.

"Oh, Miss Woodhue, this makes me look just horrible!"

"You'll look fine under the lights. Sit still a minute, can't you? If you get too warm all this stuff'll run together on you. Look at Martha. She hasn't any trouble sitting still."

Boxes of flowers began to come in. The girls exclaimed and giggled and hid the cards significantly. Most of them had come from their relatives.

"Here's some for Martha!"

"Hurry and open them."

"They're red roses! Look! About a million of them. Who are they from, Martha?"

She smiled up at them. "My father." The roses made her want to cry. She thought of her father stopping in at the florist's on his way home from the shop.

"What do you have, Mac? My little girl's the lead in the senior play tonight. Like to send her something nice."

She'd been too busy to get over to see him as much as she usually did and now she was sorry. He'd be out in front watching the play. He was probably sitting out there now, with his wife and Penny, and he'd applaud louder than anybody at the end of each act. Of all the people in the world, Daddy and Grandmother loved her best. They'd given her everything she had, they never asked anything back. When

33

you were young, and especially if you were quiet and reserved, there was hardly any way to show them how much you cared for them too. But someday when I'm older, Martha thought, I'll show them. I'll prove that all this wasn't wasted on me!

The play seemed to be over as soon as it had begun. It had been just another rehearsal except for the paint stiffening your face and the strange clothes and the audience laughing at lines you had forgotten were funny. But two exciting things happened after the play.

Martha was in her own green voile dress, dabbing at the last of the paint on her mouth, when Miss Woodhue came in with a tall, slim gentleman who wore spectacles.

"This is Mr. Keenan, Martha. Professor Keenan. He has charge of the dramatics department at the university. He was visiting the Kanes and he came along with them. We're very honored that he liked the play."

Miss Woodhue had patches of red in her cheeks and her breathing was labored. She was tired enough to drop, but relief that the long strain was over gave her vivacity. Seven voices now hailed her at once and she moved away with a mechanical sprightliness. Professor Keenan leaned against a desk and smiled.

"Now, Martha," he said, "let's have no secrets from each other. The play wasn't good. It was a rotten play to begin with and Miss Woodhue, God love her, didn't do it much justice. But you were good. You were fine. You stood out like a sore thumb. Where did you learn to move all in one piece like that?"

"I've had dancing lessons. Maybe that's——"

"Lots of girls have dancing lessons and they're awkward as cows. Now here's what I came to say. What are you going to do after high school?"

"I'm going to college. I—I want to be a teacher."

"A very worthy ambition which, God send, you may not achieve. Come up to the university anyway. They won't let you into my courses the first year, but I'd like to see what I could make you do on a stage when you do get in. I don't go around the country scouting talent, don't get that idea, but—well, you've got a lot of what it takes and I'm always desperate for a good character woman."

Martha tried to match his lightness, his casualness. "I'd like to. I'll come."

She was wild to get home and tell Daddy and Grandmother. She

34

threw her things into the suitcase and bumped into Jimmy Riley at the door.

"Coming to my party, Martha?"

Surprise made her recoil as though he were a rattlesnake. "Why, no. I didn't know I was supposed to."

"Aw, now, listen. It's for the whole cast. You must have known about it."

"I heard them talking about it, but I didn't think I was supposed to——"

Jimmy was, in his turn, surprised. He had spoken idly to her at first, but, being a handsome, popular boy, he made a point of not being refused. Although he had never paid any particular attention to this quiet little girl before, it seemed to him now that it would be ridiculous to have his party without the real lead being there.

Martha recalled the green evening dress which Elvira would, undoubtedly, leave on. She pictured the hideous moment when the rugs would be rolled up and she would not be asked to dance.

"Thanks, Jimmy, but I can't. My family's having a little supper at home for me."

"Aw, but listen——"

She hurried through the warm, dark streets, sniffing the late spring fragrance of the shrubbery by a hundred porches, her roses clutched in her arm. Yet when she sat down at the dining-room table, spread especially in her honor, all she could say was, "Professor Keenan from the university was there tonight. He said I was good."

"Of course you were good," said her father. "You were wonderful!"

"He wanted to know if I was coming to school there and I told him I was."

Grandmother nodded proudly. "And glad they ought to be to get you!"

Somehow she could not bring out the rest, the remarks about the way she moved and her having talent. It would have seemed like bragging, and there was always the chance that she wouldn't turn out to be as good as the professor had thought and then they would be disappointed. She locked the warmth away inside her and gloated over it only when she was alone.

The rest of the semester whisked by. There was the Junior-Senior Prom, which was a dinner, followed by a dance. It was held in the gymnasium, decorated for the occasion with crepe paper, artificial flowers, and paper lanterns. Martha sat at the speakers' table because she had been assigned to give the farewell speech for her class. She kept it short and to the point and there was applause. There was more applause, however, for the senior class president, whose speech appeared in toto on the front page of the next night's *Herald*.

"The class of 1924 in this, its last hour of its high school history, bequeaths to the junior class a rich legacy of ideals. Not always have we been conscious of their presence or attained unto them. Nevertheless for the past four years, like a mantle they have been about us. Now it becomes yours by the due right of those who will work out the high purposes of life better than our own class.

"Ours has been a mantle of *earnest endeavor*. We have worked with the charm of noble purpose. The studies have become not so many books to be conned but guides to the building of Character. We have had more in view than the mere finishing of a four years' course; we have worked in the light of fulfilling a greater destiny. This we knew meant constant and consistent labor. We confess the striving has not always been pleasant, but its value was evident to us. Life gets its richest elements through struggle. We at least have made an honest effort and realized with Tennyson: 'Men may rise on stepping-stones of their dead selves to higher things.'

"Our mantle may be known by the idea we have sought to maintain for *high honor,* which is ever a sign of nobleness. The honor of each has led to appreciation of another's work. Whether in the recitations or athletics or any activity we have desired to be honorable. This aim we hope will fall in a double portion on the juniors.

"Our ideal has been *symmetrical growth*. We have been aware that, though we were in preparation for life, meanwhile we are living our best years. The wise purpose of our school, to develop the moral and physical sides of our existence as well as the mental, has not been futile. In handing on to others this mantle I speak for all of my classmates in wishing that the mantle of larger and truer ideals may be yours."

Martha left immediately after the speeches. She had figured out long ago, quite sensibly, that the way to avoid being a wallflower was simply not to be there. The next day she heard that Jimmy Riley had been looking for her to dance with, that he had said the only thing he didn't like about Martha King was that she thought she was better

36

than other people; ordinary ones weren't good enough for her. She was glowingly pleased that he had missed her and aghast at his misinterpretation of the reason. She wanted to explain it to him, but, on thinking it over, she realized that nothing she could say would be right. If she told the truth he would either think she was fishing for reassurance or he would conclude that any girl who was so unpopular that she knew it wasn't a girl to be interested in. If she said, "I'd have stayed if I'd known *you* wanted to dance with me," it would sound too pushing, too affectionate. There wasn't a thing she could do.

Grandmother resented the fact that Martha's speech had not appeared in the *Herald,* but she had to admit that the president of the class had made a fine oration. Martha was bewildered. The president's speech seemed to her even emptier in print than when she had heard it. What on earth was it but a collection of old bromides and affected prose? It didn't actually say anything except that the seniors were leaving and the juniors would then become seniors. But, with the whole town admiring it, she was probably wrong. Maybe, without knowing it, she was jealous. Anyway, since so many people were on the other side of the fence, she kept her opinion to herself.

She worried a little about the quotation that would appear beside her name in the annual. She couldn't get an inkling beforehand as to what it might be. The worst that could happen would be a slogan chosen for politeness' sake, meaning that, as far as the class was concerned, the individual on whom it was bestowed had so little distinction of face or personality that no positive remark was possible, to wit: "A man's a man for a' that" or "We would not have her otherwise" or "A maiden of thoughtful temperament." After all, she had not achieved any more intimacy with the high school pupils than she had with the children back in grade school. Try as she might, she hadn't found any common ground on which she could meet them.

She breathed easier when the classbooks were distributed and by her picture were the lines: "For thou shalt find she will outstrip all praise, and make it halt behind her." Well, they had been kind, generous. They had given her credit for more than being Eleanor King's kid sister.

She looked around the study hall, and in her head the words spun themselves out: "The seniors were busy with the annuals, leafing through them, studying every page on which their pictures might conceivably appear. There was much giggling, much calling out, 'Oh, don't I look terrible in this one,' much whispered reassurance. They passed their books around, collecting signatures busily, importantly. They wanted all their classmates' names down in their own various handwritings, and this was a serious goal. Ten years from this day they would pick up this same book from a dusty shelf and say, 'Who in the world was Martha King, and why is her name in here? I never knew any Martha King.'" She repressed her thoughts sternly. Something important was missing in her make-up, or she wouldn't find silly so many things that the rest of them considered vital.

The Commencement address was given by the Rev. Dr. Haines on the class motto: "To strive, to seek, to find, but not to yield." He said that he hoped this generation would do better than his generation had done, and not allow themselves to be overcome by doubts and fears. It took him two hours to say it, and the class sat forward, drinking the heady liquid of the power over destiny so shortly to be theirs. Martha thought that Dr. Haines and the senior president would make a good pair. They both took so long to say so little.

Then the principal arose to make the scholastic awards, and Martha found that she was being graduated summa cum laude. She had thought she might get it, but she hadn't been sure. Her father and grandmother, sitting down there in the fourth row, would like that. They wouldn't realize that such a distinction meant that something was missing somewhere else, that it came from the same part of you that made you so deplorably different from your classmates. She had read somewhere about a man whose virtues sprang from his faults, and that came pretty close to being her own case.

Well, high school was over. She could hardly wait to see what the university would be like.

4.

St. Aubens was a beautiful school. Eleanor liked it at once: the gray, ivy-covered masonry, the long formal gardens, the little ceremonies of tea and dinner, the strict polite routine of the days. Aunt Ann was far away, but the headmistress and the code of school rules took her place. Except in her own room, a girl was never alone. "Out of bounds," one shopped and rode and walked in groups, supervised by one of the faculty. But from four to six each afternoon the girls were free to visit among themselves, to stroll in the gardens, or to take tea in the main drawing room. There were no uniforms. "After all, this is a school, not an *institution!*" the headmistress said. "Part of a girl's education is to look lovely at all times, and she should wear whatever pretties she pleases. As long as they are in good taste, of course."

The studies were not too difficult. The headmistress, Mrs. Mc-Masters, saw to that and it was not always easy to see to. There was, for instance, the French teacher who could not resist emphasizing the grammatical side of language.

"Really, Alix," Mrs. McMasters would expostulate gently, "these girls don't expect to teach French nor to write books in it. A reading knowledge and a good accent, that's all they want. I know you're enthusiastic about your mother tongue, naturally, but——"

Miss DuCharme flared. "I would like to know what good an accent will do them if they can't form a correct sentence to say! These conjugations they must learn. You cannot know a language unless you know its verbs!"

"I know, dear, I know. But if you would just not stress them quite so much. Some of the girls find it boring, and their parents complain." Gaily but chidingly: "You wouldn't want our enrollment to drop off because of French verbs."

A thousand times a year Alix DuCharme felt that she would explode if she did not get away from the headmistress and find a place where the French language could be expounded thoroughly and lovingly. A thousand times a year she reminded herself that her salary was good, that her living conditions were splendid, and that it was nothing to her if these Americans wished simply to skim the surfaces of things and miss the benison of the knowledge that lay below. Furiously she tried to persuade herself that she did not care; that it was the girls' loss, not that of the language. And when she would forget and rapidly cover the whole blackboard with examples of regular and irregular verbs and their various tenses, the pretty, pink mouths of her class would begin to yawn, and the headmistress would stop by again the next morning. *Inutile, ça!* Well, one must cut one's suit to fit one's cloth.

The English instructor was more complacent. Her duties were three: to see that the girls could write a good formal or informal letter; to insist on correct speech, rigorously eliminating slang or any too imaginative or unusual mode of expression; to acquaint her charges with the standard classics, so that they might not later be embarrassed by sudden allusion, and with the "best sellers," so that they might not be at a loss for timely, bookish conversation. Happily the condensed version was coming into vogue and she employed it fully. The girls liked it. What was the sense of reading a long play like *Cyrano de Bergerac*, when you could get the gist of it in one page of Barclay's *A Thousand and One Classics in Shortened Form?* And who would ever think of Lamb's *Tales of Shakespeare* as a children's book! It was a windfall, an absolute windfall, saving pages and pages of confusing reading and dropping the main idea neatly in your lap.

Miss Smithson reluctantly admitted that there was no way of shortening poetry, but most poems were fairly short and not too many people knew much about them anyway. They learned to recite *The Highwayman* and *Patterns,* and they entered upon a lifelong appreciation of Bartlett's *Familiar Quotations*. There was a book! If some smarty said something to impress you, you could prepare yourself with a few nifties to spring casually when the moment was right.

History was the only other dull subject, though sometimes the mathematics of household bookkeeping proved a bit strenuous. But certainly no fault could be found with the natural dancing, the fencing, the tennis, the horseback riding, and the table planning and correct service courses! It was St. Aubens's boast that no girl had ever completed its two-year curriculum without having developed a good posture, excellent drawing-room manners, and an impeccable taste in dress for all occasions.

Once a year the great rooms on the first floor of the girls' dormitory were thrown open to visitors and parents. The lawns and gardens would be dotted with admiring strollers, extra tables laid for luncheon, the girls on their most ladylike behavior.

"I must say, Mrs. McMasters, you seem to have done wonders for Marianne. She's always been such a tomboy, and she was nearly heartbroken when her brothers went away to school. But now—well, she's a different person, that's all."

Little, deprecating cries from the headmistress. "Why, Marianne's such a lovely girl, she's been no trouble at all! We've been so happy to have her with us. We're already looking forward to having her younger sister."

"She'll be coming next year. Of course, now she has a silly notion in her head that she wants to go to college instead, but I say to her, 'What on earth will you learn in college that'll do you any good in later life?' I think college is all right for boys; they have to earn their living, and it's nice for them to have a degree to show around when they're looking for a job. But Marianne'll never have to earn her own living, and neither will her sister."

Sympathetic understanding from Mrs. McMasters: "Girls get some strange ideas sometimes. It's as you say, what on earth does a girl care about trigonometry or biology or physics! Not that some lovely girls haven't gone to college, don't misunderstand me. It just doesn't seem very practical to me to spend so much time on things they'll never use again."

"Well, Cynthia—she's only seventeen and you know what girls are at that age—she has an idea that she doesn't want to get married. She wants to have a career; maybe be a doctor or something."

"Oh, I hope not! Medicine, even nursing, is such an unpleasant business. She doesn't realize what it would be like. And as for not marrying, if Cynthia looks anything like Marianne she'll not be able to escape it!" Self-congratulatory laughter on both sides.

Among the girls at St. Aubens there was no talk of not marrying. It was the chief concern in each of their minds, though they managed to make light of it aloud.

"Eleanor King, the way you keep your dresser drawers makes me sure you'll be an old maid! Look, they even close without having to push anything down."

"And when your husband finds out that you never have a clean handkerchief nor a whole pair of stockings to your name, he'll divorce you!"

"No, he won't. I can cook."

"Then you'll cook and eat too much of it in the kitchen—you know how you are when you make fudge—and you'll lose your figure and he'll——"

They laughed themselves helpless over talk like this.

Mail distribution was the most important event of the day. The monitor came around to the rooms, dropping the envelopes on the proper desks, leaving a wake of rustling pages, squeals, and breathless anxiety behind her.

"The wretch! The snake!"

"Who's a snake?"

"My brother Tom. He says he isn't coming home for the holidays; he wants to go someplace and ski. Imagine! And he knows darned well that he's supposed to come home and bring his roommate with him, James Purdy, he's the most divinely handsome thing, and I've been dying to meet him and Tom knows it. I'm going to tell Mother!"

At first talk like this confused Eleanor. "That you've been dying to meet James Purdy?"

"No, silly. She knows that. Tell her to make Tom come home. He shouldn't be allowed to dodge his responsibilities like that. Did you hear from John?"

His letters had become so infrequent that often she had to pretend she had received one when she hadn't. A girl who didn't get letters from some boy was without prestige. "Yes. He doesn't say much, just the same old thing. He's busy playing football on the freshman squad, and he's made a good fraternity."

"Oh, then he'll give you his pin! Won't that be thrilling? Aren't you all excited?"

Primly: "I wouldn't be allowed to wear his pin. We're too young to be engaged."

"My goodness, you're eighteen, aren't you?"

"My aunt thinks that's too young."

"Bother your aunt! How old's he?"

"He was twenty last month. He had some trouble with his stomach when he was a youngster and he didn't start school till late, and then there was one year he went to England with his family. But we were in the same class in high school, so he has three years more of college after this one."

"Well, if you'll take my advice, you'll take that pin the minute he's twenty-one. That's a legal age."

She smiled mysteriously. "I don't know that I'll still feel the same way about him."

"Ho! If he really looks like that picture you have of him and if his family have as much money as you say, you'd better feel the same way about him. Men like that don't grow on trees!"

Weeks would pass before she saw his bold handwriting looking up at her from the green blotter on her table. Toward the last of the year she was afraid to open his letters, so marked had his indifference become.

DEAR ELEANOR:

I know it's been a long time since you heard from me, but you have no idea how busy they keep us here. Fraternity initiation was last week and I am a full-fledged member now, looking forward to next year when I can put a bunch of pledges through the same paces I had to go through. I'm glad I joined, though. They're certainly a fine bunch of men, most of them from fine old families, and I think that later on when I get into business I'll be glad I know them. Just like Mother says, part of college is the people you meet there.

I'm picking up on my tennis game a lot. Maybe we can get up some mixed doubles this summer. I say mixed doubles because mostly it's no fun playing just with girls. But there's one girl on campus—Marilyn Granger—that's as good as most men. She's got a forehand drive that really hits the corners. Laying into it is just like driving your racquet through a brick wall. I don't know how she does it, because she isn't a big girl. Looks as cute and dainty as you please. I play with her a lot.

Course, I may not have much time for tennis or anything else this summer. Dad wants me to start in at the shop to learn the business from the ground up. I'm anxious to do it, too. Since I'll have to run the thing eventually, I'm anxious to get my hands on it. But I'll be seeing you every now and then, no matter how busy I am. After all, you're my oldest friend, and it's nice to have somebody that you can tell things to without thinking every minute that they may get mad. I'm going up with Marilyn this week end to visit her folks and I'll tell you all about it in my next.

Always your friend,
JOHN

She had to wait until after "lights out" to cry. If Mrs. McMasters saw as much as a sad expression on your face you were in for an hour of consolation and good advice, and somehow your people at home knew all about it two days later. She wrote to Aunt Ann that John seemed to have forgotten all about her, and Aunt Ann's reply was encouraging.

Naturally, a young man must have his fun, but I don't think you need to worry too much. His father will not permit him to marry until he is through school. After that he will be in Ashland and so will you. He is fonder of you than he knows and proximity will teach him that.

43

When she could efface John she was happy. If only she could forget he existed, how much fun she would be having in this beautiful place! There were spring mornings when she stretched her arms to the rising sun, breathed deeply of the cool morning, and said aloud, "I don't care about him! He can live or die or marry or not, just as he pleases. I'll find somebody else, somebody who'll be crazy about me, somebody that will worry about *me* instead of the other way around!" She could tell herself this, but she did not really believe it. Marriage was a serious affair; a girl could not spend too much time thinking about it.

Occasionally she would have a letter from him that sent her spirits soaring:

To tell the truth, I was a little disappointed in the Grangers and in Marilyn too. They're nice people, I guess, and they certainly did everything they could to see that I had a fine time. But I no sooner stepped in the house than I could see that they thought they owned me! Sure, I wasn't going to have a thing to say about it, I belonged to Marilyn. First they paraded me in front of every friend they ever had. Then they left us alone so carefully and so pointedly that I was embarrassed, honestly. And the way Marilyn gushed and threw herself around was disgraceful. That's what I've liked about you, Eleanor, you've got some dignity about you. A fellow isn't sure where he stands with you, and he sure has to respect you for it.

Accolade!

Some of the girls in the school were already formally engaged, marking time at St. Aubens until their nuptial date. These lucky few were the envy of the school. They had achieved the desired goal, their troubles were over, their lives lay straight and plain in front of them. These studied negligently, allowed themselves to be admired for having been marked so early with some young man's serious approval, let themselves be coaxed for information as to how they had done it.

"Now come on, Janie, what did he say when he proposed?"

"Really, honey, I don't think I should tell you. After all, some things are sacred."

"Did he come right out and ask you to marry him, or did you just kind of drift into it?"

"He asked me, of course. He told me I was the most beautiful thing he had ever seen and would I marry him as soon as he got into

44

the bond-selling business. And I'd known him for ages, so I said yes. His mother was a Todd, one of the Philadelphia branch."

Enraptured squeaks. "I'll bet you nearly fainted! Didn't you feel just glorious?"

"I was pretty excited when I got my ring. It's beautiful, don't you think?"

"It's gorgeous! Lordy, it's big. How many carats do you think it is?"

If it was over two carats, Janie was making a superb match. They knew that without having to see the young man who had given it. They sniffed at lesser stones.

"Honest, I'd think that Sally Bingham would be ashamed to wear that piffling ring. You have to have a flashlight to see the stones in it."

Eleanor liked Sally. She was a studious girl, quiet and levelheaded. She tried to defend her. "Her fiancé is studying medicine, and you know how expensive that is. He'll probably give her a better one later on, after he has his practice."

"Doctors never have any money, unless they're famous surgeons or something. And what a life! All kinds of hours and darned little vacation, never know whether you can go out for an evening or not. I wouldn't marry a doctor. Sally could do better than that. She isn't bad-looking. She could find someone who wasn't a dub."

They could conceive of no other ambition for a woman but marriage. They measured each girl by the yardstick of her probability of getting a desirable husband. A handsome man was good; a clever man was better; a man with good financial prospects was best of all. Living in that atmosphere, Eleanor knew she must not fail with John.

Once a year St. Aubens opened its doors for a formal dance to which each young lady invited a young man. It was the most exciting week end of the whole year. Arrangements had to be made in the town near by for room for the hundred or so gentlemen who would need accommodations. There would be luncheons and dinners and tennis and riding and dancing and late hours, all under the benign but alert eye of Mrs. McMasters. The girls threw themselves into an orgy of dress buying, hair brushing, and perfume selection. They were torn between their pride at producing a seemly swain and their anxiety lest some other girl should prove more attractive to him. By the time the ball date came around the school was a tangle of nerves and bad temper.

Even Eleanor, more sedate and cool than the others, felt the strain. John had not been able to come to the dance the first year, and, though he was coming this time, his acceptance had been lukewarm. In the summer vacation his attentions to her had markedly revived. But that had been eight months ago, and he was waning again. It left her on tenterhooks as to just how she should behave toward him.

The styles that year did not become her either. Clara Bow was the popular idol, with her bouncing vitality, her mass of short curls, her excellent legs, and her pert dimples. Eleanor felt herself too willowy, too reserved, too tailored. She told herself that her hair was a good color, her waist slender, her complexion exemplary, and her legs, although she could not reveal as much of them as Clara Bow did, well shaped and graceful. None of that mattered if you didn't have It.

Her long-buried temper arose to bolster her. Whether it was good policy or not, she wasn't going to let John treat her as if she were a dishrag! If he thought he was going to stroll in here like a king doing a beggar girl a favor, he could guess again. By the time she went down to the station to meet his train she had worked herself into an indignant rage. She knew it was reckless and she didn't care. For once she felt warm. For once she felt good. When he stepped out of the Pullman car, looking so blond, so ruddy, so powerful, he glittered like a god and she hated him.

He clapped his hands on her shoulders. "Well, Eleanor! How's the girl?"

Her smile was small. "Hello," she said.

To tell the truth, John had not been too crazy about coming down. There was plenty doing back on campus and he was running around pretty steadily with Margie Richards, a sweet number, a girl whom it was dangerous to leave for a week end, there were so many fellows trying to plunk their pins on her. Still, he'd had enough good manners to know that he owed it to Eleanor to accept this dance bid. And here was the thanks he got for it! She kept walking along about half a step in front of him, not smiling, just barely answering when he spoke. Just who did she think she was, anyway!

"What's the matter with you?" he asked abruptly.

"With me? Not a thing."

46

He took her arm and pulled her over to a stone bench under one of the trees at the entrance to the grounds.

"Let's get this out of your system. I didn't come down here to fight. I came to have a good time."

"You'll have it. There are some very pretty girls here. I'll see that you meet every one of them. Of course you'll have to spend *some* of the time with me, but I'll make it as little as possible."

"What the hell! I came down here to see you!" He was so emphatic that he believed it himself. He was convinced that he had spent weeks looking forward to this day and here she was, spoiling it.

"Did you?" she said carelessly. The sun struck copper from her hair, her eyes were cast down, the wind lifted a corner of her skirt and showed a shapely knee. The combination of her desirability and distance made him tremble. She felt it through his hand on her arm and knew that, amazingly, she had done the one thing that would pique his interest.

"That's polite, that is! I'm surprised at you, Eleanor King! You used to know how to behave better than this. I can't see that your precious school has done much for you."

"Oh, people change." Lightly. Significantly.

"Meaning?"

"Whatever you want it to." She looked at him for the first time, and the look of reproach on that well-remembered face smote her, but she held firm. "What's the use of pretending, John! We don't feel the same about each other. I don't know why I asked you here, but now that I have, let's have a nice time and call it quits."

He leaned back and lit a cigarette. "All of which means that there's another guy."

"Well?"

"That's a woman for you!" he said bitterly. "There you are. Here's a girl you think you're engaged to, you might even marry her, all of a sudden she starts treating you funny and you say, 'There's another fellow, isn't there?' and she says, 'Well?' That's nerve, that is!"

"I'm sorry, John."

"Who is he?"

"You don't know him."

"I'll bet I don't. And I bet I'm never going to. Because if I meet him I'll break his neck, see?"

She smiled demurely. "He may be bigger than you are."

47

John's competitive spirit raged like a forest fire. "He won't be too big! Listen here, Eleanor, are you trying to sit there and tell me you're not engaged to me?"

She turned toward him, her face distressed. "I don't know *what* to do. I thought when I saw you I'd know, but I don't at all! I don't want to be two-faced or mean, really I don't. But I don't want to make a mistake either." She seemed ready to weep.

John put an avuncular arm around her. "Well, it's just about time I came down here to put a stop to all this nonsense. Before I go back I want you to call up this fellow, see, and tell him it's all off with him."

She wilted into his shoulder. "Oh, I couldn't do that! I simply couldn't. I—I don't know what he'd do if——"

"Never mind. Whatever he does, I'll be right here to look after you. Here." He fumbled at the jeweled pin on his vest. "You wear this now. That means we're engaged. Wear it all the time. Don't take it off. And when I get out of school we'll be married right away. Though, my God, if you can't stay true to me from one summer to the next I'll have to watch you like a hawk for the next two years!"

She adjusted the pin on her dress. She smiled at him through tears. She looked like a pretty, frightened girl who had been saved from a dragon. "I guess I just don't know how to handle men. They get serious and I don't know what to say."

"Now you'll know!"

It took the other St. Aubens girls just half an hour to figure out what Eleanor was up to. They saw the fraternity pin on her dress the minute she came in, they estimated her unwonted animation and the watchful belligerence on John's face. They entered into an unspoken agreement with her about keeping John on his toes, a safe thing to do, knowing where her real interest lay. They allowed her to be wonderfully appreciative of every other young man in the place. They lent their escorts, nay, shoved them off to her for a few minutes of chatty strolling and cordial pointing out of windows at the scenic marvels of the grounds.

John, coursing her, teacup in hand, would be waylaid.

"You're Mr. Kendrick, aren't you? I'm Janie Smith. You're with Eleanor, aren't you? I thought I saw you come in with her. Here, let me get you some sandwiches."

"No, honest, I don't——"

"You must be starving. It's a long way from anywhere to here. Anyway, Eleanor's kidnaped my Jim, so we might as well console ourselves with each other."

"Where's she gone? I was talking over there for a minute and when I turned around——"

"Oh, you know how Eleanor is! Here today and gone tomorrow. She's a lovely girl, but she's a little flighty. Awfully sweet, though, and so pretty." Caroling laughter. "But who am I to be telling you all this! You've known her for perfect *years*, haven't you?"

"She never struck me as particularly flighty before."

"My gracious, we have to watch her every minute. She's too attractive to *trust*, don't you think?"

He guessed he'd forgotten a lot about Eleanor. Certainly back in Ashland he hadn't had to run this way to keep up with her. Here she'd keep drifting off, on the tennis court, on the dance floor, at dinner, and he'd find her in a corner with a bunch of laughing young male hyenas or, worse yet, with one hyena after another.

"If you don't *mind*, Eleanor, this is our dance."

"I'm sorry. Of course."

"I'm not seeing too much of you this evening. You did ask me down here, didn't you? I'm not laboring under a delusion?"

"Let's not dance over here in this dark corner. Let's get out in the lights. Aren't they pretty? I believe the ballroom looks prettier this year than it did last."

"If I get you out in the middle there, some jackass will cut in. Can't we go for a walk in the garden or something? I haven't had a chance to talk to you."

"Oh, I couldn't. Mrs. McMasters is awfully strict about that. We're supposed to stay in here where there are chaperons and everything. Only bad, bad girls——"

"You're engaged to me. That ought to make it all right."

"Mrs. McMasters doesn't count an engagement until it's been formally announced."

"What do I have to do? Get up on the bandstand and scream it out?"

"No, silly. Our families have to put an announcement in the papers. Don't let's talk about it tonight. Let's just have fun."

"Oh sure. I'm having a lot of fun, couldn't have more!"

49

She leaned back to look at him. "Aren't the other girls being nice to you?"

"They're nice enough." He danced eight more bars, bleakly. "Is that other guy here?"

"What other—no, he isn't."

"I suppose you had him up here last year, after I had to say I couldn't come."

"Yes, he was here last year."

"Why didn't you ask him this time?"

"I thought I ought to ask you first. It didn't seem quite fair——"

"And if I hadn't been able to come you'd have asked him?"

"Yes."

"Too damned bad I accepted, isn't it?"

"Don't talk like that." Her voice sank to a whisper. "I'd rather have you."

"Darling, listen, I——"

A hand touched his arm. One of the hyenas had come up.

"May I cut?"

John roared. "No, you may *not!*"

But already he was alone, and Eleanor's apologetic smile and the kiss she blew over the invading shoulder did not soothe him.

Though his train did not pull out of the station until eight o'clock, he insisted on leaving St. Aubens at six. It was his only chance to get some uninterrupted time with her. They slipped away from the Sunday night supper and walked down the hill together.

In the west the sky was streaked with orange and yellow and green. In the east a big May moon climbed purple steps toward the first star. Other couples with the same idea were walking their way, their feet loud on the pavement, their voices low and intimate. The spring breeze tugged at skirts, pulled hair, embraced shoulders, and rushed off to bend the poplars into silver arcs. There was the small stone station and the glittering tracks. Beyond that there were the acres of lush green that stretched away into the summer dusk. It was a romantic setting, but John hardly noticed it. He was bent on getting things straight.

"I'll be home June twentieth," he said. "Save that evening for me. We'll do something."

"All right. Bob Johnson will be home then too. Maybe we can get him and Kate to come along."

He dropped his pigskin bag with a soft thump. He pulled her over into the shadows and kissed her. "Let's just plan to be by ourselves," he said, and kissed her again.

Crushed against his shoulder, she felt the old, lonely ache of the two years of waiting drain out of her and the warm, comforting glow of being wanted take its place. Almost she was betrayed into telling him that she loved him, that she would never love anyone else. Instead she kissed him back, putting her arms around his neck, her lips clinging gently to his mouth.

His breath came short, irregular. "That's the first time you've ever done that."

"I know."

"Been learning a lot these last two years."

She stepped away, laughing. "There was room for improvement."

"Listen, you know what that pin means. I'm the only guy you're supposed to kiss from now on."

She let her face be troubled, doubtful, looking down at the jeweled insignia on her breast. "You're sure you shouldn't take this back with you?"

Women picked the damnedest times to start things! "Don't be crazy! If I hadn't wanted you to have it I wouldn't have given it to you. I'm not a weather vane. I know what I want, even if you don't."

"It isn't that. It's just that if I go home wearing this Aunt Ann will want to know what it means, and she wouldn't understand an engagement that wasn't definite. She'd want it properly announced, and then there'd be no backing out."

That made him thoughtful. He picked up the bag and began walking again. "Well, you're nineteen or so and I'm twenty-one. We ought to know our own minds."

"Then you'll write to your parents about it, so they'll not be surprised?"

"Why do we have to talk about all this now?" he grumbled. "Here I ought to be kissing you and telling you how pretty you are, and instead we're sounding like a business conference."

She took his arm and squeezed it. "That's right, there's no use being so serious. Oh, I'm so glad!"

"Glad about what?"

"Glad not to be serious."

Her joy dismayed him. "Hey, I just said I didn't want to *talk* serious. Lord, how you've changed! I can't get over it."

She did not mention the subject again. She let him lead her to a remote corner of the station and was cozy and lighthearted and rapturous with him. When the lights of his train stabbed the night he couldn't believe it.

"That's not mine. It isn't anywhere near eight."

"Yes, it is. Oh, hurry, you'll miss it!"

He kissed her again, hastily. "I'll write to Mother tomorrow about us, and I'll see you in June."

"Good-by, John. Good-by."

The train sprang off into the darkness. He sat down in a smoky car, waiting for his berth to be made up. The grim, prosaic fustiness of the train sobered him. He lit a cigarette and began to think.

What in the world had come over him since Friday? He hadn't had an intention in the world of leaving his pin on Eleanor. She was a good kid, he'd known her practically all his life, but he'd thought he'd changed a little, outgrown her maybe. And now here he was, committed to telling his family that he had become engaged to be married, and a lot of his freedom would go out the window with that. How had he come to get himself tied up like this?

Thoughtfully he reviewed the week end, and he could find no blemish in Eleanor's behavior. Nobody could say that she had encouraged him, led him on. No, he had just realized that he liked her better than he had remembered, and the whole thing had sprung from that. She had tried to hold him back, if anything. Well, it was all right. She'd make a wonderful wife and his parents would be pleased. And Margie Richards was due to flunk out at the end of the semester anyway and wouldn't be back.

By the time he climbed into his berth he was pleased with himself again. He had certainly told Eleanor a thing or two, shown her that he was not a man to be trifled with!

Aunt Ann came up for Commencement at St. Aubens that June.

"It will be good to have you home again, my dear. Is that the pin? Mrs. Kendrick called me to say how pleased she was that John had decided so sensibly. I'm planning the announcement dinner for the first of July. We must see that you have your ring by then."

"But this pin means the same thing."

"Oh, you children! Whatever it means, a properly engaged young woman has a ring." Aunt Ann had little respect for inexpensive symbols. "I must say I'm very happy for you. I'm not getting any younger and it's reassuring to have your future settled."

"We can't get married until he's through school."

"The two years will pass quickly enough. We can get your linens ready, choose your trousseau, a thousand things." She quelled the girl's unspoken doubt. "The Kendricks are the kind of people who hold to their obligations."

In Aunt Ann, Mrs. McMasters recognized a kindred soul.

"I may say, Mrs. Emmons, that we have never had a more satisfactory girl than Eleanor. She's in the true tradition of gentlewomen, amiable and sweet and dignified. Rare, these days. Very rare."

Aunt Ann's small chiming voice picked up the obbligato. "I had advantages myself in my youth. I have tried to pass them on to Eleanor. There are certain characteristics, admired in women these days, which I find detestable. *Flappers,* Mrs. McMasters."

"Oh dear, yes. Half dressed. Throwing themselves around. Terribly outspoken. And all that horrible make-up!"

"The thing that is so regrettable is that you find them even in our best families. What can their mothers be thinking of! What man of any consequence will ever marry one of them? Or stay married to her, providing he does make the initial mistake?"

Mrs. McMasters knew of several flappers who had married very well, but she wiped them from her mind. "Of course. They don't seem to realize that a good wife doesn't just happen by accident. She must have charm, culture, training."

"Neither do I approve of women working, competing with men. There is such a thing as a woman's sphere. A woman who is not making a home, a pleasant background for her husband and children, is simply shirking her chief function."

Mrs. McMasters frowned lightly. "I have often wondered if we shouldn't introduce a course in housekeeping. Or in child psychology."

"Oh, I don't think so. After all, most of your girls will have maids, and nurses for their children. Those things will be taken care of for them. The reason I chose this school for Eleanor is that I felt that it struck precisely the right note, that of social conformity and social intelligence. The two most important things in a woman's life!"

Mrs. McMasters was cheered. "Yes. Yes. We *do* do that."

"I am more pleased than I can say with what you have done for Eleanor. She has always been a manageable child for the most part, but she could be headstrong on occasion. I can see no trace of that fault now."

"That's very kind of you. Of course her head's in a whirl, what with graduation and her engagement coming so close together. We found young Mr. Kendrick charming, charming."

"A very promising boy. His father's money hasn't spoiled him."

Mrs. McMasters's voice was respectful. "I knew he must come from a good family. I didn't know they were wealthy."

"Yes indeed. Of course that's of secondary importance."

"Of course. Well, I can't recall a girl who's better fitted to hold her own in any society than Eleanor. Ordinarily she's so sensible and competent. It's easy to forgive her for being so vague and dreamy these days, dear child."

Aunt Ann shook a playful finger. "Young love, Mrs. McMasters, young love. Not a foot on the ground, not a thought of tomorrow. Good thing they have us oldsters to stand by and be practical for them until they come to themselves again."

"It certainly is!"

They shook hands daintily over a job well done.

5.

All her life Martha would love the university with an intense personal emotion that nothing else could arouse in her. Because its chief concern was all time, it itself was timeless. Its trees grew taller, each year the ubiquitous ivy must be cut back more severely, new buildings appeared, professors changed. Yet it lay in her mind as she first had seen it, a golden dukedom whose least lane had opened staggering panoramas for her, whose treasures were for anyone's taking, whose storehouses were packed beyond any gluttony to deplete. Many years after, in the fragrant spring or the smoky autumn, an impulse would spring up in her to run, to go back, to seek the assurance that, in spite of numberless little scrabbling days, the mind of man had accomplished and would accomplish marvelous things. And on the few occasions when she could go back she stood under the elms and climbed the hills and watched the students—oh, so young now!—go by, paced by the bells from the tower, and she felt the beauty of having been young in so excellent a place, while the benediction of that far distant happiness would descend lightly about her.

At first she had been rapacious, she had taken every course she could, she could not get enough. But by the time she was in her third year she had learned that one could not major in everything. The thing to do was to get the introductory courses in the fields that were most interesting and find out enough so that going on by yourself would not be hard. Once she had seized the principles she would have libraries and a lifetime to build on them. Mathematics, however, she could not resist. She delved so far into it that eventually she found herself the only girl in a roomful of engineers, enthralled at the way her mind could be made to stretch and encompass and solve by the use of certain simple laws so hidden and infallible that they constituted a sort of black magic she never tired of invoking. She was one of Professor Rutgers's favorites, but he shook his head over her.

"What are you going to do with all this, Miss King? Even if you plan on teaching it, you've gone quite far enough."

"Oh, I'm not going to teach it. I'm going to teach English, or maybe dramatics. I just like it, that's all."

"So. You use us as a gymnasium for your mental athletics."

She smiled shyly. "I hadn't thought of it before. Maybe that's it. I don't care so much how the outside of me looks, but I'd hate a fat, sloppy mind that just lay around the house all day."

Professor Rutgers ordinarily could not distinguish one of his students from another on the street, though he could glance at a nameless paper and tell you whose it was by the processes of mind and pencil figured there. Now he took off his glasses and stared.

"How do you get along with the other young people here?"

"Why, all right. The girls at the dorm are fine. I don't belong to a sorority, of course, so I don't know any of them very intimately."

"You did not wish to belong to a sorority?"

"I didn't have to think about it. They never asked me."

He cleared his throat and shuffled his papers. "I think that someday they will be sorry they did not."

She leaned toward him earnestly. "No, they were right. You can see how they felt about it. I didn't know anyone here so they couldn't single me out for special attention. And then I'm three years younger than anyone else. Right now I wouldn't mix too well. I wouldn't fit in. They can see that. There would have been embarrassment on both sides."

"It's nice that you can justify them so happily. I doubt if they would do the same for you."

She patted his arm lightly, shyly, and, he thought, consolingly. Why is she consoling me? he wondered. I started out to console her. This girl is like no other girl I've ever met before. "Don't worry," she said reassuringly. "They don't give me a second thought."

"And that is a good thing?"

"Good or not, that's the way it is."

"You have a great respect for fact," he said dryly. "It's no wonder you do so well in my department."

She had to turn back at the door. "It's the other way around, I think. Your department has taught me a great respect for fact."

He chuckled at his papers. She had to set me right, didn't she? Couldn't leave me unless the last small thing was straight in my mind. And managed to compliment me too, in a tactful, light-handed fashion. A nice exit. Very nice. What will she be doing ten years from now, a girl like that? Teaching third-graders or ninth-graders? That'll be nice for them, but she won't need all her faculties for that job. There'll be a lot of her left over. What'll she do with that? Join women's clubs? Crusade for moral uplift? Get married? Not so likely that she'll marry, even if she wants to. It would take a brave young man to propose that she share his future when she gives every indication of being able to have a superior one all by herself. He thought fondly of his own wife, wrinkled and gay and wholeheartedly absorbed in his welfare and domestic comfort. He had made her happy for more than a quarter of a century now, simply by loving her and letting her know that there was nothing she could want that he wouldn't try to get for her. But suppose she had been a woman who was capable of getting better things for herself, without depending on him? What would be his place in the matrimonial scheme of things then? Damn it, there shouldn't be a girl in the world who'd take advanced calculus just for fun!

The routine of Martha's days was almost invariable. Breakfast at the dormitory. Out to the walk that led to campus. Wooden or marble steps to climb. Class. The tolling of the library bell. Down and out to the walk again. Another building, another class. An hour's space for the library or a cup of coffee at the drugstore or a chance to run over to the publications building to drop off an article before deadline. Another class. Back to the dormitory for lunch.

A cigarette in the lounge. A freshening up in your room. Study time if you wanted it, there or at one of the libraries. Class. Dinner. And then you signed the women's register that told the housemother where you would be all evening and flew through the dusk to a wide, stucco building whose whole third floor was a theater and the loveliest part of your day would begin.

In the two years Martha had been in play production under Professor Keenan she had come a long way in understanding all the things that went into the building of a play. She had painted scenery and basted costumes and scurried after furniture and properties. And now, best of all, she was acting all kinds of roles: the disreputable carousel owner in *Liliom*, Mrs. Hardcastle in *She Stoops to Conquer*, and Portia and Lady Macbeth. She liked the vicarious living these parts brought to her. She relaxed in the casting off of self to become for a few hours a person she had never been and could never really be. And move by move, inflection by inflection, with the thoroughness that was characteristic of her, she polished a technique that was startlingly good for an amateur.

Professor Keenan did not deceive her. When, that third year, he made her his assistant, he said, "Martha, I'll tell you that I have never had a more promising talent. And I'll also tell you that you'll never get anywhere with it. Your being short doesn't matter. Helen Hayes is short. But you're short without being small. You couldn't play romantic leads, not ever, and a youngster starting in a regular theater has to be able to play them because producers cast to type. They wouldn't let you play character parts until you're thirty, and you can't start into a business like this when you're thirty."

"You mean I'm all dressed up with no place to go." She didn't feel as debonair as she sounded, but there was no sense blinking the truth.

"That's it. We've had girls go from here to Hollywood and from here to Broadway. None of them were better than you and some of

57

them weren't as good. But their appearance fitted in with what they were going to have to do. You can't help that. It's no fault of yours." Poor kid, she works like a dog, and she's a pleasant sort to have around, bright and humble and willing. Why the hell does she have to be short and square! Four inches taller and she could get away with it, just four inches between this girl and a career, maybe. And with that face and that head, she'd have 'em in the aisles!

She sighed. "Well, maybe it's just as well." She thought of the Big Names who had visited the theater and even consented to play a role for the fun of it. They had been odd people, flighty and conceited and overvoiced and treacherously unstable when not on stage. "I guess I don't really have an artistic temperament."

Her voice sounded so doleful that he had to look up to find that she was smiling. "We'll thank God for that. Don't ever let them fool you, kid. A person can be an artist and still look and act like other people. It *can* be done. The reason it isn't is because there's a chance at dramatizing oneself that most of us can't resist; and besides, the man in the street seems to expect it, even to enjoy it. You'd never stoop to it. In fact you go too far the other way. You lie back there in ambush and anybody who wants to know what you're thinking has to be wary or he'll miss it completely. You could make a much better show of Martha King than you do."

Nothing could dull her excitement about play acting, however. To watch a play grow from two wooden chairs on a bare stage and actors stammering over unaccustomed lines; to stand impatiently, playbook in hand while cloth was fitted and basted to you; to unpack wigs and strange archaic shoes; to fit the movements, the standings, the sittings, the reachings, into a pattern that fell aptly into the whole picture; and, finally, to see the painted flats lashed into the shape of a room, borrowed furniture gathered from everywhere fitting somehow into a plausible décor; to stand in the dark wings, listening to the rustle of programs suddenly cease when, behind you, the electrician pulled handles on his switchboard and reached for the curtain rope; to step out into the lights and begin to move through the story with scarcely any will of your own, so set into rehearsed grooves had your feet and voice become—all this partook of the same black magic as did mathematics. And, as if all this were not enough, there was Bill Knight.

Bill Knight was that anomaly among men, an extremely good-looking young man who placed no particular premium on his appearance. He ignored the advantages that a spectacular physique, black curly hair, and a Grecian profile tried to confer on him. He would not stay in a frame. He worked as hard at trying to make people like him as if he had been disfigured and were endeavoring to call attention away from his shortcomings. He had a genial, pleasant manner that dissipated other men's primary antagonism to his looks as a breath of cold air clears steam from a windowpane. His attitude toward the girls was so down-to-earth and matter-of-fact that, after their initial gasps, they could not easily show their excessive admiration for him. He would not be yearned at nor gushed over. He enjoyed hard work.

He had showed up at play production his sophomore year, and Professor Keenan had doubted his intentions. Another pretty boy who wanted to get his face behind lights so that the co-eds could have a better look at it. Well, that game could be scotched easily enough. That first semester Bill didn't get on stage at all. He was set at every dirty, boring, unpublicized job that Professor Keenan could find for him. He did not complain. He did everything thoroughly, competently. And he remained friendly as a pup. He made everyone who understood what was going on a little ashamed of himself.

Professor Keenan chuckled at him. "That Bill Knight's all right," he admitted. "Nature threw the book at him and he threw it right back."

His first speaking part was in a one-act play, in which he and Martha were the only characters. Bill was a French nobleman who had been thrown into a cell by Robespierre and was awaiting execution. Martha was the marquise, his wife, who comes to visit him in a safe disguise and decides to stay and die with him. The lines were in blank verse, the theme slender but moving. The acting must be sensitive and skillful or the tenderness of the play would be muffled, lost.

The day the scripts were handed to them he came over to Martha.

"Let's find some quiet place this afternoon and run through this," he said. "Got time?"

"Yes, I—right after lunch."

"How's about one o'clock on the auditorium steps? It's so public it's quiet. Listen, don't give up anything for this. It's just to humor a budding would-be Thespian."

59

Though she was prompt he was already there, sitting at the top of the long stone flight, above and away from the crowded campus walks. He stood up and indicated a spot by the stone lion that roared perpetually and silently at the science building behind its elms across the street.

"Sit here. It may be shady later on. Now!"

He sat one step lower, his arm resting on the warm stone ledge by her knee, his head level with hers. The proximity, so casual with him, was breath-taking to Martha. Her imagination stood off and looked at the picture the two of them made, and she saw that the pose was loverlike, Paolo and Francesca reading in a book. It was hard to reconcile this romantic appearance with the practicality of the situation close at hand.

"To tell you the truth," he said, "I have my doubts about myself. This fellow in the play, he's proud and sensitive and reserved. He has to be played with restraint, I can see that. And the mistake I'm likely to fall into is to play him with so much restraint that his character doesn't show up at all, that he'll be a wooden figure you could hang your hat on with confidence. Now he's supposed to be crazy about his wife——"

She had hurried to reassure so many people that she knew she wasn't attractive, that she didn't care, that she could face her own shortcomings without wincing, that she could make allowances for their disinterest in her. Force of habit made her hurry again. She didn't want to hear him say—or, worse yet, imply—that he couldn't see her as the woman who could inspire devotion on the part of a man like the marquis.

"I'll look quite different, you know," she said. "I know the costume I'm to have because I've used it before. The tight bodice and the wide hoops make me look much slenderer and the white wig makes me look taller. I wish I'd been born in that period. The camouflage was marvelous."

He looked at her with honest surprise. "I wasn't going to say anything about the way you look. What's the matter with it?"

Immediately she saw that she had made a false step, that she had opened a door that he was inclined to force farther.

Awkwardly, painfully, she tried to close it again. "I thought perhaps you might be having difficulty imagining me as the heroine."

He frowned at her. "Why would you jump to that conclusion? Come on now. Let's have this out."

How had she managed to put herself in this horrible position? How could she have been so silly as to drag up her long-buried frustrations for scientific dissection?

She was so abrupt as to be almost rude. "We'd better get on with the play."

"Oh no. Now that this thing's been started I have to finish it or it'll worry hell out of me. I gather you don't like the way you look."

She blurted it out. "I'm too short and too wide. I'm almost a caricature."

"Well, for God's sake!"

She struggled to her feet, tears of embarrassment making prisms to split the sunlight into color. "Please, I'm terribly sorry. I'd better run along."

"Sit down."

She could not see well enough to run away. She sat down, meekly, unhappily.

"I suppose that all girls worry about being pretty, and that's all right for most of them because prettiness is just about all they have. But I can tell you honestly that looks wouldn't make any difference in your case. Anybody who's known you for a while, or watched you on a stage the way I have, would have a tough time describing you at all. What they'd remember is your voice and the way you move and the expressiveness of your face. Haven't you noticed how quiet rehearsals are when you're on stage? Don't you know it's because the kids can't help listening to you and seeing what you'll do next?"

"I'm not myself when I'm on stage. I'm the character I'm playing. What you're really saying is that, when I'm not being myself, I'm fascinating."

"If you can be fascinating one way you can be another."

"I don't want to be fascinating. I just want to be like everyone else. I'm tired being on the outside looking in."

"That's because you don't know how vapid and silly the inside really is. You'd be bored if you got there."

"This is what I call being on the inside, just talking to you like this. In all my life you're the only person outside my family that I've discussed myself with."

He brushed his hair back impatiently. "That's your own fault, you know. You find so many excuses for people not wanting to be with you that they figure the only way they *can* figure, which is that you

61

don't want them. They end up by thinking you're conceited and pretty well satisfied with yourself."

"You didn't."

"I hesitated about asking you here. You always seem to be so busy about your own affairs and so happy in your little ivory tower. But I'm brave. I thought I'd knock to see if you were in."

"So glad you came by. We don't have many callers in this part of town." She could smile at him now.

"You'd have more if you could take down the No Trespassing signs and maybe put in a doorbell."

He took that back two weeks later when they were walking home from late rehearsal. "Now that I know you better, I'll risk an opinion. You'll never be popular."

"I could have told you that ten years ago."

"Only you wouldn't know the right reason. I do. The fault's not yours, I'm happy to say."

"Thank you."

"It's because people have a picture of what girls should look like and be and do, and you have very little resemblance to that picture. You don't giggle or blush or say, 'How do you *think* of these things?' and you make no effort whatsoever to lead a young man into thoughts of holy matrimony. So nobody knows what to do with you."

She stopped at the dormitory step. "It's awfully nice of you to take such an interest. Why do you?"

"You bother me, in a way. I find myself worrying about you. I keep wondering why a girl with brains and character and personality isn't making the impression that she should. To be brutally frank, why, when I like to talk to you better than anyone else I've met here, wouldn't I dream of asking you to a fraternity dance?"

"Because I wouldn't go."

"Let's say you would. You can dance, all right, I'm sure of that the way you move. And conversation's your prime dish; interesting, witty, unexpected. But if you went the girls would let you alone and the fellows would dodge you like poison. Why?"

"My figure isn't good. That's why."

"And isn't that a silly reason? I ask you, should long legs and a narrow waist make that much difference in how a person is treated?"

"It does, though. With a girl, anyway."

Two days later he had found a ray of hope.

"Listen, I know when the legs won't matter. After you're fifty you'll be the belle of the ball. I know it's a long time to wait, but about that time physical measurements don't matter so much and your other qualities do. Yes sir, when you're fifty the world will be beating a path to your door!"

She laughed. "Stop worrying, Bill. I'm having a wonderful time. Really."

They found many other topics of conversation, to their mutual surprise.

They were together a good deal of the time.

She was writing a long narrative poem for her class in creative writing. It began:

> *Starwood is any small Ohio town,*
> *A little river winds about its feet,*
> *(Kids used to swim there; it's polluted now),*
> *Then comes the station, and the railroad yards*
> *That never sleep. You can see lights down there*
> *On the longest night. The busy trains*
> *Snake round the curve and swallow people,*
> *Mail, and baggage, tugging loaded cars*
> *From sidings fretted with Gargantuan nudgings.*
> *Then comes the green wink from a signal lamp*
> *And they go up over the hill shrieking.*
>
> *Behind them, in Starwood, a man sits, eyes shaded,*
> *And moves a little key, so all along the line*
> *They know that train is coming in on time.*
> *Main Street runs from the station to the Boulevard.*
> *You used to know the owner of each store*
> *That fronted it. "Hello, Rod. Oh, the kids*
> *Are fine. Need some new sox. Nothing wild, now."*
> *Or, "Ed, this here prescription. I've got to*
> *Have it right away. Well, she's no better,*
> *But the doctor says she's got a chance.*
> *Make it up careful, won't you, Ed? I'll need*
> *A couple of cigars too. Won't go to bed tonight."*
> *Now the clerks are smart and cheap and new*
> *And the owners live in Cleveland or New York.*
> *The chain stores undercut, penny by penny,*
> *Till even the most faithful was forced to buy*

63

From them. And Rod and Ed went out of business,
Retired to their homes, or, doggedly,
Found work at the big shops on the edge of town.
Their white hands roughened and their backs grew stooped,
But their heads stayed up and the corners of their mouths.
A man supports his family any honest way he can."

A week after she had finished it Professor Rowell called her in
for a conference in the English seminar room. He was at his desk,
a spring breeze from the windows in back of him ruffling his white
hair and the papers he held in his hand. The big room, with its plain
chairs and tables, its commodious ash trays, its thousands of books
along the walls, was empty of students. A tall yellow vase of forsythia
was the only vernal accent, except for the limpid blue of the sky
outside the windows.

Professor Rowell indicated a chair beside him. "I want your permission, Miss King, to include your poem in our yearly volume of
the best undergraduate writing."

"Oh yes. Yes!"

"It has faults, imperfections. But it was a very ambitious project,
and you've handled it better than anyone could have expected. I
knew that you wrote a very nice prose. It surprised me to have you
submit a poem."

"I've never tried poetry before. I wanted to see what I could do."

He tilted back in his chair. "Professor Keenan is a personal friend
of mine. I had understood from him that your primary interest was
in the theater."

"I enjoy it, very much. But if I have a primary interest it's in words,
the sizes of them, their shapes, their meanings in various proximities.
I've liked to play with them ever since I was a child."

He smiled. "So many years! But it's true, you have a talent, a
decided talent. What are you going to do when you leave school?"

"I want to teach."

"That's all very well. You must do something to earn a living, we
all do. But what besides that?"

"I—I haven't thought."

"Then think now. You must write, Miss King. No one can teach
you how except yourself, and you're a long way along the road to
learning. Write and correct and tear up and write again. You must
not let such an ability go to waste."

It was hard to believe that she was being encouraged to do seriously the thing she had thought of as fun, as an amusing pastime, as a game to occupy her thoughts.

"Thank you, I will. I'll try."

"You are already majoring in English, I know. Here are the courses you should take next year." He checked them off on a prospectus. "This one and this and this. They will help you, they will furnish an adequate background for the work you will later do for yourself. Whatever else you have thought of taking, you must take these. I am not usually so rabid, but when I see what you may become I cannot keep quiet. I must speak. It's too bad that you are a woman."

"I know."

"Of course you've discovered that. Well, it won't hold you back unless you marry and find yourself with a house and children on your hands. Then the writing would go out the window. I have no right to tell you not to marry, Miss King. That would be impertinent of me. But I do have the right to advise you to consider seriously before you do. Even the best talent can be stifled, stamped out, by an unsympathetic environment. Loneliness and greatness have always been boon companions."

She walked back to the dormitory for lunch, not seeing the mud and the tentative green of the trees and the students crowding the walks. She was wrapped in sudden hope and breathless ambition. Perhaps Professor Rowell had overestimated her, but she would work, oh, how she would work!

She ran up to her room to write every bit of the interview to Grandmother. But when she saw Bill at the theater she did not mention a word of it. It would have sounded conceited, for one thing. For another, it might have spoiled his concept of her as a worthy young woman whom only he appreciated. Even if that were a slightly patronizing attitude, it was a friendly one and she valued it for that. He was the first friend she had ever had; she wouldn't offend him for the world.

"Loneliness and greatness have always been boon companions." But perhaps Professor Rowell was wrong. It should be possible to have greatness and—friendship—too.

The last play of the year was *She Stoops to Conquer,* given Commencement week end. For three nights, in spite of the heat and the competition with June's roses and starlight, it drew capacity crowds. Bill played the male lead, primarily, Professor Keenan said, because he had calves to his legs.

"We could pad if we had to," he said cheerfully, "but it would worry me. The stuff might slip. We'll just let Bill be beautiful in his natural endowments, and the rest of you better act twice as hard to carry him along."

"He's a pretty good actor too," Martha said promptly.

"Partisan, Miss King?"

"Well, I——"

"Miss King does not appreciate our academic humor. For that and her other sins, she will play Mrs. Hardcastle. I wish you joy of the silly old lady, Miss K."

The last performance was superb. She knew that even while it was going on. There was no coughing, no rustling from the audience, only intent, brooding stillness and hearty gusts of planned-for laughter. She was conscious of this, but of very little more, for, with the donning of Mrs. Hardcastle's violet satin and white curled wig, she had set aside her own thoughts. Even Bill Knight had become an anonymous figure who was necessary to the weaving of the author's pattern. If there had been a flaw, a dropped stitch, a missing line, she would have come alive instantly, as herself, alert to repair the damage, to set the act straight again. But nothing like that happened. The curtain fell to applause.

They ran for the wings to get out of the way of the stagehands who were breaking the set.

"Very nice, kids. See you all back here next year. Come around for a few minutes before you leave tomorrow, Martha, and we'll put the finishing touches on the plans for next year."

"Let's go have a cup of coffee," Bill said to her. "I'll meet you at the foot of the stairs."

She hurried to the dressing room, gathering the violet satin so that its hem should not be dusty. The little bare room with its line of mirrors and its powder-sprinkled counter under a row of blazing lights welcomed her as it had hundreds of times before. This was different. This was the last time. She would tell Professor Keenan tomorrow, before her train left, that she would not be working in the theater next year; she had too many English courses she must take. She let the picture of this little room and its heavy scent of

66

lemon cold cream sink gently into her heart, feeling the sadness that attends the transmutation of an actuality into a memory.

Outside the beauty of the night touched off all the silly, light, warm emotions that she usually kept packed away in the dry ice of common sense. She felt gay and young and talented and interesting, and she took Bill's hand and made him run with her across campus to the coffee shop.

"What's gotten into you this evening?" he asked. "You seem almost normal."

"I am. I'll hate myself in the morning when my poor old paranoia knocks at the door."

"Where is it now? Don't tell me we've mislaid it!"

"I locked it up in the dressing room. Maybe it'll go home with Liana when she goes in to take her make-up off."

"It would never go home with Liana when it could wait till tomorrow and go home with you."

The coffee shop was crowded, but they found a booth in the corner. The student waiter, harried by the crowd, slopped even more of the coffee into the saucer than usual and said a less philosophical "Sorry." They put paper napkins under their cups automatically.

"I wasn't going to tell you, Martha, but I can't help it. I'm not coming back next year."

She put her cup down slowly. "Why not?"

"Mother's not very well. She and Dad have moved out to California for her health. I guess I'll be finishing school out there."

"But lots of students come here, even from California."

"It's a long story. Mother's never been well, ever since I can remember. Hypochondriac, maybe, it's hard to tell. Anyway, when I was just a youngster she started monopolizing me, telling me I wasn't strong enough to go out and play like the other boys, keeping me as close to her as she could. I was the only child, and Dad wasn't very sympathetic to her aches and pains, so she fastened on me for company. I never was a little boy."

"And you let me think that I was the one who had troubles! Why didn't you—oh, Bill!"

"I'm not telling you this to make you sorry for me. I'm just explaining how things are. Well, I started breaking away from her in high school, running around with the other kids, going to the school affairs, acting like a normal adolescent. She didn't want me to come this far away to school, but Dad backed me up and I made it."

67

"And now she wants you back again, just for her own selfish purposes. I wouldn't go!"

"There are things to be said on the other side too. She's always given me everything I wanted, spoiled me rotten, hurried to grant every wish I ever had——"

"Except the one that might take you out of her sight."

"She gave in even there. I've been here three years now. For Mother, that's being angelically patient. She can't stand it any longer, though, and I'll bet she's making Dad's life miserable nagging him about how sick she is and why should her only son be away when she hasn't many more years to go and all the rest of it. So I'll finish at a university out there."

She was dismayed at the extent of her emotion. How had he come to be so important to her in so short a time?

"I'll miss you," she said levelly.

"And I'll miss you. Funny, but you'll be the only person here I *will* miss. Of course we can write to each other."

"Yes."

He stood up suddenly. "Let's get out of here."

The streets were less crowded now, but on the steps of the girls' dormitory there were fifty couples, standing as far apart as they could, heads bent in duo, voices muffled against the publishing of the sorrow of parting.

She said, thinking aloud, "Everything will be just the same next year except that you won't be here."

"That's right."

They stood a long time, not saying anything. Then he bent to kiss her forehead. "Funny little girl," he said tenderly.

She listened to his departing footsteps until the rushing of the wind among the leaves drowned them out.

Her senior year was her most distinguished. She worked on the yearbook and the daily. She had the best speaking part in the May pageant. She did excellent work in the English department. The dormitory elected her as their representative to the student council. She was no longer a nonentity.

She missed Bill at first, but by the time their correspondence died the natural death of too great a distance she was whole again. Forgetting was unpleasant work, but by effort it could be done.

In an essay for Professor Rowell she wrote:

It is not unfeeling, it is wise to sorrow as little as you can. Grief for things past is a black patch over the eye, obscuring the beauty of the present. Presently the realization of the years imperfectly lived through regret becomes in itself a new black patch to take the place of the original one, now worn thin. And so we make our earthly journey, blindfolded and passive, stumbling in the weeds by the wayside, not seeing the glistening Parthenon to which we might have climbed.

His absence could not spoil the university for her.
She would have held Commencement Day back with both hands if she could.

The graduating class was assembling on the library steps for the final march to the stadium. The black cap felt unsteady on her head, the tassel kept swinging around to her eyes, the gown billowed in fantastic fashion with the summer wind. Hundreds of other black caps and gowns swarmed over the lawn, gathered in bunches, were herded into seemly academic line.

"You've got my address, Sarah. If I don't see you later, don't forget——"

"Lord, I feel like a clown! When I go up those steps to grab my sheepskin I'll fall flat on my face."

"Which way did they say this tassel should be?"

"Don't forget, will you, Freddie? Don't forget."

Don't forget! Her eyes were gathering up every corner of the campus she could see, dropping each detail down into her memory beside all the other precious things stored there, staying quietly on their shelves until the rainy day she would have time to get them out and sort them over again, evoking their scents and textures and emotional connotations in a drearier time.

"Good-by," she called silently to each building, each landmark, each tree along the way. "Good-by. Stay there till I get back. Don't change. Don't forget."

They sat in a big black square of stadium seats, the speakers' platform in front of them, the spectators behind them. Her father was somewhere in that colorful sea, neat and proud in a new gray suit with their train tickets back to Ashland in his pocket. Grandmother had not felt well enough to come. Martha would describe it in veriest detail to her tonight on the porch, making it up to her for having missed the performance. Only six hours of train time between being a student here and being a plain young woman back in Ashland. It didn't seem possible.

There were speeches. There was the granting of the Doctors' degrees, honorary and otherwise, with the ceremonial slipping of the bright hoods over bent heads. There was the processional of the Masters' candidates. They came, at last, to the Bachelors of Arts.

Hers was the first name on the list for honor diplomas. She walked up briskly, took the blank white roll with its blue ribbon, shook hands with the president, walked back as the next student came up. The sun shone strongly on her face, the applause rippled in her ears, the show was over.

There would be other degrees. She would come back.

6.

Aunt Ann's house had never looked so beautiful as that summer when Eleanor came home from St. Aubens. Its new white paint gleamed across the deep lawn, making the spiraea hedge cream-colored by comparison. Underneath the two sycamores—"dirty trees," Aunt Ann said—the grass had been swept and reseeded. The cracked flagstones of the walk had been replaced and in the star-shaped bed near the sidewalk the thousand-petaled roses spilled a fragrant pink snow with every stir of air. Since it was one of the oldest houses in town, and hence in the oldest residential section, it was forced to ignore the undesirable neighbors that had crept into its block: the dressmaking sign in the window of the old Vail house two doors down; the new gas station on the corner, with its fresh red pumps and its petunia beds. The house was equal to the situation. It veiled its eyes with green-and-white striped awnings and stretched out white pickets, aristocratic wooden elbows that held off too intimate encroachment.

"It looks simply wonderful!"

"Naturally we had to have it look well, since your announcement tea will be held here."

"That's a lot of bother just for a tea. We could have had it at Mrs. Dane's tearoom. That's what Carrie Allison did. She said it saved all the fussing at home."

Aunt Ann's voice deplored the Allisons. "I have no doubt that they did what they thought best. In my day we were taught that a girl's parties should be given in her home and that she should be married either there or in her church. Nowadays it seems as if a girl can become engaged and even married without anyone catching more than a glimpse of her home or her parents. She's courted in a car or at the club, she's engaged in a tearoom, she marries in the home of a justice of the peace. It's all catch-as-catch-can and helter-skelter. A girl's marriage is not just her own affair, it is her family's, and I do not intend to evade my responsibility."

"And two new chairs! Such big comfortable ones!"

"My things are good, but they are getting old. If we are going to have John here every evening we don't want him to have to perch on the edges of things."

"It's so good to be home! I think I'll run upstairs and get into some old things and go out and dig in the rose bed."

"I'm glad you feel that way, my dear, but really you mustn't. We don't want you all sunburned as a piece of leather the very summer you should look your best. Go upstairs and lie down and rest. After lunch we'll go shopping. I saw a brown-and-white cotton in the window at Spring's that ought to look well on you."

"And I want to run over to Dad's and see him and Penny. Martha won't be home till next week. They'll be coming to the tea, won't they?"

"Your father will be working, and I see no particular reason why we should ask Hetty, since she is no blood relative of yours and her friends are not ours. Penny is too young for such an affair, but we'll have Martha, certainly."

Penny wept over being excluded. "Why can't I come? I have a darling white piqué to wear, and when you're thirteen you're not a child! It'll be all women, and they won't mind, and I want one of these darling little corsages that Aunt Ann's going to give everyone that says 'Eleanor and John' on a little card in the middle."

She made a special pilgrimage to the big white house and was so

71

demure and shy that she quite won Aunt Ann's heart. "Can't I come, Aunty, please? I've never seen a really grand party in all my life. Hetty wouldn't know how to give one. I'd help pass the sandwiches, and I wouldn't be a nuisance, really."

"If you have your heart set on it we shall be happy to have you, Penelope. It's high time you learned how these things are done, and it's quite true that you'll never learn it from Hetty."

And on the day of the big occasion Aunt Ann knew she had made no mistake. Watching Penny's pretty deference to her older sister, seeing her enthusiasm over her corsage, noticing how she jumped to her feet to get another cup of tea for Mrs. Hopkins, Aunt Ann debated with herself whether she should not take the child under her wing once Eleanor was safely launched. The girl was going to be an absolutely breath-taking beauty and from somewhere she had developed a social conscience that made her pleasant company. How different from Martha, who was sitting quietly in the corner by the piano, looking as though her unaccustomed hat would leap from her head, finding very little to say even to Mrs. Price, who was cordially relating the details of her own announcement party twenty years before. Martha simply didn't fit into these nice little gatherings, though thank heaven she was reserved and gave evidences of good breeding. Aunt Ann sighed. The other two girls would have to look after themselves. She was too old to start all over again.

"King-Kendrick," Mrs. Hopkins cooed. "You know the old saying, 'Change the name and not the letter, change for worse and not for better.'"

Aunt Ann laughed her high company laugh. "We've decided to risk it, Mrs. Hopkins."

The ladies murmured amused agreement, and Mrs. Kendrick said, "Yes, we gave that matter a great deal of thought, I tell you! But Eleanor is such a lovely girl that we thought we'd chance it."

Mrs. Wendell leaned to Aunt Ann. "My, I think that younger sister is going to be even prettier than Eleanor. Good thing she isn't older. Her sisters might find that she'd be stiff competition."

"She is very lovely. Unfortunately she will never have Eleanor's advantages."

"Well, of course! So few girls have had. Now Martha——"

"Martha's the ugly duckling, I'm afraid. But she's charming and very intelligent."

72

"Oh yes, indeed. Too bad, though, that she couldn't have been more like her sisters."

The talk rose and ebbed, the sandwiches were all eaten, the last cup of tea poured. On the careful stroke of five-thirty John came to take his mother home. Eleanor, properly flushed and tremulous, announced his arrival.

"John's out in the hall waiting for you, Mrs. Kendrick."

Little cries from the ladies. "Well, bring him in. My goodness, John, imagine hiding from us like that." "Oh, he *says* he came to fetch his mother, but maybe he had another reason!" "It just doesn't seem possible that he's grown up enough to be married. Why, I remember when——"

Martha said, "Hello, John. You're looking well."

Penny ran over and took his arm. "You're the very first brother I've ever had. Daddy'll certainly be glad to have another man in the family for a change!"

It was a pretty picture and the ladies beamed.

Martha wasn't two blocks away before she took off her hat and sighed with relief. "If there's one thing I hate to do it's sit and eat with a hat on. Men are a darned sight more sensible. You don't catch them leaving their hats on inside a house."

Penny laughed. "Most women look prettier with their hats on. That's why they wear them."

"Well, why can't those who want to wear 'em, and those who don't want to leave 'em off? Why do we have to huddle in conformity like a bunch of witless sheep?"

"I'm kind of glad it's over too. The corsages weren't so much, and I could certainly have eaten more sandwiches if there had been any. Eleanor really ought to try to put on some weight. She's a regular slat! My figure's going to be ever so much better than hers. And my, doesn't she let Aunt Ann boss her around! 'My dear, don't do this' and 'My dear, don't do that.' I'd go crazy in a week!"

"No, you wouldn't. You'd do just as you pleased and you'd twist Aunt Ann around your finger until she thought she approved of it."

Penny preened herself in the glass window of the Smith store. "I guess I could handle her, all right. Wasn't Eleanor's diamond beautiful? That square-cut kind is awfully expensive. I don't think there's another girl in town with a ring as good as that."

"I heard Mrs. Kendrick confiding that it cost over two thousand

73

dollars. She was sitting five chairs away from me, but I dare say she didn't mind my overhearing."

"Golly, I hope I get one as good!"

"No matter what goes with it?"

Penny was surprised. "Don't you like John?"

"I guess I do. I hardly know him. What I meant was that Aunt Ann and the ring got more attention than the happily betrothed pair, didn't you think?"

"Well, if a man ever offers me a diamond like that I won't look too hard for his faults."

Grandmother wanted to know how the party had gone.

"Very sweet. Very sticky. I feel as if I'd just had a two-hour bath in molasses," said Martha.

September came and the town emptied again. It seemed to Eleanor that her life was made up of gray vacuity broken only by the bright splashes of holidays when John came home or the occasional week ends when she went up to his school for a football game or a dance. She dined with the elder Kendricks once a week. She gathered sheets and blankets and dish towels for her hope chest. She went to baby showers for her already married friends, and she played a great deal of bridge with other young women whose afternoons were free. In the evenings she stayed home, not always willingly.

"It's only an ice-skating party. Dorothy's brother's going and Dorothy will be with Jeff. I don't see why it would be wrong with a whole crowd there, and it won't be late breaking up."

"Once a young woman is engaged to be married, she does not appear in public with any escort other than her fiancé."

"But John's having fun. He's not staying home every night. He hasn't even written in three weeks, that's how much he cares about me!"

"He's very busy. It's unfortunate that you should be separated for so long, that's true, but there's no helping that. Besides, you're here where the whole town can watch every move you make, and you can't be too careful about your behavior."

"If only I had something to do, to put in my time. Why couldn't I take that job at the library that Martha had before she left? It's easy work, and the hours aren't bad."

"Really, Eleanor, you can be very trying. You ought to thank your stars that you *don't* have to work."

"Martha didn't have to either, but she did."

"If you begin modeling your behavior on Martha's you'll never marry John Kendrick, I can tell you that."

Eleanor looked out at the sleet beating down on the brown sticks of the ramblers. They're just like I am, she thought, lonesome and frozen, waiting for the sun to come out and make them gay again. Only there are some climates where the sun shines all the time.

She said slowly, "What if something happens and we don't get married? Then all this would be a dreadful waste of time."

"I don't see that. If you don't marry John you will marry someone else. A good hot cup of tea is what you need, child. It'll cure your doldrums."

She wrote something of her feelings to Martha, and Martha's replies were not reassuring:

Of course you worry, and why shouldn't you? If you base your whole life on another person's, then it must stand or fall, depending on the charity of that person. It's a humiliating position, any way you look at it. It's putting all your eggs into one basket and allowing a stranger to carry it. Suppose he doesn't know the price of eggs, where are you then? What you ought to do is give John back that darned ring and tell him you're going to keep an open mind until he comes in with the marriage license in his hand. And that, I suppose, is like asking a cripple to throw away his crutches. But you must know all this. That's the really insulting thing about people who give advice: they assume that you are too dull to have weighed the same pros and cons yourself. What I mean by all this windiness is that I am very fond of you, and, if ever you need to fall back on that, there it is.

Penny was the only one who was completely happy about the situation. "Gee, I can't see what you're crying about. All you have to do is sit around and buy clothes and enjoy yourself. And as far as going out in the evenings is concerned, go if you want to. You can always say you were somewhere else if Aunt Ann gets nosy."

"I couldn't do that. I wouldn't lie."

"If I had to choose between a lie and suffering I know which one I'd take. What people don't know won't hurt 'em."

"For half a cent I'd send his ring back to him and tell him I'd decided to wait."

"Lordy, don't do that! Even if something happens to break up the two of you, keep the ring. You won't get another one like it in a hurry."

Eleanor's twenty-first birthday came and went that spring, and John's congratulatory card was four days late in reaching her.

He came dutifully to see her, however, the very first evening of his return home that next June.

"Sure is fine to see you," he said. "Sure is fine."

He kissed her cheek on the dusky porch and they went in to Aunt Ann.

"Well, you're looking mighty fine, Aunty."

"And you look tired. Poor boy, you must have had a hectic year. Sit down, do, and tell us about it. We stay-at-homes have to rely on people like you to get our excitement secondhand. Eleanor, push that ottoman over for him, will you? There now."

Importantly he told them all the things he had taken part in, how he was a cinch to be president of his fraternity that fall, just how he had won the Thanksgiving game by his clever work in the last quarter. He expanded under Aunt Ann's gentle prompting, glowed when she said she could listen to him all night, he told everything so well.

"Eleanor doesn't seem to think so much of it, though," he said.

"Oh, I do. It must have been wonderful, of course."

"You must forgive her, John. She's so busy looking at you that she can't listen to you. Now you two just sit here, all comfy-cozy, and I'll go get us something cold to drink."

Eleanor knew they would not be alone long. She said hastily, "Could we go for a drive later on, John? I'd like to talk to you about something."

He pulled her into his lap. "Didn't even bring the car. We can talk right here, can't we? What's wrong with this?"

"Let me go, please. She'll be back in a minute."

"We're engaged, aren't we? I guess she wouldn't mind."

She managed to get to her feet. "That's what I want to talk about. I don't think we should be engaged any more."

"Listen, I know how you feel. It hasn't been much fun for you, sitting at home here. But let's wait till the end of the summer and then see how we feel. Get a chance to know each other all over again."

"I don't see why we should put it off, if we're going to break up. I should have thought that you'd be glad to get it over with."

"You're sore because I didn't find time to write more often and I should have done it, I admit. But if we break up now we won't have any fun all summer. There isn't another girl in town I'd take to a dogfight, and we run around with the same people and we'd be bound to meet each other and everything would be stiff and strained all around. Sure, I don't mind saying I've had my doubts about us too, but there's no use flying off the handle like this. Let's wait."

"I'll feel exactly like a package on a shelf, waiting to be called for."

"You'll have fun. You'll see."

He was right about that. The summer was a long, glorious romp. They were asked everywhere together, and now their social group was a more sophisticated one. The young married crowd, backbone of the country-club set, pounced on them with the glee of a weary producer discovering a fresh new act.

"Here come the bride and groom. Give them a cocktail, Tony, they look pale."

The men ogled Eleanor hopefully. "I'll tell you what. Let's you and me go over here in the corner and I'll give you the real lowdown on this young fellow you're making the great mistake of marrying."

"I'd be afraid to listen."

"Even if I held your hand?"

"Now listen here, Jeff, you stay away from my girl, you old lady-killer! This guy's broken up more marriages in this town than——"

"I resent that. I call on my wife to bear me witness, I am never out and abroad after nine o'clock at night."

They howled. They had another cocktail all around. At eight o'clock someone would suggest dinner.

"Food! That horrid stuff? Never touch it."

"John, I'll take Eleanor in my car. You take Sally."

"None of that. She came with me and she'll leave with me!"

"We'll let the lady decide for herself. Which one of us do you want to drive with, honey?"

"I guess I'd better go with John. He has such a dreadful temper."

The banter made John feel seasoned and masculine. "I've got her trained, see. 'Get 'em young, treat 'em rough, and tell 'em nothing,' that's my motto."

"Sure, she's scared to death. You think."

They would go on to dinner and out to someone's cottage by the lake and stop for a nightcap and a hamburger on the way home. Their cars were big and shiny, their clothes tailor-made, they allowed themselves to become gay but not maudlin, they kept a careful eye on respectability while they dangled just the tips of their toes in the waters of dissipation. Only occasionally did someone go too far. They forgave him, but if he persisted in his error they dropped him like a hot potato. They were not going to get themselves talked about.

They moved so fast, so constantly, that sometimes Eleanor wearied. "Let's not go tonight. Let's just sit here and take it easy. I haven't been in bed before two any night this week."

"Time enough to sit around when we're old. Come on, let's get going."

Always Aunt Ann sided against her. "After all, John's only here for the summer. You can rest in September after he's gone."

Somehow she always had a better time than she had thought she would. Yawning against John's shoulder on the way home, she would admit that he had been right.

"I'm glad we went. Jeff is an awful clown, isn't he? I thought I'd die when he took the Spanish Shawl off the piano and went into his dance."

"He's a card, all right. Got a good business head on him too, Dad says. Hey, you going to fall asleep before I get you home?"

"I'll try not to, but I won't promise."

"Better get some sleep in the morning. Club dance tomorrow night."

"You must be made of iron!"

"Darned near it."

"We haven't had our talk yet, and August is almost gone."

He had forgotten all about it. "Let's skip it. We can't break up now, can't you see that? Girls sure get silly notions when they're left to themselves."

"You said you had your doubts too."

"Well, I had to say something. I couldn't very well get down on my knees and say, 'Darling, forgive me, take me back,' could I?"

"Then you really want to get married next June?"

"Sure I do. Then we'll have our own place and we can ask the crowd in and have a fine time. I can hardly wait."

In the reassurance that flooded her she did not notice that, in his proclamation of intentions, he had omitted any statement of affection.

Her feeling of security was short-lived. In the last—and worst—period of waiting, his letters followed the same ominous pattern, long and enthusiastic for the first month or so, short and casual after that. He did not come home for the Christmas holidays, saying that he was a little behind in his work, that he had to cram for midyear exams. This year her birthday did not draw even a belated card.

For the town's benefit she appeared calm and confident. At home she ate little, slept less, and spent hours alone in her room. There was no use talking things over with her aunt. She would only be called fanciful and lovesick and melancholy. But every passing minute made things worse. He was going to jilt her and, the closer she let herself get to the altar, the worse it would be when the blow came. Sometimes she thought that all her life had been spent waiting for John or worrying about him.

Aunt Ann, though Eleanor would never have guessed it, was uneasy too. The elder Kendricks remained cordial and polite but she had sensed an embarrassment in their manner to her, and there could be only one reason for that. John was changing his mind and they knew it. The young man would have to be brought to his senses!

She sent him a wire asking him not to tell Eleanor but to come to the house as soon as he could: there was something she wanted to discuss with him. Within three hours she had his answer: "Skipping Commencement. Will be home Friday next week. See you at eight." She had been right. A combination of curiosity and manners was bringing him.

She said nothing to Eleanor about his coming. At seven-thirty she sent the girl next door with a glass of jelly for old, loquacious Mrs. Thomas, who was in bed with arthritis. That would give her plenty of time to get John settled.

He came up on the porch, serious-faced, hurried. "What in the world's the matter? Where's Eleanor?"

"I sent her out on an errand, John. Come in here and sit down."

He sat down in a carved rosewood chair, twisting his light hatbrim between his hands. Good Lord, what was this all about? He had some pretty important things to say himself, and this wasn't making it any easier for him. He could have told Eleanor simply and plainly enough that he thought the marriage should be called off, that there was another girl, and that he was sorry. It wasn't going to be so easy to break the news to this kindly, gentle old lady who had always been

79

so good to him and who was pretty bothered about something herself.

"I may as well tell you directly, John. Eleanor wants to break the engagement."

Surprise snapped his head back. "She does?"

"I know it must be a shock to you. Eleanor's so quiet about her personal feelings. Well . . ." She threw up her slender hands and her rings flashed. "I've done my best to change her mind. Now you'll have to try."

"Well, but if she's——"

Aunt Ann didn't hear him. She had to tell about her disappointment with Eleanor. "I've asked her to consider what people will say. After all, you both have to live in this town. You associate with the same people. It's going to be awkward, running into each other everywhere with a thing like this between you and everybody knowing it. And what your family will think of her, I don't know! I've tried to explain to her that an engagement is a contract and that you can't just walk out of a contract any time you've a mind to."

She went on and on, and he thanked God a thousand times that he had not blurted out the truth, that he was as anxious to end the thing as Eleanor was. He had been smart, too, in not telling his family straight out or making things too definite with Mae. Now the whole thing was going to solve itself. Eleanor had decided not to have him! As Aunt Ann talked he shook his head and looked sad and rejoiced in the crown of martyrdom she was pressing upon him.

"But you must admit, John, you haven't treated her so well this last year."

"Oh, I know. I thought about her a lot, though. All the time. I never expected a thing like this."

"How could you have? Everyone knows you've been in love with her for years."

"That's true. All the time in high school and ever since. It's not going to be easy to face people after being thrown over like this. Especially when I've done nothing to deserve it. I'll admit this last year was too frantic for me, but I thought she knew how things were. I didn't dream . . ." He succeeded in bringing a choke into his voice.

Eleanor came in, blinking at the sudden brightness after the dark street outside. Aunt Ann rose, a thin gray lance in the firelight.

"Eleanor," she said firmly, "John and I have decided that we've both had enough of this nonsense. He's terribly sorry for the way he's neglected you, but you're the only girl he's ever cared anything about. Now you stop your moping about and start behaving as a prospective bride should. I'm going out to make some coffee for the three of us."

Eleanor didn't know what had happened. The shock of seeing him there so unexpectedly, the fact that he had evidently declared himself again, made her start to cry openly, foolishly. He put his hat down and came over to her.

"Hey, don't do that. There's nothing to cry about."

"I don't mean to, it's just that I've been so miserable. Oh, John, are you *sure?*"

There was nothing left for him to do or say. As he took her in his arms and stroked her hair he reflected that it might not work out so badly. He told himself all over again that she was a handsome girl, that his family liked her, that they'd have a good time in Ashland with the gang. Wryly he reminded himself that he might as well make the best of it; he certainly couldn't tell them now what he had come to say.

In the mirror across the room he saw that the two of them made an attractive picture. And Eleanor had been crazy about him ever since they were in high school. It was only natural that, no matter what silly ideas she'd had in her head, they should disappear the minute she saw him. Poor kid, she sure depended on him, thought he was the kingpin of the universe. John and Eleanor. This was the way it ought to be. Why did he keep forgetting?

They were married at high noon in the Episcopal Church exactly one month later.

7.

Penelope King was dressing for a dance. Her stepmother sat on the edge of the white enameled bed and tried to be casual, as though this were any other evening, as though this were not Penny's first formal affair. But Hetty Saunders King was not really calm. She had never been able to look at the beauty of the daughter that Fate had bestowed upon her, completed and ready-made, without sucking in her breath sharply. She couldn't get used to it, even living with it every day. Her vast pride shone through the maternal mask till her homely, rugged face seemed about to break into laughter. For here was the first of the Great Occasions; there would be a thousand or more of them before Penny settled down in a home of her own and was lost to Hetty's gloating, in which the second Mrs. King would live vicariously the moments of power and romance of which she had been cheated by an unfortunate face and early poverty.

Penny, conversely, was genuinely calm but was trying not to appear so. Like most exceptionally handsome people, she was not troubled by any powerful emotional stirrings of her own. The best she could do was to respond faithfully to the emotions she sensed in others. Right now she was acting pretty confusion and artless girlishness for Hetty's entrancement. She caught her full lower lip with perfect white teeth in a picturesque exasperation over a stocking seam that would not come straight. She furrowed her brow a little over the perking of the ribbons that ran through the neckline of her white organdy. She stamped her foot when her copper curls refused the discipline of a brush. And all the while her dark blue eyes stared levelly at the picture she made in the tall mirror and found it good. Certainly no one at the dance would suspect that she was only fifteen years old and just about, a bit tardily, to enter high school. Downstairs she heard the doorbell ring and the rustling of the newspaper in her father's hand as he went to answer it.

"There's Henry," she said indifferently.

"Well, you're all ready. I've got your coat laid out in the hall."

"And the beaded bag? With all my make-up?"

"It's all there. The white chiffon handkerchief too."

Hetty was standing up, apprehensive of a waiting male. Penny caught up both her hands. "Can I wear your diamond, Hetty? I'll take awfully good care of it. Please."

"I don't mind your wearing it, but it isn't suitable. Diamonds at your age!"

"Oh, who cares? It's so pretty. Please let me."

Hetty tugged at the diamond cluster mounted on tall golden prongs. Penny slipped it over her slim finger and held it up to catch the light. If you weren't real close you'd swear it was one big diamond!

"It's lovely. Thank you."

"Penelope King, you put that on your other hand! That's your engagement finger."

Penny shoved her lips into a luscious pout. "It won't show there at all. That's the hand your partner covers up when you dance. I want it to be on his shoulder where you can see it."

"But there'll be older people there, and some of them will know you. It'll make talk. It's bad enough that you should be wearing such a ring at all without——"

Penny hugged her. "We don't care what a bunch of old fogies say, do we?"

"Well, just don't let your father catch sight of it when you get downstairs."

As she came down the stairs in a froufrou of silk slip and stiff organdy, she paused to catch her full reflection in the mirror on the landing. Yes, there she was, tall and slender, auburn hair brushed into short, silky ringlets, a little smile dimpling the perfect cheek, the narrow silver slipper extended for the next step. Over her shoulder she caught the brooding adulation of Hetty. As she rounded the balustrade she saw seventeen-year-old Henry Mason standing in the hall below, engaged in arduous conversation with her father.

"Hello," she called at him, and was careful to pause until he had turned. She was rewarded by Henry's gasp as the picture she made hit him in his visual midriff. He walked over to the foot of the stairs, holding a glazed white box before him, tripping on the rug.

"Watch out, there," she sang. "I don't want to get to the country club and have nobody to dance with!"

It was unfortunate that Henry's voice was in the croaking stage, but the admiration in its inflections made it almost pleasant. "I guess you won't have to worry about partners, anybody that looks like you."

She came down, being careful to keep her left hand hidden in her skirts. The white box held a corsage of baby roses. She pinned them on, laughing and chattering, and preened herself, throwing little flirtatious glances at her father and longer, more significant ones at Henry. The two of them helped her into her wrap, handed her the beaded bag, consulted with each other as to whether she would be warm enough. It was cool for June.

"The car's right outside, Mr. King, and I'll park close to the door at the club. I think she'll be all right."

"I won't be cold, Daddy." She nestled her head against his shoulder, briefly. You know I like you best, the gesture said. Henry's just the boy I'm going to a dance with. He doesn't mean a thing, really. And even while her head was down she raised her long lashes to look at Henry. Daddy thinks I'm still just his little girl, the look said. I have to humor him, he's wonderful, but I can hardly wait to get to the dance with you.

"Don't keep her too late, Henry."

"The dance is over by eleven-thirty. I thought we might stop at College Inn and have something to eat——"

Jason looked doubtful and Penny had to rush at him with a hug. "School's out, Daddy. I don't have to get up in the morning. Please. It won't hurt me to have one grown-up evening."

Her father's face relaxed into indulgence. "Well, come home right after that, then. We'll be in bed, but we'll leave the front door open."

She kissed Hetty, she patted her father's arm—with her right hand —she took Henry's arm and swirled him out the door. It was not dark yet, and a white moon was rising in a sky not cleared of sunset flare. The neighbors were all out on their porches. She could almost feel the way their heads were snapping toward her as she came down the walk to Henry's father's big black car. She stood back to let him be assiduous at the car door.

"Well," called Mr. Jenkins from over the hedge, "somebody's stepping out tonight, I see."

She smiled at him deferentially and shyly, the smile she kept for men of her father's generation. "I'm going to my first dance, Mr. Jenkins." Her voice was clear and carrying with just the proper amount of girlish excitement in it. "Wish me luck."

"If I were young enough to go myself young Henry'd have to hump himself to get a dance with you."

She winked at Henry. "I wish you were going, Mr. Jenkins. I'll bet you're a good dancer."

"In my day, young lady. In my day." He waved benignly, paternally. He, too, knew that the neighbors were looking. "Have a good time."

He went on clipping the hedge, watched the white ruffles tucked into the car, watched the car drive down the street. That youngest King girl was a darned nice girl. Treated you like a man, by God, and not like a whited sepulcher. Such a pretty youngster, too, you wouldn't think she'd bother to be extra nice to a forty-year-old gent. Maybe she wasn't with all of them. Maybe she really thought he was some guy. You couldn't know. Once in a while some kid really admired an older fellow. His own daughter, now, she was older than Penny, but she acted like he was just somebody to see she had food and clothes and a place to live. Never thought of him as a person who might be going to a dance and shaking a mean foot. Didn't believe that he could appreciate a pretty girl and a beautiful June night. Not in any wrong way, of course, but gosh! You could be a father and a family man and still be human.

Mrs. Jenkins came down from the porch and stood beside him. She was a tall, thin woman who wore glasses and knitted interminably.

"Well, what do you know about that!" she sniffed. "I declare, Jason King is losing his mind. I didn't expect anything better from Hetty, she's silly about that girl, but Jason ought to know better than to let a fifteen-year-old start going to public dances. I'll bet the Masons don't know who Henry's taking. They'd be wild."

"Only fifteen, hey? I'd forgotten. She looks more like eighteen. Darned pretty girl, anyway. Best-looking girl in this town."

Mrs. Jenkins stiffened. "Pretty enough, but what's that going to get her if she loses her reputation before she's grown up?"

"I don't see how going to a dance at the country club is going to lose her reputation for her. They have chaperons there and everything."

"You're just like all men. If a girl's pretty enough, whatever she's doing is right. Well, I didn't let Joyce go out alone with a boy until she was eighteen years old!"

"We didn't exactly have to fight 'em off. Joyce isn't as pretty as Penny. I don't notice that anybody's breaking down our doors even yet."

"Oscar Jenkins, what's gotten into you!"

"And as far as age goes, I don't believe you were even twelve that day your folks came to visit us on the farm and I got you down to the barn to see the new kittens and——"

He chuckled at her retreating back. It was a wonderful evening. He hadn't felt so good in a long time.

Henry Mason leaned against a doorway and scowled at the dance floor. He was not having a good time. Oh, it wasn't Penny's fault. She tried to be with him every minute she could and she was always a little angry when anyone else cut in, which they did about every ten steps. These other fellows were being such pigs, that was the trouble! Why didn't they go dance with their own girls? Course, a lot of these cheapskates hadn't even bothered to bring a girl. They just stood in the stag line and cut in when they wanted to. There ought to be a law!

Perry Wilder, his family's dentist, stepped up to him and asked for a match.

"Gosh, I don't—here's some, over here."

Dr. Wilder looked different in a tux than he did in his white dentist's coat. Impressive, kind of. Younger, somehow. From force of habit he watched Dr. Wilder's hands, though, in case one of those little torturing icepicks should suddenly materialize therein. But Dr. Wilder put his hands in his pockets and leaned back against the wall amicably, puffing at his cigarette in an experienced fashion that Henry couldn't keep from envying.

"Why aren't you out there dancing, Henry? I've been watching you stand here for half an hour."

Henry's wrongs spluttered through his vocal cords. "Because there's nobody to dance with, that's why! They won't let me dance with my own girl, and they didn't bring any girls of their own that I could swap off with. Honest, Dr. Wilder, wouldn't you think at a formal dance like this the committee would make a rule that stags couldn't come?" Discretion laid a cold hand on rhetoric. "You brought a girl, didn't you, Dr. Wilder?"

"Oh yes. I'm in much the same case as you. They won't let me dance with my girl either. Sue Manning. There she is over there with Tony Fox."

Sue Manning was a small, black-haired girl who leaned back from her partners to look up at them. This had the double effect of pressing the lower half of her body closer against them and of giving them a flattering illusion of greater height than they possessed. She laughed and talked without a letup. Penny, swirling by, looked cool and distant by comparison. She stood remotely within the black circle of male arm and she kept her eyes down except when she raised them for her brief, lovely smile.

"That's mine. In white. Penny King."

"Oh, one of the King girls. I know Eleanor a little. I can't place this one. Has she been away at school?"

Henry guffawed. "I should say not. She's been right here all the time. She's just finished the eighth grade at Linden School!" He was enjoying the sensation of fellowship with an older man. He was ready to go on with the details about how his family had used to live next door to the Kings and how he knew Penny was crazy about dancing and how magnanimous he had been to extend this invitation.

But Dr. Wilder's interest in him seemed to have waned. He said, "Oh, that young, hey?" and turned and went into the smoking room where a poker game was organizing.

Over a fresh masculine shoulder Penny watched him go and frowned. She had seen Dr. Wilder on the street and she had tried to get her father to let her change dentists ever since. But Daddy had known old Dr. Krim for a coon's age and he wouldn't hear of changing. It didn't matter to Daddy whether a dentist were good-looking or not married or chased after by every girl in town.

"A penny for your thoughts, Penny," said Tony Fox.

She gave a sudden little laugh, as though the witticism were brand-new and overwhelmingly original. "I was thinking how good the music is. We have a Victrola at home, but it's old and scratchy and you have to use your imagination if you're going to dance to it."

"I don't know where you live. Matter of fact I don't even know your last name."

"King. Penelope King. I live near Arch and Cambridge. Maybe you know one of my sisters. Eleanor—she's going to marry John Kendrick. Or Martha; she's away at the university."

"I know Eleanor. Funny she's never had you around. Even if you are still in high school, you'd be ornamental to any crowd."

"Thank you." Her eyelids fluttered down again. She hadn't told him she was in high school, but she wasn't going to deny it. She was having such a wonderful time. It was almost like the kid parties she'd been going to all her life. All the boys had always run after her there too. It didn't seem to matter whether the boys were older or younger, bigger or smaller, they liked you if you were pretty enough. Only here they didn't try to drag you out on the front porch so they could kiss you. They tried to find out your name and address so they could call you up and make a date or two, and somewhere in the midst of the calling and going and coming they would get you out on a porch or in a car and kiss you. It all boiled down to the same thing in the end. This way was nicer, though, because the girl got something out of it—dinners or dances or movies. The only thing you got out of

87

being kissed damply by a grade school boy was a feeling that you ought to go home and wash your face. She wasn't crazy about being kissed, or mauled around either, and she permitted as little of it as was necessary to get what she wanted, which was to be the most popular girl in town with the boys. Girls didn't count. If you were popular with girls it usually meant that there was something wrong with you, that you were ugly or dumb or too standoffish with fellows. Girls never liked you if they thought you could get ahead of them.

The big drum with the red light inside illuminating the picture of the Hawaiian girl painted on it stopped short. She was ready to step back and join the spatter of applause, but Tony kept his arm around her.

"Stop me if you've heard this one," he said. "You're the loveliest thing I ever saw. I'm going to give Eleanor hell for keeping you under wraps!"

Oh dear, that was the bad feature of it! They'd all go talk to Eleanor or John or Henry Mason and they'd find out she was only fifteen and she'd have to wait years and years before anybody paid her any attention again!

"I wish you wouldn't. She'd think I was too young to be here."

She pushed him away gently and the diamond ring sent up little Roman candles of color. He picked up her left hand.

"Engaged, Penny? If you're too young to be here you're certainly too young to be engaged."

She looked beseeching. "Was it wrong of me to wear it? I've had it for such a long time, and of course the family doesn't know. Fred—the man who gave it to me—is away at college, and I thought tonight it wouldn't matter if I put it on. Oh, I know I can't get married for years and ages, but the ring's pretty, isn't it?"

"You can get a prettier one by waiting awhile." He frowned paternally. "Listen here, Penny, you don't want to go getting married before you're twenty or so. No use tying yourself down to one man with years to wait. The thing to do is send him back his ring and tell him you want to window-shop for a while. Who does he think he is, putting a 'No Trespassing' sign up on you and then romping off to have fun for himself? Because, mark my words, Penny, he *is* having fun. He's not sitting at home evenings knitting!"

They were moving slowly toward the doors to the veranda. She was enthralled with the implications of the scene she was playing now. It

88

was just like being a heroine in the movies. If only Henry wouldn't appear, yawping and stammering at her heels!

She put a distressed hand on Tony's arm. "Oh, I don't think he'd go out with another girl when he's engaged to me. He told me——"

"Sure he did. They all tell you that another girl would turn their stomachs. That's the bait that's supposed to keep you hooked. But put it down in your book that he's not running away from any pretty girl he meets that'll give him the time of day. So why should you sit at home and mope? You should be out having a good time too."

The darkness of the veranda enveloped them. Penny waited for a patch of moonlight before she let tears come to her eyes. Lovely tears that paused on the lashes and did not roll down to disfigure the pink of her cheeks.

"I can't believe it! Would—would you act like that if you were engaged? Would you still keep going with other girls?"

He sat down on the balustrade facing her. He was a dark, powerfully built young man who helped his father run the most successful automobile agency in town. He knew that his masculinity, his poise, his assurance, must be impressive to this pretty child. She would believe anything he chose to tell her. He could see, too, that she was thinking how kind it was of him to dismiss more important things from his mind and focus his attention on her small problems. Well, darn it, he'd tell her the truth!

"Listen. We're not all alike. I just happen to be a one-woman man. Not that I've found the woman yet, but when I do she'll be the only one who'll take up a minute of my time. But most men aren't like that. They don't have enough character to resist a woman who really sets out after them. I'll admit it isn't always easy, but if you're really in love with a girl I think you should be true to her."

"But then—but then a man like you is the only kind I should—any girl should—get serious about."

He smiled at her. "That makes me sound pretty conceited." He watched the shadows of wisteria leaves flutter on her white shoulders. His hand longed to touch the red silk of her hair. Lord, what a beauty! He'd been thinking Sue Manning was pretty, but she wasn't a patch on this girl. He'd asked Sue to go out to dinner with him next Saturday, but maybe he could get out of that and ask Penny instead.

"Oh, I don't think you're at all conceited. Conceited people always want to talk about themselves and all we've done is talk about me."

Sue Manning flounced out on the porch in a temper. "I can't find Perry anywhere," she said. "Young Henry Mason says he's in a poker game in the smoking room. Go and get him out for me, will you, Tony?"

Penny drew back shyly, a person unwanted, eliminated. Tony wouldn't have that. Who did Sue think she was, stamping out here as if she owned him, making Penny feel like an outsider! He took the hand with the diamond on it and drew her back into the circle.

"Sure, I'll go. This is Penny King. Sue Manning."

Sue threw her a brief glance of unadulterated hate, and Penny smiled serenely. She must be even more popular than she had thought to make such an attractive girl dislike her so thoroughly on such short notice. It was the highest moment of the evening for Penny.

She had to stay pretty close to Henry for the last hour of the dance, because he was getting really annoyed.

"You didn't have to go outside with him," he kept saying. "He should have brought you over to me. I was standing right there in plain sight!"

"Henry, we didn't see you. Honest. And I was so warm after all that dancing that I wanted to cool off a little."

"You could have come over to me and I'd have taken you outside."

She widened her eyes in amazement. "Why, Henry, you talk as if I wouldn't much rather have been with you! Tony Fox is so *old*. My goodness, he must be ten years older than I am. It's just like talking to your grandfather!"

Henry was mollified. "Well, I didn't have any idea when I brought you here that you were going to turn out to be a belle or something."

"But I'm not! They're being nice to me because of you, don't you see? They know who you are and your family and all, and they think they're pleasing you by dancing with me."

Had that been too thick, too overdone? No, Henry had relaxed. He was smiling and there was a glint of pride behind his thick glasses. It was too bad that, out of all the boys she knew, Henry was the only one whose family belonged to the country club, and worse yet that he should be sort of silly and have pimples on his forehead.

Now his voice carried a revived authority. "You'd better hang around with me from now on. These older guys, they've been drinking. By the end of an evening they're likely to be acting pretty fresh."

She trembled a little. "I haven't seen anyone drinking."

"Of course not. They all have flasks out in their cars. They keep going out and taking a nip here and there, and some of the girls go right along with 'em."

She pressed his arm. "I'm glad you don't drink, Henry."

"What I say is, a fellow who has to follow the crowd isn't much of a man. Most guys don't have any self-restraint, that's all."

"But *you* do." It was a mere breath of admiration.

He patted her hand. Good night, but she was pretty! Those wide dark blue eyes, so serious now, the tall grace of her walk, the arm-impelling curve of her waist and, best of everything, her naturalness. She was completely unconscious of what a picture she made. His sisters, for instance, were always diving at mirrors and slapping powder puffs on their faces and looking to see if anything was showing below their dresses. He hadn't seen Penny look at a single mirror yet, or pay any attention to what the other girls were wearing, or say what thick ankles So-and-so had, wasn't it a shame. Just a nice, natural kid, that's what she was.

He tried to look potent but controlled. "If I didn't have plenty of restraint I'd kiss you here and now!"

Now he'd scared her, for her hand dropped from his arm as though he had stung it. But then she saw that he'd been joking, for she laughed and twinkled at him. The music began and he swept her into his arms and started off at a trot.

Penny kept smiling, but she was provoked. In the first place she was too tall to look her best doing a short, quick, bouncing step. In the second place she could see that Henry was planning to do some necking on the way home, and in her present exalted, triumphant mood she had no intention of being mussed and crushed by a mere boy. Tony Fox, now, would be a different matter, or Dr. Wilder.

"I saw you talking to Dr. Wilder," she said.

"Yeah. He came with Sue Manning, but he got disgusted waiting for her and went in to play cards. I almost did myself."

"Sue was looking for him later."

"I know. She asked me where he was. Oops, sorry. Guess my foot slid. He wanted to know who you were." He laughed his horrible croaking laugh. "Thought you'd been away to school somewhere. I told him you'd been right here at Linden all along."

She could have killed him where he stood! That was why Dr.

Wilder had walked away without waiting to be introduced to her. Her voice was almost sharp. "You don't have to tell everything you know, do you?"

It threw him off his stride and he nearly crushed her instep. "It's no secret, is it? It's the truth, isn't it? Gee, everybody who knows your family at all must know all about you, or they could soon find out if they wanted to."

Well, that was true enough. How silly she had been to make up that story about an engagement for Tony Fox! What good was it to get him interested in stealing another fellow's girl when all he needed was a minute with Eleanor to find out that the whole thing had been a lie? But for a minute she had been carried away, she had imagined that she was as old as these other girls, just like Tony had taken her to be. She'd have to make that up to him somehow. After all, it would be only two or three years before she'd be old enough to be taken seriously.

Henry was croaking again. "Listen, Penny, it won't be so long before school starts this fall and even though you'll just be a freshman you're going to be pretty popular, I expect. I want to ask you here and now if you'll come to the Junior Prom with me in December. Of course it isn't supposed to be proper for me to take anybody but a junior or senior, but there isn't any law against it. You'll be the only freshman there, probably. Will you come?"

"I'd love to, but that's a long way ahead, isn't it? I mean, you may want to take another girl by that time."

In his mind's eye he could see the two of them dancing together in the school gymnasium, the paper decorations fluttering over their heads. He could see the rush of the other boys to him to get their names put down on Penny's dance card. He could hear himself saying, "I tell you, I've put myself down for only four dances with her. I'm *not* being piggish. I've split almost all these dances already, and I tell you there isn't another one left!" Oh, he guessed he'd have plenty of attention that night from all the fellows who'd been thinking he was a dull thud! He'd show 'em Henry Mason wasn't so slow, he knew how to pick 'em. One of the ways you judged a boy's prestige was by the attractiveness of the girls he could get to go out with him. There weren't any girls more attractive than Penny.

"Listen, I don't change my mind. Honest, I want you to say you'll go!"

She didn't want to commit herself. In the time from September to December she was pretty sure she could get somebody else to ask her. Almost anybody would be better than Henry. Still, she couldn't afford to shut him out completely. She smiled shyly at him. "If we both feel the same way about it by then I'll go."

He missed the word "both." He considered that she had given an unqualified assent.

Eleanor and John stopped in for the last few minutes of the dance. They had been playing bridge at the Johnsons', and it had been an unfortunate evening. Mrs. Johnson had been visibly and audibly pregnant, and John had been bored into a temper.

"For God's sake!" he had exploded to Eleanor in the car "The minute some of these women know they're going to have a baby they expect the whole world to be interested in it!"

"It's only natural with the first——"

"Natural! To expect your husband and your friends to seal up the doors and sit down and listen to every little symptom and get all excited about whether it's to be a boy or a girl and how many diapers to buy for it? I need a nightcap to get the taste of condensed milk out of my mouth. Let's go over to the club. There's some kind of a shindig going on."

So now she stood at the door of the ballroom, wishing that her head would stop aching, looking around to find somebody she knew, feeling John prance with restlessness at her elbow.

"Hey, there's Penny," he said. "Say, she looks all right, doesn't she? Believe I'll give her a surprise and go over and cut in. You'll be fine here for a minute, won't you?"

She sat down in an uncomfortable wooden folding chair to wait. She suspected that what John had really wanted was to see the pretty young girls slipping so lightly across the floor, to erase from his mind the picture of the swollen, sedentary Mrs. Johnson, who until a few months ago had been as gay and agile as these.

Really, it was absurd for Penny to be here. She would have to speak to Hetty. Watching John's big shoulders move expertly through the crowd, seeing the delight on Penny's face as she recognized him, observing how well their steps seemed to fit together, she felt a small sick envy. Penny had no imminent marriage to worry about, no anxiety about accumulating duties and responsibilities, no cares beyond the immediate present. Had there ever been a time when she herself had been as young and free as Penny?

She was glad when Tony Fox came over to talk to her.

"You came just in time," she told him. "I was sitting here feeling a thousand years old."

He talked so fast that it took her five minutes to discover that he had a wild idea that Penny was engaged and should be persuaded out of it.

"Tony, don't be crazy! Of course she isn't engaged. I don't know who could have told you a thing like that. She's just entering high school this fall and she's only fifteen years old. Engaged! I ask you!"

She did not see his jaw drop. She was watching John convoy Penny over to her, gathering in young Henry Mason on the way.

"We're all going out to have something to eat," John boomed. "College Inn, Henry, and it's my party! It isn't every day I get a chance to impress my pretty prospective sister-in-law this way."

Wearily she got to her feet. At least at the inn she would be sitting down. John didn't want to be alone with her. He must be finding her pretty dull if this pair of youngsters could so divert him. Tonight she didn't care. If only she could get to bed!

Penny darted away from the little group to catch Tony's arm.

"I'm sorry I lied to you, Mr. Fox. I guess it was because I thought —if you knew how young I was—you wouldn't pay any more attention to me. And—well—I liked you so much and——"

Tall and gallant and brave and young, she stood, eyes cast down and tears not far off. What the heck, you couldn't blame the kid. She'd just done what she could to make him notice her. There was no crime in that, even if she *had* taken him for a little ride. He patted her hand and forgave her.

"Don't try it with anyone else, though," he warned. "It's not every fellow that would understand."

Laughter made a prism of her tears. "Oh, thank you, Mr. Fox. I wouldn't have any reason to do it again. It was your fault, really. If you hadn't been so nice to me and said all those kind things I wouldn't have tried to make you keep it up." She added childishly and gravely, "You see, you're the very best-looking man I've ever met."

He watched her go down the stairs with Eleanor and John and young Mason. Poor kid, she had a case on him. Puppy love, of course, and she'd get over it. No harm done. Still, in two or three years from now she'd be a mighty nice number. Darn it, it was kind of flattering even now to have her admire him so.

He turned and went to hunt for the girl he had brought to the dance. He hadn't thought of her for the last hour and a half.

8.

Mother Kendrick was a plump, pink, decisive woman who meant well. Intelligent, uneducated, emotional, she was stubbornly sure that everything she had ever done had been right. She had a mind like a commodious cupboard, sparsely furnished with prejudices, old wives' tales, superstitions, second guesses, and opinions picked up from her husband that she could voice but not substantiate. At fifty-two, with her five children grown, the menopause past, her household running smoothly under the guidance of a housekeeper she had "trained herself," she had twenty years of good health and leisure ahead of her and nothing to do with it. Proudly, she had never read a book in her life. She had "never had time for reading." She liked to play auction bridge, but only "for fun," which meant that no one should be so unkind as to play too serious or clever a game.

"These people who play cards as if it was a matter of life or death make me tired!" she told Eleanor, who was learning contract. "They don't want any talking at the table, and they snap at you when it's your turn to deal, and it's as much as your life's worth to get one of them to repeat a bid, and they remember every card down to the nine spots! 'Well!' I told Mrs. Markham yesterday. 'If all I had on my mind was cards, I guess I could be a shark too. I have more important things to think about,' I told her. 'I play cards for relaxation.' I must say I don't think it's *friendly* to double a bid. I've never done it in my life!"

Eleanor sympathized, while she wondered how Mother Kendrick, friendship or no, *could* double a bid when she never looked at a hand long enough to evaluate it.

Father Kendrick played a much better game, but he upheld his wife's viewpoint. He was suspicious of any woman who played a good game of cards because he felt that it must have taken a feminine mind a long time to achieve such expertness, and a woman had had to neglect something else to do it, probably her housework or her husband. He didn't like to play cards with women.

"Give me a man's game every time!" he boomed at Eleanor, when she was trying to make up a mixed family foursome. "Women don't really want to play cards. They just want an excuse to sit down and talk. Course, if they get any fun out of it, that's their business, and let 'em go to it. But I don't like a game that's all cluttered up with chitchat and 'Partner, I'll inkle a club' and 'I don't have anything, but I hated to see them get the bid.' Let the girls play by themselves, that's what I say."

Yet, when he was finally coaxed to sit down at a table with the calculating and relentless Mrs. Markham as his chief opponent, when she set him every third bid and outfinessed him two times out of three and left him three thousand points behind in the score, he was angrier still. "When women win they gloat!" he complained to Eleanor. "Oh, they don't say anything and they try to look sweet as pie, but they're gloating all the same. Women are such darned rotten sports!"

The senior Kendricks were one of Eleanor's chief problems. They were insistent upon "family." Three of their children lived in other towns, and Mother Kendrick religiously spent one month a year with each of them, straightening out their affairs, making suggestions for the better training of the children, giving excellent and unsought advice to her various in-laws. The rest of the time she was free to concentrate on John and Eleanor, and on her daughter Elizabeth, who was married to Stephen Longworth, a lawyer who was often called away on important cases on the evenings when the clan assembled at the elder Kendricks' for dinner.

When she was first married Eleanor had liked the feeling of being welcomed into the fold, the sensation of belonging to a solid group, her new official status of a wife and, hence, a representative of the Kendrick dignity. She and her mother-in-law lunched together frequently, dined together twice a week, called each other on the telephone innumerable times in between.

Mother Kendrick was solicitous concerning such things as the number of hours of sleep Eleanor got. "You young things, thinking you can burn the candle at both ends. John gets up so early, he should be in bed by ten every week night."

Eleanor took this as honest maternal anxiety and tried to conform, but John was unco-operative. He wanted to read till all hours, or go out to dinner and a dance, or play cards, or ask a few people in. He scoffed at ten o'clock.

"I've never gone to bed before twelve in my life," he informed Eleanor. "After a fellow works all day the only way to get a little fun is to stretch the evening out. Sure, I should get more sleep. I ought to turn into a little automaton that just works and eats and goes to bed. Only I won't do it."

"There's no use being angry at me, John. I don't care when we go to bed. But your mother seems to feel so strongly about it."

"She's just trying to show her authority, prove to herself that I'm still just her own little boy. I didn't go to bed early when I lived at home. And I hope you notice that when we spend an evening there we don't dare suggest going home until after midnight. It seems to make a whale of a lot of difference whose time we're sleeping on!"

He did not respect his mother, he ignored or laughed at almost everything she said, but he had an odd loyalty to her. It made things difficult for Eleanor. It turned her into a buffer between Mrs. Kendrick's mandates and John's heedlessness of them. She was constantly having to cover up for John, to be secretive about the things he ate, his social activities, the number of highballs he drank in an evening, and the time he went to bed. On the other hand she had to soften Mrs. Kendrick's pronouncements so that John would not be antagonized and furious—not with his mother but with Eleanor. It was a delicate middle ground and she could not know when she would be floundering in the swamp on one hand or catapulting down the cliff on the other. The first six months of her married life were spent in torment between John's thinking her a milksop and her mother-in-law's hinting that Eleanor might not be the proper person to have the supervision of her son's health and well-being.

The first puzzling break came in the fourth month of their marriage. They had had a two weeks' honeymoon trip, they had moved into their new house, three blocks from the senior Kendricks', the deluge of invitations due to their new marital state had subsided somewhat. Eleanor arranged a party of her own, a buffet supper for sixteen of their friends, and, to be truthful, it did not even occur to her to invite John's father and mother, nor that they would wish to be asked to join a group thirty years younger than themselves. The affair was successful and gay, and Eleanor congratulated herself on the smoothness with which it had come off.

The next day Mrs. Kendrick did not telephone. The morning after that she sent word, by Elizabeth, that she had such a bad headache that she did not feel up to having them all in for the usual Thursday night dinner. It was so unusual for Mother Kendrick to be ill that Eleanor suggested to John that they go over to call on her that evening.

John chuckled. "There's nothing wrong with Mother. She's miffed because she wasn't asked to the party night before last."

"Oh, John, no!"

"Sure. She's being hoity-toity, like a prima donna. She'll come down to earth. It'll wear off."

"But I'm sick about it! I had no idea she'd enjoy—maybe all she wanted was the privilege of refusing. I could at least have gone through the motions of asking her!"

"Don't kid yourself. If you'd asked her, she'd have come."

"Oh dear. She doesn't go to all Elizabeth's parties, does she?"

"Nope. But Elizabeth's her own daughter and Mother knows she can walk in there any time she wants to."

Eleanor sat down in the light blue chair that Mother Kendrick hadn't quite approved of. "It'll soil so easily, oh, it's pretty enough but chairs without arms are never comfortable, I suppose styles in furniture have changed since I was setting up housekeeping, we have the same chairs we bought when we were married and look at them!" Eleanor had, and they looked exactly like chairs that were thirty-odd years old and they were not down in the living room, they were scattered around upstairs in the darker corners.

"They don't make furniture like this any more," Mrs. Kendrick had said, affectionately tucking a bit of stuffing back into a small gap. "You may have this chair if you'd like. It would have to be done over, naturally, but the frame is wonderful."

Eleanor was tactful, hastily. "Thank you ever so much, but we couldn't think of depriving you."

Mrs. Kendrick had looked as sad as the round pinkness of her face would permit. "We won't be needing them so many more years. I sometimes think I should begin dividing my things now, so I'd know that the proper people got them. Mr. Kendrick's made his will, but that just takes care of the shop and the real estate and this property. I'd hate to think of the children all squabbling over the household things."

From where Eleanor stood she could not see a single thing which would inspire any desire for possession. She found herself in the position, however, of having to accept the chair. The cost of having the springs brought back to life, the wood polished, the frame tightened, and the whole thing reupholstered was not much more than the price of a new chair. And though it was a massive thing and entirely out of key with the rest of the furnishings, it sat, perforce, by the fireplace in Eleanor's living room. Mother Kendrick always sat in it when she came, making some small remark like, "Ah, an old friend," or "Best chair in the room for the oldest lady, isn't that right, folks?" And somehow the impression crept around among Eleanor's friends that the elder Kendricks had given them all their furniture and wasn't it nice of them, you didn't often find in-laws as generous as that.

Eleanor frowned at the big awkward thing now as she addressed the back of John's newspaper. "Your mother must know she's always welcome here too."

The newspaper came down, noisily. "Let's not start that, Eleanor. When my two brothers and their wives were still living here in town I watched Mother overrun them, and I made up my mind then and there that when I had a home of my own Mother wasn't going to take over my social program for me! Sure she's always welcome—except! Except when we're planning a special affair, and there'll be lots of 'em, when she'd be out of place whether she knows it or not. She'll have to learn, that's all!"

"If you could sort of explain that to her, John——"

"Oh, *I'm* not going to get mixed up in it. That's your department. I'm just telling you how it's got to be. I can't run the risk of offending Dad, that's true, because I'm still working for him, though what he'd do if he didn't have me would be quite a problem, too, he's slowing down so. But you manhandle Mother so Dad won't get sore, and that's all that's necessary."

Around that faint and wavering beacon Eleanor planned her social life. Occasionally the light went out and John would say irritably, "Mother's being awfully good about this whole thing. I don't think it would have hurt you to have asked them for last night."

"But, John, we'd planned it for the Markhams because of that dinner they gave us last month, and you know that neither your father nor your mother likes the Markhams."

"Well, things are coming to a pretty pass when outsiders like Markhams can crowd my own parents out of my house!"

Then Eleanor would plunge dizzily into a phase during which the elder Kendricks would be included in every invitation, until John, closing the door behind the final guests one night, would turn on her in a rage.

"Honestly, Eleanor, your judgment must be slipping! Why on earth did you ask Mother and Dad tonight? Mother sat there counting the highballs I drank and when Dad came out to the kitchen and found me out there with Clarissa—nothing wrong with it, she was just helping me with the glasses and things—you should have seen his face! They don't belong with this crowd, and everybody seems to know it but you!"

She did her best with it, and she pleased no one. Mother Kendrick alternated between comments like, patiently, "Let's see, we haven't been here since September twentieth, that was two months ago, my, we're almost strangers." Or, playfully, "I know it's been a long time since we've seen you. Well, we always come when we're asked." Or, with fake humility, "Family dinners must be tiresome for *you*, Eleanor, but see if you can arrange for you and John to come."

Eleanor was driven nearly to distraction. "How did your mother treat her own mother-in-law?" she asked John once.

John laughed. "Why, they fought like cats and dogs," he said with a disconcerting note of pride in his voice, "and finally Mother just forbade the old lady the house and we all had a little peace!"

"How did your father feel about it?"

"He never said anything that I can remember. Why should he? He could always go see his mother if he wanted to. There wasn't any reason why she should be inflicted on the rest of us. Of course she wasn't nearly as pleasant a woman as Mother."

By this time Eleanor was feeling Mrs. Kendrick as a silent, steady burden, but she envied her her courage in that ancient affair. Funny how women forgot how tiresome and boring their own mothers-in-law had been when they came to fill the role themselves. To herself she vowed that she would be the best mother-in-law in the world when her time came. She would understand that the children wanted to please her but that they were of a different generation and had their own interests. She would not demand anything but would wait until it was offered. She would not insist on gratitude or family connections or duty. She would take it for granted that her daughter-in-law would not be too crazy about her.

Meanwhile, with the time she spent thinking about Mother Kendrick and her hurt feelings, she could have built a city or taken a two years' vacation in Europe.

At the time of her marriage Eleanor had been pleasantly vague about sexual matters, wholly ignorant of love as a physical delight or a mental concord, uncertain as to whether babies should be considered a penalty or a reward. In her first ten months as a wife she learned a great deal.

The first thing she discovered was that love, as she had met it in the popular magazines, did not exist in marriage. When John came home it was not in a glow of anticipation to see her. He wanted a well-kept house, a neat, anonymous wife who would smile and listen to him, a cocktail before dinner, and Emma to get that dinner on the table on time and smoking hot. After that, while Emma cleared the table, he and Eleanor would sit on the sun porch or in the living room, he reading the paper, she with a magazine on her lap and a look of sprightly interest ready to put on should he have a sudden comment to make on the newest baseball scores. Not for a minute did she admit to herself that this was boring. It was the way married people acted. And they did go out quite frequently, John grumbling that there was darned little peace and quiet around home for him, his wife was always trotting him out to this and that; yet when she had taken him seriously and refused invitations for a week he was wild. "My God, Eleanor, are we going to turn into vegetables? It's dead as a doornail around here. Let's ask Sue and Doc Wilder over and have a little bridge and a drink or two."

The one thing they never did was talk to each other. All their conversation was on the level of "May I have the butter, please?" and "Hurry and take your shower, John, they'll be here in twenty minutes." She had found that asking John if he loved her simply made him cross. If he hadn't loved her he wouldn't have married her! Women couldn't take anything for granted, it wasn't enough for them that a man worked his heart out trying to give them everything under the sun, they had to have a lot of gush to go with it!

Yet there were the evenings, when John had had an especially good time and one more than the three drinks that constituted his usual quota, when he would put an affectionate arm around her in the car coming home and tell her how nice she had looked, that she made the other girls look like a load of hay! And in their bedroom he would stroke her hair and smooth her arms and call her "You darling" and "Precious lamb," which was flattering and almost satisfactory. Almost, because after the brief and vigorous gust of his desire had passed and he slept, she lay awake, uncomfortably stirred, with all her body whispering to her that there should have been something more, that there was an emotion that she might have felt had there been more time.

About having babies she learned much more. That it was painful to have them. That it ruined your figure. That nursing them would ruin your figure even more. That it was almost too much to ask a woman to go through. That, their births concluded, it was smart to hand them over to a "woman" to take care of, because it wasn't fair not to go on being a companion to your husband. That everybody loved babies, women especially.

She kept her first suspicions to herself, but the third week in March she went to Dr. O'Malley. He was a big, brown man with an impersonal manner, a sharp eye, and an overwhelming contempt for women, which he suppressed successfully most of the time. He had the reputation of being the best obstetrician for miles around.

"So you think you're going to have a baby, Mrs. Kendrick. Well, it's customary with young married women, I understand. We'll see. We'll see."

Her hands and feet were ice-cold as the nurse helped her to undress. She climbed up on the table and was grateful for the sheet over her. Numb as she was with nervousness, she did not realize that the sheet served purely psychological purposes—that, with her feet in the metal stirrups, her knees up, and the bright light blaring down at her, she had as much physical reticence as a butterfly on a pin.

Dr. O'Malley came in briskly and held out his hands while the nurse put on his rubber gloves for him. So this is young Kendrick's wife, he was thinking. Which kind is she going to be, a whiner, a complainer, or one of the silly, careless, or hysterical brands? She doesn't talk much, has some dignity, that's in her favor. Doesn't look stupid, either. Wonder if I gave her a book on infant care, would she

102

read it? With the Kendrick money, I don't suppose for a minute she'll take care of her own child. That'd be too much to look for. Still, she might. I keep hoping. After all, it's none of my business. All I'm supposed to do is get the baby here and have it healthy when it comes. After that, as long as its body functions well, I'm not expected to concern myself. Go right ahead batting yourself against a stone wall, O'Malley. You'll never learn, no matter how often it's shown to you, that there isn't one woman in a thousand who'll take an intelligent personal interest in her children. Those days are gone forever, if they ever existed. Women used to take a personal interest, I believe, but I doubt whether it was very intelligent. How could it be, when even the doctors didn't know anything about nutrition or psychology? Well, now we know and we're anxious to spread it around, and now the women have lost the interest. Don't anybody ask *me* why we have a conglomeration of spindly, weak-minded, unadjusted citizens, because I'm apt to tell 'em! Women!

Under the sheet he probed and punched and felt. Perfectly healthy young woman. No physical abnormalities. Too thin, of course, but she has a good, wide bone structure. Oughtn't to have too much trouble. He emerged from the sheet, scratched Eleanor's arm with a sterile needle, and walked out. She lay there, stunned and mystified, with the nurse smiling down at her.

"You can get up and get dressed now," the nurse said. "Dr. O'Malley will talk to you in his office. Hup! There we are."

She didn't want to go into the office and face him, but she had to. She sat down in the red leather chair across the wide desk from him and strove to look anywhere but at his face. He came around and looked at her arm.

"No doubt about it, Mrs. Kendrick," he said, "and congratulations. I suppose you want a boy. They all do."

At the warmth of his tone, at his assumption that something wonderful had just happened to her, she found that she could smile at him, shyly. "I don't care. I'd just as soon have a girl. I have two sisters."

"No brothers?"

"No."

"Well, it doesn't matter. As long as you don't try to make a girl out of a boy or a boy out of a girl. The thing is to be satisfied with what you get. You have to be anyway."

He sat down and began writing on a form he had in front of him. She answered his questions briefly and competently, wondering at the fact that having a baby entailed so much information. When he had finished he pushed the paper away from him and sat frowning down at it.

"I'm going to say some things, Mrs. Kendrick, that may sound a bit previous to you, but they're important. Do you intend to nurse your baby?"

"I—I'd never thought of it one way or another. Whichever is best."

"Good. We've found it's better if mothers do nurse them. Oh, we can get along without it. We've grown pretty clever with formulas and other tricks. But—well, there it is. Babies just somehow get along better if their mothers can furnish their food for a while. Know anything about babies?"

"Nothing, really. I've seen them, held them. I've never taken care of one."

He slid a small book across to her. "You'd better read this, then, and don't let it get you down. If you just start out with the assumption that taking care of a baby is hard work, careful work, strenuous, unselfish work, the most important work in the world, you'll get through somehow. The reason most women don't like to do it is that they can't see any results from it. It's true, the results are slow in coming, but they're worth it when they come. If you can promise me five years of careful care and teaching of behavior and attitudes, I can promise you sixty years of rewards. That sounds like a good bargain, doesn't it?"

Oh, she liked Dr. O'Malley! She would work! She'd have children that she and John could be proud of the rest of their lives! "I'll do my best. I'd like to."

He was pleased, she could see, as he ushered her out of the office with her diet list and the baby book clutched to her. "See you next month," he called after her, "and drink your milk and get a lot of rest and keep cheerful."

"I will. Oh, I will."

The doctor walked with her into his waiting room and swooped two-year-old Tito Marnelli from his mother's lap. Mrs. Marnelli watched with pride as the tanned, rosy-cheeked Tito gurgled and laughed and waved his strong little arms and legs vigorously in aerial antics.

"Whew! This young man weighs a ton. Here's a bouncing boy for you, Mrs. Kendrick. Guess this is the last time I'll be throwing him around much. How's the training going, Mrs. Marnelli?"

"Dry always in the daytimes. Still not at night."

"That'll come. He's a co-operative youngster. Taking him up before you go to bed? That's good. Always, mind you, not just now and then. Well, if he's dry when he's three, we won't complain."

Trotting after them to the examining room, carrying Tito's hat and coat, Mrs. Marnelli gave her proudest piece of news. "We've moved, Doctor."

"Good. Where?"

"Out on Maple. My man says I try to see how far I can get from his work. I say, 'Which is best, that you should have to use your lazy legs or that Tito should have a yard with sunshine instead of that old smoke from the tracks?' So we move."

He turned at the door. "Good-by, Mrs. Kendrick. Wave bye-bye, Tito."

As he looked down the throat and into the ears of the brown, squirming cherub on the table and listened to Mrs. Marnelli's soft voice relating Tito's marvelous skill in picking up both American and Italian sentences, his mind was busy with Eleanor Kendrick. Handsome girl. Knew how to dress, gave the impression that she'd always had everything. Hard to tell how strong a character she might be; mental pallor and reserve looked like the same thing until you got to know a person. Ordinarily he despised the women of the town's small moneyed set. Bunch of shellacked sheep. This just might be the one who'd show the rest of them up, make herself useful, bring up a swell kid like Tito here. That he'd know, one way or the other, long before the delivery date.

The difference in the opinions that were expressed to Eleanor on the announcement of her pregnancy threw her into a state of nervous confusion. Coming home from Dr. O'Malley's office, she had felt so braced, so anxious to do the right things, so certain of her own powers. She stopped by at Aunt Ann's and told her first. Aunt Ann kissed her cheek warmly and drew her to the fire. The old attitude of pupil and teacher had changed with Eleanor's marriage. Her great-aunt now spoke to her as one woman of the world to another.

"Well, dear, it can't be helped. It's a shame it should happen so soon. You and John have scarcely had time to get settled yet. But as I've observed this childbearing business, it seems to me that the sooner it's over the better. You'll still have plenty of time for yourselves and be young enough to enjoy it too."

Eleanor felt some of her joy slipping away in the face of this gentle commiseration. "I don't mind. I haven't enough to do as it is. It'll be fun having something that needs me."

"It's wonderful that you can look at it in that way. Of course your capacity will be purely supervisory. We'll have to find you a good nurse."

"I won't need one. Emma takes care of the house and the meals. I want to look after the baby."

Aunt Ann's smile was indulgent. "You don't realize how much work and time that would take. After all, you can't give up John and your friends and your way of life simply because you want to take care of the baby. And you've had no experience. You wouldn't have the least idea how to go about it."

"I could learn."

"That's noble of you, my dear, but I think that a few months of diaper washing and formula making would bore you to death. Then you'd give it up anyway. It's much better to start out the way you're going to keep on. Thank heaven you can afford all the help you need. Some girls *have* to do it all themselves, and you've seen the poor creatures. They're either leaning over a washtub or they're out wheeling a carriage, and they let themselves go so dreadfully. Hair any which way and homemade manicures. And so dead tired at night that they fall into bed at eight o'clock. No wonder so many husbands lose interest in their wives about that time."

There was the warning note. There was the thing Aunt Ann had been leading up to. Choose between your husband or your baby: you can't have both satisfactorily. Well, there was something to it, Eleanor conceded to herself despondently. John was impatient and demanding, there was no gainsaying that. But maybe he'd be so delighted at having a child that he'd be willing to take a back seat for a while, just for a few years really. It didn't seem like much to ask.

She told him after dinner that night, keeping her voice factual and emotionless until she could determine what her mood should be.

"Well, say!" he exclaimed. "That's great! Dad'll be tickled to death. He's a great believer in the family man, you know. But why on earth did you go to O'Malley? We can afford to send you to some big man, in Cleveland, maybe."

"I have to go every month now, and oftener later. I'd sooner have somebody right here. It'll be uncomfortable to travel toward the last."

"O.K. Anything you say, Mama. Say, me a father! What do you know about that!"

He rubbed his hands. He called his family to tell them. His warmth and pleasure revived her and she told him all the things Dr. O'Malley had said.

"Nurse the baby? You mean you told him you were going to nurse the kid yourself?"

"He says it's better for them that way. He says——"

"Say now, let's settle down here. That's all very well for O'Malley to say, but he isn't going to have to put up with a wife that has to drop whatever she's doing every few hours of the day or night and run home to give the kid a meal! We couldn't even go out in the evening. You'd have to turn around and run right back home."

"It's only for the first seven months or so. And of course I may not be able to nurse it. You can't tell that until it gets here."

"Yes, we can. We can tell that right now. My God, it sounds as if you were a cow or something!"

"But your mother——"

"Sure. But they didn't know any better then. They've got it fixed now so a woman can be a mother and still be a human being!"

Reluctantly she gave up the idea, all the lovely, serious, thorough-going plans she had made at the doctor's office. She'd get a nurse. She'd go on looking at the back of John's newspaper. She'd go out and play bridge in the afternoons and mill around in general with the rest of them. Maybe Dr. O'Malley was wrong anyway. Children seemed to grow up in the families she knew, just as they did on the other side of the tracks.

John insisted on mixing a drink. "Special occasion," he said. "Have to celebrate. I've always been crazy about kids. Somehow never thought about having a boy of my own."

She didn't ask him what he would think of having a girl. Something sweet and open in her spirit had closed and turned to stone. She didn't care about the baby. She didn't care about anything. She wished that she were dead.

She took the glass he handed her doubtfully. She had read the diet list. "I don't think——"

"Oh, come on, be a sport! Can't hurt you. We have to drink to the baby, don't we? Don't be a wet smack."

She drank and her mouth was bitter, but not with the taste of whisky. "Sure, we have to drink to him. That's the least we can do for him."

"Atta girl!"

While he was at the telephone giving the great news to his sister she took the diet list and the baby book and threw them into the wastebasket by the desk. It made her think, somehow, of scattering flowers on a grave. She would wait to cry until John was asleep, until it was so dark that she wouldn't have to face her cowardice in not telling the lot of them that she was going to do exactly as she pleased about the baby and they could all go to hell! Her mind recoiled from the word. It was the first time she had ever thought it.

But she smiled brightly at John when he came back, and he did not notice the slight diffidence with which she allowed herself to be pulled into his lap for fifteen minutes of alternate jests and endearments before the Pearsons came by to take them to their weekly poker game.

9.

Laketown Teachers' College sprawled its yellow brick buildings over a city block in the middle of Laketown itself. Every semester it swallowed hundreds of new students, digested them through its class mill, and spewed them out, state teaching certificate in hand, to find positions in the vast educational system of Laketown.

Martha had wanted to stay in Ashland, to live in Grandmother's house, to teach at Ashland High School. Her father and grandmother decided against that. The highest-paid teacher in Ashland was paid a hundred dollars a month, and for that magnificent salary she was expected to dress well, take summer classes at the state university to "keep up," be a model of decorum, attend church regularly, go out very little and then only in the most respectable surroundings, and eschew the gayer social element in town and the smoking of cigarettes. Under this regime the women teachers who had any claims to charm married as quickly as they could and stopped teaching; the less charming but equally progressive ones found jobs in other towns, other fields; the unattractive and unambitious ones formed the nucleus of the Ashland teaching system, and Ashland was not satisfied but could not discover what was wrong.

Laketown spread over the lower half of the adjoining state with a population of more than two million. Along its shore line rose the tall stone spires of business enterprise and on its outskirts were many smoke-belching chimneys. It possessed immense libraries, used by only a fraction of its population; an art museum (sometimes a hundred people visited it in a day) so photogenic that pictures of it were in every second rotogravure section; twelve high schools; almost two hundred grade schools; parks that covered green miles where there was barely a trace of the exhaust gases from the cars humming and honking on the impatient streets that began again the minute the trees left off. It was inhabited by Captains of Industry, Wizards of Finance, Rising Young Men, Taxpaying Citizens, Labor, the Great Middle Class, and the Unfortunate. Surely the school system of such a city must be manned by gods!

Yet in 1928 Laketown did not demand that its grade school teachers possess college degrees. They could come from high school, spend two years at Laketown Teachers' College, and begin teaching. Academic degrees were preferred, however, and the owners of these need spend but one semester at the teachers' college before they also could teach— in the grades. Transfer to a high school was considered a promotion and was not attained until a teacher had spent eight or ten years in the grades and her habit of speaking to anyone as if he were a twelve-year-old, or less, had become thoroughly ingrained. Adolescence was not regarded as a special and difficult age that called for special teacher training. As character attributes for its teachers Laketown demanded good references and no behavior spectacular enough to be noted by the more sensational press. As to personality, there were no demands at all. A state certificate and a number of years of service guaranteed personality enough for all educational purposes.

To Martha, Laketown Teachers' College was puzzling and dreary and offensive. In the first place she disliked the other students: the giggling, silly, unhandsome girls just out of high school with no knowledge of typing or they would have been secretaries instead and no hopes of marriage or they would have been hunting part-time jobs to tide them over to the marital date; the young men, very few of these, who were seeking a "sure thing" for their life's work, evidently distrustful of their abilities to succeed in a competitive field, unbearable in their masculinity, which, weak as it was, was sufficient to make them cherished and fawned upon by girls and faculty alike; the bespectacled misfits from all walks of life who were looking for positions of authority, albeit only over children. Only occasionally was there a personable young woman who honestly thought she had the qualifications for a good teacher and was interested in the work. Only infrequently was there the genuine scholar whose love of books and study had drawn him to what he thought would be a lifetime of it.

The six weeks of classes came first. Martha learned that the good teacher planned every lesson and wrote down the plan under three headings: stimulation, presentation, and response. "Stimulation" might consist of the teacher saying "How many of you have ever been on a train? Oh, that many! Where did you go on the train, Johnny? Did you eat on the train, Mary? We've all seen trains going by, haven't we? Or we've heard their whistles and wondered where they were going. Today we are going to read a story about a train." "Presentation" meant that the class would open their books, look at the pictures of the train, pointed out with many small ejaculations from the teacher, and read the story aloud. "Response" would be a few oral or written questions on the story. If most of the class knew the story about the train the lesson plan had succeeded.

Mrs. Stanton, the white-haired, motherly woman who taught the course, looked so approachable that Martha made bold to ask her in private, "I don't mind writing these plans out, Mrs. Stanton, but do you mean to say that there are people wanting to be teachers who are stupid enough not to know that a subject should be led up to first and checked on afterward?"

Mrs. Stanton's vague smile congealed and her voice was quite sharp. "It doesn't hurt to be meticulous, Miss King. And there's always the possibility that some substitute might have to be called in. The written plans would insure your work being carried on properly in your absence."

"I'll grant that she should know what lesson the class was to have, but my method of stimulation and so forth might not be hers at all. Shouldn't she use her own judgment in that case?"

"Decidedly not! She should follow to the letter the written plans you have left. I don't wish to be unkind, Miss King, but you people with college degrees are always so ready to assume that all you need to teach material is to know it yourself. Believe me, that's not enough. There are techniques in teaching, and they must be learned."

"The same technique for everybody?"

"Why not? Teaching is teaching."

To Mary Dobbs, a girl from the University of Minnesota with ideals about the nobility of the teaching profession, she said wonderingly, "They don't want you to be an individual here at all. They want you to be a form letter. How can you take seventy-two different kinds of temperament and expect to pour them all nicely into one mold labeled 'Good Teacher'?"

"Well, they try, but it doesn't work out that way in the long run. Oh, you have to try to conform the first year you're out of here, because the supervisors come around and the principals check back. But after that you're left alone and then, if you're good, you branch out on your own. If you're poor you stick to the forms until kingdom come. They're the salvation of the bad teacher. I substituted for a year back home so I know how it works."

Classes, classes. Droning theory. Lesson plans. Stand straight. Dress neatly. Enunciate distinctly. Be sure your writing slants the right way. It has been found to be better to grade papers with a red pencil rather than a blue pencil. What is the grading curve? Make sure there is ample light in your classroom but no glare. Sign this card saying that you will always support the Constitution of the United States. How can you make your classroom attractive on George Washington's birthday? At Christmas time? Study this sample note to parents whose child is failing in his work. Turn in your notebooks.

At the university Martha had taken but few notes, going on the assumption that the more in the notebook the less in the head. Here notebooks were an end in themselves and the high school girls labored over them with different-colored pencils and beautiful penmanship. Martha's was spare and accurate, and Mrs. Stanton was caustic.

"You certainly haven't spent a great deal of time over this, Miss King."

"I saw no reason for writing it down, particularly. It's all very clear in my mind." Yes, and it would have been clear in my mind twenty-four hours after I walked in the front door, but you chose to take six weeks in pointing out the obvious.

An angry red mottled Mrs. Stanton's face and her lips pouted like a small girl in a temper. "If you don't wish to follow our procedures, why did you come here? If you're so sure that you are always right, why do you need us?"

Martha smiled. She was contemptuous of Mrs. Stanton's monotonous, shapeless schemes, her avidity for flattery, her crooning over pretty nothings. That a person could teach lesson planning and plan his own lessons so uninterestingly! "Because I can't grant myself a state certificate, Mrs. Stanton."

"That's almost rude of you, isn't it?"

"I'm sorry if it's rude. It's true."

"May I say in turn that I have never met a girl who thought herself so superior to others?"

"You certainly may. And may I say that ordinarily I have no occasion to feel superior but that I would have to close both eyes or shoot myself to keep from knowing that I'm better educated, better read, and better suited to teach than nine tenths of the students here?"

"In the final analysis it is the faculty who will judge that," snapped Mrs. Stanton.

"I am perfectly willing to trust myself to a fair and impartial judgment, such as I am sure the faculty's will be."

Mary Dobbs was aghast at the account of this interview. "Good night, Martha, do you want to end up teaching in one of the colored schools? That's where they put the teachers they have to pass but don't like. They're in the poorest parts of town and the children are wild little ruffians and even a good teacher burns out there in three years. You've got to be careful until you've got your job!"

"That's just why this is such a silly place and such a waste of time. Everybody's being careful. Everybody's pretending that the classes are doing them a lot of good and that every word that falls is a pearl. And so the place goes on being the same year after year, sillier and sillier. If a few people would blow off steam there might be some reformations."

"Oh, now you're going to change the whole teachers' college!"

"It wouldn't be hard. In the first place nobody should be admitted here without a degree. I know that most of them will teach in grade school, but they ought to have as whole an education as they can get so they know where each part on the way up should fit. Then the faculty here could teach us some real child and adolescent psychology courses, instead of this pap they have to give out now, because too few have had the beginning courses in general psych to understand any more. I had a psych minor and I've done some extra reading on the side, thank heaven, or I wouldn't know *anything* about it. And somewhere along the line there ought to be some weeding out of misfit, awkward, impatient people who'll never be good teachers and shouldn't be inflicted on children——"

"My, my, my!" said Mary.

"How many of the teachers you had in grade school or high can you remember now? One or two, maybe. And why can't you remember the rest? Because they were so colorless, so ineffectual that in a whole year, standing in front of you and talking to you every day, they couldn't make any impression on you! And why was that? Because they all came from teachers' colleges like this one!"

The next twelve weeks were devoted to practice teaching, and Martha was soothed and violently interested. The student teachers were sent out into the Laketown school system and each was assigned to a "critic teacher." The critics were supposed to be the best teachers Laketown had, and they drew extra pay for the chore of supervising the work of the students who taught classes in front of them, and for reporting the progress each was making back to the faculty at Teachers'.

Martha's first contact was with a third-grade room. The critic teacher was Miss Moss, a nice-looking girl, thirty years old, patient and soft-spoken.

"You'll watch me for a few days," said Miss Moss, "and then you'll take over the morning lessons for the next four weeks."

Here, at last, there was a great deal to learn. There were forty-five third-graders in the room, and the chairs were pulled around to form three small groups of fifteen each. This was because of the Laketown device, which Martha approved highly, of sorting the children into X, Y, and Z groups. The X's were the superior pupils, the Y's the average, the Z's the poorest. All their lessons, even the texts they used, were different. To get a high mark in spelling, for example, an X would have to learn to spell a hundred and fifty words a semester; a Y could get the same mark by learning eighty or ninety; and a Z by spelling forty or fifty. Thus the brighter child was not allowed to romp away with all the high marks but was forced into competition with his kind; while the slower child did not turn hopeless in the struggle against better wits. Each could function in his own element. The only drawback was that, with this classification in effect, two children could be graduated from a grade school with report cards that looked alike, but one would know three times as much as the other. This was a minor defect but confusing to the lay mind.

It was a pleasure to watch Miss Moss manipulate the schedule. While the X group studied spelling words by themselves, a Y pupil pronounced other words for his own group to write down, and Miss Moss worked with the Z's on their new words. Fifteen minutes of this, and the Z's were left to write the new words over and over, the Y's exchanged papers and corrected them by a key, and the X's took a quick written test on what they had studied. Miss Moss was continually in three places at once and knew everything that was going on in the far corners. All this on top of pencils to be sharpened, blackboards to be erased and covered with new writing, children who wanted to go to the bathroom, children who felt sick at their stomachs, and children who didn't want to pay attention, preferring to look out the window. Came the reading period, and Miss Moss flashed about the room, passing out books, answering questions, appointing monitors, passing from one group to the next. Penmanship, recess, the music teacher, arithmetic—Miss Moss kept them all going as neatly as a juggler keeps twelve balls in the air at once. Occasionally she had a moment for Martha.

"You see, this is a good class," she said. "No discipline problems to slow you down. I've been in plenty of rooms that couldn't be handled like this, but they like to break the student teachers in under the most ideal conditions they can find. Now tomorrow you take over the reading. Here are the books so you can make out your plans for it. We'll add the other lessons gradually until you're doing a full morning's teaching."

It was hard work, nerve-racking, neck-breaking, brain-wrenching work. It called for all the wits you had, all the composure, all the presence of mind. It kept you hopping like a cat on a griddle. By noon your dress was wrinkled, your face was pale, your hair was hanging in wisps. You wondered how Miss Moss had kept it up, morning and afternoon, for eight years!

By the end of four weeks she was getting the hang of it, even enjoying it. For one thing, she knew all the children by name then, and she found them adorable, with their smooth pink cheeks, their quick laughter, their brown scraped knees, the habit they had of slipping a hand into yours when they walked beside you or of leaning on your lap when they came up to ask a question.

"I don't want to leave," she told Miss Moss. "I don't want to go on. I'm homesick enough for Ashland, and now I'll have to be homesick for Sylvia and David and John. I'd like to stay on and teach these children right through eight grades."

"I know. There are always some you hate to lose. But after you've been at it as long as I have you'll know that children just as lovable will be coming along. You couldn't possibly keep them all." She pulled a paper from her drawer. "I want you to read this, Miss King. It's my final report to the teachers' college about you. I always let the students read them. I think it's only fair that you should know how you've done."

So lost had Martha been in her work that she had forgotten that Miss Moss would grade her on it. Now she read:

Miss King has succeeded well with these children. Not only do they respect her, they are very fond of her. She is patient, amiable, and conscientious, quick to sense a situation and resolve it. At this moment she could tell exactly how much each child under her jurisdiction knows about each curriculum subject, and she has a warmth of personality that makes it easy for her to teach, not subject matter, but the child himself. I have never had a more promising student teacher.

Martha raised her eyes to find Miss Moss smiling at her. "Thank you very much," she said. "I hope you're right."

"How you talk!" said Miss Moss. "Don't you know that critic teachers are always right? Of course all I've said here is that you have the equipment to teach children and to teach them well. Unfortunately there is more to being a teacher than just that. I can't say how tactful you'll be with injured parents. I can't tell whether you have administrative ability enough to please the administration, which consists of your principal, your assistant principal, your supervisor, and whatever member of the downtown hierarchy happens to be around. I don't even know how accurate you'll be at filling out the two thousand forms that you'll have to fill out each year. All I can say is that the teaching part of the job you've done well."

"But that's the most important part, isn't it?"

Miss Moss gathered papers from her desk and stacked them neatly. "Sometimes I wonder," she said. "Sometimes I wonder."

Martha's next "contact" was with a fifth-grade room in the same school and her critic was a Miss Ogle. She had not been there two days before she was wretched and floundering desperately, working so hard that her memories of Miss Moss's praise faded completely away. Miss Ogle was a tall straight woman of forty-five with an expressionless face that she occasionally stretched into a formal gesture at a smile. She had light brown hair rolled up in an old-fashioned style and glasses that clipped onto the bridge of her nose. For every day of the four weeks Martha was with her she wore the same dress. It was a well-cut black sheer which she enlivened with a rope of small pearls that dangled nearly to her waist. And the pearls and the eyeglasses and the hair were always trembling a little with the cold fury of their owner.

Miss Ogle did not throw Martha on her own and let her struggle through to her own solution, as Miss Moss had done. Miss Ogle wanted Martha to be Miss Ogle and was enraged that she remained Miss King. The first concern in this room was not that the children were learning. It was that the books should be neatly racked and labeled, that the bulletin board should be covered with new pictures every day even though the children were never granted a minute to look at them, that the blackboards be written over with material that would look well to the principal if she should come in, that forms meant for office attention should be filled out as carefully as if many lives depended on them. And all this must be done exactly as Miss Ogle would do it.

"Your handwriting, Miss King," she said, "leaves a great deal to be desired. Handwriting is so important. Yours is plain enough, but it doesn't slant as it should and the loops of your *l*'s should be taller. Now just erase that board and fill it out more legibly this time."

Martha tried her best to be Miss Ogle. She was careful to pass papers from the left instead of the right, she did not smile at a fifth-grader when he smiled at her, she allowed not the slightest whispering in the line that marched out to recess. And always at her elbow was Miss Ogle, criticizing, nagging, raging. What Martha taught that grade in four weeks, or whether she taught them at all, she never knew. She could not remember one of the children's faces, much less their names, for always between her and the pupils Miss Ogle loomed, to be placated if possible. The student teacher assigned to Miss Ogle in the afternoon had a nervous breakdown after two weeks of it. Martha plowed through somehow, making herself as thick-skinned as she could, losing ten pounds in four weeks in the agony of trying to conform to the senseless tyranny. The little third-graders she had left behind made things no easier. They would come to peer in the fifth-grade door on their way to the drinking fountain. They ran to walk down the halls beside her. They followed her around the playground, or nodded and smiled to her from any distance, their faces like pink peonies bowing in the rain. Miss Ogle sniffed at these demonstrations and nagged more furiously than ever.

How Miss Ogle rated her on her teaching possibilities Martha never knew. She went to her third and last critic hopeless, discouraged, and pretty sure that she had chosen the wrong profession. Mrs. Vincent had a seventh-grade room. She was short and round and rather pretty, and she began by being apologetic.

"You're to have my third-hour English class," she said. In the seventh grade the pupils went to different rooms and teachers for each subject. "They've given me an English program this year, and I've never taught English before in my life. I'm a music teacher, but my arthritis has grown so bad that it's hard for me to play accompaniments any more. I don't know much about teaching English and I thought I'd better tell you before you found it out. I'm not a regular critic teacher either. There are just so many of you folks this year that they had to put you somewhere. Well, we'll see how we make out."

They made out well enough in one way. At least they got along. Mrs. Vincent took Martha as a boon from heaven and promptly disappeared for a rest as soon as Martha's class came in. She would appear just before dismissal and make a despairing gesture at her desk. "Look at all those papers I have to grade!" she would exclaim. "Five English classes certainly snow you under. And me not knowing the first thing about it!" It became an unwritten agreement between them that Martha would grade all the English papers for all the classes.

"Oh, you do them so beautifully, Miss King. You must know a great deal about English. I went to Teachers' College right from high school—I'm an old-timer, you see—and somehow I never got my apostrophes straight. I hate to load you with all this work, it's just a favor to me really, but I don't know what I would have done without you. Be sure I'm giving the principal a good report of you!"

The worst part of this last four weeks was that it took just that long for Martha to find out that Mrs. Vincent had taught the English class exactly no English in the first two thirds of the semester. Then she felt that it might be insulting to take them back to the beginning of the book where they belonged, that Mrs. Vincent might be offended, and she wasted her days trying to build something on top of nothing and, of course, came to grief there too.

Quickly the practice teaching was over. The college called in all the student teachers for personal interviews and, possibly, permanent jobs in the Laketown system. It was a tense week. Martha was so sodden with fatigue that she sat in her cubbyhole in the dormitory, looking out at the January blizzard, smoking one cigarette after another—We Permit Smoking in This Room But We Do Not Approve of It—and thinking of nothing except how quickly she could get back to Ashland and find a job clerking in a store. She was pretty sure that in spite of her tremendous effort she had not made the grade. Teachers were made of different stuff than she had thought. She was not cut from that length of cloth.

Behind closed doors, in the most intimate sanctum of the college administrative offices, a faculty committee was meeting. There were Mrs. Stanton; Dr. Hayworth, head of the history of education department, a comparatively young man with dangerously liberal views on a great variety of subjects; Miss Judd, who represented the Board of Education and had a list of teacher vacancies in her hand that had to be filled; and old Dr. Riley, who headed the psychology department. Before them lay the reports of all the critic teachers on all the students who were about to be sent out to teach. The discussion was lively and personal.

When Martha's name came up Mrs. Stanton spoke first. "I'm not even sure she should be given a certificate," she said, "much less assigned to a teaching post here. She's such an opinionated young woman that it doesn't seem to me she'll adjust well."

Dr. Riley picked a paper from the desk. "Miss Moss seems to think well of her. And here, even Miss Ogle admits that the girl might turn out all right. Coming from Miss Ogle, that's the equivalent of a Croix de Guerre."

Mrs. Stanton related the story of the notebook and Dr. Hayworth laughed. "Well, it's about time someone kicked about those precious notebooks of yours, Elizabeth. You know what I've always thought of them!"

"John, you know very well——"

"Sure, I know the high school kids love it and maybe even learn something from it for all I know. But this girl! Just look at the record she made at her university: mathematics, English, philosophy, science, everything. And you want her to turn in seventy-five pages on stimulation!"

"It's important to——"

"Elizabeth, let's grant that we're from the old school. There's nothing wrong with that unless it fails to keep us abreast of the times. You can't stand over pupils any more with a club in your hand and make them bow down to your judgment. The kids this girl is going to meet are different. They're going to have to be interested, they're going to have to be made to like what they're doing, they're going to want a teacher to be a person, not just a shell with authority. Discipline in the home has changed and our discipline is geared to it. Look at the words Miss Moss used. 'Patience,' 'warmth,' 'personality.' Says the girl teaches not the subject but the child. Well, there's the exact thing we're looking for in new teachers!"

Dr. Riley raised his head. "Brilliant mind, Miss King's. It's a pleasure to teach her, and if I could have had her in a classroom by herself, instead of having to keep her slowed down to a snail's pace because of the group she was with——"

Dr. Hayworth was leafing through papers. "I want to take a look at her I.Q." He found a small card and whistled at the figures in the corner. "Wow! No wonder. She's smarter than I am, which is practically an impossibility, wouldn't you say, Elizabeth?"

"I'm not saying she isn't a bright girl. I'm just saying that she's not my idea of a teacher."

Miss Judd cleared her throat. "This Miss King has had dramatics, English, and mathematics?"

"All kinds of it," said Dr. Hayworth.

"I have an opening that calls for those three things. It's unusual to find that combination. Ordinarily, of course, the girl should start out in the grades, but this situation calls for special dispensation. You know how Mr. Trent is. . . ."

Mr. Trent was the irascible, dictatorial principal of the new Devon High School, which had opened its doors the previous September. His thunderous voice could be heard, not only on the third floor of his own building, but its echoes frequently carried to the Board building downtown. They all knew Mr. Trent, though they did not pale at the mention of his name, as mere teachers always did.

"He says he doesn't want some 'old dodo' in there to manage his brand-new auditorium. We've combed the teachers in the system and none of them suits him. So we have to find someone from here. You know how it is in a new school: the classes are small at first until we get their district lined up for them. So, besides the dramatics, there'll be English and mathematics for her to teach for a while, until attendance grows. It calls for some versatility and intelligence. Mr. Trent is not easy to please."

Mrs. Stanton was smiling. "I'm perfectly willing to have Miss King assigned to Mr. Trent's school."

"Why, Elizabeth, you vixen!" Dr. Hayworth was laughing too. "You're willing to give the girl a darned good job just so Brother Trent will have a chance to beat her down! Tell you what, I'll bet you any amount up to five dollars that the girl makes the grade, that she isn't booted out at the end of the first year."

"Or that she won't quit? I'll take that bet."

The next day a dignified committee informed Martha that she was to be granted her certificate and that a teaching position was waiting for her in a new high school in one of the best sections of the city.

Martha wrote to her grandmother:

I can't understand it. Nobody starts in a high school. Only me. I couldn't have been that good, but I'm not asking any questions. It's a marvelous place to begin. I'm going out to look at the school tomorrow and find a room in the neighborhood, and I'll be sending you a check every month now. You see, you have to keep your health to give me time to pay back all the money the university took away from you. Oh, Grandmother, I'm so pleased! Even Mrs. Stanton was smiling when they told me!

10.

Tony Fox knotted his tie in front of the mirror and wished that he had the courage to take a drink. Couldn't, of course. Not with a high school commencement to sit through and his father on the school board. Why in God's name did he let himself be herded into these things? Why should he have to sit through two hours of monotonous speeches and fluttery kids, just because his father would expect to see him there and because Sue had a cousin who was finally managing to get a diploma? The cousin was a leggy girl with prominent teeth, but from the fuss the Mannings made over her, you'd think she was Venus de Milo. Sometimes Tony wished he hadn't married Sue Manning. She had so many relatives who were always dying, or on the verge of it, graduating, marrying, giving birth!

He wrenched the tie loose and began all over again. In the mirror he could see his brown, unsymmetrical face, his dark, deep-set eyes, the strong chin with a cleft in it, the way his hair sprung up to short, black waves. One good thing, he'd never be bald. John Kendrick, now, he was a couple of years younger, and already his hairline was slipping back a bit farther every year. The thought pleased him, gave him a feeling of superiority. He smiled at himself and was more patient with the tie.

To get back to the Mannings. They were a nice family, he hadn't a thing against them except their penchant for making special occasions out of episodes that other people regarded as trivial. And there were so many Mannings! Five married daughters and two married sons, all living in Ashland and all circulating in the same crowd. It didn't give you a minute's privacy. You couldn't go anywhere without meeting a relative who, by family privilege, would usurp your time and attention until your own friends slipped away and pretty soon they were just acquaintances who felt kindly toward you but knew you had no time for them. He was being smothered by a dreadful intimacy not of his own choosing and he was getting tired of it!

Sue came in briskly. "Tony, for heaven's sake, we'll be late!" She was dressed in a white summer flannel suit that was tailored to make her look taller. Against the white her skin and hair looked darker than ever, vivid, shining.

"Just have to put my coat on. I suppose I do have to wear a coat, even though it's hotter than blazes."

She sat down and examined her lacquered nails, ignoring him as if he were a naughty child. It made him resolve to be as annoying as he could. He threw himself down on the bed and put his arms under his head.

"It's too hot. I don't think I'll go at all."

"Oh, Tony!" Her voice was patient but ragged. "We've been through all this a thousand times. Of course we have to go."

"Why do we?"

"Your father, for one thing."

"He'll live."

"And little Peggy would be heartbroken if we didn't——"

He snorted. "*Little* Peggy, indeed!"

"If ever you find a member of my family that you like, let me know, won't you?"

"I will. Immediately."

"I'll do the same for you."

This was open warfare. Sue didn't usually go this far. He rose to one elbow. "There are only three of us. Just what have you got against Dad and Mother?"

"That they had an only child and spoiled the daylights out of him."

He lay back again, more pleased than angered. Being spoiled was an attractive trait. It meant being pampered and catered to, that you expected it and got it.

"I'm not so spoiled."

"Not much! Now come on, Little Caesar, stop being antisocial and get up off that bed. Joe and Doris will be here in a minute."

Doris was the most attractive of the Manning girls and her husband wasn't too bad. Still, he felt it his duty to groan, "Joe and Doris!"

Sue rose. "All right, if that's the way you feel about it, you can stay home and rot. I'm going."

He followed her down the stairs. "I don't know what you're so sore about. I'm coming. I always meant to."

"Sure. After you'd been coaxed enough. Does it ever occur to you that I get sick of begging you to do the things you ought to be able to do all by yourself? I have to beg you to get up in the morning and plead with you to come in the house when it's dinnertime and entreat you to go the places you're obligated to go. You're a big boy now. You ought to be able to make yourself do these things all by yourself."

Instantly he was furious, as much at her tone as at the words. Sue was a bright girl but not bright enough to be patronizing to *him*. Before their marriage she had treated him like a man, all right, or he wouldn't have had anything to do with her. She had been gay and deferential, jokingly derisive or frankly complimentary, flirtatious, mysterious, and, above all, superbly feminine, which meant to Tony that she had given him to understand that, in the last analysis and with all bluffs called, he would be the master in any situation that concerned the two of them.

It was the last quality that had suffered during the three years they had been married. It was partly because he couldn't make her understand that in his position he didn't have to be a slave. His hours and his choice of work were his own. Dad didn't care when he came in; in fact he thought it was pretty nice that Tony worked as hard as he *did*, seeing that he wouldn't even have to worry about where the next dollar was coming from. Sue couldn't get that through her head. "Tony, you won't get to the office before ten if you don't hurry." "I don't know why you were so unfriendly with the Bates man. He could be a good customer of yours." "For heaven's sake, Tony, get out to see Mr. Carlisle! He's been calling up for three weeks now and you haven't been to see him yet." As if he didn't know enough to run his own business.

Sure, he could work harder, make more money, but it wasn't necessary. And even if he had tried to please her in that regard she'd have had plenty of other things to criticize. Three years ago she had thought him a prince of a fellow, a promising young man, a romantic fiancé, an excellent husband. Now she thought he was lazy and selfish and careless and a bum. Well, he wasn't going to stand for that!

He pulled her around to face him on the stairs. "I got along all right even before I met you, sweetheart."

"You could always have done better."

"Which brings us up to a question. What have you ever done that's so startling that you can tell everyone else what to do?"

123

"I wanted to go into nurses' training, but Mother wouldn't let me. Then I married you. I know it's silly to talk about ambitions that were never fulfilled, but at least I *did* have the ambition."

"Yeah, and you'd have lasted about six months if the going got tough."

Her face crinkled and he saw she was going to cry. "I don't like to quarrel like this, Tony. I don't want to be a nagging shrew. Since I can't do anything myself, isn't it natural that I should want to drive you into something worth-while? If you'd co-operate a little it would be so easy. If I were to get fat you'd nag at me until I did something about it, wouldn't you? If I were to wear dirty underthings you'd speak up fast enough, wouldn't you? Well, that's what I'm trying to do for you. If I didn't care anything about you I'd shut up. It's just because I do care that I go through a horrible hour like this."

She was crying a little now and it served her right. "What you really want to do is make me over. If you didn't like me the way I was, why did you marry me?"

"I did like you the way you were. I think we'd both like you better the way you could be. If you weren't rude to people, if just once you'd do something you absolutely hated to do, if you didn't always act as though you were doing everyone a favor by being with them——"

"Dear me!"

Anger dried up the tears. "All right, you're perfect. We'll play it that way and I'll keep quiet. I'll thank you to return the favor and stop screaming about my family and my friends. Let's be a mutual admiration society for a while and see how we make out."

So automatic had her responsibility to him become, however, that before they left the house she had found his cigarette case for him and reminded him about the letter he had wanted to mail, and neither of them thought of these small insertions as veiled judications.

The one hundred and fifty graduates who composed the class of June 1931 sat on the stage, not too comfortably, on wooden folding chairs. The girls wore white, the boys wore dark coats and white flannels. The girls tried to sit still, worrying about the wrinkles in their dresses when they arose to walk across the stage to get the diplomas. The boys fidgeted, cleared their throats, tried to be indifferent to the occasion. In their midst, two black swans among the white ducklings, sat the principal and the speaker for the evening. Programs had been distributed among the audience, but the principal arose to announce each number anyway. The high school orchestra in the pit led off with the "Star-Spangled Banner," invocation followed, and there was an immense rustling as everyone sat down and prepared to give respectful attention to the unwinding of the scholastic ritual.

Tony mopped his forehead with his handkerchief and kept his arm stiffly away from Sue's. He was certainly not going to listen to the speeches. He'd heard them all hundreds of times before. He knew all about how these young people were about to go out into the wide, wide world and how it was their job to do better than the generation before them had done and how they were leaving now the happiest days of their lives. There was nothing else to do but look at the graduates.

He saw her immediately. She stood out in that immature, unpolished group like a fragment of marble in a heap of brass. She sat in the second row of folding chairs, so he concluded that she had attained no scholarly distinction. The honor students always sat in the front row. But, boy, anybody who could look like that shouldn't waste time studying! She'd never have to. The beautiful coppery hair made little curls around her face, though she had tried to draw it back smoothly. The widely set dark blue eyes were demure. Even at this distance you could see the luster of her satin skin and catch the red promise of her mouth. Her dress was white, but it didn't look stiff like the other girls' did. It was of a soft stuff that clung to her shoulders and rippled a little with the lightest current of air. It was the girl who had fooled him about being engaged. What was her name? Penelope King. That was it. Eleanor Kendrick's sister, Penny. She must be eighteen years old by now. He could not take his eyes off her.

He was surprised when the orchestra swung into "All for Thee, Sweet Ashland" and Sue stood up.

"Gee, for once they made it short and snappy," he said.

"It was the usual two hours. You were asleep for most of it."

Like hell he'd been asleep! "Let's go backstage and say hello to Peggy," he proffered amiably.

"Why, Tony, that's awfully nice of you!" Sue was smiling at him now. "She'll be out soon, though. I know how you hate pushing through a mob."

He took her arm. "Never mind me. Come on, honey."

He was charming to Peggy, overlooking her strident, overwrought laughter, the ugly crimson that splotched her neck when she was excited, the teeth gleamings at his shoulder when she chose to languish against him in cousinly fashion. Then, politely, he made way for fifty more Mannings, detached himself deftly, and started on his search.

The auditorium had emptied into this big study hall. It was packed with small intersecting groups whose nucleuses were graduates. There was much calling back and forth, a great deal of handshaking, an incense of pride and complacency that rose in heat waves to the ceiling. Penelope stood alone in a small triangle of empty corner. She was unpinning her corsage, gathering her purse and coat. Poor kid, where were her people? In all the room she was the only one who had no one around her.

"Hello, kid."

"Oh, Mr. Fox! How nice to see you again."

Her smile, her radiance, reminded him of a child looking at a Christmas tree. At this close range she was more flawlessly beautiful than ever. You kept looking at her to find some imperfection, and there was none, and you had to keep on looking. She was as guileless, as sweet, as unaffected as the gardenias she carried.

"All grown up now," he said.

"Nineteen last month." The long eyelashes lowered, but the mouth smiled. "I'm not as foolish as I used to be."

"What? Still not engaged?"

Her hand flew to his arm like a dove in distress. "You haven't held that against me. You've forgiven me?"

He patted the hand, thinking how gentle, how tender, how easily hurt she was. "Of course. We had a lot of fun, didn't we?"

A rather good-looking boy sidled up to them. "Say, excuse me, Penny, but I'd like to have you meet my folks. They're right over there, and——"

"I'll be along in a minute." Tony could see that she was annoyed at the interruption, but she was too polite to hurt the kid's feelings. "Is your wife here with you, Mr. Fox?"

"Listen, you can call me Tony, everybody does. Yes, Sue's right over there. A cousin of hers is in your class, and we came around to see her."

"Oh, Peggy Manning. She seems like such a—pleasant girl."

He grinned at her effort to find an adjective that was flattering but apt. "I guess she's pleasant enough. I don't know her very well."

126

"Neither do I. We don't seem to travel in the same crowd."

"I should think not! Because your crowd must be full of young men, and they wouldn't hang around Peggy."

She discovered that her hand was still on his arm and she took it back with a small, flustered smile. "You know," she said confidentially, "it worries me a lot. I mean, I haven't any girl friends, not a single one. And the boys—well, they take me out to dances and things, but I can't talk to them about things. They don't want to talk and they don't know much anyway. I guess I'd have to say that I don't have a friend, not one."

"How about your sister? Eleanor."

"She's a darling, but she has the two babies now and she and John go out a lot and she hasn't much time for me. And Martha's teaching in a high school up at Laketown and comes home in the summers, but all she wants to do then is read. I like to talk to Daddy, but he thinks I'm still a baby, so that doesn't help much, and Hetty—that's my stepmother"—she smiled apologetically—"well, you know what stepmothers are. They're not interested in you like your own mother would be."

"Poor kid." It was incredible, he thought. Here was this beautiful child, eating her heart out in loneliness, like Cinderella in the ashes. He had an inspiration. "Look here, you have me. Why can't I be a sort of young uncle or something? Any time you need advice——"

"Oh, I didn't mean—oh, no, it's sweet of you, but I couldn't."

"Why not? I have a little common sense and I've had a lot more experience."

A lovely pink blush, completely unlike Peggy's red splotches, crept into her face. She could not look at him. "You won't be angry?"

"No. Promise."

"Well, I could never think of you as an uncle. You're much too handsome, and——" He laughed at her confusion and then she could look at him again. "It's terrible of me to be so frank, but I promised myself four years ago, when you were so kind to me, that I'd never lie to you again."

"There's no law against thinking a guy's handsome."

"Well, you're married," she said shyly, "and you know how people talk. I couldn't even have a soda with you, much less——"

The good-looking youth came back and urged her away. She looked back over her shoulder. "Good-by, Tony," she called. "Thanks anyway."

Even after she had gone out the door her presence lay around him like a perfume and he had to shake himself to dispel it. Thank God, the Mannings were still at it. Sue hadn't even noticed where he had gone. She'd have had plenty to say if she had. There sure was a lot of difference in girls. Penny, now, you couldn't imagine her being bossy or nagging or critical. She'd always be sweet and kind and lovely and grateful for little things. Whereas Sue, no matter how much you tried to please her, it wasn't enough.

He sighed and walked back to his wife.

Penny stood out in the hall being pleasant to Jack Morrison's father and mother. In the glass cases that lined the wall she could see, dimly, the reflection of herself. Yes, her hair was perfect. All the little careless curls she had worked over so carefully were in place. Her make-up was still a masterpiece. What a bit of luck to run into Tony Fox like that! She'd made her father and Hetty promise to wait outside for her in the car, because she didn't want anyone around to scare Jack away, and while she'd been waiting for him to get up his nerve Tony had come along. It would be years and years before Jack could get married, but Tony was adult and had money besides. Unfortunately he had a wife too. In any case she was sure she'd be seeing him again, and almost anything could happen now that she was a seemly and eligible age.

"We're having a little supper out at the house," Mrs. Morrison was saying. "Won't you join us, Penelope?"

That was a concession, even a reversal. Penny knew that Mrs. Morrison had been worried that Jack was seeing too much of her, that, to put it bluntly, the King girl had been chasing her precious son. She'd make them try harder than that. Besides, she wasn't so interested in Jack any more.

"Thank you, Mrs. Morrison, but Daddy is waiting for me in the car, and I know he wants me to go home with him."

"Aw, Penny!" Jack was dismayed. Penny had told him just the day before that if he could make his mother ask her she'd come.

"I'm sorry, Jack. I'd like to but——"

Mr. Morrison cleared his throat. "Perhaps if we went out to the car and asked your father——"

"Oh, if you asked him he'd say all right. But he'd be hurt, I'm afraid." She smiled charmingly. "Parents are so darned nice, it's a

128

shame to take advantage of them, don't you think? Thank you so much. Maybe there'll be another time."

"There certainly will be," said Mr. Morrison gallantly.

Penny held the outside door ajar for a minute after she passed through it. "I've surely been mistaken in that girl!" she heard Mrs. Morrison say. "I can't think what Mrs. Mason was about, to tell me that she was a boy chaser, that all she wanted was to get out of them what she could."

Mr. Morrison grumbled. "Probably Penny had turned down the sainted Henry. You women are all alike. You've got your knives out for any pretty girl that comes along!"

"She's nice, isn't she, Mother? Just like I told you, isn't she, Mother?"

"I must say she isn't at all as I thought she'd be. Most girls that pretty are vain and conceited and not happy unless someone is running after them. This one doesn't seem to be that way at all. Certainly she's thoughtful of her parents, and that's usually a good sign."

Penny ran lightly down the walk to where her father and Hetty waited in the car.

"Have you waited long, darlings? I hurried as fast as I could. The Morrisons wanted me to go home with them, but I said I wanted to go home with you."

Jason and Hetty smiled at each other. "Now, Penny, you could have gone. They're nice folks."

She lay back and sniffed at the gardenias. "I'm with nicer folks," she said.

She cranked down the window to get the breeze. Her father drove as if he had all the treasures of the Indies in the back seat, taking the curves slowly, apologizing for every bump. The evening had been a great success.

She was looking out the window, though anyone coming suddenly into the room would have thought that she was studying a picture which hung a good three feet away from the embrasure. Tony's light green roadster was circling the block the third time. He'd been driving for a week without catching a sight of her. Today she'd give him a chance. In the glass within the picture frame she saw that she had never looked better. The yellow wash silk was perfect for her, cool and so simple that it detracted no iota of attention away from its wearer. These women who hung themselves with furbelows and bangles were trying to call attention away from their shortcomings. She had no shortcomings to hide.

She had not walked for more than a minute when the roadster pulled up alongside her.

"Well, hello!" Tony called.

"Why, Tony, what on earth are you doing way over here?"

"Had to call on a prospect. Let me drive you where you're going."

She hesitated a moment. "Well, it's just over to Eleanor's. She isn't home, but I like to see the babies."

It was the nicest car she had ever ridden in. The upholstering was a soft brown leather, the motor purred powerfully, the roughness of the road was imperceptible.

"What a beautiful car!" she said.

"The only kind to buy. When you get ready to own one, call on us."

"Don't worry. I'll never be able to afford a car like this."

"Who knows? You may marry a millionaire."

"Sometimes I think I won't ever marry anyone."

"Don't tell me that, with your face and at your age, you've lost hope already!"

She wished the wind would not blow her hair quite so much, but it couldn't be helped. "It's Daddy, you see. Oh, he's awfully sweet, but he's a tiger where I'm concerned. Any young man who comes to the house, Daddy's so severe with him that he doesn't feel like coming back. Well, you can't get married like that."

"Can't you talk to him?"

"You know how fathers are. They always think nobody's good enough for their children. Daddy wouldn't even like it if he knew I was in this car with *you*."

"Is that a fact? Well, say, we'd better make sure he doesn't hear about it."

"I guess he won't object too much, if it's only once."

"I kind of hoped it could be more than once."

She looked away, and her voice was soft. "I know, I feel the same way. But it wouldn't do any good. There'd be no future in it. If I'd been nineteen when I first met you four years ago——"

"I wouldn't have married Sue, maybe."

"You mustn't talk like that! That's a dreadful thing to say."

130

"Listen, you don't know." It all spluttered out of him, Sue's lack of affection, her bad temper, her constant fault finding.

Penny nearly wept. "Oh, I'm so sorry for you! I had no idea it was like that. How can she treat you that way? It would be different if you weren't a good husband. But you work hard and you don't drink or run around and you've given her a lovely home. What more does she want?"

"I don't know," he said grimly. He'd never told anyone all this before, and now he was glad he had. It just confirmed his opinion that Sue was being selfish and unreasonable. From now on he was going to stand up for his rights, he wasn't going to let her keep getting away with it!

"Did you know each other long before you were married?"

"I've known Sue all my life. I guess we just took each other for granted."

"That's such a mistake, isn't it? There used to be a boy who lived next door to me—well, Henry Mason, you know—and because we knew each other so well he just imagined that we'd get married someday. Then when I told him I wouldn't he was furious. I guess he thought he owned me." She laughed a little. "Imagine, Henry Mason!"

"I guess that's what Sue thinks, all right, that she owns me."

"Surely, if you explained how you feel about it, she'd try to change."

"Not Sue! She'll be the same till the day she dies."

He went into Eleanor's with her. The two-year-old was in the back yard in his play pen, but Baby Alice was waving her small pink arms in a basket on the sun porch. Mrs. Church, the nurse, looked surprised when Penny walked over and picked up the baby.

"Oh, Mrs. Church, isn't she sweet? She's getting bigger every minute. You must take awfully good care of her."

Mrs. Church softened. She hadn't thought young Miss King gave a snap for babies, she'd never paid much attention before, but she knew a healthy baby when she saw one.

"Oh, we have our hands full, I tell you!"

"I'm sure you do. I don't know much about it, but if you need any extra help I'd be glad to try sometime. I'm just crazy about babies!"

What a picture she makes, Tony thought, standing there with that lovely Madonna look, catching a small hand to kiss, smiling into the little face. He quite forgot that ordinarily he disliked children, that he had told Sue that they ought to wait a couple of years longer be-

131

fore they had any, that he had said they ought to have some fun out of life before they settled down to taking care of a bunch of kids.

Penny put the baby down. She hoped the horrible little animal had not wet through to the yellow wash silk. No, it was all right. Funny how homely babies always were and how they smelled of sour milk no matter how well they were looked after. "It's selfish of me to pick her up and spoil her nap."

"That young lady'll sleep right through it. She's never going to be bothered by insomnia the way it looks now."

The two of them walked into the big living room where venetian blinds turned the bright sun into a pale translucence.

"Sit down a minute, Tony. I'll go make us some lemonade."

This is domestic, nobody scolding you for being home in the middle of the day or shoving a lawn mower at you; this is wonderful, he thought as she came back with two frosty glasses of lemonade that the cross cook had taken time out to make for her.

"Here you are. If I say so myself, I'm especially good at making lemonade."

It was delicious. He sipped and admired the glints the one direct ray of sunlight that had forced its way past the blinds was making in her hair.

"When can I see you again, Penny?"

She held her pose, though the sun was making her head uncomfortably hot. "We can't. It wouldn't be right."

"But if I happen to run into you somewhere . . ."

She smiled. "Perhaps. If it's purely by accident."

Purely by accident he overtook her on the street the next morning, and, since Sue was at a bridge luncheon, he drove Penny out to the Country Inn for lunch.

At first Sue's references to Penny had been jocular. "Grave snatcher," she called her, which was supposed to be an amusing reference to Tony's thirty years, and "wondrous child." By the time two months had gone by she had stopped referring to her altogether. By the end of four months she was in an honest rage.

She came into his study one rainy evening and dropped down in the green leather chair. "We have to talk this over," she said. "Might as well do it now."

"Talk what over?"

"Don't play dumb. We have to talk about Penelope King. You know, the girl you meet on street corners."

"I don't meet her on street corners! She's not that kind of a girl."

"Oh, you call for her at her front door?"

There was no use trying to explain to Sue that Penny hadn't once come out of her way to see him, that it was Tony who had made all the opportunities. She would have thought that the girl should have left town or shut herself up in her room or something.

"Anyway, there's nothing to talk about."

"Yes, there is. At least the rest of the town is talking. Why not we?"

"They have darned little to talk about if that's the best they can find."

"It's always amusing to see how much of a fool a man can make of himself. But that's not my affair. What is my affair is that you're not going to make a fool of me."

"I don't see why you should begrudge me a little harmless, agreeable company. You talk as though I was carrying on an affair or something."

"The whole thing really boils down to one question. Are you going to stop seeing her?"

"No."

"Then I'll want a divorce."

He was unprepared for that. He had expected a quarrel, tears, his recriminations for her doubt in his virtue, her apologies, a reconciliation. Good Lord, he'd joshed with Penny a lot, a fellow had to say nice things to as pretty a girl as she was, but he hadn't intended to reorganize his whole life for the kid. Sue had taken it all wrong.

"You're just sore because she doesn't seem to find me as unappetizing as you do. Jealousy, that's all it is."

"It's the gossip I'm objecting to, primarily. If you want to know the truth, I don't think the girl gives a rap about you. I think she has you down for an easy mark, a chauffeur for the country, a payer of luncheon checks."

"Sure. You would think that. Let me tell you, the kid understands me a lot better than you do."

"I've never made a specialty of sympathizing with your faults, that's true."

"If you loved me——"

"If I didn't love you I wouldn't bother talking this over with you,

133

I'd just have walked out. It hasn't been easy for me, these last four months, trying to keep people from telling me about you, laughing it off when they were tactless enough to come out with it anyhow. I've stuck it out because I thought you'd get over it. But it's been too flattering for you, being married to one not unattractive woman and being chased by another more attractive one. It looks as if you weren't going to get over it. Well, I can't be a complacent wife any longer. I want a showdown."

He was caught in a dilemma. He wanted to tell her that Penny didn't mean a thing to him actually; he had liked to look at her, that was all. But that admission would make him seem weak. It would convince Sue that he'd jump any time she wanted to snap her fingers. He couldn't have that. Let her worry and stew about him for a while. Then he'd take her in his arms, magnanimously, and assure her that she was the woman he really loved. That was the truth too. Oh, he blew off a lot of steam about her, she had her faults, but she was, nevertheless, the only woman in the world he'd give a nickel for. He'd let her know that, in time. Right now he was busy teaching her a lesson.

"If you'd try being a little more bewitching yourself, maybe I wouldn't have to try to find somebody who'd give me a kind word now and then."

"That's exactly like you, Tony. No matter what happens to you, it's always somebody else's fault. Don't cast me for your whipping boy this time. I'm not in the mood for it."

Was he going too far? Hadn't he better give in right now, tell her that he'd behave better? His mother and father wouldn't like a divorce. The Mannings would be enraged, gathering Sue tenderly back to their fold, roaring social damnation for him everywhere they went. Besides, damn it all, Sue was his wife and he was fond of her! Aw, she didn't mean it. She *couldn't* mean it. She was simply trying to bring him to heel, and he'd show her that she had taken much too severe a line.

"I wouldn't saw at the rope quite so hard if I were you," he said. "It might break."

"You fool! You're the one who's doing the sawing and in spite of it you're convinced the rope will hold. I can forgive you for being weak—I knew that when I married you—but it's hard to overlook your being—insane."

"You say the nicest things! It's no wonder I'm wild about you." He made his voice girlishly falsetto.

For a minute he thought that had done it, that she was going to break down and cry and then things would progress satisfactorily to peace between them on his terms. But her eyes were dry and hard.

"You can have a week to make up your mind. After that you'll be an honest man. Honest to me or honest to her, I don't care which, but honest at last you'll be!"

He thought he was righteously indignant. Actually, as the door closed behind her, he was closer to panic.

Sue had gone home to her mother, and he did not dare to brave her in the Manning den. He took to driving around the town in the evenings in the hope of an accidental meeting with her. He was ready to concede now, to give up his braggadocio, to admit that he had been in the wrong. In a town this size a man couldn't carry on a harmless flirtation; to the older residents there was no such thing, he knew that. Sue must have put in a tough six months or she could never have been so sore.

It was Saturday night when he went into Kernson's to buy a package of cigarettes. On a Saturday you were apt to see everybody in town at Kernson's, at one time or another. The white-coated clerk, who had been in Tony's class in high school, slapped the cigarettes down on the glass counter top and asked him how he liked the Yankees *now*. He had never paid much attention to the clerk before—he knew his first name was Don—but tonight he was glad to talk to him. He leaned on the counter and discussed the major leagues at length.

He did not see Penny come in, but the clerk did.

"Someone to see you," said the clerk, and went away.

He turned and she was standing, pink and hesitant, by his shoulder. This was bad, this was very bad. He calculated the number and caliber of the people in the store. Nobody he knew, but the chances were some of them knew him. The strangest people took an interest in your affairs. A man his father had sold a car to. A woman who had served at the same counter of the church bazaar with his mother. A boy whose older brother had played on the same basketball team with Tony. All these felt that they owned a little part of you, it made them violently interested in your every act, and there was no way of spotting them. They were absolutely anonymous.

"Let's go outside," he said.

She followed him obediently out to the car. "I don't think I should get in, Tony. I've never——"

Apprehension made him savage. "Get in, damn it! Let's not stand here arguing until we have a crowd around us. I'll drive you home."

She climbed in, tucked her hair more closely inside her white turban, arranged her lovely legs. He cursed his luck that the top was down, but everybody in town knew his car anyway and if they got a look at the girl at all they'd know she wasn't Sue. Main Street was crowded, all the lights were on, the traffic was slow because the farmers were in town, driving carefully down the middle of the street. He turned off on Linden and headed up the hill toward the residential section.

"You're angry with me?" she said.

"No, I'm not. Not a bit of it. It's just that I don't think we ought to be seen together when there's such a mob around."

"We've been seen together lots of times before. There's nothing *wrong* with it."

"Of course there isn't, but you know what this town is. They can't imagine a man and woman being friends with nothing more to it than that."

"Sue's been talking to you."

"Well, yes, and I can see her point of view in a way."

"I'm so sorry for you, Tony."

"No reason to be."

"Yes, there is. You live such a miserable, lonesome life, never able to do what you want to or say what you want to. Oh, don't try to hide it. Everybody knows that Sue has you under her thumb." She put her hand over her mouth. "I shouldn't have said that, it wasn't nice. What I mean is, you're so wonderful and nobody appreciates you."

He laughed, briefly. "She's trying to get me out from under her thumb now, all right. She wants to divorce me."

Her face bloomed with rapture. "Oh, I'm so glad. At last you'll be free of her! Aren't you happy?"

"Well, but say, I don't——"

"Of course right now it's a shock to you, but after you get over the first hard part you'll see how lucky you were to get out of it. All these years of trying so hard to please her! She'll never be able to say it was your fault anyway."

He began to feel a lot better, righteous, vindicated. "She thinks I'm seeing too much of you, that's the main trouble."

"Why, we're just friends. She understands that, doesn't she?"

"I guess not."

"Aren't you even allowed to have friends unless she approves of them?"

He pulled in to the curb, a careful block away from Penny's house. He opened his package of cigarettes and lit one, frowning over the question. "I don't think it's Sue so much as it is what all her friends have been saying to her. I'm trying to be fair about this, you see."

"You're being wonderfully fair. But if I thought enough of a man to marry him I wouldn't care what anybody tried to tell me about him, I'd trust him!"

He hadn't thought of that and it was a point. "Sure, that's right. Trust is pretty important. Can't have much of a marriage without it."

"And if she doesn't trust you now, she never will, and you'll live a perfectly dreadful life until you die. You're going to let her divorce you, aren't you? You're not going to go on trying to live with her?"

"It's a serious decision. I'm trying to give her the benefit of the doubt. She went over to her mother's a week ago and I haven't seen her since. Naturally I didn't want to run in on my folks because they'd have wanted to know what the matter was. I didn't want the news to get around as long as there was a chance of patching it up. So I've been eating out, sleeping in an unmade bed—you know how it is when a man's trying to keep house for himself."

"Oh, why didn't you let me know? I could have slipped into your house while you were out and cleaned it for you and washed the dishes and made your bed. I just love to putter around a house."

"That's darned nice of you, but I couldn't let you do that. A pretty kid like you ought to be out having a good time and not sit around worrying about an old man's problems like this."

She threw him a quick, laughing glance. "Old!" she said reproach-fully.

Uneasily he looked at his luminous wrist watch. It was almost nine o'clock, just the time when those who had been in time for the first showing of one of the movies would be trudging back home up the hill again. He wanted Penny out of the car before that happened. Too many cars were beginning to go by already, and the foot travelers would have an even better chance at observation.

"I'd better run along, Penny," he said. "Thanks a lot."

"I can't bear to think of your going back to your lonely house."

"That's all right. I don't mind. I'm getting used to it." He could hear feet on the cement sidewalk several blocks below him. They were coming now. He opened the door for her.

"Whatever happens, you know you can count on me, don't you? Whatever happens, we'll be friends."

"Sure. You bet." Beautiful as she was, he was glad to see her get out, stand on the strip of grass between the curb and the walk.

She caught her breath on a sob. "I don't think you care whether we're friends or not. I think you just want to get rid of me."

"Aw now, listen! I——"

"You don't have to worry. Daddy wants me to go away to school this fall. You won't have to see me again if you don't want to."

"It isn't that, Penny. But what, for God's sake, do you want me to do? I can't——"

Mrs. Fannie Parsons, elderly widow and writer of the social notes for the *Herald,* came by slowly enough to take in the car, the girl, and the tears. Of all people, Mrs. Parsons, the most wicked mind and pointed tongue in town!

"Well, Penelope," she said, "and Mr. Fox. Lovely evening, isn't it? I declare I was nearly suffocated in the Lyric. Been for an airing?"

By the glee, the licking-of-the-lips quality in her voice, he knew how thoroughly he was lost.

Penny shut the car door. "If you're going right past my house I'll walk with you, Mrs. Parsons."

He wanted to call her back, warn her that Mrs. Parsons would wring her dry, misconstrue every word she said, count every tear. Why in hell hadn't he taken her straight home? Trust Mrs. Parsons to put the worst interpretation on his letting her out a block away. And with that for a starter, the Lord alone knew what tall tale would be circulating in Ashland the next day! Sighing, he turned on the ignition. Maybe the poor innocent kid would have sense enough not to be fooled by Mrs. Parsons's amiability. Maybe she'd keep her mouth shut.

He never learned what Penny had said to Mrs. Parsons. Sue left to

138

visit an aunt in another state the next afternoon. Within three months he was a divorced man.

They drove up in front of the King house early one spring evening. A sleek, beautifully dressed Penny ran up the walk, burst into the house, and threw herself into her father's arms.

"Oh, Daddy," she said, "don't be angry with me. I'm so happy. I never thought I could be so happy. Tony's not an ogre. He's an angel!"

In the hall mirror she could see her bright, penitent face over her father's shoulder as he hugged her. The pear-shaped diamond she had made Tony buy for her glistened like a captured meteor.

"Penny, you didn't have to run away to get married. Why didn't you give us time to know the man? Why couldn't you be married at home? It was hardly decent, so soon after his divorce."

"He hadn't lived with his wife for ever so long before. They'd never been happy together." She threw herself against Hetty and sobbed into her shoulder, "Daddy's cross with me, Hetty. Make him understand. You're not cross at me, are you, darling?"

Between them they stilled her tears. By the time Tony came in Jason could be almost cordial. "Well, young man, what have you to say for yourself? Though I guess it's too late to say it now. We'll have to find out the worst for ourselves."

"That's right, Mr. King. I hope you're not too sore."

"No sorer than your own folks are going to be, I bet."

"Just wait until they meet Penny. Then they'll love her. They can't help it."

Jason put a hand on his new son-in-law's shoulder. "There's one thing you'll have to remember. She's not much more than a child. Take good care of her, won't you?"

"You bet I will," Tony promised. "I sure will. She's helpless as a baby."

Jason turned to his daughter. "Hear that, Penny? Your husband says you're helpless as a baby."

"Why, I am *not!*" she said with dainty indignation.

The two men smiled at each other over her head. They knew better.

11.

John Kendrick's father died of a heart attack in 1929. It was an excellent year to quit the world. Real estate values were skyrocketing downward, the factory had to close most of its doors for lack of orders, the clang of the big hammers no longer sounded faintly over the town at midnight, and the eerie, blue-white light that had flooded out of its windows on sweating summer nights blinded passing drivers no more. The brawny men who, stripped to the waist, had coaxed and commanded the restless, bellowing machines now sat on their porches and wondered what the hell a guy was going to do to feed his kids and what kind of a country was it when a man was willing to work, had worked all his life, and, all at once, couldn't find work for love or money?

They tried everywhere, these men. First they made the rounds of the shops in the smoky part of town across the railroad tracks. They stood for hours under the giant "No Hiring Today" signs in the hope that somehow something would turn up. They no longer mentioned the classifications of which they had been proud: mechanic, draftsman, checker. "Anything," they said now. "Anything." But there was nothing. Door by door the shops shut down until, in most of them, there was left only a small office and maintenance force.

People sniggered about the WPA, made jokes about it, jeered: "Shovel leaners." These men were in no position to make light of any financial plank that was held out to them. They spent their savings, they borrowed on their insurance, the meals on their tables had shrunk to poor quality and small servings, their landlords had lowered their rents to twenty-five, to fifteen, to ten dollars and were having to wait for their money at that. One by one these men went to the WPA office, picked up shovels, and went out to work on the roads. It wasn't like having an honest job. The government wanted you to work just enough so they'd have an excuse to give you money to keep you from starving. Fast, competent work was frowned on. The job had to last. This labor was simply a token of your self-respect; the government paid you because you were a citizen, not because you worked well. It was hard for these men to slow down, to take it easy. All their impulses were in favor of doing a good job, fast. It was harder to stand around all day than it was to work. They longed for the day when times would get better and the shops would open again. They smiled grimly over the editorial worry, expressed over and over again in every newspaper, that if men were once given a pittance for not doing very much they would never again want to do an honest job and the nation would have spawned a breed of loafers. Christ, that was dumb! What guy would squeeze along on twenty dollars a week when he could make seventy, eighty? Who didn't want a chance to send his kids through school and dress pretty well and go to the movies when he wanted to and see that the wife didn't have to worry about where the next groceries were coming from? A few bums, maybe. Not these men.

In Ashland the joking about the WPA died down. In Ashland the WPA saved lives.

In the big houses farther up the tree-decked hill the pinch was felt too. The elder Mrs. Kendrick collected her husband's insurance and moved in with her daughter Elizabeth, though Eleanor had dutifully offered her a place in John's home.

"It's kind of you, my dear," Mrs. Kendrick said, "and I appreciate it. But Elizabeth's husband is going to have a hard time of it, and I may be able to help out a bit. There isn't going to be much call for lawyers for a few years, the way it looks. John, now, will manage the shop, and he'll be all right. I'd like to sell the old house, if I could get anything for it. It would be silly for me to keep it up by myself in times like these."

John could not find a buyer for the old Kendrick house. "It cost twenty thousand dollars to build," he said. "I'm damned if I'm going to give it away for eight. And nobody can afford to rent the place. We'll just close it up, Mother, and wait for things to get better."

He had always been a hard worker. Now he worked fanatically, traveling to scrape up orders for the factory, making all the business friends he could in the hope that one of them might throw something his way. He came home only to eat and to sleep.

They gave up their membership in the country club. They dropped their subscriptions to the book clubs whose books they had seldom read but had valued highly on their shelves as symbols of literacy.

They told the man who worked on the yard not to come back. The housekeeper had to go in 1930. The nurse in 1931.

"It's going to be tough on you," John told Eleanor, "but I can't help it. We've got to cut down. I hate to dump the house and the kids and the whole works on your hands this way, but we've got to protect our investments and sit this thing out. No more elaborate entertaining. If our friends want to see us they can drop in for a cup of coffee or a highball and we'll let it go at that."

She watched his body sag as he walked over to his chair, dropped into it with a sigh of fatigue, and reached for the newspaper. John was only twenty-nine and he looked five years older than that! His ways had grown older too. He didn't talk much any more. He moved only when he had to. He ate rapidly and in silence. He went to bed early. For the first time in her life she felt sorry for him, and it made her feel strong and equal to any emergency, as she had felt that day long ago in Dr. O'Malley's office. "I'm sure I can manage, dear," she said.

But the feeling of competence faded as she tackled the job. The house, perhaps, she could have managed; the house plus four-year-old Sonny and two-year-old Alice was too much for her. She worked like a maniac, struggled like a drowning man, and wept a little sometimes when her aching bones refused to carry her another step. Aunt Ann, a withered leaf whose hold on the bough the first strong wind would break, tried to help.

"I can come over several hours a day and watch the children for you," she said. "I don't know much about children, but I can keep Sonny from breaking his neck. And you'll forgive me for mentioning it, my dear, but you should really try to spend a little more time on yourself. When did you have a manicure last?"

Eleanor giggled hysterically. "Why, about a year ago. Oh, I've given myself a coat of polish now and then when I had a minute, but it doesn't last long when your hands are in water all the time."

"You simply can't go around looking like a washerwoman. What John and his mother must think——"

"Don't worry. John doesn't have time to look at me, and Mother Kendrick is carefully staying away until after the children are in bed, for fear she'd be asked to do something."

"Well, naturally, you wouldn't expect her to——"

"I don't expect her to come and sit in my house for three hours at a time and think that I'm going to treat her like company, anyway, with the living room dusty and a washing waiting to be done in the basement and the two youngsters screaming and crying at the tops of their lungs! The least she could do would be to follow me around while I work, and she doesn't want to do that. She wants the two of us to sit there, all immaculate, and have a cup of tea and a nice cozy chat!"

"That's the sort of thing she's used to. You can't blame her, dear."

"It's the sort of thing I'm used to, too, but things change. If she can't stand our desperate family routine she'd better stay away."

"I hope you didn't forget yourself so far as to say anything like that to her."

Eleanor shifted the squirming Alice to her other arm. "Oh no," she said wearily. "We're still the well-meaning, openhanded mother-in-law and her devoted daughter by marriage."

Aunt Ann's sitting with the children those few hours a day helped amazingly. Eleanor could keep up with the washing and ironing, do more of her housework in the morning, spend more time on the preparation of dinner. She was not very good at any of this, and, though her skill increased with the years, her meals were inclined to be taste-less and watery, and she never learned a sound, tight method of bed-making. Her working schedule was formless, and she was always robbing Peter to pay Paul in the matter of time.

When she and John quarreled it was always about the children. When was Sonny going to stop wetting the bed? Why couldn't Alice leave his desk alone? Shouldn't they, by God, have learned to eat properly by this time? Eleanor was just wearing herself out on the darned kids, and she shouldn't do it!

She tried to tell him. "I don't spend *enough* time with them, John. It takes time to teach them all these things. Most evenings I forget to pick Sonny up at eleven, I'm so tired. If you'd only remind me——"

"Sorry. I've got more important things on my mind. If all I had to do was to manage a couple of kids I'd be ashamed to squeal about it. Just what is it you do all day?"

She would have liked to say, "Why, nothing much. I get up at five forty-five and get dressed any old how and come downstairs and start breakfast. While it's cooking I get Alice and Sonny up and dressed without disturbing Your Highness and get them fed early because you don't like them at the breakfast table. Then I get you up and have

143

breakfast with you while I sit on the edge of a chair and wonder whether Sonny is climbing the fence or throwing sand in Alice's eyes. After you go I take them both up to the bathroom. Oh, I've heard of toilet training, though I'm not so good at it! Then I do the breakfast dishes, straighten the house, do a washing or ironing, take the children along when I go to the store, come home and get their lunches, clean them up and put them to bed for their naps. While they sleep I do the luncheon dishes, put toys away, and scrub or wax a floor or two. Sonny gets up first, and I dress him and turn him loose. Of course on bad days he's under my feet every minute. On good ones he plays outside, but I have to keep an eye on him and on whatever neighbor kids are around. Then Alice has to be bathed and freshened. Then the washing has to be taken in or the roses sprayed or the clothes mended. Along about that time it's six o'clock. I give the children their suppers and get dinner for you. Then all there is left are the dinner dishes, and the children to be cleaned up again and put to bed. By that time it's nine-thirty and I can sit down. Oh yes, every two hours all day long I have to remember to get the children to the bathroom. And if they hurt themselves or get sick I have to take a lot more time out to take care of them. I know all this can't compare with riding around in a car and talking to businessmen, but I call it a day's work!"

He wouldn't have listened. Already he had gone back to his eternal paper and his eternal snarling over Roosevelt. She sat quietly, looking down at her horrible hands. John was right in one respect: the children weren't well trained. What had the nurse done to them to make Sonny a bad-tempered little tyrant who went into screaming tantrums when he couldn't have what he wanted? He was mean to younger children and impudent to adults. He was capable of rolling himself in his clean clothes in a puddle if he were angry with his mother. One day, to her horror, she had found him tormenting a stray sick kitten. No, Sonny was not a nice little boy. And Alice, conversely, was a little whiner and storyteller.

But what John didn't realize was that the way to change that was not to suppress it, shove it out of the way, sit on it. That corrected nothing. It carried the assumption that, as long as the children weren't actively bothering you, they were all right. What was needed now was an intensive period of retraining in habits and manners. If she didn't have the housework she might be able to do it. She would have to spend all their waking hours within ear and eyeshot of them for a while and divert their attention into different and harmless channels, praising, frowning, judging. Right now that was impossible, but if you didn't do it now, before they got to school, when was it going to be done? Puzzling over this, she fell asleep in her chair. By the time she got upstairs Sonny had wet the bed again.

In the spring of 1935 Aunt Ann died of pneumonia. There was no long invalidism, no messy chores for anyone to do for her. She left life as politely and formally and properly as she had lived it. A few very old ladies came to the funeral, and a few old gentlemen who had known her husband. There were a great many flowers from the Women's Club and the church associations to which she had belonged. Martha came down for the funeral and stayed at her father's house.

"I don't know why you didn't come to us," Eleanor said. "We have a lot more room and I know you don't care particularly for Hetty."

In spite of her smart clothes, her fashionable coiffure, and her new coupé, it was the same, honest Martha. "I care even less for John, honey."

Eleanor wasn't listening. In her grief her mind jumped aimlessly from one thing to another. "I do think Penny might have made an effort to come. She's out East with some friends. She's never home. I don't think she and Tony are getting along."

"They wouldn't. Unless he's prepared to set her up on an altar and spend all his days burning incense to her. Expensive incense, besides. No cheap stuff for Penelope."

"They've been married only three years, too." She began to cry. "You'll come and spend this summer with me, won't you? I'm so lonely. Now that Aunt Ann's gone there's not a soul I can talk to."

"I'll be at Grandmother's. I'll come over every day."

"You don't know how hard the last six years have been for me. It's easy for you. You have a job that keeps right on going, depression or no, and you have that lovely vacation in the summers."

"Oh, there's a little work connected with it." No use explaining about her full teaching program, the extra work that her promotion to being a critic teacher entailed, the long rehearsals of school plays that took up evenings and Saturday mornings, the rush of trying to make the night classes that would eventually give her a Master's degree. All Eleanor would see was the clothes and the car. You had to give her credit, though. "I know it's been tough, Eleanor. I didn't think you had it in you."

145

"I did my best, but . . ." Fresh tears flooded her slender face. "The children aren't turning out well at all, and I don't know what to do. Sonny's going to be in third grade and he can't read a line and doesn't want to learn. And Alice is going into first, but she wept all the way through kindergarten, and she hates school."

Martha permitted herself a small irony. "What does John suggest?"

"Oh, gracious, don't mention it to him! He'd be wild. As long as they leave him alone in the evenings, that's all he asks. I don't want him all stirred up about it."

"Dear John. Well, I'll do what I can with them this summer. I'm used to bigger children, but I guess teaching is teaching."

She helped Eleanor put dinner on the table and she managed to look pleasant when John came home.

"Glad to see you, Martha. Thought maybe you were going back to Laketown without giving us an evening."

"I'm going back in the morning."

"Driving?"

"Yes. It takes about five hours."

"You career women, roaming all over the country by yourselves! I don't know as I'd like to have Eleanor make a jaunt like that all alone. What if something happened to the car?"

"I'd do what most men do. Have it hauled to the nearest garage to be fixed."

"Yes, well, uh . . ." He glared down the table at his wife. "Have you been crying again? Martha, can't you make her stop? She's been crying for a week! I tell her everybody has to die sometime."

Martha smiled beatifically at him. "Sometimes," she said, "that is the only thought that sustains one."

Ruffling his after-dinner paper angrily in the living room, he heard the two of them laughing and talking in the kitchen. That Martha was a fresh thing. Didn't care what she said. Pity the guy that married her. She'd never get married, though. Most unwomanly woman he'd ever met. Glad she didn't live around here. First thing you knew she'd be putting ideas into Eleanor's head.

A cardboard airplane sailed past his nose and spatted against his paper. Sonny came in from the dining room to get it.

John roared at him. "Can't you sail these damned things somewhere else? Can't I have a minute's peace in this house?"

Martha came quietly around the corner, tea towel in hand. "Come away, Sonny," she said. "Your father doesn't like to have you around."

"I *do* like to have him around if he could behave himself for five minutes in a row!"

She ignored him. "Come on out in the kitchen, Lindbergh. We've just built a brand-new landing field out there. That's the place to land these damned things."

"Martha!" John was horrified.

She was rounding the corner after Sonny, but she paused to look back, amiably. "The moral is obvious," she said, and went on to the kitchen.

Now there, that was what he meant! In three minutes she had given Sonny the impression that his father didn't like him and had rebuked that father for using bad language in front of the child. He *did* like Sonny, of course he did. All fathers liked their children. You couldn't go around grinning at them all the time or they'd lose respect for you, think you were an easy mark, run all over you like they did their mothers. And as for the language, all right, he shouldn't have used it, but what business was it of that old-maid schoolteacher's anyway?

He tried to take her down a peg or two on the only grounds he could think of. At the door, as she was leaving, he said genially, "S'pose you'll be getting married soon, Martha. Lot of beaux coming around?"

"No, not many. Though when I see how happy all married women are and the easy time they have of it, I'm sometimes tempted." She looked at him gravely and her voice was innocent. "You know, John, I've thought and thought, and I can't see one advantage to marriage— for me. I live in a pretty apartment with maid service, I have all the clothes I need, I like the work I'm doing, I don't have to bother my head about pleasing anyone but my principal. Now just what could marriage give me that I don't have already?"

He stumbled over it. "Love," he said.

She laughed. "Oh, John dear, I'd bet you my last dollar that I could get more of that unmarried than I could married. That is, if you're referring to the physical aspects of love, which I suppose you are. That's what most men mean by love, isn't it?"

He was shocked but he tried not to show it. "Children then. You can have those too, without marrying, but it's more convenient the other way."

147

"Children? You mean those little savages who can't behave themselves for five minutes in a row? Besides, I have children, over two hundred of them a day. Good night, Eleanor." She kissed her sister's cheek. Then she turned back to John. "If you had said 'companionship' I wouldn't have had any answer except that, in most marriages, that seems to be extremely rare, wouldn't you say?"

He could hardly wait until the door had closed after her. "If you have any plans for seeing a great deal of your sister this summer, forget them. I won't have her in my house!"

Eleanor looked better than she had in a long time. Her color was livelier, her eyes animated. "Martha said that you'd say that. Don't worry about it. She doesn't like to come here either. The children and I will go over and visit her."

Under ordinary circumstances he would have argued with her, but he felt uncertain, chagrined. Perhaps Martha had told Eleanor what he was going to say for the next two days! He wasn't going to be a ventriloquist's dummy. He kept quiet.

By the summer of 1935 John could relax a little. The shop was going again, all the shops were going again, the men had given back their shovels and come home to the drafting board and the machine. Back came the yardman. Back came the housekeeper and cook. There were two new cars. The children were to go to an expensive summer camp.

Eleanor was almost delirious with joy and relief. "Oh, darling, how wonderful! But I'd rather keep the children here. There are a lot of things I'd like to do with them."

"Listen, if you're thinking of dragging them over to Martha's and having her say a magic word or two over them that will clear up all their difficulties, think again. In the first place she'd be relieved not to have them. In the second, this is a darned good camp. I've looked it up. They'll learn a lot there and have fun besides. Anyway, I thought you and I would take a vacation up North somewhere. We certainly have one coming."

"John, so much money all at once! How did we get it?"

"Why, we got it because your old man was smart enough not to spend the first nickels he started to make. We could have had all this three years ago, but it would have been on a shoestring. The way I've got it fixed now, we won't have to worry for the rest of our lives."

She exclaimed and marveled over him, and he lounged importantly in his chair.

"Oh, we have the world licked from now on, all right. I've worked like a dog and had a little luck besides. We're going to build a much bigger house farther out. We'll have a whole staff of servants. We'll send the kids to a private school. We're going to live like white people, you bet!"

"I'd like the children to stay home and go to school here, just like they're doing. Martha says it's bad for them to——"

"Martha, Martha, Martha! Whose children are they, mine or hers? We'll pick a good school, not just any old place. They'll be fine."

"Alice is only five, dear. That's awfully young to be sent away. She's just a baby. I don't think there's a school that takes them that young."

"Sure there is. There must be."

There was.

"She's so little," Eleanor sobbed to Martha. "I don't see how I can bear to see her go."

"Don't let her, then. I think you're smart. It doesn't take long for children to figure out, if they're always being sent away from home, that their parents don't want them. That's not a good way to make a child feel."

"Well, John says——"

"Tell him you've changed your mind. Don't be so mousy with him. He's not Lord God Jehovah. It's your fault that he's as bad as he is. If you'd stood up to him about things in the beginning he wouldn't have turned so grouchily omnipotent by this time."

"I can't quarrel. I hate trouble. And, after all, he's given me so much."

"Too bad he didn't give you a housekeeper three years ago, when he says he first could have afforded it. You were dashing your brains out against a stone wall then, but he thought too much of his precious business to see that you had help. Moral: If things get tight, sacrifice your wife but never your investments."

"I don't mind, now that it's over."

"The work didn't hurt you. Everybody ought to work. But he should have explained the situation to you and given you a chance to make the choice yourself. That wouldn't be like John, though. He has to wait until he can take all the credit himself and then come flouncing in throwing roses and playing Lord Bountiful."

149

"Anyway, everything's all right now."

"Till next time. He'll sacrifice you again, one way or another, you'll see. You've let him get away with it so often that he's got the habit." Martha laughed. "The woman John should have married is Penny. Wouldn't she have shown him a thing or two!"

Eleanor repeated some of this to John in their luxurious rooms at the hotel in Quebec later on.

"Don't quote Martha to me any more," John said. "If you had any sense at all you'd see that she's jealous. That's what makes her talk like that. You're married and she isn't. You have everything given to you and she has to work for what she gets. She'll end up on a teacher's pension and you'll end up in a palace. Naturally it makes her a little sour to think of it."

She thought aloud. "But she does have her independence. She can say what she wants and go where she wants and do what she wants."

"And I suppose you can't? Maybe you'd rather have stayed in Ashland than come up here? Well, go on back. I won't stop you, if that's the way you feel!"

"I love it here, of course. I didn't mean that."

"God knows what you mean! Women are all alike: they never know what they want. Here you are, couldn't earn a dime on your own, and yet when your husband works and slaves to give you everything in the world you aren't satisfied. I don't ask much from you, Eleanor, but I do think you might show a little appreciation now and then."

"Dearest, I do appreciate it, honestly. I think you're—well, you've done wonderfully well."

He was mollified. He picked up her hand for a minute. "Say, those are your aunt's diamonds, aren't they? Tell you what we'll do. We'll take them to a jeweler here and have him make up one big ring out of them. They'll be a lot more impressive that way."

"Wouldn't it be too much? These stones are pretty big. If they were put together the effect might be almost—vulgar."

His laugh boomed through the cool, quiet room. "It's pretty hard to make a thing look vulgar if it costs enough. Here, give 'em to me. I'll see to it."

The ring was a fabulous thing. It was composed of many small diamonds, two larger ones, and a very large one that John had bought himself to crown the effect.

"There, that ought to make 'em sit up and take notice," he said.

"I'll bet there aren't many women in the Middle West who have a ring as fine as that one."

"It's gorgeous. I can't imagine an occasion grand enough for it."

"What do you mean, occasion? You'll wear it every day."

She laughed, watching the white stones burn in the sun. "I couldn't wear it with casual clothes. I wouldn't feel right about going shopping in it. And imagine how it would look with my sun suit."

Somehow, though, since he was always asking about it, she fell into the habit of wearing the ring. She wore it all the time in New York, where they went for a shopping trip before returning to Ashland. She saw women's heads turn around as she passed them on the street, their eyes sharp with evaluation. As she handled satins and linens, as she tried on dresses with original labels, as she stroked mink furs appraisingly, she noticed the salesgirls' glances at her hand, an added deference in their manners, their respect for a woman who commanded such a ring as this. The genie of the ring made taxi drivers and waiters assiduous, shopkeepers genial, beauty operators anxious to please. At first it made her laugh to think that, if all these people could have seen her six months ago with her hair skewered to her head while she mopped a kitchen floor, while she hauled babies to the bathroom, while she rushed out to buy two pounds of steak, they would not have given her a second thought. She marveled that a collection of hard little stones could so make a Somebody out of a Nobody. Then she forgot it, took it for granted.

John did not forget it, however. He made sure she had it on when they dined with business acquaintances of his. He did not like her to wear gloves.

"Make sure that Martha sees it before she goes back to Laketown," he said. "I'd like to hear what she has to say about it. She'll never have one a fourth as good herself, that I'm sure of!"

She asked Penny and Martha over for tea the very afternoon of their return. Penny was trim and impeccable in white sharkskin, Martha mussed and sandy in blue denim overalls.

"I'm a sight!" she said cheerfully. "I've been gardening and I didn't have time to change. If you girls are going to be formal I'll go home and get into a better number."

"Sit down, silly. Who cares?"

Penny pursed her lips. "Though I must say, Martha, since you do have beautiful clothes, I don't see why you don't wear them."

"Because I have to be dressed up every day for ten months of the year, that's why. I get sick of it. Right now I'm relaxing—unpicturesquely."

"The people around here will begin to wonder. They're bound to think you aren't doing very well if you persist in looking like this all summer."

"Oh dear, that *would* be dreadful!" Martha leaned forward with mock anxiety. "Do you think they're talking much, darling? Really, I wouldn't be able to sleep nights if I thought——"

"Don't quarrel, girls."

"Then will you kindly point out to the beauty of the family that the people who like me will go on liking me in spite of my choice of wearing apparel, and that the people who don't like me do not concern me?"

"There's such a thing as keeping up appearances!"

"There's also such a thing as just being yourself. I doubt whether you've ever heard of it."

"For heaven's sake!" Eleanor wailed. "I asked you two over to show you all the things I'd bought and to have a long chat with you, and now—you haven't even noticed my ring!"

"I did," said Penny. "It's gorgeous, of course. I suppose you put it on just to show us. I mean, it isn't the kind of ring you'd wear at an informal tea."

Eleanor was apologetic. "I thought that myself, at first, but I seem to have fallen into the habit of wearing it all the time."

"Why shouldn't you?" said Martha. "If I had a ring I was crazy about I'd wear it whenever I wanted to, and the devil take the hindmost. John give it to you?"

Eleanor explained about Aunt Ann's rings and the stone that John had added. "He's as wild about it as I am. As a matter of fact he *insists* that I wear it."

"I see," said Martha, and lost all interest in the ring.

They admired her other possessions, and Penny tried on the mink coat, with the corners of her mouth turned down a little. "You certainly are a lucky girl, Eleanor. I'll never get anything like this from Tony."

Martha blew smoke at the ceiling. "There aren't many things I want," she said, "and ordinarily, while I admire baubles on other women, I have no wish to own them. But someday before I die I'm going to buy myself a really breath-taking star sapphire. Strictly a burnt offering to my material side."

"You'll have quite a time affording that out of a schoolteacher's salary." Penny's voice was sharp as she laid the dark fur back in its box.

"I may not always be a teacher. There's such a thing as rising in the world too, pet."

"For men. Not for women. If you aren't married to a man who's getting on you'll never get anywhere."

"I like to think I can get the same places on my own."

Penny sniffed. "For a smart girl, you can sound awfully stupid."

Eleanor poured oil on the troubled waters. "I don't see why Martha shouldn't be able to do just about what she wants. She's smart and she has a good education. That's all most *men* need to get along."

"Good heavens, there's no place for a woman to *get!*"

Martha sat up. "That's all you know about it. There are women physicists and women doctors and women——"

"A bunch of old maids who couldn't find anything better to do!"

"Some of them are married. Just because a woman is capable it doesn't mean she has to be a spinster."

"Well, Eleanor and I are satisfied to be just women. We stay home and manage things——"

"You never managed a thing in your life, and you know it. Eleanor does, but you don't."

Penny smiled. "There's an art to managing husbands too."

"Sniveling, underhanded way of making a living!"

"But easy."

Eleanor said, "I guess that depends on the husband. It's far from easy to manage John."

"You're not a manageress like Penny, dear. You're a worker like me. The only reason Lovely Legs here respects you more is that you're being paid more than I and by your husband rather than an impersonal employer."

Penny smiled down at her legs. "I respect you all right, Martha. I'm just sorry for you."

"How do you like that for nerve! I dare say it wouldn't matter if I were another Mme. Curie—and *her* husband didn't give her much but a chance at a lot of hard work—you'd have the consummate gall to pity me!"

153

"All Penny means," Eleanor explained, "is that it's a hard life for a woman, this making her own way. Not many of us would have the strength to do it, even if we wanted to."

"It's not a hard life. It's exhilarating, it keeps you on your toes, it's fun!"

John came in, highball glass in hand, to see if Eleanor's show was impressive enough. He smiled at his wife, chucked Penny under the chin, said a brusque hello to Martha. He reorganized the conversation into a monologue on his New York activities.

There was only one bad spot in that Cinderella summer. Early in September came the day when the children left for their new school, and Eleanor thought she couldn't bear it.

"They're so little," she sobbed to John. "Can't you see? I know the school's only a hundred miles away, but it might as well be in Mars! If they could stay home for a few years yet, maybe——"

"We'll drive up to see them every week end that they don't come home. You don't have to act as if they were dying. They'll have every care, every attention——"

"If we had a governess here——"

"There you are," he said. "I spend a lot of thought and good money besides on a school for them, and what thanks do I get for it! You act as if I were trying to murder them. I don't know what's gotten into you. You used to be reasonable. When they were babies you didn't see them for more than ten minutes a day and you didn't seem to mind. I don't know what's come over you now."

"But I've been with them for the last four years, and I've seen how awful it was of me to neglect them so. This is just another way of neglecting them, if the truth were told."

"Martha said that?"

"No, she didn't. Can't I say something that makes sense by myself once in a while?"

"Well, it isn't like you." He did not mean to be insulting. He was daydreaming about the year ahead. "Honestly, honey, we can't have them home this year. In the first place the new house will be being built and we'll have to move into it, and that'll keep things torn up for a while. Then I'm going to be doing a lot of traveling, and I'd like to take you with me. It helps a man along in business if he can trot out a wife that other men's wives will like or even, maybe, be

154

jealous of. If I go by myself I stay at a hotel and meet them at their offices. But if you're along they ask us out to their houses to dinner, and that's the way you get to know them, really make friends with them. And when they visit Ashland I want to be able to bring them up to the house without having to wonder whether the children have the mumps or are going to start yelling for you just as we sit down to have a drink."

It was the longest speech he had made to her in years, and she was flattered. "I'm glad you want me to come along, dear. But I could do that and still have a governess who would——"

"And it's just possible that we might have to spend a couple of months in Europe. There's a man over there who has some patents—— Well, I may have to go. So you see you wouldn't see any more of the kids if they were home than you will if they're away. You wouldn't want me to go trotting all over the world by myself, would you, worrying about my laundry and having nobody to look after me?"

"Europe! Oh, John!"

"Never thought when we went to the high school dances in that old Buick that one day we'd be traveling to Europe in style, did you? *Parlez-vous français, madame?* How's that for speaking a foreign language?"

Yet after they had driven the hundred miles and left the children in the brightly antiseptic rooms of the new school she went over to Martha's to weep where John couldn't see her.

"I felt as if I'd never see them again, Martha. I feel as though they'll never come back."

"They won't, in a way. At least they won't be the same children who went away." She put her arm around her older sister and kissed her gently. "Don't cry, Eleanor. Don't cry so, dear." And added, queerly, extraneously, "Everything has a price, remember that."

12.

Winter slush covered the streets of Ashland, and as early as six o'clock in the evening the street lights were turned on to push the purple shadows back. Snow drifted gently down past the yellow globes and spatted on Tony's windshield, from whence the fussy wipers threw it back into the cold, damp air or packed it down into icy triangles that melted gradually against the warmed glass.

The streets were treacherous, and he drove slowly, his shoulders drooping under the three-year-old topcoat. Eight years ago he wouldn't have been seen dead in such a coat. He ought to have a new one, a fellow who was trying to sell cars ought to make a prosperous appearance, but he simply couldn't afford it. The depression had hit him hard and he hadn't been able to bounce back. First no one had had the money to buy cars. Then, when they had, somehow they had bought them somewhere else. That had been his fault, maybe: he hadn't tried to make friends, he hadn't followed up his prospects, he hadn't been too obliging to his customers. He was trying hard enough now, and things were bound to pick up in a little while.

He was sorrier for Penny than he was for himself. She hadn't any more than married him before his financial substance began to come apart at the seams. She was an extravagant youngster and she had a right to nice things. He didn't like to curtail her, but he had had to. She'd been sweet about it, but it was hard for her to understand. Every month some bills would come in that he didn't know anything about, and it would turn out that they were for things that she just couldn't resist.

"You said yourself it looked sweet on me, Tony."

"Darling, anything looks sweet on you. That's not the point."

"Don't you *want* me to have nice things? You wouldn't want to be ashamed of me, would you?"

He would kiss the adorable, pouting mouth. "How could I be ashamed of you when you're the most beautiful thing in the world!"

Somehow he always found the money. That was the reason his old coat was still seeing service. That was the reason why he had had to sell his house and move back with his father and mother, who had made a three-room apartment for them on the top floor. Penny had not seemed to realize that this was a comedown. She had been delighted.

"Since we can't afford help I'd much rather live in a smaller place," she said. "Anyway, I adore your mother. She and I will be able to do up the housework in no time, the whole house, I mean, for of course I want to do something to show how much I appreciate what she's doing for us. And we'll be taking our meals with them, so I won't have to cook. I'm such a wretched cook! Do you think I should offer to help with the cooking, darling?"

"Heaven forbid! Mrs. Rafferty, the culinary institution in Mother's kitchen, wouldn't let you within three feet of the stove."

"That's wonderful." She settled back more comfortably in his lap. "Then all I'll have to do is make beds and dust and sweep and clean."

"And get me up in the morning."

"Oh dear, that's the one thing I can't do. I simply can't wake up in the morning myself!"

That was true enough. Morning after morning he shut the alarm clock off and went back to sleep. Morning after morning his mother crept up the stairs to tap at his door and whisper that it was after eight o'clock. He hadn't wanted to put her to that trouble—her heart wasn't too steady—so he had finally disciplined himself to early rising. Penny would kiss him good-by drowsily and fall asleep again before he had closed the door behind him. She didn't eat breakfast anyway. As a matter of fact she didn't eat much of anything. Worse than anything in the world she dreaded losing her figure. He often kidded her about it.

"What are you going to do when we have our baby?" he would ask. "What will happen to your precious figure then?"

"Darling, don't joke about it. Naturally for a baby I'd be willing to give up *everything*. But until then I intend to look as nice as I can."

Well, she did look nice, and he knew she kept their three rooms neat as a pin. He could see that his mother was a little jealous of Penny, a little edgy over Tony's adoration of her. Just let him chance to remark how nice the rooms were looking, and his mother would say, "I cleaned up there myself today."

Penny laughed with him about it. "I do the cleaning, darling. I work myself into a lather for three hours, and then she comes upstairs and pulls a chair here and straightens a curtain there, and she thinks she's made all the difference. Let her think so, poor soul, if it makes her feel better."

Scowlingly he remembered what Mrs. Rafferty had said to him that morning. She had halted him in the cold draft from the grade door and her manner had been surreptitious.

"I don't want to interfere in anything that isn't my business," she had said, "but I've worked for your mother a long time and she's a wonderful woman. I hate to see her working herself to the bone for a woman forty years younger than herself. She'll die of it without opening her mouth, so I thought it my duty to say a word."

"What do you mean, Mrs. Rafferty?"

"That wife of yours. She lays in bed until noon and then gets up, dresses herself like a million dollars, and goes off for the day. Doesn't even make the bed, mind you! I've been up there myself, hanging up her things and emptying ash trays to make the place neat before you came home. Seems like, with just that much to take care of, she ought to be able to do it."

"I think you'll find that she does take care of it, Mrs. Rafferty. Mother's apt to make a mountain out of a molehill, you know."

You had to make allowances; women didn't like Penny. Sometimes he missed the old days, when he and Sue had the gang in at least once a week and had, in turn, been invited so many places that they couldn't get to half of them. Golden sun or flying snow, there had been laughter around him then, and bright faces and warm hands and the fun of being part of a friendly crowd. All that was gone now. He and Penny weren't asked anywhere.

It wasn't just because of the divorce, either. Of course Sue's family and her more intimate friends had sided with Sue so thoroughly that they didn't even speak to him on the street. But there had been others, the kids he had grown up with, the young couples who had married about the time he did; these had stuck by him for a while.

He didn't exactly know why they had dropped off, why he didn't see them any more; but it had something to do with the fact that Penny and the women didn't get along. Their husbands had been interested, all right! They had swarmed around Penny, laughing at her unsophistication, paying her extravagant compliments, each one insisting that he should be the one to dance with her or sit next to her at the table. And Penny, poor guileless kid, hadn't known how to handle them. She couldn't keep them on a bright, humorous plane where their wives could laugh at their antics too. Sooner or later she had had to come to him, troubled and embarrassed.

"Tony, I don't know what to do! Bob keeps calling me on the phone all day long, and if Helen finds out about it she'll kill me."

"Humm. What's he calling about?"

"He wants me to go out to the beach with him or dinner or to a movie. He must use the phone at the bank and somebody'll be sure to hear him and it'll get back to Helen as sure as you're born."

"Well, as long as you keep giving him the busy signal she oughtn't to have any complaints."

"You don't think it's my fault, do you, Tony? Honestly I haven't done a thing to make him think——"

"I know that. What you can't realize is that there are some guys a girl simply can't be friendly with. You've got to keep them at a distance. Bob's one of my oldest friends. I can't go to him and say, 'Look here, I want you to stay away from my wife,' when all he's done is ask you to have lunch with him. You'll have to do the discouraging yourself."

It was unfortunate that she was so incapable of complicity. The very next time they were with Bob and Helen, Penny forgot and said, "It's just as I keep telling you on the telephone, Bob——" Her gasp of realization had made things worse. Helen's mouth had set itself in a straight line, and that was the last they had seen of the Blazers.

When you came right down to it a man had to depend on his wife to keep his social life going. Men saw each other at the office or the golf course or had lunch together. But it was the women who planned the dinners and the beach parties and the dances and the barbecues. If the women didn't like you, you were out. Maybe it was just as well. When you accepted invitations you had to return them, and that cost money he couldn't spare right now.

He watched the red reflection of a stop light on the ice at a crossing. If the women could know what he knew about Penny they wouldn't be so anxious about their darned husbands. Penny wasn't— well, sexy. She liked to be admired, she loved cuddling as a kitten does, but beyond that she was reluctant. Much as she loved him, she kept his ardors infrequent and tolerated them badly. She didn't mean to, but she made him feel base and earthy and a little ashamed of himself. Sue, now, had met his passion halfway. No matter how sharp her tongue had been, her body had always welcomed him, sometimes with a touch of high romance, sometimes with simple necessity.

He had seen Sue just yesterday, walking down Main Street looking in the shopwindows. Home for a vacation probably; he hadn't asked. He knew that she had completed her nurses' training and worked in a hospital in Cleveland, but he hadn't expected to see her looking so much the same. The turn of her dark head, the lift of her walk, her habit of fingering her wrist watch were so familiar to him that his eyes felt suddenly rested and pleased. But he hadn't let her see him. He didn't want to pass her with a friendly "Hello, Sue. How are you?" That might be modern, but it was silly. It would carry the implication that marriage was merely an affair of the law and that legal dissolution could wipe out all its personal, emotional, intimate concomitants. That would be an insult and a falsehood.

Not that he wished he were still married to Sue, he thought hastily. He was a great deal more peaceful with Penny, and it wasn't Penny's fault that peace and loneliness were sometimes indistinguishable.

He pulled up to the curb in front of the dentist's office and hoped that he was not late. No, there she was, just coming down the steps, and Dr. Wilder was beside her. She must have been his last appointment for the day. Tony cranked down the windows.

"Hello, Doc," he called. "How're things going?"

The two of them came over to the car, Penny with her chin tucked down into her silver fox scarf, the doctor clutching his hat against the snowy wind.

"Fine, Tony. Good thing you're on time. I was going to ask your wife to ride home with me."

"As if I would have!" said Penny. "After the way you're always making my teeth hurt? Not much."

"That's the way to treat him, honey. After all, he always gets half my salary. No use being nice to him too."

She climbed in beside him, tucked her hand under his arm, and smiled at the doctor out in the snow. "I'll see you tomorrow," she said.

160

"My God!" groaned Tony. "This goes on and on. When are those teeth of yours going to be fixed so I can start to take things easier and not have to run around selling twice as many cars to pay for 'em?"

Penny laughed, but the doctor looked startled and a little embarrassed. Better not kid him so much about his bills, Tony thought. He doesn't like it. Gosh, he must know I mean it as a joke.

"Good night, Doc," he said with extra cordiality. "Run up and see us sometime. Always somebody home."

Dr. Wilder waved and stood there, alert and impenetrable, until the snow swept him from sight.

Penny was ill. Her face was flushed with fever and she tossed and mumbled and refused to have a doctor.

"Tony, no, I'll be all right. Just let me alone. Doctors are so terribly expensive, and I don't want to be a trouble."

She could scarcely keep from slapping his anxious face as he leaned over her. It was all his fault! If he weren't always wanting to make love to her she wouldn't be suffering now. Because of him she had had to slip in at the back door of Dr. Temple's office late in the evening and submit her fastidious self to exploratory probing and messy minor surgery. She hadn't worried about it at all, because Dr. Temple was a reputable man still, though whispers about where most of his practice came from were growing; and the time she had gone to him two years ago everything had been all right; she hadn't had a minute's worry. Now there was this!

"I'm going to call a doctor. You're too sick to know what you're saying."

"Call Dr. Temple, then. I don't want anyone but Dr. Temple."

The doctor arrived, septic and sedate, and even Penny, who was watching for it, could see no inner disturbance behind his professional mask.

"Now if you'll all go out of the room," he said firmly. "I'd like to make a complete examination and she's been disturbed too much already."

He did not dare lock the door behind them, but he kept glancing over his shoulder as he worked.

"You're going to be all right, Mrs. Fox. Just stay in bed a few days. I'll call again in the morning. I'm pretty sure we got it in time. I don't have to tell you how wise it would be to keep your own counsel about this."

He covered her carefully and opened the door. "May I have a glass of water, please? Here, Mrs. Fox, take these tablets. They'll bring your temperature down and make you sleep. If you are uncomfortable or wakeful in the night, take two more." He turned to Tony. "I think your wife has a touch of flu. Nothing to worry about. What she needs is rest and complete quiet. I'll be back in the morning."

Comfortable and sleepy as he had made her, Penny had to admire his nerve. He certainly pulled it off in fine shape! He was even accepting a fee for it. It would take a much smarter man than Tony to be suspicious of so smooth a maneuver.

She felt so much better the next morning that she tried to sit up when Mrs. Fox brought in the breakfast tray.

"Never mind," said the old lady shortly. "You'd better just keep on lying down."

"But I feel so good! Isn't Dr. Temple wonderful?"

The white pompadour trembled a little. "That's as may be. I just want to tell you that I won't give you away. I'd hate to have Tony know. But if ever again you say in my hearing that there's nothing you'd like as much as a baby I shall vomit!"

"Mother!"

"Never mind the 'Mother.' If I'd had a daughter like you I'd have drowned her at birth. You'd better start making up one of your long stories for Tony as to why you'd like to move out of here, for I've stood you in the house as long as I can. At first I thought it was because you were so young that all you could think about was your face and how sheer your hose were and whether you were being flattered enough by everything that wore trousers. But you're twenty-five now and you're just the same as you were at eighteen. You haven't grown up. You'll never grow up, because growing up means exchanging privileges for responsibilities and that's the last thing in the world you'd ever want to do."

For a minute Penny was minded to tell this old hag a thing or two. What has growing up and accepting responsibility done for you, Mrs. Fox, except give you a chance to work your head off and buy marked-down clothes and worry about your son? I'm happier than you are, because I'll never do anything I don't want to do. I don't have to. I'm beautiful, and there's nothing men won't do for you if you're

162

pretty enough. Which of the two of us does Tony prefer, for instance: you, who can't do enough for him; or me that he likes to look at? I'm careful to keep myself so he *will* like to look at me, so other men will look at me and Tony will see them doing it and realize that they envy him for having me. That's all I have to do, Mrs. Fox, and you're jealous because it's so easy for me!

She said nothing. After all, she might need Mrs. Fox one day. There was no sense in making her mad. But oh, how tired she was of this dreary hole! How tired she was of Tony, working all the time and never having much money, not giving her the attention he should, not seeing that she got to the places where she wanted to go!

She kept her face sorrowful and pensive until Mrs. Fox went out. Then she sat up and ate her breakfast with interest. It made her smile to think how long a daughter-in-law of her own would have to wait until Penny would bring her breakfast in bed, sick or well.

Someday she would have a child, after she was older and not having so much fun. It would be a boy, a handsome boy, and he would think that there was no one on earth as beautiful as his mother. They'd go places, the two of them, and she would be mistaken for his sister, and the younger girls would have to be pretty darned attractive to make him look at them twice. What was a good name for a boy? Peter? Michael?

"Isn't your mother the most gorgeous thing, Michael? Honestly, you'd think she was your sister!"

"Yes, she is. I've never been able to take my eyes off her since I was a little boy. Guess I'll go see if I can dance with her, though with the crowd that's around her now, I probably won't get a chance."

The pretty girl would seek to detain him. "And the next one's mine, Michael, don't forget."

But Michael was moving off through the crowd, engrossed in the vision of his mother's radiant head, the calyx in a black lily of tuxedo coats. He would stand before her, tall and young and radiant and possessive. "This is my dance, Penny." He wouldn't call her Mother, that was an old woman's name. He'd think of her as Penny. "Sorry, gentlemen." He would sweep her away on his strong young arm, and the gentlemen would smile and shake their heads. "That boy of hers certainly admires her. Can't say I blame him."

She roused herself from the reverie, much as she would have liked to go on with it. Ordinarily she mused on these imaginary scenes for

163

hours. Sometimes the hero was an older, fascinatingly sophisticated man; sometimes a young playboy; sometimes a handsome woman-hating bachelor. But the heroine was always Penny, and the point of each little drama was the way in which her beauty bowled them over and won their unstinted admiration. But today she had other, less pleasant things to think about.

They would have to move. That would be bad, in a lot of ways. As long as they lived here she had an excuse for not entertaining, for not asking people back, for not having to go to all the mess of mid-night lunches and cleaning the place next morning. And she had been able to allow Bob and the others to be as flirtatious as they liked, knowing that she had a stronghold into which they could not follow her. Now she and Tony would have to have an apartment of their own and there would be lots of work to do and much less money to spend. It was a dirty shame that Mrs. Fox was so strait-laced!

The new apartment was small and dark and not in a very good part of town. Even Tony, usually unobservant about such things, was de-pressed.

"I don't see why you're so set on this," he said. "We were much better off where we were."

"But I've been longing for a place of our own where I could have you all to myself. Your mother was wonderful, but she was always *there*. It'll be so much nicer this way. And I'm afraid that, being sick and all, I might have been a trouble to her. And oh, how sweet it will be to cook your meals for you myself, and mend your clothes, and take care of you without any outsiders around!"

As it happened, they ate out a great deal.

"I get so tired of the house, darling. It's such a treat for me to get away from it, and it's so good of you to take me, when I know you'd rather be home by our own fireside. You're an angel."

"It's expensive, eating out. I don't know that——"

"Oh, it won't be for long. I'll get over being lonesome and settle down. You'll see."

And after he had eaten thirty of her badly cooked, poorly planned, thrown-together-at-the-last-minute meals, he was reconciled to the restaurants.

"Why, there's a button off your coat. I'll sew it on as soon as we get home. Why didn't you tell me! I can't have you going around looking as though your wife didn't *care* about you."

"Well, I did tell you, twice. And about those holes in my socks, and the——"

"Sweetheart, I could cry! I'm not a very good wife to you, am I?"

He took to slipping away to his mother's house, the damaged clothing rolled up under his arm, and his mother would mend them while they talked about Tony's business and the weather and anything but Penny.

Two weeks of that summer she spent in New York, going with John and Eleanor on one of their trips, and she was careful to wear her least striking clothes.

"Now I'm going to be pretty busy," John told them, "and you'll just be seeing me at dinnertime. So you girls have a good time. Go out and buy up the town. Eleanor, you see that Penny gets some pretty things. Can't have my own sister-in-law going around as plain as that, just because her husband is no great shakes as a money-maker. Say, I've been meaning to ask you, do you think Tony would consider a different kind of a job? I have something in mind for him, if he'd be interested."

She was tired of Tony, she was almost through with Tony, what was the use of doing the Fox family a favor?

"He wouldn't be, I'm afraid, John. He thinks he has to stick by his father."

"Well, that's fine, but it's kind of hard on you."

"I don't mind. I'm used to it."

"By golly, you'll not be used to it while you're with us! We travel in style, don't we, Eleanor?"

Penny could not conceal her admiration. "But there aren't many men like you, John, successful and generous besides. Eleanor's the lucky one in our family."

"Oh, now, I don't know if I'm as good as all that."

Alone with Eleanor, he said, "It's going to be hard to make Penny take things, she's such a proud little soul, but you make 'er do it. Shame we haven't been home more. We might have been able to do a lot for her, maybe introduce her to some men that'd be worth her time. She could do a lot better than that worn-out prep-school article she's got."

165

It ended with Penny buying more clothes than Eleanor. The beds were drifted over with white satin and lace and pale silks and autumn-colored wools.

"It's like a trousseau," Penny said. "I never had a trousseau before. I'm afraid you'll be a poor man when we get through, John."

"It'll take considerably more than a few trinkets like this to break me."

"It must be wonderful to be able to afford every single thing you want and know that you earned them by your own efforts."

"I've never been afraid of good hard work. That's what it takes."

"Brains too."

He laughed deprecatingly. "Well, they help."

They were a much-observed trio in the dining rooms which they frequented: John, big-shouldered and ruddy, his tailoring faultless, his manner imperial; Eleanor, smart and cool and slim, with her patrician face and her winking jewels; Penny, breath-takingly perfect from the top of her auburn head to the rhinestone heels that helio-graphed the ultra symmetry of her legs. Men who knew John sought their table almost before they could sit down. They had a small retinue with them wherever they went.

It was like one of her reveries come true: the admiration, the grace-ful compliments, the quick attention to her every word, the added prestige of being a relative of John Kendrick's. If only they lived here and it could last forever, instead of only two weeks, a time so short that it was impossible to make any real headway with these men!

She asked John, "Haven't you ever thought you'd like to live in New York?"

"Not me. Too many big men here; I'd be lost in the shuffle. I prefer to stay out in Ashland where the competition's easier. Anyway, Mother's living with us now, you know, and she wouldn't like to leave Ashland."

"That's thoughtful of you. But the first reason's silly. You'd be a big man anywhere."

He beamed, and she thought how easy it would be to interest him, involve him in an affair. The trouble with that was that it could never go any further than the affair stage. She had a pretty good idea that Eleanor would never give him up, and she'd be silly if she did. No, John would have trouble marrying another woman, no matter how badly he wanted to. There was no use wasting time on him, except for being a gracious and appreciative younger sister to whom he would like to keep on giving things.

For one day she thought she might be able to stay on in New York by herself. Mr. Andrews, who owned an agency for models, told John that he thought she would photograph marvelously. She went over for the tests.

"Perfect, just as I thought. Young lady, if you're willing to work we can see that you get a chance. You're exactly the person we're looking for this minute for the *See Book* cover. How about it?"

It would be splendid publicity to be the girl on *See Book's* cover, but she was cautious. "I don't know. You see, my husband lives——"

"Yes, but you're here right now! Let's try the cover pose, shall we? It'll only take a day and you can see whether you like it or not."

She hadn't. For half a cent she would have walked out on them after an hour of it. There she stood for aching ages in raspberry chiffon ruffles, holding a big straw hat to her head, clutching a basket of artificial flowers. Technicians, a thousand of them it seemed, rushed around, putting down grass mats, placing big lights, fooling with the camera, turning on the fans that made her skirts blow and ripple against her limbs. She might as well have been a wax dummy for all the attention they paid to her.

"It isn't right. Let's try 'er this way."

"Listen, Mac, that arm of hers is stiff as a poker. See if you can get a better line on it. And pull that pink collar down a little. She's swathed like a mummy."

"I'm tired," she said.

"Lord, don't get tired now, we've just started. Change the fan over there, will you? We don't want the skirt to billow. We want it to mold."

The lights were hot. She could feel perspiration washing her make-up down in streaks. The basket of flowers weighed a ton.

"Now smile! Not that way. You're on a windy hill, see, and maybe your boy friend is coming along pretty soon. You're thinking of him and smiling—well, I guess that'll have to do."

Mr. Andrews saw her for a minute in his office afterward.

"Of course there are a great many things you have to learn before you get to the top in this business. Dancing and fencing lessons would help you stand and move better. And before we could use you for any of our movie work you'd have to have voice training. Your

167

voice is too high and thin, though the quality is sweet. But your face and figure are good enough to tide you over until you learn the ropes. It isn't a bad life. The two main requirements are that you have an extensive wardrobe and that you should be on call any time we want you. We work all hours at this place, you see, and we don't always do our work in the studio. Sometimes we go down to the beach—bathing beauties on the sand—or out to the park—lovely girl rides merry-go-round. You've seen the sort of thing."

"I hardly think . . ."

"How old are you? Twenty-five? Well, you may have ten good years yet. Think it over. Oh yes, I'll mail your check for today to you, and watch for yourself on the newsstands."

She took a taxi back to the hotel. Well, that was out! She couldn't see herself hanging around in a hot little room waiting for the phone to ring to call her to work at any hour of the day or night. She didn't like being pushed and pulled around as though she were a head of beef. She had no intention of filling her life up with lessons in this or that. And worst of all, while she had been in there she had seen at least twelve girls go by, each one as pretty, if not prettier, than herself. John was right. There was less competition in Ashland.

She explained prettily to John and Eleanor, "They were kind enough to think I could make quite a success of it, but it wouldn't be any kind of a life for me. I'm domestic, I guess. I just want to be married and have a nice home and maybe a baby or two, if I'm lucky enough."

She went back to Ashland determined to improve her position. She'd have to get rid of Tony: he'd never be able to do anything for her. Dr. Wilder was a bachelor, he traveled in the best company in Ashland, and he had money. He'd flirted mildly with her in his office, and some of it might be made to sound pretty serious. All that talk about her being his most beautiful patient and his jokes about the frequency of her visits would be significant to anyone who didn't see the smile that went with them or the painstaking drilling that followed. She was glad now that she had made him send his office girl out so often so that she might confide in him.

"You're the only person in the world I can tell my troubles to, Dr. Wilder."

"If I do this filling in a hurry we'll have ten minutes left and you can tell away."

"Will Miss Hoffbrau have her ear glued to the door?"

"I'll send her out on an errand if it'll make you feel better."

She might be able to do something about that. Dr. Wilder.

She timed her next visit to his office for the week after her picture on *See Book* was on the stands. The town had rushed to buy up the copies.

"That's Penny Fox. One of the King girls. Eleanor Kendrick's sister."

"Jason, you old fossil, how did you ever come to have a daughter that looks as good as that? She's a stunner!"

Tony was proud with reservations. "You look swell, sure, but it shows an awful lot of your legs, the way that skirt wraps around you. How much did they pay you for it?"

"Enough for me to buy all those clothes I brought home with me." He would have been furious had he suspected John's patronage. Might as well let him think she'd done it on her own.

"Well, that was a good round sum, sure enough."

There was an article in the Ashland paper: "Ashland Girl on *See Book* Cover." Little flurries of excited recognition followed her on the streets.

"I wish I hadn't done it," she said to Eleanor. "I can't go a single place without being pointed at and whispered over!"

"Stay in the house awhile. It'll soon blow over."

"I'm sure I hope so. And I suppose I can't blame them. After all, it's quite a thing to be a cover girl."

Eleanor smiled absently at her and went on adding up check stubs. She's jealous, thought Penny. Imagine, my own sister is jealous of me! The idea made her smooth her smart suit down across her flat stomach and smile ravishingly. "I must rush, darling. Have an appointment with the dentist. My teeth may *look* good, but they certainly require a lot of attention."

Dr. Wilder met her at the door of his inner office, throwing up his hands in a pretense of being blinded. "Pull down the shades quick, Miss Roberts! 'Euclid alone has looked on Beauty bare,' and all the rest of it."

"Perry, you idiot!"

"Come on in. Impressed as I am by *See Book's* façade, there may be a cavity or so lurking beneath it. You run on out, Miss Roberts, and buy yourself a malted milk or something. You look tired."

The door closed behind the winging Miss Roberts and Penny frowned. "She's a new girl, isn't she?"

"Yep. Miss Hoffbrau moved to Oklahoma or somewhere."

"She had a talk with Tony before she left."

He closed the door of his instrument rack slowly and carefully. "What do you mean by that?"

"She told him how you always sent her away when I came and about the times she had overheard you telling me how crazy you were about me and about how——"

"Good Lord! I never said that! I don't believe it."

"Yes, she did." She put her handkerchief to her eyes. "It's been awful, Perry! Tony's just beside himself. He's a devil when he's worked up like this. That's why I went to New York, hoping it would bring him around, but it hasn't. He's wild, I tell you!"

He was studying her sharply. "What does he intend to do about it?"

"He won't live with me any more. He wants me to go back to my father's. But he says you'll marry me or you won't have any practice left in this town. He says if you acted that way with me you've acted that way with other women and he's going to find out who they are and make an awful mess. Oh, I didn't want you to know. I've tried to spare you——"

Damn it, he thought, I haven't done anything to deserve this, but the town'll never believe it if Fox is going to yell his head off about my professional and personal integrity. But I don't want to get married, not to anybody. Hate to be tied down. It's better than being out of a job, though, and maybe having my head smashed in besides.

She buried her head against his shoulder and the fragrance of her hair stirred him. "It's all my fault. I shouldn't have kept coming up here. I tried to stay away, I did really. If you hadn't been so kind, so wonderful to me, so awfully interesting to talk to, I might have been able to do it. I finally told Eleanor how I felt about you, and she said, 'I think you're married to the wrong man, Penny. Why couldn't you have waited for someone like Dr. Wilder?' Oh, why didn't I, why didn't I!"

Eleanor. So the Kendricks knew about this, did they? And they evidently thought pretty well of him as a prospective brother-in-law. It certainly wouldn't hurt his standing any to be affiliated with the Kendricks. There might be some sense to a crazy deal like this. He made up his mind.

170

"Don't cry, darling. You run along home and tell Tony that there's nothing in the world I'd rather do than marry you."

She raised her head like a blind person seeing the dawn break for the first time. "Honestly, Perry? You don't hate me? You're not angry with me?"

Lord, she was lovely! "How could I be? But we'll handle this thing carefully. Tell Tony, but don't say a word to anyone else, except Eleanor maybe. Then go home and live with your father until the divorce is final. I'll take it from there. Guess I'd better start house-hunting and looking around for a housekeeper. Have to have a place your sister won't be ashamed to come to."

Miss Roberts came back just in time to see Dr. Wilder bid young Mrs. Fox a remote and dignified farewell.

She had her suitcases packed by the time Tony came home. He threw his shapeless hat and his shabby coat over a chair and stared.

"What's all this? Where are you going?"

"Come over here, dear, and sit beside me. I'm leaving, darling. Not because I don't love you, you mustn't think that, but because I'm too much of a burden to you. I can't do any of the things that would help you get along. You've been sweet about it, but I can see how it is. You'd be much better off living at home where you'd be more comfortable and wouldn't have the expense of keeping up a wife and a separate establishment."

He was so tired that he couldn't take it in. "What will *you* do?"

"I'm going to Dad's for a little while. Then I'm going to New York and take that modeling job with Mr. Andrews. I want to work! I want to feel that I'm of some good in the world, and I'm not very good at what I'm doing."

"You mean you want a divorce?"

"I'm not coming back to Ashland, ever."

Dazedly he drove her to her father's. Then he went to have dinner with his father and mother and tell them that he was coming home to live, that Penny and he had agreed to a divorce.

"I suppose I don't quite realize it yet," he said, heaping his plate with Mrs. Rafferty's miraculous mashed potatoes. "I haven't had time to feel sad or anything. That'll come later, I suppose."

He ate a tremendous dinner. His father brought out some brandy to go with the coffee. The three of them were very gay. When he

171

went up the stairs to his old room he turned to look back at the two of them. "Gosh, it's good to be home," he said.

"You've been away only six months," said his father. "You took that foolish apartment just six months ago."

"He means really *home*," said his mother.

Jason King sat listening to the pathetic story his youngest daughter was telling him. Tony had neglected her, abused her, finally refused to support her!

"He can't behave that way, Penny. There are laws that take care of that. I'll see him tomorrow and——"

"No, no. That's the last thing I want. I'm so glad to be rid of him. I'm so happy to be here with you."

He stroked her hair. "We haven't seen much of you for the last four years, that's a fact."

"He never wanted me to come. He's always been nasty if I spent time away from the housework or the cooking. I haven't had it easy, Daddy."

"I suppose not. Well, you'll have a better time here. Hetty's just dying to get a chance to wait on you again. She's always been foolish about you."

She could hardly keep from yawning. She had had a strenuous day. "I've always been crazy about her too."

Jason, white-haired and too thin, sat there trying to make up his mind about another matter. "Don't go to bed yet, Penny. There's something I want to say to you. Perhaps this is a bad day for it, after all you've been through, but you'd have to hear it sooner or later."

"What?" She hoped it wouldn't be one of his long, bookish harangues.

"I'm not well. The doctor says—well, there's no cure for me, it's too late for that. Cancer, to put its ugly name to it. Anyway, I don't have much more time. No use crying or making a fuss. I don't want any of that. That's why I haven't told Eleanor or Martha yet. They'll have to know soon enough. But I have a favor to ask of you."

"Anything at all, Daddy, anything!"

"Hetty'll be pretty lonesome after I'm gone. She won't have to worry about money, because there's the insurance and Eleanor'll help her if she needs it. But she never had a chance to know the other two girls very well. You're her favorite, and you know how she's always done everything she could for you. If she'd been your real mother she couldn't have tried harder. I want you to promise me that, no matter where you are or what you're doing, you'll come to see her, often."

"You know I will! But, Daddy——"

"I never made any of my girls cry before, and I don't want to start now. Please, Penny."

Going up the stairs to her room, she wished that her father hadn't told her. Just when things were going so well with her, wouldn't you know that something like this would come along! There was nothing she could do about it anyway, except feel depressed. Dear Daddy, he had meant well, but he should have realized that she was too young, too blithe, to be burdened with so heavy a knowledge.

She lay in bed for half an hour, but she could not get to sleep. It was unbearable, this strange, heavy feeling in her chest, the tears that kept stinging her eyes. She couldn't stand it. She must think of something else.

Perry! He was the one to be thinking about. So good-looking, and the town thought well of him professionally. He'd give her lovely things and they'd go everywhere together and have a wonderful time. That crazy old Mrs. Fox would see that Tony was far from the best Penny could do!

She'd tell Eleanor about Perry in the morning. That would make it official, kind of, and oblige Eleanor to sit up and take notice besides. Eleanor had a lot of things any woman would envy, but she had to work hard for them. The way she slaved over John and that house, not daring to call her soul her own! And men didn't appreciate that kind of thing. They'd rather just have their wives pretty and cute and amiable. Of course she was prettier than Eleanor, and that gave her the advantage. As long as she kept herself so easy to look at she'd never have to work, or worry either.

It was a good time to do her deep-breathing exercises. In the darkness she tightened and relaxed her stomach muscles vigorously. A twenty-three-inch waistline was unusual enough to be worth the trouble. And if your waistline weren't small you might as well not try to get good-looking clothes. No matter what you bought or how much you paid for it, you'd look like a bale of hay tied in the middle.

Like Martha. Poor dear that she was, nobody would ever take a second look at her. She had a nice face—that sculptured quality was

173

very smart now—but the short, square stockiness of her body neutralized it. She bought good clothes, she kept herself well groomed—when she wasn't "relaxing"—but none of it helped much. Martha would end her days a schoolteaching spinster with her hair in a bun on the top of her head, eyeglasses, and sensible shoes. Her wildest excitement would be to live next door to a library or go to Europe, tourist class, in the summer. Penny was as fond of Martha as she could be of any woman. There was absolutely nothing for which she could envy her, no way in which Martha could possibly be her rival.

She yawned and stretched, feeling the length of her long white limbs against the cool sheets. Tomorrow morning she would put on her yellow wool coat and do Hetty's marketing for her. The whole town was still buzzing about her picture on the *See Book* cover. It was only fair to give them a chance to see the original. She must remember not to seem too lighthearted, though, because the news about her split with Tony would be leaking out soon. She must appear serious, a trifle sorrowful, a thought bewildered. It was really too bad about Tony. She had tried so hard, put up with so many adversities, and he hadn't done anything for her in return. Well, she certainly couldn't blame herself for Tony's being a failure. She had given him some of the best years of her life.

The sound of her father's feet coming up the stairs to his room banished her feeling of sleepy well-being. Listen, you have to be reasonable about this, she told herself. You can't let your mind dwell on his dying, that's morbid. Older people were always exaggerating their illnesses anyway, and doctors didn't know everything. Daddy might be too thin, but otherwise he looked healthy enough. Probably the situation wasn't nearly as serious as he had been led to think. That was it! The doctor had been trying to scare him into taking better care of himself, that was all.

She felt immeasurably better. As she turned over on her side and closed her eyes she hoped that Perry was finding a really nice house for her.

It had taken her exactly twenty minutes to rationalize away the first real emotion she had ever entertained.

13.

When Grandmother died, Martha wrote in her journal:

One grows up whenever the time comes when there is no one left to whom to run when things go wrong; whenever absolute self-sufficiency is imposed on a nature; whenever, in all the world, there is no one in whose thoughts and plans and interests one comes first. I reached my adulthood last week when Grandmother died. I am twenty-eight years old.

This sounds formal and stilted because it is hard to translate an emotional state into reasonable words. An emotion can be written best in action. So this one cannot be read from paper but from the way in which my stomach despises food, my eyes quarrel with sleep, my feet move me about without purpose, my mind is drugged with the poison of grief.

Death is the supreme insult to the insolent Brain. It is a door slammed in the face of conjecture. There is no peering over the walls, and all your pounding and twiddling of the knob will bring no answer. The agile, active mind stands outside, baffled and still. Here is no problem to be solved, no situation to be manipulated. In all of life here is the one cold, stark Fact which carries irrevocable acceptance with it.

I forgot that her death was so important only to myself. As I raced through all those dark little towns on the way down I was surprised that they could be so calmly asleep. I wanted to shout, "Wake up! The day you dreaded is here. My grandmother is dying!" Yet all these people had lived through the days they dreaded most, alone, as I was now.

She smiled at me. She spoke my name. They wouldn't let me talk much to her, and it was just as well. I wanted to pour out, quickly, all that I was grateful to her for, all that she had meant to me, how her kindness and serenity and wisdom had shaped the world for me. There was no time. And anyway, I guess she knew.

She closed the book and wiped her tears away with her hands. She poured herself a cup of coffee, lighted a cigarette, and began pacing the apartment. Tomorrow morning couldn't come too soon. The doors of the school were a haven. Once inside them, dealing with the thousand and one details that sprang up under her nose like mushrooms in rainy weather, gathering literature or drama from textbook pages and cramming it into heads of varying capacities, feeling the push-pull of five thousand other personalities, she was safe. With that much demand on your abilities, you had to check your personal problems on the front walk and not pick them up again until you came out. The eight hours of her working day were the only assuagement for her pain.

But now it was only ten o'clock, and the people who lived below her would think they had a caged lion over their heads. She sat down and opened the journal again.

The first page was dated seven years back, her first working day at Devon High School, when she had decided that the best way to keep thinking from being fuzzy was to harden it into words. She had written:

Mr. Trent is the principal. I think I shall like him very much. He says things in a plain, forthright way, and you can't know him for ten minutes without comprehending his philosophy of education. He is all for the pupils and not very much for the teachers unless they, too, are all for the pupils. That sounds like common sense to me, and a far cry from the meaningless ritual that the teachers' college used as a substitute for thought. Mr. Trent says that the children are in school to learn; anything that a teacher does which contributes to that end is good; anything that does not is bad and he won't have it. He turns quite purple when he says this, so I judge that he *doesn't* have it and that this is a good school for honest instruction.

This is a tremendous place. Three floors, hundreds of rooms, an auditorium, swimming pools, gym floors, shops, cooking rooms, two hundred teachers, and the Lord and Mr. Trent alone know how many pupils! It will take me years to con all the physical properties of this place; I hope to catch on to the mental ones much sooner. Mr. Trent says, "I am not impressed, Miss King, by pretty bulletin boards and writings in colored chalk and tricky arrangements of crepe paper. I don't want my teachers to waste their time batting erasers and washing boards. We have janitor service for that. What does impress me is the preparing of a youngster for a higher course just a little better than can reasonably be expected. If you can arrange matters so that the children will hurry to your class as they would hurry to a football game, keep quiet and highly interested while they are there, and leave feeling sorry that it's over so soon, I'll give you the building!" I don't expect to get the building right away.

Met Mrs. Stanton in the hall this morning—she was there in some supervisory capacity—and told her how much I thought I was going to like teaching here and what a fine man Mr. Trent seemed to be. Perhaps I was too enthusiastic, for she kept looking at me in a peculiar fashion and her smile was pretty weak. Next time I shall be dignified and sedate. I'd like to please her for two reasons. First, she's an old woman, not equal to her job. Second, she never held the differences we had against me, and she might easily have done that. If it weren't for her agreeing to it I wouldn't be in this best of all possible schools. I thanked her for it three times, so I guess she knows I'm grateful.

After that first interview she had not seen Mr. Trent for two months. Then he walked into her room, right in the middle of a ninth-grade grammar lesson. The class was reading sentences and telling what part of speech each word was. " 'The boat was in dry dock and men were painting her sides,' " a boy was reading. He analyzed the sentence, sat down, and Martha opened her mouth to call on her best student.

Mr. Trent picked up the grammar book. "What's a dry dock?" he asked the class. They didn't know, and he told them. He spoke of all the trades that went into the making of a big boat and the care that must be taken of a ship to keep her serviceable. For ten minutes he discussed boats with them. Then he thanked Martha for allowing him to interrupt and walked out.

So now I know that one lesson can serve many purposes and that it is wasteful not to use all the by-products. I will never be able to teach mere parts of speech again.

Discoveries like that one gave her the courage, two years later, to take Shakespeare into her own hands. The twelfth-graders had to read *Macbeth* and they hated it. They were given copies of the play so annotated and footnoted that Martha feared the reading would be almost too simple to be interesting. To her dismay, she found that the class was not understanding either text or footnotes. They persisted in considering the end of each line of verse as the end of a sentence, making a meaningless hash of verse and plot alike. For a month they sat, sluggish and bored, while she tried to prick them into comprehension. Then she could stand it no longer.

"Close your books," she said sharply. "Go on, close them. Now! Forget everything you think you know about *Macbeth* and listen to me."

177

Rapidly, economically, she sketched in forceful words the picture of a powerful general in the king's favor, how he listened to the witches, how he yearned for greater power, how his wife steeled him to get it. She acted the play before their eyes, pacing the floor in front of the desk as though it were a stage, now using the actual words of the play, now paraphrasing them but keeping their mood. The classroom metamorphosed into the cold, drafty halls of old castles, the flapping window shades were wavering tapestries, the little blond woman was a tall king, a murderous queen, the kindly Banquo, the insistent Macduff, the dying Macbeth. The twelfth-graders were so entranced that they did not hear the gong that signaled their dismissal.

Neither did Martha. The magic of the play, the feel of her audience in the palm of her hand had driven away all concept of schools or gongs. The sight of new faces in the open doorway, peering in, wondering what was going on and when this class would vacate the chairs that were to be theirs for the next hour, brought her back from early England in mid-gesture.

"The homework for tomorrow," she said, "is to get yourselves back in here so I can finish the play for you. And the next one of you who comes up to me saying that he doesn't understand Shakespeare and that *Macbeth* is dull will be struck lightly on the head with my leather-bound edition."

Why, it was as good as a movie, they told Martha. Who'd ever have thought that there'd be so much action and swashbuckling in an old Shakespeare play? They became Messiahs, explaining the fine points of *Macbeth* to their friends in less fortunate classes. Encouraged, Martha did *Julius Caesar* and *The Taming of the Shrew* for them in like fashion, though the twelfth-grade curriculum did not call for them. They soaked it up.

Early the following September Mr. Trent called her into his office. "Just what is going on in your English literature classes, Miss King?" he asked her. "Never mind giving me an outline of the course of study. I am interested in your approach to Shakespeare, a man who has been dead in these halls for many years and seems to have had a strange resurrection of late. What kind of smelling salts did you use on him?"

"I acted him in modern English, except for the most beautiful passages. I left those in."

178

"Could you give me a sample?"

She got to her feet promptly. "Which play shall I do?" she said.

"Oh, you have a repertoire? Well, I haven't heard *Hamlet* for a long time. He isn't in the course of study."

"First I'll set the stage for you," she said. "Since there's no changing scenes successfully in the old plays, a stage can be devised that will take all the scenes, with just a touch of lighting and a few props to help out here and there. Here's one level of the stage. From the center at the back a short flight of marble stairs goes up to a terrace . . ."

Mr. Trent sat back and listened. The curtain went up. The gaily colored court and the black-clad Hamlet moved about. The ghost came in, seen as a mere glinting of moonlight on steel casque. The troubled king, the guilty mother, the soft, distracted Ophelia talked and moved and filled the small room to overflowing with their plaints, their tempers, their gentler moods.

When she broke off in the middle of Hamlet's soliloquy and became Martha King again he felt the impact as the bludgeon of reality crashed his concentration.

"It hasn't done me much good to see it," he said finally, "though why you aren't an actress instead of a teacher I can't imagine. What I was looking for was a method that other teachers could use. I forgot that you were our dramatics teacher too, and that you have training and talents beyond your literary functions. I'm afraid not many of my other English teachers have the qualifications for such a presentation. Most teachers are shy birds, anyway. They like to keep print between themselves and their students. They couldn't come out in front of the page the way you do."

"I like to do it. I've always liked it. I know it isn't orthodox procedure, but the class seemed to get a great deal out of it."

He touched some papers on his desk. "These are letters, Miss King, letters from parents asking that their children be put in your classes next semester. We like to be obliging, but you understand that we can't turn our whole schedule upside down just to route these pupils to you."

Her face was radiant. "Honestly, did those kids think enough of those plays to go home and—well, that's wonderful!"

"I see that I can't depress you with administrative problems," he said, "so let's get down to brass tacks. If we can manage to throw

179

all the twelfth-grade literature classes into the auditorium for an hour a week could you do your Shakespeare for the whole lot at once?"

"Of course I could. Five hundred is no different from fifty."

She opened the door, but he called to her.

"Miss King."

"Yes, Mr. Trent?"

"I'd like to say—well, nothing, I guess. That's all."

The implied compliment was tremendous.

The summer was coming on, and she dreaded it. She could not go back to Ashland, not yet. Uncle Lewis had rented Grandmother's house. She could stay at her father's or at Eleanor's, but she had to put time between herself and all the dear, familiar things of childhood or the weight of them would crush her heart, not stiffened enough in this short time to bear reminding. She would go to her second home, the university, and begin work on her doctor's degree. That would take a great many summers and make her exile as pleasant as any exile could be.

She wrote to Penny:

I am sorry that I can't come down for your wedding, angel-face, but right now I couldn't be festive. What would you like for a present? Do you have a sterling pattern? Or a dinner set you favor? Speak up if you have, because I'm flush. I have just discovered that Grandmother deposited to my account the checks I've sent her monthly for all these years, and so I have five thousand dollars or so I didn't know I had. She was wrong to do it, dear soul. It would give me so much pleasure to think that she had spent them for little luxuries that otherwise she couldn't have afforded. So, instead of being satisfied, I am merely rich.

Perry Wilder seems to me an excellent man, although I know him only slightly and I don't suppose he remembers me at all. I used to see him in the Carnegie Library, choosing an armload of books to take home, and, from the kind of books they were, I judge that he is widely read and somewhat of a thinker. Hence I always discounted the rumor that he was a bit of a gay blade with the ladies. He is an immeasurably better bet than your poor, bewildered Tony, but he'll take a little living up to. You might try reading a book or so yourself, just to be companionable. I don't want to preach, but just being pretty won't be enough to satisfy him for long. If you're very much in love with him, as you say you are, you'll make the effort. You almost have to. There is no use keeping on "seeking monogamy from bed to bed." It can't make you happy and if you make a few more marital changes it is going to be obvious that the blame is yours. I don't say that it was in Tony's case. I know nothing about that situation. I am croaking warning at you in typical schoolmarm style, and you'll have to forgive me.

Is anything wrong with Dad? I keep asking him and he keeps writing that there isn't, but he didn't look at all well at the funeral. See if you can get him inspired to make a trip to a good clinic. I'll foot the bills. I'm bound to spend this money on somebody. It's no good to me just lying around in the bank.

My best wishes for a silver anniversary for you, and all my love. Your sister-under-the-skin,

MARTHA

All the time she had spent writing long, newsy, amusing letters to Grandmother she diverted into writing to her sisters and her father. It helped, but it was not quite the same. She and Grandmother had had their own private jests, their personal crusades, a mutual esteem for each other's opinions. There was no companionship in the letters now, no long intimate friendship behind them, but they were better than nothing and they took up time.

Time was the thing you had to spend to purchase emotional peace. She was a critic teacher now, and she devoted much attention to the problems of her student teachers. She graded stacks of papers more meticulously than ever. She went to concerts and ballets and movies, sometimes by herself, sometimes with one of her faculty friends. She thanked God for her old habit of reading everything on which she could lay hands. Laketown had fifty good libraries, and she kept cards going at three of them. She made careful appointments at beauty shops and she forced herself to be interested in her wardrobe.

She attracted no attention as she went about the big town. Her figure, as always, made her look older than she was, and with heels she was only five feet three inches tall. Not a height to command attention when your bones were too big to make you shapely. Her lovely yellow hair was swept up under a smart, dark hat. Her clothes were expensive but simple. Above all, there was an air of independence about her that discouraged easy acquaintance. She did not know this and she could have done nothing about it if she had. She did not know either that to the school children she was beautiful; that

181

when her face was animated, when her luscious voice poured out in expertly modulated and chosen words, she carried an aura of glamor with her that Helen of Troy would have envied, she created a fire at which the coldest and most ignorant could warm themselves. The school children could not tell her this, and they were the only people who really knew her.

She was deep in the production of *Quality Street* for the school when the letter came from Eleanor.

We've kept it from you as long as we could, because he wanted it that way, but Dad is dying. He knew almost a year ago that he had cancer, but he told us just last month when there was no concealing it any longer. He has the best of care, a nurse is there all the time, and Penny and I go over often. He is drugged most of the time and does not know we are there. You had better come soon.

She barely waited to notify the school. She got into her car and drove to Ashland, pushing from her mind the awful similarity between this trip and the one she had made not a year before. Jason King died twenty-four hours after her arrival.

Eleanor took her home with her. "Martha dear, you look so dreadfully tired. Stay with us awhile and get rested. The school can get along without you for a month or so, can't it?"

"I have to go back right after the funeral." Oh, I must go back, I must leave this town where even the maple trees bending over the streets hurt me more than I can bear, where I dare not look at the sunset through a certain window, where there are flowers in a weedy garden that I must not touch, where there is a cemetery that now holds more of my own flesh and blood than I can spare. I must drug myself with work.

John was pontifical but kind. "Well, Martha, this is a sad occasion for you. Your father was a wonderful man, worked hard all his life, never owed anybody a nickel. He——"

"Don't talk to her about it, dear," Eleanor said hastily. "I want to get her to bed."

Numb as she was, Martha wanted to tell John a few things. Yes, her father had been wonderful, but not in any way that John could appreciate. He had sacrificed his own wishes for the good of his daughters, he had not complained of loneliness, he had been proud of their slightest achievement and sympathetic with their failures.

He had asked nothing of them except that they be happy and he had tried to build for himself a life as happy as he could so that they should not be burdened with anxious thoughts about him. There were not many fathers like that. And how could John, selfish, have-to-come-first John, take Jason King's name in his mouth so lightly!

Eleanor tucked her into bed. "Take one of these tablets. They're all right. I often take them myself when I can't get to sleep."

"I wouldn't have guessed that you had trouble sleeping. What's the matter?"

"Nothing, really. It's silly of me. John says that when women have nothing to worry about they have to find something. I lie awake and plan menus and invitations and wonder whether the chauffeur is taking the cars out by himself at night and how much Mrs. Moppleby is cheating us on the grocery bills. Things like that. And I think about the children. Heavens, they're not really children any more! Sonny is nine."

Martha raised up on her elbow. "I've never dared ask before, Eleanor, and you can tell me it's none of my business if you want to. Are you really happy?"

Her older sister sat down in a puffy pink chair by the window. In her elegant black suit with the ruby clip on the lapel she could have been an illustration out of the fashion magazines, save that her face was not scornful or pert or blank. She had always been a pleasant, courteous woman. Of late she had acquired a composure that gave her a vast, simply dignity.

"I should be, surely. I have everything."

"That's a nice evasion. It isn't an answer."

Eleanor smiled. "What makes you think I'm not happy?"

Martha lay back and studied the ceiling. "I don't see how you could be. What's the stuff your life is made of? Well, it's being a backdrop for John, primarily, but for other people too. You see that everyone who comes here is made comfortable. You order food, hire servants, buy linens, see that you and your family have the proper clothes, consult about slipcovers and train tickets and laundry soap. You arrange social affairs and sew for orphans and are seen in the right places. And always and always and always you are Friday to John's Crusoe. Does the great man have a headache? Drop everything and run to rub his brow. Is he troubled with indigestion? Reorganize the month's meals around him. Does he require mountain air? Leave whatever you are doing and escort him to the more healthy spot, relieving him of the tedium of choosing it, getting there, and selecting the best hotel. You're a combination of housekeeper, valet, nurse, treasurer, and social secretary."

"You make me sound very efficient."

"You are. You've schooled yourself to be. But where are *you* under all this pile of good works? Where are *your* opinions and desires and wants and whims? You've submerged yourself so completely that you've lost your individuality. I don't know you any more. If someone were to ask me what you think about anything I wouldn't know what to tell them, because you've never said. You must think. You must feel. You must have some kind of private life of your own, I know that. But if you have you're an expert on camouflage, because I can't see a trace of it."

"I'm a cipher?"

"You're the cipher that lifts the numeral that precedes it to a higher power than it would ever have by itself. You're the zero after John's number and you certainly step up his potential. But suppose the number were to be taken away? Would you still be a cipher? That's what I want to know."

"Let's say it's my way of earning my board and keep."

"That's fine. But most people earn their board and keep and still have time left over to do exactly what they want to do with part of their lives at least. You don't. Take the children, for instance. You've always wanted them with you. Have they ever been? Do you insist on their being? No."

"I would like them home, that's true. I don't know that I could do better by them than their school does. Perhaps I wouldn't have been a very effective mother."

"You had a right to try to find out, if you wanted to. And you're not at all stupid. I think you could always have been anything you wanted to, granted the practice at it." Her indignant eyes were closing in spite of her.

Eleanor's voice came from far away. "I was brought up to think that a woman's chief aim in life was to help her husband and to please him. If I had had the courage to make a stand or two when I was younger things would be better. But when you've been taught to believe that women are inferior to men you don't trust your own

184

judgment against your husband's. And it hasn't turned out so badly. I have everything."

Martha snorted sleepily. "You keep saying that! You have a lovely house and a few pretties, I'll grant you. And for that you've had to live a life of self-sacrifice, subjugation, and contrivance. Slavery was abolished in the States a long time ago, haven't you heard? Sure, you have everything . . . except yourself, except . . ."

She was asleep. Eleanor tiptoed over to pull the down comforter over her. Then she went quietly downstairs to pacify John, who was inevitably aroused to obscure fury by the sight of Martha.

The teaching, the long letters to Eleanor and Penny, all the extra social activities she could find were not enough. There were always two or three hours in the evening when she sat as if in a vacuum under a glass sky.

The typewriter solved her problem. She pulled it out of its alcove one evening and began to write about the various theories of education that she had heard expounded and seen practiced. She began with no thought in mind but to crystallize her own opinions and, perhaps, to have a paper ready, should the evil day for delivering a paper at a teachers' meeting ever arrive; but as the sheaf of paper beside her grew she saw its possibilities. It might be interesting to a great many people, this information. Teachers were usually busy teaching; ordinarily they talked shop only among themselves. The general public knew almost nothing about what went on in the schools nor why it did nor what purpose it was to serve. They might like to know.

Here was what she had been looking for, an activity that would call for every ounce of concentration and ability she had. As she wrote and edited and polished she had no room left over for anything else. This was her old word game, but now she was playing it with a purpose. The informal essay grew and flourished; some nights it scintillated and made her laugh at its bright aptness; some nights it lay on the typewriter spiritless and dead. Even when she was in school she would find her mind hard at it, shaping and pointing and revising. When it was done she sent it to the New York *Chronicle*, because she had such a respect for their Sunday magazine section, which had, and deserved, a national reputation. Within two weeks she had from them a letter of acceptance and a check for three hundred dollars.

She was vastly pleased, but briefly too, for the typewriter had not stopped. She kept it going all that summer in her little apartment, putting off the work on her Doctor's degree until the next year for the ecstasy of working at this fascinating, difficult business of being articulate in print. She had rejections, but they did not depress her. By the time she was twenty-nine she had been published in five leading literary magazines, and her skill in the essay form was beginning to attract comment. "A new Repplier," someone said.

Miss King is an intelligent woman who has read everything and built up highly individual and stimulating principles of logic and living. Though her essays are brilliantly terse, shot through with high humor, she is at heart a poet. For what is a poet but one who puts the keenest of observations into the fewest and best and most beautiful words? We'll wager that Miss King would scan well, were she so minded.

A publishing house wrote to her to say that, if and when she had enough material for a book of her shorter forms, they would be very interested in seeing it first. The Laketown *Times* ran a story about her successes, inferring that Miss King was typical of the general caliber of teacher in Laketown.

When she left herself a moment to think she was surprised that her life remained so much the same. Somehow she had imagined that the people who wrote the words she had read on countless pages must lead momentous lives in a constantly benign social climate. She wrote in her journal:

I might have known better. I knew that Shakespeare had had his ups and downs and that Milton was known to his neighbors as a pious but crotchety blind man. You can go right through the literature books and not find two authors who had more than a year or two of what the average person means by happiness. But within themselves did they feel marked, superior? I'll bet they didn't, any more than I do. Nor do I shrink from making the bold comparison, for, no matter how minor or major, human beings are human beings; their mental wealth may differ vastly, but their emotional small change is common currency. So, Shakespeare or Milton or I, we all worry about the rent and we try to find work that will pay us while we try to write ourselves into the happy situation where our writing will be our main work and not the gleanings of our grudging spare moments. And those who read us will think, "Ah, if I could only write, how different my life would be," whereas they would find that their lives remained exactly the same, even could they set their thoughts on a page.

There is no profession that leaves one's daily living so untouched as authorship. There is no stigmata to the trade. A lawyer may become wordy and argumentative, a teacher dictatorial, a doctor quick to the pulse and veins and hard to physical frailties; an engineer must break things down to arithmetic and stresses and be practical; a politician must try to be popular. But everyone writes, in some fashion or other, and there is sometimes little distinction between the writing that gets published and the writing that does not. Thus everyone considers himself a potential author and sees small difference between himself and the man who signs his name to an article.

The typewriter tapped out the minutes, the months, the year. She combed her journal for ideas. She wrote voluminously, but she mailed parsimoniously. Four fifths of her work saw the wastebasket or the file. She did not dare read so much now. It was too discouraging to see how easily other writers could flip a phrase, how beautifully they integrated their paragraphs, how effortlessly they said precisely what they had intended to say.

Actually she was a lonely woman. She knew many people in the schools, but most of them had private obligations or relationships that took up their time. The women she knew, who lived alone like herself, were occupied in chatter with other women whose extra hours coincided with theirs or in a struggle to attract the not impossible He. They gave gossipy luncheons or giggling, erotic cocktail parties, and the presence of a man, however stupid or brutish or emasculated, in the same room with them robbed them of all desire for thought. They became exclusively haughty or hectically gay or ebullient or simpering, whichever antic might attract his attention most fully. Their educations, their salaries, their little luxuries had not sufficed to obliterate the fact that no man had wanted them on honest terms; and this supreme humiliation drove them to fantastic gyrations for the benefit of the male.

They're fine in school and I like them. They know a little about almost everything, and a lot about their particular subject. But they're such unhappy women! Some of them are bitter, some restrained, some whining or neurotic. They all want to be married and they're miserable because they aren't. The fact that they have everything else to make life pleasant and enjoyable doesn't seem to matter. They want a marriage certificate to hang on the bedroom wall, reassuring them that they are just like other women.

I can honestly say that I have always been too busy and too diverted to

187

worry about getting married, and that right now I have the raw material for happiness for the next fifty-five years, even if I have to live them quite alone. *Especially* if I live them alone, I should say, for that way one gives no hostages to fortune.

Blindingly golden summer faded into apricot-tinted September. Sumach burned in the drying grasses. Road stands burgeoned with baskets of purple eggplant and crimson tomatoes and yellow squash. Along the country roads the apples and pears fell with a deep, rich sound. In Laketown autumn came in the falling of frost-painted leaves, the light blue haze that hung over the water, and the children going back to school.

Martha couldn't believe that it was time to go back to teaching. She had not seen the roses and delphinium come and go, the fleecy dawns, the riotous sunsets. All she had to show for the summer was an essay or two and a slight double furrow between her eyebrows.

"Enough's enough!" she told herself. "I won't touch the typewriter till after Christmas. It's about time I stopped going to extremes and found a good, healthy, middle ground. Trouble with me is I've always been as wholehearted as an ingenue."

She moved to a larger apartment with better maid service and a pretty view over the park. She allowed herself the luxury of reading again. She took herself out to dinner. She drove around the countryside, admiring its colorful tapestry, lugging pumpkins and black walnuts home with her. The grade-school children pasted turkeys on their windows and she began work on the high school Thanksgiving program.

Two pleasant things happened the second week in November. The first was the Handsome Stranger, as reported by Miss Bricker, the chief clerk in the school office.

"He came in right after you'd left for the English meeting, and when I told him you were out he said he'd like your address at home. I hated to tell him that we couldn't give out that kind of information about our teachers, but you know how the rules are. Oh, Miss King, I wish you'd been here! He was a big man with dark wavy hair and the grandest smile."

"What did he say then?"

"He said, 'Your Miss King is a short, blond Miss King, isn't she?' And I said yes, you were. And he said, 'Well, she isn't in the phone book and I'm anxious to see her.'" Miss Bricker giggled. "Then he leaned over the counter and said, 'I suppose you're too ethical to let me bribe you.' Honestly I nearly came right out and told him where you'd moved to."

"It wouldn't have mattered if you had. He's after some other Miss King. I don't know anybody who looks like that. Didn't he leave his name?"

"I asked him if he wanted to, and he said no, he was going to be a surprise. 'Just tell her that a former student was asking for her.' But he's older than you are. And if there'd ever been anyone around here who looked like that I'd have remembered 'em!"

After a beginning as exciting as that it was a distinct letdown to have the school day pass uneventfully and tranquilly. But when she reached home the second out-of-the-ordinary thing was waiting for her. It was a cheering letter from Perry Wilder.

I know that the first Thanksgiving and the first Christmas after a death in the family are hard to live through. How about spending Thanksgiving with Penny and me? We'd see that you had a good time, big dinner, football game, and the whole works, and I'd get a chance to tell you how much I've liked your *Chronicle* stuff. You can't refuse a brand-new brother-in-law, can you?

Eleanor and John will be in California all winter, so you won't see them. Sonny and Alice will be home for the holidays and Mother Kendrick will look after them. I think Eleanor wanted to stay home—she's always managed to be home for vacations with them—but John insisted that she come along with him. Anyway, we can go over to the house and see the children.

Did you know that Hetty is living with us now? Penny thought she might not want to, felt queer about asking her for some reason, but I took the bull by the horns. After all, she was always good to Penny, still is for that matter, and we have more room in the house than we know what to do with. It's worked out fine. She runs the house and Penny and I can come and go as we like. And it seems that we like to go a great deal. Occasionally I'm bored by our little social treadmill, but Penny thrives on it.

Try to come, won't you?

Penny had added a postscript:

Perry's been after me for weeks to write this letter, but I couldn't get around to it. We'd love to have you. There's bound to be a lot going on that won't interest you, such as the dance at the country club Thanksgiving night, but Perry will be delighted to stay home with you and talk your ears off.

Everyone down here is anxious to see you again and the library has all your articles tacked up in one of their little showcases with your picture in the middle. At least so Perry says. He's made a collection of your things all by himself, and I'm going to read them the first evening I have a minute.

We're planning a big picnic for the Saturday after Thanksgiving. Jerry Auld—he's John's new plant manager—lives here in town now, and he's in on all our affairs. You might be interested, darling. He's terribly handsome, almost forty, and not married. John says he's very capable, and I believe it. Perry says he's a conceited ass, but you know how husbands are—from observation at least.

The bite in the last line made her laugh. Penny was finding it hard to forgive her for getting her name in print. Well, she couldn't go. It was too far for such a short stay. Maybe Christmas she would. She'd like to talk to Perry. He was most certainly cordial, and already a little lonesome too, if she had the tone of his letter right. It was almost as if he were telling himself that, with a sister like Eleanor and a sister like Martha, Penny couldn't be so bad. And Jerry Auld. What was Penny up to with him?

The next Saturday morning she got out of bed at eight and opened the venetian blinds. It was snowing, big soft flakes that the still green park absorbed without a trace, like blotting paper. She took a quick shower, brushed her hair, zipped herself into a striped Roman silk housecoat. As she set the breakfast table she kept glancing out at the snow, thinking how much like a stage setting her little dining room was: white cloth, soft pink light from her table lamp, furniture set just so, and beyond the wide window a gray cyclorama down which a stagehand was blowing white scraps of paper.

There was a knock at her door. The caretaker, probably, about something or other. She crossed her living room to open it and said, "Good morning," briskly. She did not know the man who stood there smiling at her. He was tall and wide-shouldered and very good-looking. He had his hat in one hand and a big bunch of roses in the other.

"Here, take these," he said. "I'll have to brush myself off before I come in. It's snowing harder than it looks."

She took the roses, stupidly. "I'm afraid you've made some mistake," she said.

"You bet I have. But I'm going to make up for it now."

His black hair, dampened by the weather, lay in unruly waves. His gesture as he ran his hand over his head revealed him to her.

"Bill Knight! It is, isn't it?" Tears stung her eyelids and she didn't care. Here was an ambassador from her youth, from the university, from half the golden days that there was no one left to remember but herself.

Over the breakfast table they talked like two machine guns let loose. First it was "Do you remember?" Then it was "Whatever happened to——" and then it was "What are you doing now?"

Bill was a salesman. "Not the kind who goes from door to door, nor the kind that stands behind a counter. I'm a 'business representative' of Mayhew and Sons. See, it says right here on my card. That means that when you want a couple of miles of pipe or any other engineering supplies we make, I come and explain all about it to you and why you should buy ours instead of anyone else's. Just was transferred to the office here last week. I've been all this time looking you up and planning today. Took an awful chance on finding you home."

"Not such a chance. I don't go out much."

"Well, we'll rectify that."

He had not married. He had lived in California until three years ago when his mother died. Since then he'd been traveling for Mayhew. Made a very respectable salary. Spent it all, of course.

"How did you ever find me, Bill?"

"Oh, I knew long ago that you were teaching in Laketown. One of my fraternity brothers heard it somehow and wrote it to me. He lives here. I finally shook your exact street number out of the Laketown Board of Education, after convincing them that I was a sober young man with immaculate intentions. Do you like teaching as much as you always thought you would?"

"Yes."

"Did the 'former student' baffle you? I am a former student, you recall."

"Not of mine."

"We could argue that, but not today. And how's your paranoia?"

"I'm working it out by writing in my spare time."

"Writing? Like what?" She told him. "Well, that's fine. Have to read it sometime."

She sat and admired him while he talked. All the light in the room seemed to have focused on him, on his black curls, his white teeth, his well-cut suit. He was gay and quick and alive. He quoted from the old plays and she made the right answers. He told her about his mother's death and she sympathized. He related his ambitions and she marveled. But he had not lost his old, gentle sensitivity.

"Happy, Martha? I've wondered. You were such a strange little girl."

"I'm happy." But never as happy as now.

She suspected, knowing his love of drama, that his first visit had been intended simply to give a little girl a great big thrill. But he kept coming back, first once a week, then twice, then every evening. They ate their meals together; they went nowhere except with each other.

"Why not?" he said. "I don't know a soul in town outside of the office people and an old college acquaintance or two. And I'm companionable. I hate doing anything alone."

"You'll never get to know new people if you spend all your time with me."

"Sure I will. We'll get to know them together." He looked at her sharply. "If you're being tactful it's going over my head. Do you mean you're bored and would like me to give you a rest?"

"Silly. I'm having the time of my life."

That was true, partly. But she had no time for writing now. Bill wouldn't let her.

"Listen, you can do that kind of stuff when you're old. It's bad enough that you have to work all day. I'm not going to let you work all night too!"

Women watched them wherever they went, their eyes wide at Bill and narrow at Martha.

"They're all saying, 'What does he see in her?'" she told him.

"And if I'm right about Mr. Trent—that's your principal's name, isn't it, the guy we saw on the street the other night?—he was thinking, What does she see in him? That makes us even."

In March he asked her to marry him. She wrote in her neglected journal:

In a way I'd like to, very much, but I'm afraid of it. For one thing, Bill's going up the ladder, and everything will have to come second to that. Well, I have a ladder of my own to climb. How will we work that out? I'd have to stop teaching—state law—but what about my writing? What happens to that? Bill says I can go on with it, but he doesn't realize how much time it takes. He's sociable, people like him, the house would be full of guests all the time. That's hardly the setting for serious literary effort.

In the second place I'm used to making my own money. I'll hate being financially dependent, and I would be, because no one gets rich on the kind of thing I do. Prestige, maybe. Money, no. And I'm extravagant because money has never been important to me. I've always been able to make more.

In the third place I'm not very optimistic about the institution of marriage itself. I can't say that I've ever seen *one* that I considered an unmitigated success. One of the two partners may be happy, but both seldom are. And I'm thirty years old and adjustments may not be so easy for me to make.

For another six months she kept firm in her refusal. He was alternately furious and humorous about it. He quarreled with her for being a saint. He kissed her for being a fool. And a year of seeing him constantly began to make him seem indispensable to her. She worried about the time when some other girl would marry him. She dreaded his being transferred to another city. Finally she could not bring herself to imagine either contingency.

She did not go back to school that next September. She had become Mrs. William Knight, suburban housewife.

14.

Mother Kendrick sat at the breakfast table, concentrating on her grapefruit. Mrs. Moppleby was a prize among cooks. Everything she sent to the table was a picture out of the magazine ads and tasted good besides. The yellow fruit sat in a bowl of crushed ice; powdered sugar frosted its translucent surface, and a fat red cherry marked its cut-out center. Food meant a great deal to Mother Kendrick these days. Since her eyes had been failing her so badly and her neuritis was worse, meals were the exclamation points in her day. Eleanor was lucky in having Mrs. Moppleby.

She took two eggs from the platter Hilda held for her and stole a look at Eleanor, ready to excuse her greediness by saying, "My, I certainly am hungry this morning. Everything looks good to me." She said this almost every morning, and Eleanor always replied, "I'm so glad, Mother. You must eat enough to keep up your strength. Have another piece of toast, do." But Eleanor was reading a letter and had not noticed.

John would be down in a minute now. No matter how Mother Kendrick tried to dally with her breakfast she was always finished before John made his appearance. He hated to eat alone too. Well, Eleanor always waited for him. Sometimes she'd drink as many as three cups of coffee before he came, but she'd always have her toast and orange juice with him. John didn't eat much these days, his stomach was troubling him so, poor boy.

"Ulcers," she had said when he first complained of it.

"No, it isn't, Mother. I've been to the best doctors there are. They say it's nervous indigestion."

"They're just trying to make you feel better. I tell you it's stomach ulcers. Old Mr. Spring—you remember him—started off the same way and within three years——"

"I tell you I don't have ulcers! Eleanor, will you kindly tell Mother——"

"You see, Mother, for years John has rushed through his meals. He's worked too hard and he hasn't slept enough and he's had a great deal on his mind. All of that's bound to upset digestion. A condition like that might develop into ulcers; you're right there. But John's caught it in time. If he takes his pills and watches his diet and tries to slow down a bit he'll be all right."

John's face had smoothed again, and Mother Kendrick had said to herself, Eleanor knows I'm right, she just said it might be ulcers. They both had felt vindicated.

Eleanor looked up from her letter and laughed. "Martha's married," she said.

"My land, it's about time! How old is she now? Thirty?"

"Almost thirty-one. Penny's twenty-eight and I'm thirty-four. It doesn't seem possible."

"Well, she's old enough to know her own mind, anyway. Who'd she marry, a professor?"

"No. A businessman. And she sounds so puzzled and uncertain about it, and a little humorous. Says she can't figure out how it happened, but so far she feels all right about it. Not exactly a bridal rhapsody, is it? But you know Martha, she always has to have a reason for everything. 'Do people ever get married because they're lonesome?' she says. And in one paragraph she's talking about how good-looking he is and what good company, and in the next she's saying that if it doesn't work out all right she'll always be able to support herself at any rate."

"She may not stay married long. Women who can support themselves usually get a chance to do it." Mother Kendrick's voice was slightly bitter. Until her husband died she had never had a penny that she could unreservedly call her own.

"Oh, I hope it works out for her! I've worried about her. She's been alone so many years."

John came in, pink and immaculate. "Good morning," he said shortly. He sat down and shook his napkin over his knees. His tablets were beside his plate and he took them with his orange juice. His look flickered over his mother's plate. Fine, she'd finished eating. He'd told Eleanor that he couldn't stand watching the old lady eat, the way she wolfed her food and the combinations she insisted on mixing up on her plate. This system of their starting ahead of him was working out pretty well. Course it meant some extra sitting around for Eleanor, but she didn't mind.

"What's the news?"

"Martha's married. To a Bill Knight. She knew him at college."

He snorted. "Well, what do you know! I always swore there wasn't a man in the world who'd want to marry Martha. I suppose he's some little moth-eaten specimen who doesn't expect to call his soul his own?"

"No, he's a big man and very good-looking."

"Then he probably hasn't much of a job. Martha can swing her own weight financially, you've got to give her that."

"He has quite a respectable job. Martha's had to quit teaching, of course."

"State law there just like here, eh? Well, that's right. No use paying a woman if a man's already supporting her. Well, I'll stop by and see 'em next time I'm in Laketown. I want to see the guy that's willing to take a tiger into his house and try to live with her."

Eleanor smiled. "You've never been quite fair to Martha."

"Fair! Good Lord, you don't have to be fair to a woman who can take her own part as well as she can! And I do admire her writing. I told you that."

"You've never read any of it."

"And when do I get time to read, may I ask? But I tell all my friends about it. It's something to get published in the *Chronicle*. I'm not dumb enough not to know that."

"I've always thought I could write," said Mother Kendrick. "If I could write the story of my life it would make a book ten times as good as this drivel you read nowadays."

"But your eyes would never stand it, Mother," said Eleanor. "You really mustn't try."

Mother Kendrick looked faintly martyred. "That's right, of course."

John got to his feet. "I'll wire you from New York, Eleanor. Don't know just when I'll get back."

"Try to be back for my party Saturday, won't you?"

"I'll try, sure, but I may not be able to make it. Fact is, with this war that's going on in Europe, my nose is going to be tied closer to the grindstone than it ever was before. Can't let these Eastern fellows put anything over on me because I'm a hick from Ashland."

His mother pushed back her chair. "Oh, I guess they'd have quite a time putting anything over on you."

"Anything you want to remind me of before I go, Eleanor? You'll take care of the checks, won't you? And the tailor will be sending my suits one of these days. And tell——"

She followed him to the door as the stream of directions swirled around her. She laid a hand on his arm.

"Don't stay away any longer than you have to, dear."

He was gratified. "Well, after the war—because we're going to get into this war before it's over, you'll see—after the war I'm going to settle down and never leave town again. Except for a trip to California now and then, or Paris or Cuba. Have Jerry Auld up to dinner while I'm away and be sweet to him. I want to make sure that boy stays in town. He's worth his weight in gold, the trouble he saves me."

He climbed into the car and waved at her from the rear seat as Benson let in the clutch and started down the drive.

Mrs. Moppleby was behind her. "Mrs. Kendrick, if you'd just step into the kitchen a minute. I'd like to have you see what the butcher is sending us for chickens. And Mr. Perkins says he'd be obliged if you'd step out to the garden as soon as you have a minute. Those flats have come and he wants to know where to put them. Is Hilda working out all right, or——"

Her day had started with a bang.

There were benefits to John's interminable absences. For one thing she did not have as much to do. The house ran more simply with him away. There was no accepting or giving important invitations without him. She had not had to open the summer place.

She had looked forward to having the children with her for July and August. In her imagination she had seen them and herself picnicking under the trees, strolling through the country, driving down to the beach, three contented souls asking no more than to be together. At long last she would be able to talk to them without interruption, cuddle them to her heart's content, inspire them to being better children. Their arrival, their actuality, had shattered her graceful picturing.

Nine-year-old Alice resembled John. She had his light curly hair, his decided chin, his wide shoulders. She did not have his indomitable spirit or his energy. Whatever the school was doing for her, it had not taught her to have resources of her own. She missed the other children and wept for them. She did not know what to do on a rainy day.

"Why don't you read one of your nice books, dear?"

"Reading's for school. I don't have to read in vacation, Mama."

"Shall I ask Janie Price and Stella Maddox to come over?"

"I don't *know* them."

"You soon would."

"I don't *want* to!"

"You could go over to the pool in the park and swim."

"I don't like to swim."

Exasperated, Eleanor would let her alone. Every hour Alice would find her. "Mama, what shall I do? There's nothing to *do*."

They usually ended by going to a movie. Alice was mad about movies, especially the violent or highly romantic ones. Sonny preferred Westerns and football heroes. Combining these tastes called for a judicious selection of double features.

Sonny found plenty to do, most of it bringing repercussions in its wake. There was a wild recklessness about him that the other boys admired. They gasped at his impudence to gardeners, passing civilians, and strange little girls. They resented his trying to boss them, but they were inspired by his bragging. He would spend hours of their time relating his past escapades, ending up with "Well, I certainly told *him* off! He wasn't so quick to bother me the next time, I tell *you.*" Eleanor was always answering telephone calls which told her what Sonny was up to now, how he had encouraged several other boys to see how many things they could take from the dime store before they were discovered and had to run, how he had threatened Billy Maddox with a baseball bat because Billy would not let him pitch, how he had driven the Princes' car out of the drive where it had been left and smashed into a delivery truck at the foot of the street, how—there was no end to his genius for troublemaking. She alternated between fervently wishing that John were home to settle him and thanking God that he wasn't.

Sonny looked like his mother, tall and slender, with fine features and a wide brow. The schools had taught him manners; they could not teach him a consistently creditable comportment. He regarded his mother as a very likeable servant and most of the time he was gracious to her, even when she lectured him on such dry subjects as improving his grades so that he might stay in the same school for another year at least.

"You've been expelled so many times. I don't know where we could find another school that would take you."

"The dump I'm in now is about as good as any. They've got a swell basketball coach. I learned a lot from him."

"That's fine, darling, but basketball won't get you into a university."

"You think not? Listen, Mother, I don't even know that I want to go to a university. I can get educated plenty of other ways. Travel, now, I'd like to travel. Maybe go around with Dad a little bit, meeting nice people and everything. These days it's not *what* you know, it's *who* you know, and we know just about everybody, don't we? Honest, I don't care much about books."

"You used to. When you were a little boy you used to beg me to read to you, and I did whenever I had the time. I didn't have enough, though. That was during the depression, and I was working pretty hard. I wish now——"

198

"Listen. *I'm* all right. There's nothing the matter with me."

Emboldened by John's absence, she took a transcript of Sonny's school record to the superintendent of the Ashland schools.

"I'm thinking about keeping the children home with me this year," she said. "I think they need to live at home for a while, and Sonny has only one more year to go before he'll be in high school. I'm putting all my cards on the table. I'd like you to accept him, but there are some fairly unpleasant letters from headmasters in that packet and I want you to read those too."

He read them judiciously. "We will accept him if you insist, Mrs. Kendrick. By law we'd be obliged to. But may I give you a bit of advice from long experience with all kinds of children? I don't think he'd last more than a month in the public schools here. Then he'd be expelled, and you'd have to put him in a private school again. You see, he's been in six different schools in the past five years, and each time he's been sent home for a serious infraction of rules. Private schools are more patient than public ones. They have fewer pupils for one thing and for another they depend on tuition and they like to keep up their quotas. They don't expel lightly. Here we have so many pupils that we cannot afford to let one stay if he is infecting or disrupting a group, and I'm afraid your boy might do just that."

"He's not a stupid boy," she pleaded.

"I'm quite sure he isn't. It takes intelligence to think up deviltry, as much as it takes to be a model scholar. Somewhere along the way his energies were misdirected, that's all, and so far no one has been able to discipline him, make him fall into line. I hate to confess that I don't think we'd have the time to do it for him."

"We tried a military school, and the rules there were very strict. He didn't last a semester."

"The stricter the rules, the greater the challenge to him, perhaps. The truth of the matter seems to be that children learn respect for law and order before they're of school age, or they have trouble learning it at all. And without that respect a child is like the big gun that got loose in a heavy seaway: no good to anybody, rolling about the ship crushing men and battering anything that got in its way. The saddest part is that it hurts the gun as much as it does the ship."

She was sorry she had come. She might have spared herself this extra reproach, this last humiliation of town knowledge. "It's a shame that children are ordinarily born to young and inexperienced parents," she said lightly. "If I had been old and wise twelve years ago there are a great many mistakes I wouldn't have made."

He was being as courteous and considerate of her as he could be with that dreadful messy record on the desk between them. "I don't think you should blame yourself entirely, Mrs. Kendrick. The child had a father and some other relatives and playmates who must have made an impression on him."

Her hands shook a little as she put the cards and letters in her purse. "The worst part of making mistakes with children is that you can never live them down. You have to see the results of them going on and on as long as you live."

The house was in a turmoil when she got back. Alice had taken over the kitchen to bake a "play cake," and Mrs. Moppleby was frantic. Sonny had tormented Mother Kendrick into her room and a bad headache.

Alice was persuaded from the kitchen reluctantly. "I'll be glad to go back to school, Mama. There's just nothing to do here at all. I wish I'd gone to camp with Gladys. I wish Gladys was *here*." She wept.

"Perhaps we can get Gladys to come stay with us for a week or so before school starts. Would you like that? Sonny, go out and ride your bike awhile. You're making so much noise we can't hear ourselves think!"

Just as Martha had reminded her on the day she first sent them away, everything had a price. John was a stormy man, a difficult man to live with. The price tag on peace with John had been exorbitant, but she had met it. It would have been better if she hadn't, Martha would think, but Martha was not conventional. What the children had become was part of the price, the only part she regretted having paid. Yet what purpose would it have served had she stubbornly kept the children home with her where she and they would have been in eternal conflict with John and John's demands? Martha might have carried off such a situation, but Martha wouldn't have married John in the first place.

The children went back to their schools in September.

She spent much of her time outdoors that autumn, wandering in the orchard, watching the birds at their feeding stations, sitting in

200

a chair under the biggest oak. Sometimes Mother Kendrick joined her, when there was a lapse in the Women's Club programs or an unpleasantness among the elderly group of women who were her friends. Occasionally Penny and her husband came to dinner and that was diverting because Dr. Wilder was an intelligent and entertaining conversationalist. Penny was losing her looks a little. She was still one of the handsomest women in town, but some of her peachblow bloom had now to be supplied by artifice. Her manner left something to be desired too. She was not interested in talk about anything but local personalities, fashions, or herself. If any other subject were introduced she yawned openly and declared herself bored. She was so openly contemptuous of Perry that Eleanor was shocked.

John wrote occasionally about how busy he was, how beastly the weather, how much he had enjoyed a short yachting trip, what the imminence of war was doing to the stock market. He managed to come home one or two days out of each month, and he did not look well. His nervousness was increasing, he ate scarcely anything, he wandered about the house like a lost puppy. For the first time in his life he was impatient at sympathy. "Don't worry about me!" he said irritably. "Just let me alone." She laid that to his indigestion.

Sitting in the last of the year's sunlight under the oak tree, she mused that she had come a long way from the quiet, reserved girl she had been, living in Aunt Ann's faded house, uncertain of her capacity to face maturity. She had become an excellent household manager by engaging inimitable servants and learning from them. But heavens, she thought, if I were thrown into actual housework again I'd be just as bad at it as I was those horrid, scrabbling six years. There's a vast difference between knowing how a thing should be done and doing it yourself! Still, other women had servants and their households creaked along instead of running on ball bearings as hers did.

She had traveled to so many beautiful places that she had never thought to see: Paris, Los Angeles, London, Naples, New Orleans. She hadn't seen enough of them. There had always been so much wiring ahead for reservations, so much consulting with headwaiters and chambermaids, so many purchases to make, so much laundry to count, the problem of finding and staffing a house if their stay were a long one, the arranging of dinners for John's business friends and their wives. She would like to go back to those cities someday with nothing to do but really look at them.

Today she refused to think about the children, because she wanted this warm, self-congratulatory glow to last. She would think of John and all the lovely things John had given her: her jewels, her furs, the properties and money that were in her own name. He had been generous, and in turn she made his life easier, more comfortable than he could have lived it anywhere else. There were, after all, rewards for not being demanding.

She wrapped her gabardine jacket more closely around her and smiled at her own good fortune.

John came home the first week in November. She sent Benson to meet him at the airport. It was a cold, blowing autumn night, but she would have preferred to go herself if John had not specifically told her not to. The wire said:

HAVE BENSON MEET ME. I WILL HAVE HAD MY DINNER. ARRANGE SO THAT WE CAN HAVE A TALK ALONE.

She went upstairs immediately after dinner to put on her purple taffeta tea gown. She brushed her hair so that the few white ones did not show. She moved about the room, closing slatted blinds against the dark, pulling the blue draperies together, lighting the small pink lamps, refolding the afghan on the chaise longue, pushing the puffy gray satin chairs into their proper positions, straightening the flounces of the cover on the big double bed. It was a perfect room, though she could have done greater things had it belonged to one or the other of them instead of to both. As it was, she had had to combine masculine severity with feminine fluffiness, and of course the bed was old-fashioned. People used twin beds now or had separate rooms, but that John would not tolerate.

"Think I want to have to come padding through cold halls to find you, like a damn hotel?"

That had settled that. To be sure, John snored and pulled blankets out of any mooring and took up most of the bed and threw his clothes around and left wet towels all over the bathroom, but that was not too much to endure for the compliment of being indispensable to him. Being needed was the greater part of being loved. Though John loves me too, she thought hastily. Thank heaven she could take things like that for granted, now that she was older and had more sense. It saved a lot of thinking. How many years had it been since she had thought about anything more vital than the proper choice of schools for the children or the capabilities of her laundress? Let the men do the thinking.

John strode in, rubbing his hands, making the little knickknacks on the dressing table jingle.

"Cold out," he said. "How are you, my dear?" His cold face brushed her own.

"I'm very well. Did you have a bad trip? Have you really eaten? Would you like——"

"Where's Mother?"

"Having dinner at the Branningans'. I didn't tell her you were coming, so we'll have to pretend it was unexpected. I thought if you wanted to talk to me you could do it better this way."

"That's right." He sat down and lit a cigar. "Close the door, will you? I don't want the servants to hear all this."

She closed the door quietly, but underneath an uneasiness began to stir. John had never acted like this before. Now that she had a chance to look at him, his face was drawn and wretched, his feet pranced even while he sat in his chair. No man not yet forty should look as old as he did!

"What's the matter, dear? Trouble with your stomach again?"

"Lord, yes, but that's not it. I—this is a very difficult thing for me to do, Eleanor." He looked at her reproachfully.

"What is?"

"Well, I——" He got up so suddenly that sparks from his cigar flicked the gray satin of the chair. "I should have done this months ago, but I've been putting it off. First time in my life I've ever been a coward about anything. The truth is—well, I want a divorce."

There was a roaring in her ears as the main scaffolding of her pretty life tore apart and crashed around her head. Her hands and feet turned into ice. Her heart thudded a rapid, light, strange rhythm. She could feel her smile of welcome still on her face, and she left it there. There must not be a scene. Mother Kendrick. The servants. Conventions. Etiquette.

Now that he had the worst of it out he plunged on. "It's nothing against you, Eleanor. It's not anything you've done. It's just that I—there's someone else I want to marry."

"Who?"

"You don't know her. She lives in New York. Her name is Mary Wendell, she's a widow with one child, very respectable, has money, right in the social swim, all that kind of thing. I've been seeing a lot of her, and—well, I want to marry her. You see, I'm putting all my cards on the table. I'm being honest about it."

She said slowly, "I'll have to think it over, John. This has all been a little too quick for me."

"Sure. You can let me know in the morning. I have to fly right back. You can keep the children, though I hope you'll let me see 'em once in a while, and you'll never have to worry about money. I'll take care of that."

She was coming back to life a little now, and a demon of malice pricked her. "Is she pretty?"

He looked distressed. "I don't think it's very good taste for us to discuss her, Eleanor. It's bad enough that——"

"Oh, come on. Just between friends, is she pretty?"

"Beautiful."

"You don't happen to have a picture of her, I suppose?"

"Listen, this isn't—well, here."

"In your billfold? Oh, John, you should have it pasted in the back of your watch. So much more secretive and traditional. But you're right, she is pretty. Is that hair bleached or is it real?"

He snatched the billfold away. "I must say I don't know what's gotten into you. You're not acting——"

"You mean you want me to cry. I will if you insist."

"I don't know how Mother will take it."

"We'll worry about that in the morning. Right now I think you should be getting some sleep. If you'll take your bag to the front guest room Hilda will unpack whatever you need."

"Guest room?"

She laughed. "Darling, you can't stay here. It wouldn't be proper."

He looked at the bed reluctantly. It was a wonderful bed. "I don't see where one more night would make any difference. I don't like to sleep in strange rooms. I won't lay a hand on you if that's what you're worried about. And there's no use letting the servants in on this till we have to."

"They're bound to know sooner or later. Off you go."

He picked up the bag. "This has all been rather a shock to me,

Eleanor. I thought you cared for me, that you'd be sorry about our breaking up, that——"

"We haven't broken up yet."

She was puzzling him. For the first time in years he was seeing her as a person, as an individual separate from himself, and he was confused and troubled. "You have too much pride to live with a man who's in love with someone else. Haven't you?"

"I haven't had time to think about it, John. When I find out you'll be the first to know. Good night."

At last she could take the smile off her face, strip the meringue from her distress. Sobs crumpled her up on the wide, desolate bed. What was going to become of her? Where would she go? What would she do? All she had said to him had been a kittenish attempt to strike back, to hurt him a little, to break down his complacence. She would have to give him the divorce, naturally. You couldn't live with a man who didn't want you.

She sat up and saw her sodden face in three mirrors. Crying wouldn't do any good. She would have to make plans. Reno first, since this state had strict divorce laws. Then an apartment somewhere, or a house. Not in Ashland. She would not be able to face Ashland after this. She writhed as she imagined what the town must have been saying all these months.

She knew the kind of things they had said in the old days. "John's twice the man his father was." And "You have to say this for the Kendricks: they may have money, but they don't get their names in the papers and they mind their own business." And "I guess when John gets to talking with those big shots out on the coast he makes them sit up and take notice. Nothing slow about him, and he works like a horse, always did. Got a nice respectable wife too. One of the King girls, she was."

Now they were whispering, "He's never at home, is he? Nothing going on up at the big house. Must be pretty lonesome for her." And "Harry Martin says he was sitting in the Trocadero last week—that's in New York—and in walks John Kendrick with the swellest-looking babe you ever saw. Not a tramp, Harry says, but a real good-looking woman with plenty of class. What do you make of that?" And "Kendrick's getting around the foolish age. Hear he's going to ditch his wife and marry some New York woman. That'll mean he'll probably move away from here. Wonder what his wife'll do."

205

By midnight her grief and humiliation had ebbed, and a small but growing rage had taken their place. How could John be so unfair! How dared he dismiss her with no more reluctance than he would have shown with a good servant for whom there was no longer room! Did he consider that all her years of thoughtfulness for him, catering to him, humoring his slightest whim had been bought and paid for? There was no payment high enough for that brand of service, didn't he know that? Mary Wendell wouldn't do it for him. He'd be wretched inside of six weeks with her, and it would serve him right!

"If you base your whole life on another person's, then it must stand or fall, depending on the charity of that person." Martha had written that to her long ago, and how true it had turned out to be. Nevertheless it was the way most women had to plan their lives, around someone else's; there was no other choice. And when she had seen marriages fail she had always, in her mind, blamed the woman. If she had made herself and her home and the mutual plan of their living attractive and intelligent enough the man would never want to leave it. Now there was this, and her fury grew to see how easily a new sex impulse and the thrill of novelty could outweigh years of devotion and self-effacement.

She threw the tea gown over a chair, turned out the lights, climbed into bed. For the first time in years she omitted the ritual of brush and cleansing cream and the puttering little beauty jobs that had always attended her retiring. What was the sense of looking well if the one person who mattered no longer cared to look at you! She had been a mannequin long enough, a showcase for John's gifts, a testimonial to his prosperity. It was time that she gave some thought to being herself.

The idea came to her all at once, and she rose to a sitting position in the darkness and clasped her knees. A wife had rights, legal rights; there were laws that protected her from this kind of thing! She did not have to give John a divorce at all. She could stay right on here, being Mrs. Kendrick the rest of her days!

Her pride whimpered, and she stilled it sternly. It took pride not to stay where you weren't wanted; it took even more pride to hang on, survive the storm, allay the gossip, show the world that you were playing your part correctly to the finish. She would stay.

But was pride enough to bolster her when he had made her hate him so? Always, from now on, she would judge him in the light of this evening. Never again could she listen to his bombast with awe, never again could she trust his strength, knowing this weakness. Even if in time he came back to her, what value could she put on that, having seen how easy it was for any woman to win him?

Her mind moved, and immediately she had the perfect answer, the one that would satisfy both her pride and her hatred. She would stay with him for five years, get him back, stay him with comfort, still him with even more devotion than he had known before. He would be over forty by then, no vast age for a man, but each year would lessen his flexibility, sober him, settle him down to the sober canter of middle age. And *then* she would leave him, walking out of the house calmly some morning without so much as a good-by.

She smiled in the darkness at the picture of his mortification and rage. He would hunt her up, demand an explanation.

"For God's sake, Eleanor, what's gotten into you to do a thing like this? Come home where you belong."

"Don't you remember you wanted me to leave you a long time ago? I'm just getting around to it now."

"But that's all over and done with, years ago. Why did you stay with me if you didn't love me, forgive me, want to be with me?"

"I stayed because I hated you. The only satisfactory time to leave a man is when he doesn't want you to. Clever little revenge, isn't it? Amazing that such a stupid person as I could think of it."

Perhaps some other woman would marry him then, but the colossus, set in the marble of habit, would not find a new regime to his liking. A harness worn long enough, no matter how loosely, becomes not a burden but a necessity, a reason for being. And John was not ordinarily a woman's man. The chances were he would never find another Mary Wendell.

Thank heaven, too, that Mary Wendell was the kind of woman she was—respectable, rich, social. There could be nothing less than marriage with a woman like that. She would not have the taste or the facility for a backdoor affair, and, attractive as she was, she would not wait five years for any man. No, John could never marry Mary Wendell if Eleanor stood firm now.

Her smile tasted bitter on her lips. If she could only be patient enough she would live to see the day when John would have to drink from the same cup he had proffered her so blithely tonight. She felt she could bear anything for the satisfaction of witnessing that day.

He came into her room sheepishly at seven-thirty the next morning. He had not slept. He looked ill. Looking in the mirror, she thought how much younger she seemed than he. Of course he had not rubbed pink cream on the dark circles under his eyes, as she had. She adjusted the last button on the yellow wool dress and turned to him pleasantly.

"Good morning, John."

"Well, I suppose you've thought out all the details by this time. I must say, I'd have had a better night's rest if you hadn't been so anxious to keep me on the fence. After all, there's only one thing to do in a case like this——"

"Yes, I know. I'm not going to give you the divorce, John."

He couldn't believe it. He turned to stone. His face flushed, his voice stuttered, he was a helpless moth impaled on the pin of fact.

"I—I don't understand."

"It's very simple. I have no intention of giving you a divorce. A wife isn't like a pair of shoes that you can discard when the new styles come in. She has privileges and rights. I am going to be unkind enough to insist on mine."

He exploded. "You can't force me to stay with you if I don't want to. I'm not a child! I won't live with you. That's all! I've told you that I'm in love with another woman. If you had any pride at all——"

"I haven't, you see."

"There are legal ways to get around this thing. I'll find them."

"It's possible that you might get some cheap, easy divorce, but it won't be the kind that would suit Mary Wendell. I imagine that she'd like to be sure her marriage was pretty generally considered legitimate. This state will never recognize her at all."

She could tell by the way his face clouded that the two of them had discussed her possible connivance, that Mary Wendell had insisted on no unpleasant fuss or publicity, that John had assured her that Eleanor would offer no trouble at all. If anything could have made her angrier this knowledge did.

She said composedly, "If you're coming down to breakfast you'll have to pull yourself together. There's no need to upset Mother with our private difficulties."

It made quite a game, this playing of roles for the benefit of Mother Kendrick and the servants. If the old woman noticed any alteration in her son's behavior she laid it to his illness. And as a matter of fact rage had made him really ill. He took to his bed and stayed there three days. His mother and his wife hovered over him with apparently equal solicitude.

When he was alone with Eleanor he raved at her like a demented man, and his threats and tortured cajolings stoked the fires of her anger into a holocaust that she could scarcely keep hidden under a patient, dignified exterior. If he had approached her differently she might conceivably have broken and crawled away to some distant part of the country. As it was, calluses formed over the tender spots, and she even grew to enjoy baiting him under the screen of wifely martyrdom.

"You'll thank me for this one day, John."

"The hell I will! Don't think you'll get away with this. Before the next year's out you'll be the one who'll be asking for the divorce!"

He came very close to being right. The next ten months were almost unendurable. He came home for Thanksgiving and Christmas and Easter because of his mother. He openly moved into the front bedroom, as far away from Eleanor as he could get. He was surly and unpleasant with the servants and the children, whenever they were home. To his wife he did not speak at all, unless Mother Kendrick were present. He had taken an apartment for himself in New York from which he wrote short letters to his mother, none at all to Eleanor.

There were many nights when she wept. There were many days of sick indignation. She imagined the growing of talk in the town, Penny's jealous delight were she to hear it, Martha's pity were she to catch a suggestion of the real state of affairs. She pictured John reassuring an impatient Mary Wendell that things would be all right soon, that his wife would not hold out much longer. She set her chin and waited.

15.

Penelope Wilder reached for the small enameled clock on the table by her bed. Eleven o'clock. No wonder she felt so marvelously rested. She opened her mouth to call Hetty, but she closed it again. On weekdays she could coax Hetty into bringing her her breakfast in bed, but this was Sunday, and Perry was home. She'd have to get up. He said it made him sick to see an elderly woman lugging a tray up the stairs to a lazy wench one third her age. Well, she'd get Hetty to do it tomorrow when Perry was safe at the office.

She lay back and looked out at the sky. It was an April day, cool and blue and windy. The perfect day for her new blue suit. She'd look so well in it that even Perry would have to admire her, and while he was in a good mood she would show him the bill. Husbands wanted you to look nice, but they never wanted to pay for it. Lucky thing it was so easy to get around them.

To tell the truth, she was disappointed in Perry. He wasn't at all the gay, openhanded, worshiping admirer that she had thought he'd be. He was generous enough in a way. Look how he had insisted that Hetty come to live with them when Penny was all against it. He'd been right too. Hetty took all the housekeeping off Penny's hands and stood as a buffer between her and the horrible, practical side of domestic routine.

"She *likes* it," she told Perry when he protested that the old lady was overworked. "She wants to do it. It makes her feel less like an object of charity."

"I don't object to her doing little things if she wants to. But there's only Emma to help out, and between the two of them they manage this big house, the washing, the ironing, the mending, the cooking——"

"Oh, for heaven's sake, you don't have to go through the whole list. Everybody knows housework is a detestable job. But Hetty *likes* that kind of thing. She's used to it."

"If you'd take only a little of it off her hands I'd feel better about it. The way it is, I'm embarrassed when I think what *she* must think about my asking her to come and live with us."

"Why, darling, I direct things, you mustn't think I don't. I keep Emma on her toes. I don't let her slacken up for a minute."

That was true too. If the white sauce was a trifle lumpy Penny always made a point of saying, "Really, Emma, this sauce isn't fit to bring to the table. I thought your recommendations said that you were a good cook. You must have forged them." And really, girls these days were so lazy! If Emma couldn't get sweetbreads the first two places she asked, she'd give up and come home with calf's liver. Penny never let her get by with it. She always gave her a good talking to.

Perry was too exasperating. "It's easy to criticize, my dear, but in the long run it boils down to a case of do as I do, not do as I say. If you're not willing to take over the smallest household function you can't expect Emma to break her neck showing an interest."

"She's paid for it."

"To put it crassly, you are too. At least you're getting your room and board and clothing and spending money besides. There are those who would think you ought to make some kind of return for it."

She laughed. "But you give me those things because you love me, don't you, darling?"

Lately she had not ventured to ask that question. In the old days he had answered it by putting an arm around her waist and saying, "I suppose I must, you beautiful creature." Then there was a period when he had said, "I can't think of any other reason why I live with you."

Now he said, "*And* I suppose you love me?"

"Of course, silly!"

"Strange that I should have to ask to find out. You'd think there'd be something in your behavior that would tell me."

"Why do you suppose I try to keep myself looking pretty if it isn't for you? Why do I get us invited everywhere, even when I'd rather stay home, if it isn't because your practice——"

His quotation was impolite. " 'What you are stands over you the while, and thunders so that I cannot hear what you have to say to the contrary.' "

"What on earth are you talking about?"

"That's Emerson, my little ignoramus. An American essayist and poet. You should read his *Conduct of Life*. Especially where he says, 'Make yourself necessary to somebody.' There's something you've never tried."

"Well, really, if you're determined to be insulting——"

There was no use trying to please Perry, he didn't appreciate it. These days she didn't bother to practice her fascinations on him. More and more he sullenly refused to be budged from his chair with the book-heaped table beside it.

"I will *not* go to another country-club dance, my pet. There is something a mite ridiculous in the sight of a forty-year-old dentist prancing and sweating around a crowded floor for the second time in a week. It looks as though he couldn't find anything better to do. But you run along. Those affairs are strictly on your mental level. Besides, Jerry Auld is sure to be there."

This was more familiar territory. "Darling, you're jealous."

For a minute he seemed about to retch, but all he said was, "Am I?"

"And you mustn't be. Jerry admires me, likes to dance with me, pays me silly compliments. But that's all there is to it, honestly. There's nothing *wrong* about it."

"You don't have to tell me. No one knows better than I that you'd never give even a kiss away if you could help it. Don't flatter yourself that it's because of your high principles either. It's your magnificent selfishness. I suppose that's what passes for virtue in a good many women."

"We can't talk to each other for five minutes without quarreling. Your disposition——"

"Is not improving with age. But then neither is your character, so that makes us even, doesn't it?"

She had learned, finally, to let him alone. They appeared in public together on occasion. Otherwise they led separate lives. At table, with Hetty, they talked noncommittally about inconsequential things. In the mornings Penny shopped for clothes and bangles, or played tennis or swam. In the afternoons she played bridge or drank cocktails with whatever group of unoccupied women she could find. In the evenings she went out with a crowd or with some temporarily unattached male. When there was positively nothing to do she watched Perry putter in the garden and went to bed when he picked up one of his everlasting books.

She had objected when he first suggested having separate rooms.

"Really, Perry, I won't bite you! And I'm not as unpleasant to look at as all that."

"On the contrary, you're too pleasant to look at. Weren't you a cover girl a few years ago?"

"Well then . . ."

"Well then, I'm only human. You make a point of sheer lingerie and bewitching negligees. You flaunt yourself in them until I'm thoroughly aroused. You can see that and you like it. It flatters you. But you don't want to do anything about it. And I'm tired of being merely tolerated. So I am removing myself from the sphere of influence. In short, I am willing to be a cat's-paw in many other ways but not sexually."

Surprisingly, she liked it better this way. It was almost like being a woman with an independent income, because Perry supported her well and made no demands upon her. It would have been better to be divorced from him and living on alimony, but she couldn't see any way to get that. Yet oh, to be single and have the house and clothes and money that she had now! There would be no place she couldn't go, no end to the men she could charm once a forbidding husband loomed no longer in the background. Well, one couldn't have everything.

The "crowd" had saved her life. With the exception of Jerry Auld, they were all young people in their early twenties. Not many of them were indigenous to Ashland. They had moved in with the expansion of the industrial and commercial life of the town. The men were engineers just out of school, or store managers or accountants or technical clerks or the owners of budding business enterprises. Their wives were smart young women who dressed well, drove their own cars, amused themselves with cards and gossip and movies and trips to the beauty parlors, and avoided churchgoing, civic enterprises, and work. They lived in furnished apartments and spent as little time in them as possible. Except for a toasted sandwich at midnight, they ate out. They were a gay, nomadic tribe, ready to pick up and go at a moment's notice should a better financial opportunity arise in some other community. "Of course we want children as soon as we can afford them," they said. "It isn't fair to the child to bring it into the world if you can't do anything for it." Penny had given Dr. Temple's name and address to several of them.

Anyway, they were the only people in town you could have fun with. Perry's stodgy, professional circle consisted of the forty-year-old lawyers and doctors, teachers and merchants of the town. They lived in suburban houses, with great lawns and gardens that ate up their time. Their children, ranging in age from seven to sixteen, kept them tied down at home. Carefully planned, their daily schedule permitted no spontaneous, idle hilarity.

She had tried to stir them up. Calling on one of the women whose husbands had shown a signal interest in Penny's charms, she had cried, "Oh, drop everything, why don't you, and let's go to a movie and have a sundae afterward!"

"I wish I could, heaven knows I could do with a little spree, but the children will be home from school any minute and I have to be here, anyway, because the plumber's coming. The drain in the kitchen——"

Once or twice she had responded to their urgings to "stay awhile and keep me company." She sat in the living room with a glass of iced tea or a cup of coffee in her hand and a smile on her face that there was no one to appreciate, the mistress of the house having to get up every other minute to answer the children's wants or check on her frozen dessert in the refrigerator or direct some tradesman or go to the telephone. And their eyes would creep to the moving hands of the clock, planning to the split second a last-minute rush to the grocery store and the possibilities of a change in dinner menu that would compensate for the time lost on this unexpected guest.

It wore her out to watch them. She grew accustomed to the idea that their hospitality functioned best by invitation only. And since their conviviality must be forecast, with "sitters" and weedy gardens and children's temperatures as bad-weather portents, she had dropped them altogether and found the "crowd," whose women had time to lavish as herself.

She sat up on the edge of the bed and ran her hands through her heavy auburn hair. In the days of the long bob she had let hers grow. It fell to her waist, thick, coppery, shining. It took an hour to arrange it on the top of her head in an upswept pompadour, but the singularity of the style was worth it. There wasn't a woman in town who didn't envy that coiffure; there wasn't a man who could resist looking and looking again at those dark red coils that made her neck look so slender and revealed the perfection of her pink ears, her brow, her oval face.

She creamed her face thoroughly. Water was so drying, even though Perry said that it was unnatural to go through life as greasy as a mechanic. A brisk rub with an old towel brought the pink into her cheeks. She reached for her rouge, bending forward to the mirror, frowning in concentration. Those horrible wrinkles around her eyes—how had they come there in spite of the wonderful care she had taken? She must consult Anthony about them the next time she was in his shop. With all the marvelous inventions people were making nowadays, you'd think they would have found something to do about wrinkles!

In just an hour and a half she was ready to go downstairs. All she had done to her costume of nightgown and slippers was to slip a piqué housecoat over her head and zip it snugly to within a careful five inches of the throat, an amount of exposure which she had determined by experiment gave the maximum of prettiness for the minimum of revelation. That had taken two minutes. The rest of the time she had spent on her hair and face.

Perry was reading the Sunday papers in the sunroom off the dining room. Hetty and Emma were rattling around in the kitchen, probably preparing one of their horribly abundant and hearty Sunday dinners. Years ago she had suggested that they do away with the huge Sunday meal.

"There's no sense in anyone eating so much," she had said. "It isn't healthy to overstuff yourself like that. Just to look at that table makes me ill. Let's have a late breakfast and a light supper and call it a day."

It was Hetty who, for once, had balked her. "That's all right for *you,* my fine lady. You don't get up till almost noon and you don't do anything all day long. But the rest of us get up early and put in a day's work just like any other day. The way Perry works in that garden he's got a right to a little nourishment."

She hadn't made a point of it, and she always sat down to the dinner with them, even though she had just finished breakfast. She ate nothing, but she felt that she should be there to preside, to contribute a gay note, to show that she was interested in them.

"Perry, you don't want *another* helping of meat! Oughtn't you to be thinking about your blood pressure?"

"Darling Hetty, how can you expect to lose weight if you keep eating potatoes?"

And later, out in the kitchen, to the furiously trotting Emma, "Great heavens, Emma, is that all the roast that's left? It looked quite healthy when it left the table. I'd like to have some sliced cold for supper if you feel you could spare it."

Certainly they couldn't complain that she didn't *try* to take care of them.

She stood by the table, drinking her orange juice and looking out at her husband. He hadn't seen her yet, and she had a chance to observe his face in repose. He was a good-looking man, big, dark, with nothing soft or heavy about him. In spite of his uncongeniality at home he had the biggest dental practice in town. People had confidence in him, liked his reserve, admired his honesty. The good Lord knew, he certainly was honest!

Still carrying her orange juice, she walked out and stood by him, dropping a light kiss on the top of his head.

"Thank you. Thank you very much," he said humbly. "To what do we owe the honor of so much sweetness and light this early in the day?"

"I want to ask you a question, and I want a straight answer."

"All right." He put the paper down and folded his hands. His eyes, clear as amber, held no mockery for once.

"Am I looking old?"

He was thoughtful. "You look older than you used to, but you don't look your age. What is it, thirty? You don't look thirty. Neither do you look eighteen."

"You'd guess me in the early twenties?"

"In the middle twenties, maybe."

Content, she moved to a window and looked out at the blue squills in the border. What a ravishing shade for a dress!

His voice came quietly from the chair. "You worry a great deal about your age, don't you?"

"I'd like to keep looking young. That's only natural."

"I know that it's fashionable. I don't know that it's natural. Everyone gets older all the time. I don't understand this intense preoccupation with youth. It's as if it were an end in itself instead of a pleasant phase through which all of us pass too briefly."

"You can afford not to worry. You're a man. As long as you're clean and well dressed and not too fat, that's all anyone asks of you."

"It just occurred to me that we're going to be a funny-looking civilization, with all the men looking their age and all their wives trying to look like their daughters."

He was puzzling her again. "Isn't it right to try to look as young as you can? I'm prettier that way."

"It isn't worth the six hours a day you spend on it, no. It isn't that important. If you spent the same amount of time on your mind or your personality you'd be a world-beater, and you wouldn't be wasting your chips in a losing game."

"Losing game?"

"Sure. Eventually you're going to get old and you're going to look old, no matter what you do. Whereas if you lay up treasures in heaven——"

216

She was at the wall mirror. "I don't look old yet," she said with satisfaction. "I won't look thirty for years yet."

He smiled briefly. "Then there's no more to be said about it. You're happy."

"Aren't you?"

He did not answer. He went on reading the paper.

Tony Fox came into Dr. Wilder's office at five o'clock on a September afternoon.

"Thought you might be able to work me in about this time of day, Doc. I have one that I think needs to come out."

"Just ready to shut up and go home. The girl's gone already. Step in here and we'll have a look."

It was a nervous job, preparing to do an extraction on your wife's first husband and not being sure just how he felt about you. What in the devil had brought Tony in here? He hadn't seen him for years. Still, he looked spruce and healthy and happy, just as he had looked in the old country-club days.

"We'll give the novocain a chance to work. Rest of your teeth look good."

"I don't have much trouble with 'em, that's a fact." He hesitated a moment. "While we're waiting around there's something I'd like to get off my chest. I'm going into the Navy next week and I may not get another chance. Well, what I want to say is, if there'd been anything wrong with my teeth before, this is the place I'd have come to."

"Thank you."

"What I mean is—I don't want there to be any hard feelings. There aren't, on my part. Penny had a hard time of it with me, poor kid. I didn't have a dime in those days. She wanted to go to New York to work, that's why she left me. Some people have said that it was a put-up job, that she knew she was going to marry you when she walked out. I never believed that. You're not that kind of a guy."

"Well, it's nice of you——"

"Sure. I know how it was. You'd liked her, maybe, and when you saw she was free there wasn't anything to hinder you from asking her to marry you. And she—well, New York was a long way away, and even though she had a wonderful future before her she isn't a very independent girl. Penny's awfully feminine. How is she?"

217

"Fine. Wish there were time for you to drop up to the house and see us."

"There isn't. Really." His regret was merely conventional however. Behind the politeness you could see that he had completely forgotten Penny, hadn't missed her for a minute.

"So you're going into the Navy. Beating the gun a little, aren't you?"

"Not by much. We'll be in this thing by next year, I figure. The Navy didn't like my age much, but my education's all right. I got a junior grade out of it." And Sue, the independent little idiot, already overseas as a nurse. Perhaps he'd run into her again after all. She'd be standing on a beach somewhere and he'd come riding up the waves in a battle wagon and . . .

"That's fine. Now if you'll just open your mouth we'll have a try——"

He said casually to Penny that evening, "Saw Tony Fox today. He came into the office and wanted me to pull a tooth for him."

Her glance flicked him, trying to gather his intent. "How is he?"

"Fine. Going into the Navy next week. He must be in the bucks again. He looked prosperous."

"What did you talk about?"

"Just things in general. He wasn't at all ferocious, said he bore me no ill will, that kind of thing. I asked him to come up to the house for a minute if he had time."

"You didn't!"

"I did."

He was enjoying her discomfiture, her flurry of anxiety, her uncertainty. She deserved this and more besides. What a simpleton he had been to fall into her little, pink, lying hands, the minute she made up her mind to have him! How had she kept from laughing at the marriage ceremony, seeing what a timid, trembling ass he had been? And because of that clever trick of hers he had kept her in comfort for all these years, never getting anything, not as much as a sensible word, in return. He didn't even like her, any more than he could have liked a wax doll. There was no warmth to her. She couldn't inspire affection if she tried, which she wouldn't. The only reason she might want anyone to love her was so that she could put him on her sucker list, see what she could get out of him; but she didn't want that so badly either that she'd work at it.

She was going to evade him. "I'd better go upstairs and get dressed," she said. "A bunch of us are having a steak roast down on the beach. Want to come along?"

"Thanks, no. You know—who better—how much my respectability means to me. I can't afford to be seen cavorting in drunken beach parties."

"They're not drunken. Oh well, some of the bunch drink a lot, but I don't, and you wouldn't have to."

"There's nothing so boring as watching other people lap it up when you can't have a drink yourself." Wearying, this business of trying to communicate with a vapid, shallow mind. He longed to pick up a book, lose himself again in a world where, by a writer's careful selection, he could find sense and logic to living. But he tried to be polite to her. After all, she was his wife. "Anyway, the crowd's a little too young for me."

"Jerry Auld is almost as old as you are."

"Ah, Jerry Auld, the perpetual gilded youth, the perennial Peter Pan!"

"You're jealous." The smile that always accompanied that pat opinion!

"Somehow I guessed you'd say that. I'm getting psychic in my old age."

Irony could not dent her marvelous complacency. Her mannequin's exit was unhurried.

He reached for a cigarette and frowned. What a mess marriage could be without a hint of it showing on the outside! He'd had a premonition, before he'd been married a month, that it wasn't going to turn out well. But he'd thought that she'd grow up, that he could make her love him, that maybe they could get on some sort of working basis. He knew by this time that they never would.

His talk with Tony had changed his mind about Penny. He had rated her as innocent and ignorant; he had not suspected shrewdness and treachery. Oh, he'd seen through plenty of her little, more harmless tricks. The way she'd run downstairs in a particularly revealing nightdress and be surprised to run into Jerry Auld in the hall. Her contempt of all other women behind their backs and her guilelessness to their faces. The little games of There's Nothing Wrong with It that she played with various husbands on moonlit porches or in dusky corners. Her scorn for card players after she had tried to learn bridge herself and failed. Little things like that—painful but no bones broken. He now knew that she was capable of trickery on a cosmic scale. Even that he would have tried to overlook had there been one single thing he could point to and say, "Well, she did *this* for me. Shows she's trying to pull her own weight."

She came back ostensibly to tell him that she was taking the car but really to give him a chance to see how well she looked in the new tailored slacks and the too snug sweater. Seeing her smile, he realized that she was thinking of nothing but how pretty she looked and what a wonderful time she was going to have. Infantile, that was the word for her. Some men might find that refreshing. Unfortunately he found it revolting. In a thirty-year-old he liked maturity.

"I'll be home early, dear, but don't wait up for me."

He hadn't waited up for her in years. She was still at her play acting. "If you come home with Jerry you do the driving. He's apt to take a few too many."

Suddenly his curiosity pricked him and he called her back. "Just what is the score between you and Jerry, if you don't mind my asking?"

"We just have a lot of fun together. We like the same crowd and the same movies, and he dances divinely."

"I don't want to be stodgy about this, Penny, but——"

"Darling, there's nothing *wrong* with it."

"When all you can say about a thing is that there's nothing wrong with it, it usually means that you can't find anything that's right with it. I know you haven't slept with him, if that's what you mean. I just wondered what you hoped it would lead to, all this seeing so much of him. Not marriage, I can tell you. Jerry's a cagey boy, and he's pushing forty. If he marries it will be somebody who can do something for Jerry, in the way of money or family or background. He isn't going to sign himself over for a thrill or two. I thought you ought to be warned."

"Angel, how can I marry him when I'm already married to you!"

She ran out, convinced that she had answered his every doubt.

Jerry had had too much to drink, but he insisted on driving.

"Never let a little lady get calluses on her pretty hands when I'm around. Move over, precious."

He drove expertly, as he did everything else, and with the moon as bright as it was, there was really no danger. Perry was an old fuss-budget.

"A penny for your thoughts, Penny?"

She laughed. "You say things so cleverly. Who else would have thought of saying that just that way?"

"Oh, I'm a clever guy, I'll admit it. But that doesn't tell me what you were thinking about."

"I can't tell you. It would make you conceited."

"If you don't I'll stop the car, and little red hen will not get home tonight."

"Horrors, Perry would be furious! Well, I was thinking that there wasn't a place in the world I'd rather be than right here."

"Beside me?"

"Are you conceited?"

"No. I'm delighted."

She patted his arm briefly. "You're nice," she confided. "You're the nicest man I've ever known."

"I don't like to introduce unpleasant subjects, but there's something I'm curious about."

"What?"

"Your husband. Where does he stand in all this?"

"Oh, Perry's all right. It's just that he works so hard and is so tired by dinnertime. He hasn't any time to play with a young, foolish wife who likes to go places and do things."

"But he doesn't object to your finding other playmates?"

"Oh no. He's not at all Victorian."

"Nor jealous?"

"Maybe just a little bit," she confessed prettily.

"And why do you suppose I'm out driving with the gorgeous wife of a jealous man who's twenty pounds heavier than I am? Because I'm crazy."

"Crazy?"

"About you."

Sudden exaltation abolished her breath. He had not committed himself to anything definite before, in the several years she had known him. There had been long meaningful looks and small private jokes and transpicuous smiles between them. It was generally understood that they were great friends, that they liked to dance together, that they singled each other out in a crowd. The women had intimated to Penny that this was natural, seeing that she was his boss's sister-in-law. The men had professed great worry that the two of them were on the verge of elopement. "And then Doc would pull every tooth in Ashland just to get even," they said. "Don't you kids skip town and leave us to a fate like that!" The implication of romance, the hint that Jerry was damming up his emotions because she was un-attainable, had thrilled her. There was not an unmarried girl in town who would not have liked to be in Penny's shoes.

For Jerry Auld was above the usual run of men. His tastes were fastidious, his clothes quietly elegant, his pronunciations crisp, his mind tremendously shrewd and aware. Yet he was not a reader or philosopher. He was a man of action. In his worship of motion he had acquired a facility at bowling, tennis, wrestling, baseball scores, and football standings that commanded the respect of other males with mellower muscles. He treated women as though they were tender darlings that he would be happy to cherish if only he had the right. Thus he was really at his best with married women. When speculation was made on his bachelordom he sighed, as at an old sorrow, and refused to talk. It was inferred that he had been madly in love with a girl in his youth and that something tragic had happened. Actually the confinement of the marital state was unthinkable to him, and he was privately scornful of the men who had allowed themselves to be led inside the stone walls.

Tonight he had drunk more than he usually permitted himself, and the liquor and moonlight conspired to addle his brain. To think that this beautiful girl should be tied to a tired, grouchy old dog of a husband who let her find her own diversions, like a lonely child.

"Poor kid, you don't have much of a life, do you? It's a damned shame."

"I'm used to it, Jerry dear. Oh, I used to hide myself and cry my heart out because there was nobody who really cared about me. If Perry only gave me a kind word once in a while I could stand it. Or if I could have had a little boy to take care of, to laugh with, to put to bed at night." She sighed. "Perry doesn't like children."

"Why do you stay with him? Why don't you go live with Eleanor? She'd take you in."

"That would be worse, really. Eleanor's wonderful, but she's so strait-laced she'd never let me outside the door without her. And I do so enjoy my little brand of harmless fun, being with a crowd and *doing* things. Of course I should have stayed in New York and modeled, as they wanted me to the time I was on the cover of *See Book.*"

"I heard about that. What on earth made you give up a wonderful chance like that?"

She smiled and made a helpless gesture with her hands. "I fell in love, or thought I did."

He swung the wheel of the car and muttered, "We don't have to go right home, do we? Let's go down to my cottage and have a nightcap. You've never been there, have you? It's a nice little place, not far from here."

"Oh, I shouldn't. It's almost midnight."

"Well, from what you tell me, I don't think Perry cares whether you come home or not. There won't be any harm in it. I'll just show you the place, we'll have a drink, and we'll leave. I've never taken anyone else there before."

Her eyes glinted beneath their luxuriant lashes. "I almost believe that you're lonely too. Poor us, each trying to bring our empty ships ashore."

"Almost seems as though we ought to get together, doesn't it?"

She laughed, mischievously. "What would young Nancy Holzworth say to that?"

"Good Lord, she's just a kid! Only reason I see anything of her is because she isn't one of those dead fish that like to sit around in deck chairs. She moves."

"She's young, spirited. Nineteen, isn't she? Four whole years younger than I."

"Listen to the old lady! You know you're ten times as pretty as she is."

"I don't see how I can be. She's led such a protected, sheltered life, and I—well, I've had to pretty much make my own way. It hasn't been easy."

"It's just about time you had a little fun!"

He pulled the car into the shadows of a grove of trees beside the sandy road. They had arrived at the beach. Before them stretched a row of cottages, discreetly spaced. They were all of natural wood, all dark, all alike. The nearest one was some ten feet away.

She got out of the car and stretched her arms to the moon. "Isn't it a gorgeous night, Jerry? I feel as if I'd just been born tonight."

The lines of the upflung torso took his breath. "You're lovely. You're the most beautiful thing I've ever seen."

"You mustn't. You mustn't say things like that."

"Why mustn't I? Say, let's pretend we're kids again. Let's go for a moonlight swim."

She thought unpleasantly of what the water would do to her hair. "We haven't any suits."

"There are some in the house. And what if there aren't? Nobody comes down here at this time of year."

She had a sudden vision of herself walking across the moon-silvered sands, white, flawless, the wind lifting her long, dark red hair, swirling it around her graceful shoulders. Jerry would crumple at her feet, murmuring, "I knew you were beautiful, but I never dreamed you were as beautiful as this. Oh, my darling, leave Perry and marry me."

"Oh, I don't think we . . ." She acted a pink, small confusion.

"Tonight there isn't anyone in the world but just ourselves." He swept her up in his arms. "I'll carry you over the threshold, just as if you were a bride. You'd make such a lovely bride."

"Jerry! How strong you are. Darling, be gentle with me."

He strode down the flagstones, carrying her lightly, and as she nestled against his shoulder she was impassioned, not by his physical presence but by the meaning of his thus throwing his hat over the steeple. In all the hours she had spent musing over him she had never dared hope that he would declare himself in any such open fashion. She had reveled in his flattery, his singling her out for extra attentions, his acting as courtier for her. Since she had estimated her chances of marrying him as forlorn she had been satisfied with the distance between them. Now that the distance was lessening by leaps and bounds she did not object as long as it brought her goal in sight. She was not going to lose her head. When he tried to make love to her she would be hurt, distracted, grieved that he had assessed her so wrongly; and he would hurry to assure her that he wished only to marry her, that the reason he had held off this long was because he had thought his worship hopeless.

She let her hair brush his cheek, wondering whether he would catch her perfume over the liquor on his breath. "So strong!" she repeated against his light shirt.

He squeezed her quickly in corroboration. "There," he said, putting her on her feet by the door of the screened porch. "That'll teach you not to talk back to the master of the house. Enter, Venus!"

"I will, my lord."

As she stepped over the sill the lovely dream turned into a nightmare. Scores of people, herds of them, rose from chairs on every side, and all these people were screaming and chattering and laughing as though they would die of it.

Jack Nixon's voice rose above the rest. "Say, my lord, you've got the wrong cottage. Your place is next door, in case you're too far a-swoon to realize it yourself. But welcome, welcome. And you, Mrs. Wilder, are perfectly free to take that moonlight swim. There are suits in the house, but what if there aren't?"

"Ah there, Venus, will you let me carry you over the threshold?"

A woman shrilled, "Nobody comes down here at this time of year, you know. Nobody except the Women's Club and the Rotary and a few old family reunions!"

"Oh, Jerry, you great big strong boy, you!"

"Be gentle with me, angel, I might break in two!"

Jerry was trying to get them in hand. "I swear there's not a place in town where you can have a minute's privacy, not even the house next door to the one you own! Jack, you didn't ask my permission to have this gang down here. If I'd known they were here I'd have come sooner. Hello there, Jim. Ah, Mrs. Willoughby, can I entice *you* next door?"

They were good-natured, they liked Jerry, they would have sobered down in a minute or two and been good sports about keeping their mouths shut later. They did not want publicity themselves, the Nixon beach parties being notoriously rowdy. But they must have their joke, they must tell how they had seen the car drive up, wondered who it was, and then listened to every word, keeping quiet as mice.

Penny couldn't stand it. She kicked the door open and the look in her eyes drove the laughter from their faces. "I won't stay!" she said. "I'm not going to sit around with a bunch of cheap, spying sneaks. If Jerry wants to associate with riffraff that's his business. I'm going home!"

She flung down the path, listening to the quiet she had left on the porch. Just before she got in the car she heard a man's voice, made small, say, "Izzums mad, then, Daddy's little precious darling?"

She drove away from their new spasm of mirth.

225

For two days she stayed in the house, not daring to brave the amusement of the streets. The news had spread around, all right. Eleanor had brought it to her the afternoon of the next day.

"How could you have been so terribly indiscreet, Penny? You have no idea the awful things people are saying, and how much Jerry is distressed about it. He says it's his fault, he shouldn't have taken you down there in the first place, but that it would have been all right if you hadn't lost your temper. What on earth did you say to those people to make them have it in for you like that?"

"I told them they were a bunch of cheap, sneaking spies, and I'm not sorry. Nobody'll pay any attention to what they say anyway!"

"Well, it's an unfortunate thing all around. When it first began to spread it was a ridiculous joke, but the further it goes the more bite it will have to it. And you don't have many friends stanch enough to stand up and deny it for you, so it will grow and grow from something funny into something hideously immoral. I hope Perry understands about it."

"I haven't mentioned it to him. It's none of his business."

"It would be better if he heard it from you before he hears it from anyone else. He's bound to, you know."

"I don't care if he does. I don't care what he hears or thinks or says. If he hadn't neglected me all these years I wouldn't have been out with Jerry!"

"Penny dear, you won't find much sympathy for that point of view. I do hope you're not planning on talking like that to anyone else. People will say——"

Penny threw back her head defiantly. "I don't have to care what people will say. Jerry just as good as asked me to marry him, and I'm going to do it. I guess they'll laugh on the other side of their silly faces when they know that!"

"Are you sure he—Jerry's a great hand for implying things he can't be held to."

She was in no mood to listen to Eleanor's carping. Jerry had said he was crazy about her, hadn't he? The only reason he hadn't telephoned or tried to see her was that he was waiting for her to make the right move. How could he make her a genuine offer of marriage with Perry still on the scene? That was it! How silly of her not to have seen it before!

Immediately she felt relaxed and blooming and sure, instead of tight and nervous and faded. Perhaps it hadn't been so foolish of her to lose her temper, after all. The more talk there was, the more Jerry would see that there was only one way out of it. She'd tell Perry Wilder what she thought of him this very evening, and then pack her bags and move in with Eleanor. After that Jerry would feel free to communicate with her and they could make plans. She stretched and smiled, visioning the marvelously improved life that was opening ahead of her.

She was packing her bags when Perry came home at six o'clock, and she made enough stir about it so that he paused at the door of her room.

He was not surprised. He said dryly, "Running out? Can't face it?"

She was glad that he knew. It saved explanations. "I'm going to live with Eleanor for a while. My lawyer will get in touch with you."

He leaned against the doorframe. "And what are you going to do after that?"

She shrugged, not looking up from the suitcases. She was taking only her very best things. From now on she could afford better ones.

He was studying her, his face unreadable. "If by any chance you're leaving to save me unpleasantness it isn't necessary. No matter how much people talk, they still like good dental work. And gossip dies down quickly. We can batten down the hatches and weather the storm."

"This has nothing to do with the gossip. I was going to leave anyway. We're just not suited to each other, that's all. You don't understand me, you've never tried to. I'm tired of being neglected or criticized. I don't have to put up with it. There *are* men in the world who like me and say so."

"Jerry Auld?"

"That's none of your affair."

"Listen to me a minute, Mrs. High-and-Mighty. We'll never get along like kittens in a basket, that's true. But I do feel a certain responsibility toward you. Pity too, because you've got such a damnably wrong slant on things. Anyway, I have to know. Has Jerry said in so many words that he wants to marry you?"

She straightened up. "Yes, he has." By this time she was convinced of it.

His shoulders lifted as though a load had been taken from them.

"It's all right then. The grief's all his. What do you want to do about Hetty?"

"Hetty?"

"She's your stepmother, remember?"

"I can't take her along to Eleanor's. She'll just have to look after herself, I guess. After all, I've given her a home for years. She can't expect me to sacrifice my whole life to her."

His smile was abominable. "I'm sure she doesn't expect it. She can stay right here, as far as I'm concerned. I like her."

She commended him, reservedly. "That's nice of you, Perry."

"Don't mention it. Well, I might as well go downstairs and have my dinner."

It was sweet and pathetic of him to mask his grief with this indifference. "I'm sorry, Perry. I loved you a great deal when I married you. I've tried to be patient and thoughtful. Even the greatest love can be abused until it dies."

"Don't give it a thought." He grinned impishly at her around the corner. "Your *really* great love will never die until you do."

She went downstairs and out to her taxi quietly, while the rest of them were eating dinner. No one will ever know, she thought, of this tragic moment when I crept out of the home I had grown to love without so much as a good-by from those to whom I had given so much of myself.

She walked into Eleanor's, crying, "Darling, I've crept away to you. Perry doesn't want me any more, he didn't even say good-by. Say something kind to me, anything! I've been without kindness for so long."

A week went by and there was no word from Jerry. That was natural; he was simply allowing a decent interval to elapse. Perhaps, too, he was hesitating to call her at the Kendricks', to let them in on the private arrangements the two of them must make. When Eleanor suggested that she take a furnished apartment in one of the buildings John owned she accepted eagerly.

"It would be better for me to be somewhere else when John comes home," she said. "I suppose he'll be angry with me for entangling his precious plant manager."

"As long as Jerry stays in town I don't think John will concern himself about the matter." How lucky that Penny was so insensitive to undercurrents, so blind to the strain that Eleanor was undergoing! Sooner or later, however, she would notice that something was wrong. No price was too great to get her out of the house. "You won't have to pay any rent. I can even make you a small allowance to tide you over until you see what you are going to do."

"I don't like to impose on you, Eleanor. I've never been very good at imposing on people, even my own family."

"I know, but this is an emergency. Please let me give you what I can."

She was careful to leave her new telephone number with every servant who might answer that instrument. She scarcely noticed that the new apartment was pretty and modern and at a good address. She unpacked her bags and waited for another week, leaving the telephone only for necessary trips to her lawyer's office. As far as her friends were concerned, she had dropped out of the world. Only Eleanor—and perhaps Jerry—knew where she was.

All at once she could bear it no longer. She called his apartment and there was no answer. She called him at the office and he had "just stepped out." Her rapturous dreams grew thin from lack of nourishment and she slept badly. What in the world was the matter? Why should he be so overcautious now?

On her fourth try the plant telephone operator found him for her.

"Well, Jerry," she said, as pleasantly surprised as though he had called her.

"Hello. Oh, it's you. What have you been doing with yourself?"

"I'm at the Parkside. I've left Perry."

"Say, that's too bad! I hadn't heard about that."

Her heart leaped again. "I've been terribly lonely."

"The bunch hasn't known where you were. They'll be rallying around to see you."

"I'm not much in the mood for them. I'd like to see you when you have a minute. Can you come over for dinner tonight?"

"I have a date for tonight that I can't get out of. Tell you what. I'll give you a ring as soon as I'm a bit more free."

She shivered as she hung up. She felt genuinely ill. He hadn't sounded at all as he should. Of course he'd been talking from the plant and there had been people all around him. That was it! That kind of talk had been for them and he really meant to run up to see her the minute the shop let out!

Almost gaily she spent the next two hours on her hair and face and the adjustment of the turquoise crepe dress he had never seen. Any minute now there would be a ring at her doorbell, and the sight of her would dispel all his uncertainty, if he had any. "Darling, I couldn't say a word I wanted to over that damned phone. You're looking lovelier than ever!"

The early edition of the evening paper had been slipped under her door and she picked it up as she went past. She sat down in the pink chair by the living-room window and lit a cigarette. Then she saw the front page and the cigarette smoldered away into ashes in the tray before she moved again. There were pictures of Jerry and a girl. There was a caption: "Mr. and Mrs. J. E. Holzworth announce the engagement of their daughter Nancy to Jerry Auld, formerly of New York, now a resident of this city. The nuptials are planned for Christmas week. The happy couple received the congratulations of their friends last night at a formal dinner given by the bride-elect's parents."

It was dark before she got up from the pink chair and went to bed.

16.

It took Martha a year and a half to realize that good housekeeping is a trade that requires ten years of apprenticeship for any considerable degree of efficiency and that those years, for the best results, should be early, malleable ones; that, hard as she tried, she would never be a good housekeeper; that, except for cooking, housework was dull, monotonously repetitious, and boring; that to be what the magazines extolled as a "homemaker" was to be a cheerful little drudge who gloried in getting the right kind of wax for her kitchen floor ("my neighbors couldn't believe the difference") and then hurried to smooth the right kind of lotion on her hands so her husband ("Jack was ashamed of my red, rough hands at the bridge table") might keep his illusion of her as a smooth, pretty creature who lived a life of luxurious idleness on his money.

"Though he must know his wife is doing the scrubbing," she told Bill, "because if he were paying for a maid he'd know it, wouldn't he? Still, a man who would marry a girl who spent her time worrying about what kind of soap to use for the washing and who asked for a good vacuum cleaner for Christmas would be stupid enough for anything."

Bill frowned, and she wished she had not tried to make a joke on the subject. It was a tender and puzzling spot with him. How could marrying a man who earned a good salary and was going up the ladder be a comedown to a woman? Yet for Martha it had been. Without his meaning to, without his thinking about it, he had taken her from a life of physical ease and mental stimulation to one of dirty dishes and dust on the typewriter, and that knowledge made him miserable no matter how she skirted a reference to it.

He stopped the power mower, sat down in a deck chair beside her, and gave her a cigarette. For a few minutes they watched the sunset flare across the wide lawns and burn against the old apple trees that made gracious circles around the interloping houses and then marched up and over the little hills. There was a legend that Johnny Appleseed had planted those trees, and Martha liked to believe it, even though her common sense told her that the trees weren't old enough for that.

Anyway, she loved living in Orchardia. It was a unique little town. Only ten miles outside one of the largest cities in the world, it drowsed among its cupping hills, ignorant of factory smoke or traffic noise. The old part of town, which included the grocery store, the general store, the post office, and six or seven old red brick gabled houses, was the nucleus that had caught a clever real estate man's eye. He had bought up the farm lands for miles around, parceled them into one-acre tracts, and sold them to people who worked in Laketown but loved the country. Only better than average incomes could afford this luxury, and so the widely scattered houses were big and had had the benefit of an architect's hand and skillful landscaping that blended with the intervening orchard and meadows. Martha thought it the most beautiful place in the world.

After so many years of apartment living the Cape Cod house Bill had bought for them seemed tremendous. And after so much craning for a sight of greenery an acre of your own seemed untold lavishness. Here she could watch the sun and the moon at will and see the weather and the birds and plant all the flowers she wanted. Here the snow stayed white and the only smoke was from wood-burning fireplaces or from some neighbor's outdoor barbecue rack. A dog might bark, children would laugh, bridles would jingle past early in the morning or late at night, and the quiet and serenity seemed to wrap your every nerve with plush.

She said, "Let's never live anywhere else, Bill."

"Before God, Martha, if there was a maid to be had we'd have her! You oughtn't to be sweating your life out over a house. You're *somebody* and I've turned you into a slavey. Don't think I don't know how you must resent it. Why, even if you didn't want to write, you could go out and get yourself a job that'd pay you a handsome salary any time you wanted to. Why should you have to turn into a dishwasher for me?"

"You mustn't fret. Everybody's in the same boat. When the war's over I'll find myself a housekeeping paragon and go back to writing."

He slumped down in his chair. "But the war may last for years yet, and by that time you'll hate me—not for anything I've done but for what I've kept you from doing."

"Foolish!"

"I don't know that it is. I've never yet seen a brilliant woman who seemed to be happily married. Either the marriage or the brilliance seems to have to go by the board."

"I'm not as brilliant as all that. If I wanted to work I could. We could polish the house together when we got home and eat our meals out. And we'd both be exhausted all the time and we couldn't entertain and—oh, it'd be the gypsy kind of life that I've always hated. I'd rather stick it out this way until help arrives."

His cigarette made a live arc against the dusk. "Remember that you said that, won't you?"

"I'll remember."

She could have told him about one thing that would have made her life easier, but it would have meant altering an integral part of him and she loved him too much to ask the sacrifice. He liked people, he throve on crowds, he had a habit of making friends. That much was fine. Unfortunately he liked best to see them in his own home.

"Have dinner with us tomorrow night," he would say to a couple he had met but once. Or "Let's round up a few people for a poker game." He knew everyone in Orchardia and called most of them by their first names. They thought he was a fine fellow, they stopped him for an hour's chat as he went by, they felt free to visit the Knight house any hour of the day or night.

So that first year and a half she made gallons of coffee every week, cut miles of sandwiches, whipped quarts of cream. The grocery bills were tremendous. The furniture acquired stains and cigarette burns and an aged look. Almost every morning she spent her first three hours emptying ash trays, vacuuming, washing dishes and glasses, removing the traces of the mob that had surged in the evening before.

He was contrite when she looked tired. "I'm sorry, kid. I shouldn't have asked them in, I guess. Here, you run on up to bed and I'll clear away."

"It's two o'clock. You'll never be able to get up in the morning. We'll just stack them and I'll take care of them in the morning."

"Well, don't get up to get my breakfast. I'll eat downtown. Sleep late, won't you? You look all worn out. I swear I won't ask another soul in here for a year!"

But he couldn't help it. If it wasn't friends it was his boss, or the vice-president and his family, or the men who were responsible for his biggest accounts, or the men at the office whose wives were out of town, or . . .

"I almost have to have them, Martha. This kind of thing helps me in my business."

It did, she knew. She knew also that he would have done it anyway. He was in love with the human race.

It would be easier to love the human race if you didn't have to wait on it, she decided. She did not say this. She would not have stamped out one bit of his warmth and geniality for the world. Sooner or later he would see that he was putting too great a load on an inexperienced hand. After a while he'd realize that if she were ever going to write again she'd have to have a breathing space. He was just a long time getting around to seeing it, that was all.

Physically they suited each other perfectly, and this was due to the time and trouble Bill spent on her sexual education. She had studied biology, could draw endless diagrams of various types of reproductive systems, and was as ignorant of the personal bylaws as a studious child. He was a gentle and considerate lover; he taught her

233

that, among the higher grade of human being, one must love with the mind before one could love with the body.

"There's a spiritual catharsis that goes with it," he said. "Otherwise it's no good."

From listening to the frank talk on marital relations among the women of her acquaintance she learned that she was lucky in having that part of her life on such a gloriously sane and healthy basis. Few of these women had experienced the tremendous, rushing sweep of sensation that Martha had. Many of them had heard of such a thing, and when their husbands did not arouse it they pretended it anyway.

Mrs. Burns, thirty-five and the mother of two children, was ribald about it. "Oh, I make Allen think he's a great man, all right," she said. "Actually, as a bedtime occupation, I'd prefer an apple and a newspaper."

Martha had read Freud and Havelock Ellis, but she had never thought of their case histories as commonplace, everyday records of people she might know. Now she saw that sexual maladjustment for women was the rule rather than the exception; that the male, excusing himself everything on the grounds that he was no longer brutal about it, was too careless or ignorant or self-centered to know or care whether his wife enjoyed his love-making; that if his ego had permitted him to admit that there was a lack of rapture he would be at a loss as to how to inspire it. The women, left wishful and quenchless, curled greedy fingers at every attractive man who came in sight. Not knowing just what they were missing, they still kept trying to find it.

Because Bill Knight was handsome and courteous and genial they chose him for a target. One or the other of them was always trying to cut him out of the crowd, to sequester him in the study or the kitchen. They telephoned him on the slightest pretext. They danced with him languishingly. They said, "I'm going to be downtown shopping tomorrow, Bill. Can I have lunch with you?" They cooed and crooned over him, making sly eyes at Martha to see how she was taking it.

While she was with them she pretended placidity. To her husband she raged, "How do they have the nerve to act like that under my very nose? What do they hope to gain by it? Not my friendship, certainly, nor a welcome sign on my doormat!"

It turned out that there was a code of amorous ethics that must be adhered to. A wife was supposed to be a "good sport." It was not

234

good taste for her to be jealous of or unfriendly to the women who were doing their level best to make Bill find them seductive. She should do everything in her power to make them feel pleasantly welcome while they disported themselves. If she could honestly ignore it or, better still, make herself enchanting to one of the other husbands, so much the better.

"I have to play up," Bill said. "It would look pretty silly if I didn't. A man isn't supposed to run away from these little ravishments. The other men would laugh him out of town."

"You mean they *like* to have you paw their wives?"

"Well, makes them feel the old girl still has what it takes. It's a form of flattery to have other men appear to think your wife attractive."

"How uncomplimented *you* must have been feeling! All I've rated from your gentlemen friends is a kind word or two."

He laughed. "That's because you don't invite more than that. You have an air about you, I don't know what it is, independence, reserve, a kind of integrity, maybe, that absolutely precludes dalliance. I keep wondering how I was brave enough to try it myself."

"I can understand dalliance well enough if there's a purpose behind it—marriage or seduction, or something logical like that. But these women can't marry you, and I can't think that they are seriously trying to seduce you. In fact I don't know what they're after."

"A little excitement, darling. It's just a game with them. You're taking it far too seriously."

She frowned in concentration. "And what if one of them really does succeed in making you think that you'd be better off with her than with me? Then it would be my fault for letting things come to such a pass, wouldn't it?"

"You don't have to worry about that. Anybody who's lived with you for a while would find these other women as flat as soup without salt. They're simple, uninvolved. If I live with you for sixty years you'll still be able to surprise and delight me." He drew a hassock beside her chair and sat down on it. "I love you, Martha." There was no varnish on his voice. He spoke to no one else like this.

"I know."

"Then try to take it for granted, won't you, even though I don't get around to saying it more than a couple of times a week?"

She leaned over to kiss him. "I'll try. It's just that I get mixed up."

235

"I don't blame you. It's confusing for you, because you're not like the rest of them. You're the new woman, darling. We haven't got around to making rules for you yet."

"I'm no crusader. As long as the rules around here agree with me I'm willing to let the other women work out their own problems."

"And don't let these other girls get under your skin. It pleases them too much to see they're annoying you."

She made new resolutions of tolerance and understanding, but they were somewhat marred by an incident that occurred in her dining room the Wednesday evening of that week. The crowd in the living room were clamoring for highballs, and Bill went out to the buffet to mix them. Connie Abend, one of the more relentless pursuers, slipped around the corner after him, declaring her intention to aid the host. Ten minutes later Martha started for the kitchen and the bowl of potato chips.

She stopped dead at what she saw in the shadows of the dining-room alcove. Bill was standing there with the tray of drinks in his hands, but his head was bent down with the pressure of Connie's arms and they were deep in a kiss. At her gasp they looked up, Bill with embarrassment, Connie triumphantly, patronizingly. The woman was so unafraid that she continued to let one arm lie around Bill's neck.

Martha walked over to them, smiling. She picked one of the drinks up from the tray. "It's warm in here," she said mildly. She lifted the whisky and soda and poured it on the top of Connie's head. "You'll find it cooler now, I think."

Connie hissed like a cat, leaping away, one hand endeavoring to dam the cascade that was staining her light crepe, the other shoving back her wet, straggling locks. "What do you think you're doing!" she shrieked. "Why, I never in my life——"

To the crowded doorway that faced the tableau Martha explained innocently, "She seemed to be in a terribly overworked state. I was only trying to bring her back to normal." She turned back to Connie, beaming. "I suppose you'll never forgive me. Don't even try."

Connie walked out of the house, screaming her intention of never returning, her husband trailing dazedly in her wake. Bill set the tray down and laughed until he cried. He had to explain over and over again just what had happened, until all the men were laughing with him and even the women giggled, though apprehensively. Martha went on out to the kitchen to get the potato chips and found herself a heroine by the time she returned.

"Vixen!" Bill said.

"Not at all. I thought the woman must be having a seizure."

Thereafter parties at the Knights' were conducted on more decorous lines.

They had lived in their house for more than a year before Martha met the man next door. Bill brought him in out of a pink and green summer evening.

"Dr. O'Malley," he announced. "The vanishing American. The man you never see."

The doctor smiled apologetically. "I made a bad choice in my field. There's no more interminable job than delivering babies. I can't seem to persuade the mothers to have them in my regular hours."

"He's head of obstetrics at Stoneview," said Bill. "And what do you know? He comes from Ashland!"

She liked him on sight: his quiet gravity, his quick eyes, his slow smile, his deft economy of motion. The two of them plunged into reminiscence as easily as though they had known each other twenty years.

"Your husband says your maiden name was King. I don't remember any Kings. Of course I haven't been in Ashland for fifteen years. There would be a great many people from there that I wouldn't know."

"My sister Eleanor married John Kendrick. Perhaps you knew her?"

"I know the Kendricks." He mused. "Yes, I think I recall your sister. Tall, slender, dignified girl she was. I delivered her first baby."

"She has two. They're half grown up by now."

"I imagine so. It was a long time ago. How did the babies turn out?"

He remembered a great deal more than he was pretending, she sensed that. A man like this would have had a few words to say about the regime to which the Kendrick babies had been subjected from birth. "Not very satisfactorily. About as most children turn out, let's say."

"Don't tell me that you're not optimistic about the methods of child rearing employed by most of the women of our great nation! Surely mother love is too sacred a thing to need instruction."

"I've met a good many mothers who couldn't teach a child anything —good manners or how to spell c-a-t."

He did not smile but his eyes were sparkling. "Education is the function of the school, Mrs. Knight."

"Education is the function of the home. All the school dispenses is instruction."

They did not notice when Bill went back to mowing the lawn. They were off on the subject, hammer and tongs. The doctor had a vigorous and stimulating mind and she found that there were many things she did not have to put into words for his comprehension. He got them by inference, by spontaneous thought process. With him a discussion did not plod; it ran so fast that you had to let yourself out to keep up with it.

"Why don't you write something about this?" he said. "I've read you in the *Chronicle*. I think this would be a good subject for your particular approach."

"No time."

"You must take time. Nothing can be more important to you than to go on with your work."

"Are you married, Dr. O'Malley?"

"No. I have an elderly woman who keeps house for me. She tries to keep me informed as to how the other half lives."

"Is she good at her job? Sails right through a day's work?"

"She appears to."

"Then she couldn't appreciate my problem. She's a past mistress at the art. I'm a novice. She'd laugh if she knew how long it takes me to iron a shirt."

"Just as you'd laugh if you knew how long it takes her to write a letter to her sister."

"Oh no. I don't write easily either. With me it's a long, hard, slow business."

"Could you do it in the evenings, after dinner?"

"There are usually swarms of people all over the place. And we have to make the rounds of their houses once in a while too. It makes for a full life, in the worst sense of the word."

"See them once a week and write the other nights."

"And what will Bill find to do while I'm writing?"

"His boredom is not too great an offering to be placed on the altar of the Muse."

He made it sound so possible, so plausible, that she could find but one other objection. "Well, I'd like to write an essay on the subject of women, but the theme has drawbacks. In the first place there's so much written about and for women, whole magazinefuls of it. How to be prettier, how to be a better cook, how to make yourself more attractive to your husband. The wordage is inordinate!" She paused. "Come to think of it, men don't allow themselves to be gushed over and preached at like that. I don't believe I've ever seen a single magazine article for men on how to be handsomer or how to be a better husband."

He took his pipe from his mouth. "That's because we men are all handsome, and in the few cases when we do not make excellent husbands we blame it on our wives."

"And all this preachment to women is written in a kind of baby talk, a sort of Kallikak English. Darling, ravishing, glorious, breathtaking, glamorous, the new silhouette, stunning, pert, a love of a dress—you know the kind of thing. Mine would be plain and in the mother tongue and nobody would read it."

"You'll have to find a better excuse than that."

"All right, there's this: the subject's a touchy one, likely to arouse antagonism. I don't want howling publicity and mockery down upon my head. I'm a peaceful soul."

That night, however, she wheeled the typewriter table from its corner, dusted the machine, and laid a fresh pile of paper beside it for an early start in the morning.

Three hours a day was the minimum of time in which she could produce five or six pages that might be worth reading. Morning was the best time to work because she was rested then and her faculties were at their sharpest. Evenings were no good at all; the intense concentration wilted her already fatigued body and set her nodding within an hour.

She made a rigid schedule for herself. Bill left the house at seven-thirty, and the dishes were done, the beds made, and a cursory dusting accomplished by nine. From nine to twelve she sat at the typewriter, surrounded by sheets of paper and her reference books, ignoring the telephone and the doorbell. At noon she made herself a cup of coffee and a sandwich and took them out on the lawn when the weather was pleasant. Until one o'clock she relaxed, easing the tired muscles in her neck and shoulders, making her mind idle down to the planning of her grocery list, reveling in her short hour in the sun. After that she had to hurry. Sometimes there were things to be washed or ironed—things you couldn't trust to the laundry—or the kitchen or bathroom to be scrubbed or the marketing to be done or the rooms vacuumed, and always and always dinner had to be ready at six o'clock. And after she and Bill had done the dishes there were the flower borders to weed or the beetles were after the roses again.

There were certain things that the schedule would not permit. Baking was one of them, the one she regretted most because she liked to cook, was good at it. Fresh bouquets for the house took too much time to arrange, and she let that go reluctantly too. Her other omissions weighed on her mind rather than her heart. The screened porch and the basement didn't get the scrubbings they should have; the house looked bare with its vases and ornaments put away to save dusting; the two bedrooms she had closed off upstairs hurt her conscience; and no matter what she did, she never seemed to be caught up. Sometimes she thought she was, and then she would notice that the curtains were gray and limp or that there was a sizable spot of ink on the rug or that the windows had turned splotchy with the last rain.

"You never get through," she said to Bill. "That's the awful thing about a house. You do something for it and right away it's all to do over again."

"Don't let it worry you, honey. Forget about it. How's the opus coming along?"

"Good."

"Atta girl."

She thought of the canned fruit he had had for dessert and the really noble way he had refrained from giving invitations for the last few weeks.

"You're awfully nice, Bill. There isn't another man in the world who'd put up with this."

He grinned. "That's the kind of talk I like to hear. Tell me some more about how wonderful I am."

"You are. I don't know why. Most men would be furious."

"Because the hotel service around here isn't what it used to be? I married you for company, not for comfort."

"Most men insist on both."

"What's this 'most men' I'm hearing so much about? I'm not most men. I'm exceptional. I thought you knew."

He would not let her be grateful to him. "Hell, Martha, you'd have to shove a pile of dust right under my nose before I'd notice it. I don't care if the damned house falls apart as long as we're both happy."

She appreciated the full extent of his self-discipline only on the evening she met him at the door with the news that the essay was finished.

"You don't mean it!"

"At long last. It's all over."

"Well, what are we standing here for? Let's have dinner in a hurry and run over to the Bennetts' to play some bridge."

"Wonderful!"

He broke his own record by inviting people in for six nights in a row. She baked, she cut fresh flowers, she scrubbed the porch, she opened the two bedrooms, she put the knickknacks back in place. Nothing was said about her starting on a new article. Well, that was all right. She had earned a little vacation from the typewriter, and it was fun to see Bill so gay again.

"Women and the Twentieth Century" was published in full, all nine thousand words of it, in the New York *Chronicle* magazine section the first week in October. By the time it appeared she had forgotten all about it, for once a rounded thesis left her typewriter she dismissed it from her mind.

She had written in part:

What are the commonest complaints about women? That they are vain, silly, incapable of logic; that, when they are young, they are full of romantic daydreams and resentful of any perseverance that might detract from the pinkness of their emotional haze; that, married, they make incompetent mothers and household managers; that they cannot bear to turn their grown children free, preferring to fatten vicariously on the younger lives; that they judge by foolish standards, putting baubles above kindness, "good family" ahead of character, beauty before virtue; that, after their children are married and gone, they complain that they have nothing more in life to sustain them, nothing to interest or amuse them, nothing to do with their time; that their greatest tragedy is the loss of their youthful appearance and that, in reality, they never mature because maturity is ungirlish, a sign of approaching decrepitude. Thus they have no period of mellowing that comes with the graceful acceptance of time.

The small green apples wither on the tree and finally fall, still unripe, a reproach to the blossom that produced them.

None of these characteristics are of sexual denomination, they are not inherent or hereditary. They are the products of ignorance and dependence. They are found more usually in the female because of the environment, the ideology, the training in which she is fostered. Intelligence does not enter into the question. No matter how fine the mind, if it is reared in servility and reliance it will function in those traditions.

It is easy to see why men like the idea of women being inferior to themselves and why they should encourage the continuance of that inferiority. It enables the weakest of men to be a colossus to his wife. It is more difficult to see why women should encourage a like idea, but they do. As a general rule women do not like each other very much. Among themselves they are jealous and quarrelsome. They are contemptuous of their own and other women's opinions, but they will listen with bated breath while a man talks. They envy as the gem of their sex the woman who can attract the most men, who can pick and choose from a host of beseeching beaux, who marries as shrewdly as may be, and who, by flattery and scheming, twiddles her way through life with the minimum of mental and physical effort. They have nothing but scornful pity for the few women who can and do stand on their own feet in any cosmic weather.

All this is not too far from the harem, the concubines, the favorite wife, the struggle to gain the attention of the caliph. It is the distilled essence of all slave psychology, the fawning, the flattery, the wiliness, the quick envy of the other slaves, the reliance on the master, the indifference to individual effort and self-respect.

If this is the woman you want, she is here and has always been. The faults of which you complain spring from the limitations that have bound her from her birth. Though she loves her chains and would hug them to her were you to try to take them away suddenly, time is loosening them. A few have had a breath of fresh air from the larger world outside the narrow window, and they find it infinitely more stimulating than the close, warm muskiness of the zenana. Your daughters will be more self-sufficient than your wives, and this is an excellent trend.

Why should the world be deprived of the mental strength of half its inhabitants? If woman did nothing else, there is at least one problem she could solve: if women were in equal political ascendancy with men all over the world—a right they must earn by intelligent action, for it cannot be bestowed—would there be any more wars? Never. War is an unthinkable insult to their sex, because it destroys their chief work so carelessly and lavishly. No sensible woman would—if she could contrive the power to refuse—risk exchanging her son, representative of some twenty years of her care and thought, for a slip of paper which tells her how expertly she had wrought a man now dead. Men do not know, have never known, the value of human life; but any woman can tell you its price, and her voice needs badly to be heard in this chaotic world.

Bill said, "This is a bombshell. You'll hear from this."

"Do you think it's good?"

"I don't set myself up as a literary critic, but if good writing consists in making yourself plain, then this is good writing. But a lot of people are going to disagree with you. They're going to disagree with you so strongly that I advise you to slip on a false mustache before you go to the grocery store after this."

She looked at him quickly. "You're really bothered about this, aren't you, Bill? You'd rather I hadn't written it."

"No. I'm just a little worried about the repercussions among our friends. After all, you've said that women are ignorant and that men try to keep them that way so they'll be content to play second fiddle in the race for the power and the glory. Well, that's not going to make most of the people we know feel good."

"Most of the people we know won't read it."

"Don't kid yourself. They're not as illiterate as all that."

She was aghast. "I didn't mean—it's only that not so many people take the *Chronicle* out here."

"Sometimes I think you don't give 'em enough credit. Take the other evening, when Mr. Bender was explaining about the situation in China. You kept asking him questions and getting him all mixed up until he was pretty sore. And Carl Bender's lived in China for the last ten years!"

"If he'd lived there a hundred years he wouldn't have known anything about it! Mr. Bender is the kind of man who builds a little hill of his prejudices against the yellow race, any religion but the Christian, what he thinks is communism, and anything he doesn't quite understand. And he hugs this hill to him and crouches down behind it and wherever he is the view is always the same. He didn't have a single notion that there were conflicting ideologies in China, that she's hovering between feudalism and the machine age, that——"

"All right. I'll grant that Carl doesn't have the time to read everything in the world the way you do, but there was still no reason to offend him."

"I didn't mean to offend him. I was just asking for information. When I found he couldn't give me any I kept quiet."

"What I'm getting at is that I think it's wiser to avoid controversial subjects if you want to keep your friends."

She stared at him bleakly. "All subjects are controversial. And if Mr. Bender can't take part in a mild adult discussion without being offended it's because he's too lazy to try to find some pillars of logic to bolster up those mirages that he calls his opinions. What you're really trying to say is that you wish I wouldn't talk so much."

"It isn't that you talk so much. It's the things you say when you do talk. Now I'm willing to coast along with the question of who's going to win the pennant or the best way to grow grass in the shade or the latest war news, things that most people feel the same way about. But you're always getting into something like child psychology or what the New Deal is all about or how socialized medicine is working out in Russia, and those are all subjects on which people have very decided opinions."

"I don't pick those subjects. It always starts by someone making a sweeping statement like 'Roosevelt's done this country more harm than good' or 'How'd you like the government to tell you who's going to fix your teeth or take out your appendix?' All I do is try to find out what makes them say things like that. That's permissible, isn't it? You wouldn't think anyone would start something like that if he weren't prepared to back it up, would you? That's why I like to talk to Dr. O'Malley. I don't always agree with him, but he knows what he thinks and why he thinks it and he doesn't use catch phrases and half-baked popular slogans for his opinions."

"We can't all be giant brains, you know."

She rose. "I guess I'll go to bed."

"Don't be sore now." He came over to put his arms around her. "How'd we ever get into this mess?"

"We got into it because you don't care what I think or if I think, as long as I give no indication of thinking. Considering that everything I've done in my life has been pointed toward learning to think straight and being articulate about it on occasion, it's a blow. You've made me feel like something on a soapbox, and I'm not like that at all and it isn't fair."

"What I meant was——"

"What you meant was that your wife should be sweet, bland, polite, and shallow. You want her varnished with the orthodox veneer. Well, I can act that way. I'm always willing to oblige."

She cried that night for the first time since her father had died.

The effect of this rift in the lute was to make her self-conscious. Bill's charge of mental snobbery had horrified her and, though she was positive that she had not been guilty of it, it repressed her, made her more silent, drugged her spontaneity, forced her to consider twice her slightest remark. Worse than that, Bill seemed to see no change in her. As far as he was concerned, he had apologized for his part in the quarrel and they were back on their old footing. She mused ruefully that, if she could thus conceal half herself from him without his noticing, then he must never have seen that half at all or disliked what he had seen of it. Uneasy and uncomfortable, she waited for some sign from him.

The sign was in the nature of a thunderbolt. It came on his return from a business trip that had taken him through Ashland. He had had dinner with John and Eleanor, and Penny had been there. It was the first time he had met her sisters and he could not say enough about them.

"You didn't tell me that Eleanor lived in a mansion! Kendrick must be a millionaire."

"I'm surprised that he was there. He's in New York most of the time. How are they all? I must go down. I haven't seen them in such a long time."

"You could have come with me, honey, if I'd had an idea I was going near the place. The minute all these shortages let up we'll go."

"What did they say when you told them who you were?"

"They were bowled over. Penny said that she'd begun to think I was a myth. There's a beautiful woman for you! Easy to get along with too. Talks about anything you want to talk about, laughs in the right places. Those two husbands of hers must have been awful duds. She told me that she'd been through hell. 'I've always had poor taste in men,' she said, 'but I think now it's improving.' The way she looked at me when she said it—well, it wasn't a sister-in-law look."

"I can imagine."

"She didn't bear them any ill will though. Her first husband—Tony something or other—was killed at Pearl Harbor, and she was wearing black for him. Sensitive, emotional sort of kid. What are those guys in Ashland thinking about to let a girl like that stay unmarried for the last couple of years? What more do they want?"

"Most of the men her age are already married, and the rest of them are away at war. And I guess she's antagonized a lot of people in the town, one way or another. She doesn't go out much, Eleanor says."

"She's working. Manages some of Kendrick's apartments for him, collects rents, takes care of complaints, that kind of thing. She doesn't like it much. Told me she'd rather be fussing around a house. 'I wish I were strong-minded and independent like Martha,' she said. She certainly admires you, I could tell that."

She looked at him to see if he were joking. No. He meant every word of it. Penny must be as beautiful as ever.

"We've never gotten along particularly well, except when we were children. I like her well enough. I can't say that I admire her."

He winked at her. "A little jealous, maybe? I suppose most women are."

For a moment her dammed-up honesty threatened to break through the restraining gates. That he thought so little of her capacities that he could imagine that she would be jealous of selfish, empty, man-mongering, pretty Penny!

She said quietly, "She is very pretty. I'm sorry I don't look more like her perhaps. I've always felt closer to Eleanor."

"I can see how you would. She's just about the nicest girl I've ever met. Makes you feel right at home, can't do enough for you, and the way she runs that big place is a marvel. Two youngsters nearly grown up she said she had too. Penny might be the perfect girl friend, but Eleanor's the perfect wife." He meditated this. "Yep. If a young man could get past Penny's glamor he'd show good sense in marrying Eleanor. Imagine finding two such peaches in the same family!"

"Yes indeed."

"Hey! I was being impersonal and excepting present company. I've met girls as pretty as Penny and as nice as Eleanor. I married you, thank God."

She did not thank him for the afterthought. The ache in her heart was unbearable. Always she had considered herself the luckiest of the three. She had told herself that Penny's only capital was beauty and time would spend that. She had pitied Eleanor for the thorough and ungracious way in which John had exploited her. She had believed that the treasures of the mind were the only insurance against boredom and futility. Yet this was the second time that Bill had shown her that a woman's mind was the least ornament she might possess, even a defect perhaps.

She tested this, pressing her breast against the sword. "What did you talk about?"

"You. Politics. The war. Oh, we went on at a great rate."

"Did Penny and Eleanor talk about politics?"

"No, John and I wrestled with those. But they seemed to take an intelligent interest."

She couldn't resist. "You mean they agreed with you?"

He laughed. "I guess so and ouch! Led me into that one in fine shape, didn't you?"

"It wasn't hard."

"Meeting your sisters made me feel bad though."

"Why?"

"Well, they have such easy lives. All Penny has to think about are her clothes and her facials, and Eleanor has everything handed to her on a silver platter. You have to work around here—matter of fact you've had to work for everything you've ever had—and, compared to them, you don't have anything. It doesn't seem fair."

Almost she cried out, "You fool, I have ten times as much as Eleanor can ever have, and you ought to see it and pity her, not me!" Instead she said, "Well, I'm glad you liked them so much."

That night she dreamed she was wandering weaponless on a battlefield where troops of women hurled themselves at each other and she, as the only one unarmed, was the surest victim.

17.

Secretly, resentfully, she went back to her typewriter in the mornings, this time to write and re-edit and polish a sufficient number of essays to make up the book the publishers had asked her for long ago. She did not tell Bill what she was doing, and she neither asked for nor got quarter. People came in, she and Bill went out, they kept late hours, the household chores weighed on her more heavily than ever, but stubbornly she sat down at her desk at nine o'clock every day but Sunday.

The strain made her nervous and irritable, no matter how hard she tried to conceal it. In the evenings she watched every highball glass, every dish, every fleck of ash, conjecturing how long it would take her to clean it up the next day, how much precious time it would take from the book. When Bill suggested that they buy a puppy she looked at him as though he had gone insane. The noise of a knife dropping to the floor could shake her to tears.

Bill was alarmed. "You're not a bit like yourself, honey. Better go see a doctor."

"I'm all right. Just tired."

He hesitated. "I'm not going to be around home here much for the next two or three months. Just heard today. They want to send me out to help set up the new branches, and I'd just get home week ends. It's a promotion really, but I'm not going to go away with you all sick and shaky."

He was going to be away! No more late hours, no more cleaning up after crowds, no more six o'clock dinner, no more anything but herself and the book! Delight flooded into her face, making it rosy and luminous. "Bill, how wonderful!"

He thought she was admiring his new prominence, but where she was concerned he had strong intuitions and they made him uneasy now. "It would be cheering if you could add that you were going to miss me."

"You don't know how much." She was careful to keep the irony out of her voice. Nevertheless he sniffed at the sentence as a bird dog does at a scent too far away to identify.

"It's all right with you then. I'll tell 'em I'll go?"

"Of course, silly. I'll be perfectly all right."

"Promise me one thing. Go down to the hospital with Doc O'Malley some morning and have a checkup."

"If it'll make you feel better."

With his departure she forgot that promise in the luxury of days that stretched out twenty-four hours long, to be used as she pleased. She lived in the study, the kitchen, the bedroom, and the garden. She went to bed at nine and got up at five. The book grew to a size respectable enough to be titled. *Positive Answer* she decided to call it, and she gloated over the pages, turning the paragraphs lovingly, edging the sentences, brushing away even the slightest lint of ambiguity. What they had told her at the university was the truth: the only way to learn to write was to write. Her work was improving with every week of concentration, she could see that for herself. If she could have another ten years of days like these to devote to it, who could tell? She might even be able to make a permanent place for herself in American letters!

Saturday mornings she got up at four to have the house—the infernal, the inevitable house—immaculate for Bill's arrival at noon. She enjoyed the flurry of excitement that attended his coming, she relaxed and laughed and talked and hurried and devoted herself to his company for thirty-six hours. And by the time she went down to the station with him Sunday night she was ready to have him go.

He said, "It would be nice if you could contrive to look just the least little bit lonely when you wave at me through the window."

"I keep thinking that you'll be home again next Saturday."

"You don't have to be so damned Spartan about it. Have you had that checkup yet?"

"I haven't had a minute."

"That's nonsense. You must have a lot of time on your hands. What do you——"

"He's calling your train! Good-by, sweet."

On one of these occasions he refused to budge. He planted his feet on the marble floor of the station and put both hands on her shoulders. "Is anything wrong, Martha? I can't stand much more of this. You act as if you didn't care anything about me at all."

"Bill, this is no time——"

"There's never a time. Do you love me?"

She looked up at him gravely, honestly. "If I didn't I wouldn't be living with you. I love you. You're the only person left in the world that I do love."

And, she thought, driving herself home in the car, it would be much better for me if I didn't.

"Women and the Twentieth Century" had stirred up a hornets' nest. Invitations for her to speak came in from women's clubs from coast to coast. She was urged by the Laketown chapter of the University Women's Club to join them. Two leading literary magazines solicited her for further discussion of the topic. All these she declined for the sake of *Positive Answer.*

But she could not get away from the letters. They came in a trickle at first, then in a stream, then in a tide. She read them all, out of conscience and curiosity, and they stunned and disturbed her with their high emotional pitch. Some thought she was right, some thought she was wrong, but they had in common an intensity that indicated prejudice rather than reason.

A woman in Denver wrote:

It's easy to see that you are a sour old maid who couldn't get herself a man, and that's why you're so against them. If you were a womanly woman you'd find that things are all right as they are. I don't have any letters to put after my name, I had to quit school in the tenth grade, but I have a husband and four kids who think the world and all of me and that's enough for me.

An Ohio lawyer said that he'd had a good laugh out of the article.

You certainly are right when you say that women are a featherheaded, backbiting crowd who think they're God Almighty, when in reality they're a feeble-minded lot who don't know anything and don't want to know anything and who resent being "talked down to." I don't share your optimism about their educatability. As long as there's a male who will have them for their long eyelashes, they'll specialize in long eyelashes rather than turning into citizens and digging into the world's problems.

And from the dean of women at a Western university:

We are progressing, but the progress is slow. As I see it, the problem of women might be compared to the problem of the Negro. In both cases the incentive to self-betterment (in a serious sense) is weak because, once educated or polished or well informed, there is no place for them to go. Once we get over our idea that women and Negroes should be servants, once we make their potential goals as varied and high as those of white males, we will see more and more outstanding characters rising from their ranks.

Everyone had an answer. All the answers were different.

Only three of the women she knew personally gave any sign that she had written such a thing. Sally Simpson—Mrs. Hogarth Simpson III—was prettily condescending.

"Oh, if you'd only waited until you had a baby or two you'd have felt so differently. I was restless when I was first married—of course

I was only eighteen then—and I thought I'd just die sitting around all day waiting for Hogie to come home. And his mother—yes, she lives with us—got on my nerves till I thought I'd scream! But then I got pregnant and right away nothing was too good for me and instead of being treated like an old shoe I got some consideration, believe me! And now I have the three youngsters and they're such a joy and Hogie thinks I'm so smart to keep looking young and pretty and have things fixed so I can drop everything and go with him when I want to, which is most of the time. I think a woman has a duty to herself not to get dull and stodgy and a stay-at-home. First thing you know some bright girl with a good line and a nice figure will have your husband and then where will you be?"

It turned out that Sally's mother-in-law had full charge of the children and a colored woman ran her house and another woman came in to do the washing and ironing and Sally, having delegated authority so expertly, was out and around most of the time. Her only worry was that the five-year-old had not stopped wetting the bed, and Davy ate peculiarly and remained spindly, and they all seemed to have a great many colds.

But Sally could laugh at herself. "We mothers have to find something to fret over, you know. It'll all iron itself out, I dare say."

"Doesn't your mother-in-law find the three of them a fairly strenuous job?"

"Why, they're such good children you'd never know they were in the house! In fact they aren't in the house most of the time. They're in the playroom or out in the yard, and all she has to do is sit and watch them. Once in a while she flares up at me and says it would be a good idea if I stayed home more, that it's too much for her at her age, but that's only when she's cross. She's devoted to them, really, and she hasn't anything else to do. I say to her, 'Well, Mother, if you don't like it here, you can go live with John or Emily,' and that shuts her up in a hurry. John has a dinky, dark little house in the middle of Pittsburgh and Emily and her husband fight all the time. After that she knows that watching the children isn't going to hurt her!"

Ellen Plover came to call, plunging up the snowy drive, pulling her two youngsters on a sled behind her.

"Are you busy, Martha? If you are we'll go home."

251

"I just signed off to make some coffee. Come on in. What would the children like to eat, or aren't they allowed to at this time of day?"

"They'll stay outside here and play. It isn't cold, and they've been under my feet all day. Now you let Mary have her turn on the sled, Bob, and if either one of you gets to quarreling I'm going to be good and cross."

While she took off her galoshes she watched them through the glass of the door, a tightly resigned look on her face. "They won't stay out, you know. They'll be tramping in and out for one thing or another, and finally I'll have to wrestle them out of their snow suits and then we won't be able to hear ourselves think. But maybe we can get in ten minutes or so."

"Let's sit in the kitchen. It's warmer."

"I can use some heat. That red brick mausoleum of ours hasn't any insulation. When the furnace is on full tilt the curtains are still standing straight out from the windows from the winter wind. Never let a man talk you into an old house that you're going to remodel later. When the time comes to do it you'll be too crippled from rheumatism to care."

Ellen was as comfortable as an old shoe. A Ph.D. in biology, she had worked in a government laboratory before the babies had come along.

"At least I thought I was working," she had told Martha. "After I had two babies on my hands I realized that I hadn't known what work was. Say, tell me, is there any way for a woman with two offspring and no relatives on hand to get out to a beauty shop and get her hair set? I try to set it myself and all I produce are coiffures à la rat's nest. Sally Simpson claims that I'm about to lose my husband's love if I don't do something about it."

She had let her hair grow, finally, and bundled it up in a neat but not breath-taking pompadour. She wore plain shirtwaist dresses, cotton in the summer, wool in the winter, and they made her tall, angular body look taller and thinner than before.

"But they're easier to iron," she said in extenuation. "I don't mind for myself, but I worry about poor little Mary. Why didn't the kid pick the kind of mother for herself who could make little girls' hair curl even if it was naturally straight and who was an expert at ironing tiny ruffles? Braids and sweaters and skirts—that's her future until I can afford a laundress."

252

"I don't think that's so bad. English children are kept plain and neat and they seem to turn out all right. It's only the American mothers who beruffle and becurl their little girls like dolls for a show case."

"No one will ever be able to accuse me of that! That's why I like to talk to you, Martha. You make all my shortcomings sound like virtues."

Today she sat at the kitchen table wearily and cuddled her coffee cup to warm her hands.

"Read your 'Women and the Twentieth Century' last night. I've been thinking about it all day. You know, you didn't give any solution for this problem of how a woman can be a mother and still carry on some outside work and be a citizen besides."

"I couldn't think of any, that's why. I didn't want to say that I thought she should turn her children over to some outsider, because I don't, and short of that I didn't know just how she was going to manage."

"Well, I thought of how she could do it. The thing that most people forget when they talk about child care is that the child has *two* parents. Why shouldn't the father share the care of them? I don't mean give them an occasional bath or put them to bed while Mama is doing the dishes. I mean divide the day into equal parts—Mother take care of them six hours and Father take care of them six hours. And what stands in the way of that? Because Father is working eight or more hours a day outside the house and isn't home to do his stint. But suppose that the working day should be shortened to six hours, as it will be sooner or later. *Then* Father could work his six hours and come home to look after the children for six. Mother would look after them for the six hours he was away, and after he came home she'd go out to *her* six-hour job. Ideal, isn't it? Each parent keeps on with his work, each knows an equal amount about the children and their problems, and the family income is stepped up to boot. How do you like that?"

"What about the women who don't want to keep on with a job?"

"Listen. Any woman who has had one and then gets a family to take care of knows darn well which is easier. She'd jump at the chance to get away for a fourth of a day. Look at all these women who are flocking into the factories now. To hear the newspapers talk, they're making a tremendous sacrifice in tearing themselves away from the kitchen and the kids. And you and I know that, while they wouldn't have done it if necessity hadn't forced them to it, they're having a lot better time of it than they were before. They won't want to give up those jobs and go back to staying home all day, I'll bet you a thousand dollars. You'll have to pry them loose, veterans returning or no."

"A lot of them are doing double duty though. They work and then they go home and do the washing and ironing and cleaning on top of that."

"I suppose so. Well, my scheme gets around that. Father does just as much of the housework as Mother, and with their improved income they can send the laundry out."

They looked at each other like conspirators, their eyes wickedly gleeful.

"Just one thing against it," said Martha. "If you could get the fathers to try it, it wouldn't be long before families would be getting smaller and smaller and——"

"I'm in favor of making the boys learn to take it. I had to," said Ellen. She tapped on the window and shouted, "Bobby Plover, you stop throwing snow down her neck. Stop it this minute, do you hear me!"

Horace Gamble had gone into the Army as a major. Mrs. Horace Gamble, forty, plump, and brisk, had taken stock of the remaining payments on their large house, figured the costs of college for the three children, all of whom were already in high school, estimated Army allotments, and hunted a job. She had been an efficient secretary before her marriage and she found, to her surprise, that she still was.

"It took me a couple of months to brush up," she said to Martha, "but now I have plain sailing, and I imagine I'll be made office manager pretty soon. All the other girls are either young and inexperienced or they're just working until their young men come home and their minds are with the young men rather than the work. Not that I blame them. I miss Horace too, but I've been married to him for eighteen years and that makes a difference. No, I can't stay a minute. Just dropped in to tell you how much I liked your piece in the *Chronicle*. I cut it out and sent it to Horace. He's been having fits about my working, you know. He wanted me to rent the house furnished and take the children and go live with Dad. But I didn't want to leave my home and take the children out of school, and anyway I've hankered for a long time to get out and see what I could do on my own."

"How are the children taking it?"

"Better than I thought. They each have their chores to do around the house, because it's too much for Mattie to keep up by herself, and she's getting old now and may go to live with her sister any day. Even if she does we'll be able to cope. The girls get dinner, and I was surprised! They're pretty good at it, really. And Randy can scrub a bathroom better than I can! I'm happy as a lark about the whole thing. You know what made me decide to do it? It wasn't just the money. I was thinking about my own mother. She had five of us and we lived on a farm, so I don't have to tell you how hard she had to work. Funny how you can watch somebody slave his life out right under your nose and not realize it. Mother wasn't a complainer; she always said that we girls were a wonderful help to her. Maybe we were, but every one of us was married or working by the time we were eighteen. And it took me until a few weeks ago to wonder what she had gotten out of it all. The minute we were grown we moved away, worked, and sent money home or got married and started a family. We weren't any company to her after we reached an age when she might have enjoyed us."

"She had time for her own friends after you were gone."

"Friends? She'd never had time to make any. Acquaintances, sure, but not friends. Country women are too busy to make friends. If some neighbor gets in a jam, you take time out to help them, and then you rush right back home and break your neck catching up. Why, Mom even made her own soap! And she used to feel guilty because she didn't weave cloth, the way her own mother had had to! Anyway, I got to thinking that you don't get much out of your children in the way of companionship and if you're smart you'll fix your life so you'll have something to take their place. Mine's fixed. I can go on working for the next fifteen years if I want to. And I like it. I like getting out and meeting people and being part of an outside world again. It's got bridge parties beat hollow."

"But when Horace comes home——"

"He'll just have to get used to the new scheme of things. Imagine, for eighteen years I've been ironing that man's shirts because nobody

255

else could do it to suit him! And shushing the children in the evenings! And going to bed at ten because he couldn't sleep unless I
was in bed too! I made life so pleasant for him that he got to thinking
that, from all he ever saw of it, anyone who stayed home all day
had a life that was one sweet song. Well, the worst is over now, so
he'll never know any different. But he's apt to find a few changes now
that his wife's a workingwoman; working, that is, for a different
employer. Say, that's pretty good! 'I've always been a workingwoman,
but now I'm working for a man I'm not related to.' That's the way
I'll put it to Horace when he raises a fuss."

She mailed the manuscript of *Positive Answer* to her publisher on
a Tuesday morning. Wednesday and Thursday she stretched out in
the sun and read all the things she had made herself put aside for
this gloriously idle time. Friday morning she vomited her breakfast.
Friday afternoon at the hospital Dr. O'Malley told her that she was
well along on the way to having a baby.

"Don't look so stunned, Martha. There's nothing so surprising
about it. You're married and you and Bill are not exactly ancient."

"I don't know why I'm being so stupid. Somehow I just never
thought of my having a baby."

He smiled. "What do you think of it now that you're thinking
of it?"

"I'm not feeling the way I'm supposed to feel, I can tell you that."

"How are you supposed to feel?"

"In every book I've read all my life long the heroine gets all flushed
with excitement and thrills to the knowledge of the new life so soon
to be et cetera and sprouts such a halo of unearthly tenderness that
people on the street recognize her secret. And all I feel is a little
nervous and just plain flabbergasted!"

"Don't worry about it. There have been others before you."

"Also, according to the novels, the minute the baby is born I'm
supposed to be swept over with a mysterious power that goes with
maternity and that will enable me to know exactly how to take care
of the child and just what to do for it up to the age of six at least.
Can I count on that?"

He pushed several small paper-covered books over the desk to
her. "Read these in case. They're the latest scientific word on baby
care."

She picked them up. "Put out by the Department of Labor. It's nice to know that somebody in the government had a sense of humor."

"And don't let other women scare you with their tales of the anguish of childbirth and the horrors of delivery. In fact don't let yourself worry or fret about anything. Watch your diet, get a lot of sleep, and forget that you're going to have a child until he arrives."

"If I worry about anything it won't be for the few hours I spend in having him. It'll be about whether I'll be an adequate mother in the twenty years or so after that."

On the way home she stopped in at the public library to get a few more baby books. There might be some things the Department of Labor had missed, and she had only seven months left to plot her course on an uncharted sea.

To Bill she said, "Don't look so stunned. There's nothing so surprising about it. We're married and we're not exactly ancient. And don't bother to sweep me off my feet or call me your little angel or help me into the easiest chair. The novels have it all wrong."

And later: "Funny how a thing that seems so ordinary when it happens to somebody else can be so fearfully exciting when it happens to you."

"You don't seem fearfully excited to me."

She was shy, embarrassed at being honest with him. "But you know I am, don't you?"

"Yes, sweetheart. I know."

18.

Even before Mother Kendrick became so very ill John was coming home more often. He never announced his appearances. A cab would swing around the asphalt circle, the front door would slam, there would be a muttering to one of the servants and then the sound of his heavy footsteps going up the stairs to his mother's room. John was home.

He took his meals from a tray in his own room. When he encountered Eleanor in the hall he looked straight past her. If she came into a room where he was sitting he got up and left. There was humor in the situation, something laughable in two people who had lived together so long pretending to be strangers. But she could not laugh, she was too hurt and too lonely. By unspoken agreement she left the library wing to him, had his newspaper carried there, told Henshaw to keep a fire in that fireplace. He never came into the rest of the house.

She went out a great deal, as much as she could. She rolled bandages for the Red Cross, she was a hostess at the USO, she acted as a nurses' aide at one of the hospitals. There were letters to be written to Martha and the children. There were servicemen's wives to help. She did what she could. When she came home to the quiet house in the evenings, tired and depressed, she went quietly to her own room.

"Just tea and toast, Hilda."

"And maybe an egg? You ought to try to eat more."

"An egg, if you'd like. How is Mother today?"

"Doctor says she's no worse. No better, he means. She'll be going one of these days, looks awful bad."

"Is Mr. Kendrick in there with her now?"

"No'm. He's in the library."

"Then I'll run in and see her for a minute."

The rest of the household must know how things were. There was no use trying to hide it. Many times that year she turned the pages of her calendar to see the date she had marked for her leaving. May 1, 1945. She had drawn a circle around it.

At first that day seemed a long way off, but a year ran off, a drop at a time, and she did not know where it had gone. She saw to it that the children did not come home for Christmas vacations. She asked one of her friends in Florida to invite them there, and they went. No use troubling them with their parents' difficulties; their presence would have made things unbearably painful. Their pictures showed her that they were growing up at a tearing rate. She took to going down to the school to visit them every few months, though the trains were uncomfortably crowded and hotel reservations hard to get. They did not seem to care whether she came or not, but she could not keep herself from going to them. Once she was surprised to learn that they had had a visit from their father.

"Sure, he was here last week. Spent a whole week end. Don't know how he did it, but he went next door and fished Sis out of that nunnery and we all went out to dinner and to a show. Look, he gave me a camera. Isn't it a honey?"

"It's lovely. What did you talk about?"

"Oh, whether the war would be over before I got a chance to get into it or not and what Sis and I would like to do next summer. He says he's thinking of taking me along on a fishing trip up North with him. Wouldn't that be swell?"

"Yes. You've never been anywhere with him before."

"Well, you know how it is. I don't blame him. Kids are a nuisance. Now that I'm grown-up, practically, we'll go around a lot together. I like to be with Dad. He isn't always fussing at me about my grades and things."

"I don't fuss at you because I want to, dear."

"You do, though."

"What did he give Alice?"

"About a gallon of some kind of perfume. Canal something."

"Chanel No. 5? Oh, Sonny, she's only thirteen!"

"Well, she's been going around smelling like sixty. Hey, that's a pretty good joke, isn't it, Mother? You said, 'She's only thirteen,' and I said—say, I'm going to write that one to Dad!"

There was a new picture in the silver frame on his dresser, an alarmingly pretty girl in a strapless evening gown.

"Who's that, Sonny?"

"Dixie Baker. Girl who lives here in town. I've been going around with her a little. She's a sweet number."

"I thought they didn't allow you to date here except for school parties."

He winked. "Oh, things like that can be arranged, you know how it is."

"She looks ever so much older than you are."

"Only a couple of years. She's seventeen. Now don't start fussing again, Mother!"

She worried about it all the way home. John was the one who should explain to Sonny the perils of girls named Dixie who ran around with fifteen-year-olds on the sly. Now that he seemed interested in the children, visiting them, giving them inappropriately expensive presents, perhaps she should talk to him about them. But she dared not risk another rebuff. She had all she could do to keep her head up now. She would have to wait.

259

The knocking at her door brought her out of a sound sleep. She put on the light, saw that it was three o'clock.

"What is it?"

"You'd better come. She's dying."

She threw on a robe, shuffled into her slippers, opened the door.

"Have you called the doctor, John?"

"Yes, he's on his way. That damned nurse doesn't seem to have the least idea what to do. Can you——"

She ran down to Mother Kendrick's room. The nurse was bending over the bed.

"I've done everything I can, Mrs. Kendrick. She's just giving out, that's all."

Until morning she sat on one side of the bed and John on the other. At six o'clock the heavy breathing ceased.

Dr. Rickard put a hand on John's shoulder. "It's all over, Mr. Kendrick. Go and try to get some rest. You're not in very good shape yourself."

She slipped her hand beneath his arm, led him to his own room, made him lie down while she went to get her sleeping tablets.

"Take these, John."

He lay back numbly, staring at the ceiling, while she unlaced his shoes and threw a blanket over him.

"Don't go away, Eleanor. I'm not quite clear. Is Mother——"

"She's gone. Don't think about it now."

He turned his face to the pillows and sobbed, heavy, strangling, heartbreaking sounds. She could not bear it. She sat down on the bed, leaned her cheek against his.

"Darling, don't. You were good to her, she loved you, she wouldn't want you to act like this. Please, dear."

Under the warmth of her touch, the whisper of her consolation, he relaxed, lay still, slept. He did not wake until noon, but then it was to instant consciousness.

"Where is she? What have they done with her?"

"They've taken her to the funeral home. They'll bring her back tomorrow evening. The funeral will be Thursday. I've wired the children to come home. Would you like some warm milk and crackers sent up? You must eat, you know."

"I suppose so. You've taken care of everything?"

"Everything."

"I'll be all right now. Thanks for standing by." His expression was aloof. If he remembered the previous night he gave no sign of it.

"You're very welcome," she said, and closed the door behind her.

While the children were home they took their meals, *en famille,* in the dining room, and after the children had gone again it seemed silly to change. They spoke to each other now, casually, politely. Many evenings they sat together in the living room, Eleanor with her war knitting, John with a book. With the exception of her room, he roamed the whole house freely. It took him six months more to brave this last fortress.

He wandered into her room—the door was always open now—at eleven one evening. It had been more than two years since he had set foot over that threshold, and he knew it. His manner was forcibly nonchalant.

"They're putting too much starch in my shirts again, Eleanor. Stiff as a board, can't get the collars around my neck."

"I'll speak to Mrs. Bates."

"Maybe it's because I'm getting fat. Put on ten pounds these last few months."

She looked up from the letter she was writing. Sharply, sweetly, she recognized the moment she had been waiting for.

"Sit down and have a cigarette, if you'd like. They're over—well, you ought to remember where they are."

"Rather have a cigar, if you don't mind."

He sat down, a well-mannered tiger trying to look like a harmless house cat.

"Sure I'm not disturbing you?"

"Not a bit. I can write this any time."

"That's a becoming housecoat. Don't believe I've seen it before."

"I had it sent from New York. The color's good, don't you think?"

"Swell. You know, you don't look a bit older than the day I married you."

"John!" She bent her head to the light. "I'm going gray. See?"

"I guess we all have a few gray hairs along about this time. In fact I'd settle for a few gray ones. I'm losing 'em all, no matter what color."

"Nonsense! That higher forehead just gives you a more intelligent look."

261

He looked down at his cigar, portentously. "It's just about time we had a talk, isn't it?"

"About the children?"

"About us. You must have guessed that I'm all over that other— stupidity."

She made her eyes innocent. "You mean she married someone else?"

He looked at her acutely. "I was all over it long before she married. I want to say that you've been wonderful through it all, the way you looked after Mother and everything, and I appreciate it."

"I was fond of Mother too, you know."

"Well, when I acted up the way I did most women would have given me a kick in the pants and sent me about my bullheaded business. Instead you buckled down and held things together until I came to my senses again. Why did you?"

"It was my duty," she said meekly.

"I don't know that it was. Frankly it surprised me. I didn't know you had the grit or the spunk to buck me like that. At first I was sore. Then I got to running down to see the kids once in a while— Sonny looks a lot like you—and Mother's dying—well, it brought me around."

He looked up, expecting her to say something, but she let him come the whole way. "The way I look at it is, you saved me from myself. I'd have been miserable sooner or later when I got to thinking about this house and the kids and Ashland. You were darned sweet about the whole thing."

"I'm glad you're—happier."

"And I've fixed things so I won't have to go away very much again. I've got good men in the key spots, and they can take care of things. So I thought we ought to open the summer house again this year, and plan to take a trip somewhere after the war, and have everything like it used to be."

"That will be nice."

He took her hand diffidently. "Will things be just the way they used to be, Eleanor?"

"I've always considered myself your wife, John, then and now."

"I don't have to stay in that damned drafty front room any more?"

"This is your house. I should think you could go anywhere in it you wanted to."

He pulled her into his lap. "Why couldn't you have said that half an hour ago! You know very well it's what I came in here to find out."

She put her head down on his shoulder. "It was fun listening to you get around to it."

Their laughter shook the chair. "I'm beginning to think I never knew you, Eleanor. You're a little devil!"

No, you don't know me. But you will.

They were dressing to go to the Methodist rectory to witness Penny's marriage to Colonel Thomas Ashley.

John was grumbling about it. "Why on earth do I have to get all dolled up for that stuffed-shirt colonel? I don't see what Penny sees in him."

"I don't care for him too much myself. But Penny's my sister, and it's our fault that she met him in the first place."

"Our fault, she says! Who dreamed up that job where Penny went snooping around my apartment houses? And if she'd been any good as a supervisor at all she'd have kicked him out. There must have been a million complaints about all the wild parties he was having. But oh no! She has to go and marry him."

"I don't think we could have kicked him out, John. He's here on Army ordnance. I believe he expects to be transferred to Chicago within the next month or two."

"Chicago's welcome to him! He's been pinching all the secretaries down at the plant black and blue. An old gent like that, nearly sixty!"

"As a matter of fact he's only fifty-two, and he doesn't look that. He's handsome, you have to say that for him."

"Well, I wish her joy of him!"

He was still lugubrious when they arrived at the minister's house. The Rev. Dr. Sims and his wife welcomed them into the parlor with dignified, ecclesiastic joy.

"A happy occasion," boomed Dr. Sims. "I understand that the bride is your sister, Mrs. Kendrick. Yes. I may say that I have seldom had the privilege of conducting a more suitable marriage—the brave with the fair, you know." Catching a corner of his wife's frown, he chuckled anyway. The Kendricks were Episcopalian but he had an idea that Mr. Kendrick might prefer a pastor who was less stodgy, more a man of the world, than the Rev. Bateswood, leader of the Episcopal flock. No harm in letting the Kendricks see that a man

263

could be a minister and still a good fellow. "Wonderful day for golf, Mr. Kendrick."

"I don't play. Never had time to learn."

"Ah yes, you businessmen have little time to indulge in recreational frailties. Not that the rest of us aren't thankful. It's you, with your wonderful capacity for unstinting endeavor and your quickness for detail, who enable us to carry on the present great crusade against the powers of fascist darkness. Well, here we are."

The colonel got up from the piano bench and shook hands smartly. Though he was as stiff, as military as ever, there was a heavy odor of whisky on his breath. Eleanor wondered if Dr. Sims had noticed it. He must have. But perhaps he was accustomed to grooms who had fortified themselves for their marriage ceremony. Still, she would have thought that a man who was over fifty and had been married before—the colonel had been a widower for fifteen years—would have better sense and too much regard for his new bride to give the impression that he had needed bottled courage to brave the parsonage.

Penny looked sweet in a gray suit and a hat made of blue and white violets. She stood pale and dreamy during the service and, when it was over, turned to her husband like a pleased, enchanted child. The colonel's kiss was not in key. He seized her greedily, embraced her as if they had been alone in her boudoir. Eleanor was embarrassed, but Penny, when she finally could draw away, was smiling.

"Impetuous!" she chided him.

"Can't blame me. First time you've ever let me within arm's length before." He was pleased with himself. He swaggered. All the way out to the car his hands hovered around her like vultures, touching her hair, her hands, her waist.

The colonel stuck his head in through the back window of the Kendricks' car. "Can I buy you a drink, Kendrick? We oughtn't to start off on our trip without a little celebration."

Eleanor said quickly, "Didn't Penny tell you? You're supposed to come to our house and have lunch."

"If she told me I've forgotten." He laughed. "Guess I must be as excited as a bride."

He went back to his own car, got in, smothered Penny in a series of kisses. He drove off, grinning and waving at them through the rear window.

"Oh, God," said John, "I have to give that stinker a cocktail and watch him make a Roman orgy out of a plain little luncheon! If he was so damned anxious why didn't he bring a folding bed along to the parsonage and get the thing consummated right then and there? Listen, can't you drop me off at the plant and tell them I've suddenly been taken busy? No, I won't do that to Penny. But she's made a terrible mistake this time, all right!"

"It may work out better than we think."

"What do you suppose made her tie onto that double-barreled ass, as attractive a girl as she is?"

"A girl in her thirties, especially one who has been married before, doesn't have so much choice. Most of the men her age are already married, and those who aren't don't intend to be. And Colonel Ashley has quite a nice income beyond his Army pay. He can keep her very comfortably."

"All I can say is, when it comes to practicality you women have us men backed right off the map. There's no such thing as love, to hear the way you talk."

"Yes, there's such a thing as love. And there's also such a thing as being practical about it."

"You're not speaking from experience, I hope. Were you just being practical when you married me? Or when you stayed married to me when I was giving you every reason not to?"

The question startled her. But he was not doubting his answer. His ruddy face was pleasant and complacent. She put her handkerchief daintily to her nose to conceal her mouth for an instant, her diamonds making a little rainbow against the gray upholstery.

"Sometimes—sometimes I've been practical," she said.

They were together now more than they had ever been, even when they were first married. He went to the plant in the morning at nine and came home at noon. They spent three months of the winter at the Florida house and planned a Northern log cabin to be built when the war was over. The two of them slept on beaches, lounged in gardens, paced terraces, went out seldom, came home early. He put on twenty pounds the next year.

He became addicted to the pursuit of health. "The way I was running around, driving myself, keeping all hours and gulping down almost anything, it's a wonder I'm alive at all. Quiet and routine, that's what turns the trick. Silly, all this milling around in crowds in stuffy rooms. I feel better now than I have for twenty years. Wouldn't know I had a stomach except for getting hungry every two hours or so. Tell the cook no more bread and butter on the table. I don't want to get fat!"

All the energy he had spent at his business he concentrated now on his physical well-being. The bathroom shelves filled up with vitamin preparations and iron tonics. He searched the luxury markets for health foods. He signed up for an hour a day at a gymnasium. He insisted on getting to bed well before midnight. "An hour's sleep early is better than two of them later on."

He entreated Eleanor to slow down. "What in the world do you want to rush around for, killing yourself with work you don't have to do? I subscribe a whopping amount every year to the Red Cross and I'll make it more if they'll let you off this bandage stuff, whatever it is."

"Surely it can't hurt me to sit for an hour or so a day rolling bandages. And the hospital work is active, but it isn't difficult."

"Well, you're hardly ever home. I had that bird-feeding station built and up for three days before you had time to look at it. Handsome thing, isn't it? First thing I ever tried."

"It's very nice. What do birds eat?"

He produced a book with large colored plates and explained to her about birds until ten-thirty.

She exulted over his growing dependence on her. She praised his new accomplishments, humored his fads, furnished him with amusing diversions to while away the little time she was not with him. By now she knew him so well. It was easy to sense the proper moment when he would enjoy a dinner party, to pick the movie he would like to see, to bring home new people whom he could talk to. His interests now lay at home. He helped her select the new dining-room chairs and he triumphed with her over a lovely majolica vase she had discovered. From the catalogues they chose five hundred bulbs for the garden, and, waving old Mr. Simpson aside, planted them themselves.

Melancholy found her in the little dark moments of the night when she lay awake and listened to the broken rhythm of his snoring. If they could have led this kind of life seventeen years ago, how happy she would have been! If they could have done all these things together, and with the children beside them to enjoy it too, what a mighty marriage they could have built! Perhaps it had been her fault that things had not turned out better, she had been such a mouse. That did not excuse him, though, for trampling on her, trying to throw her out of his life after all the faithful years she had put in waiting on him, thinking only of him. Though she had not reminded him by so much as a look of his dereliction, she thought of it often, and the memory would fill her afresh with the rage and shame she had felt then. What was that line she had read in a book just the other day? "To forgive and forget is dearly bought experience thrown away." That was right. That was sensible. She must remember it to say when she had left and he came after her. "I don't know how you can expect me to come back to you, John. To forgive and forget is dearly bought experience thrown away."

"Why did you stay as long as you did?"

"To make sure you would miss me when I went."

"Martha put you up to this."

"Martha knows nothing of it, has never known. I am not as stupid as you think."

Getting up to smoke a cigarette, she would riffle the pages of her little calendar. The circled date was ever so much closer now.

For her birthday in 1944 he gave her a square sapphire, set with diamonds. For Christmas there was a Russian sable stole. He had not put it under the tree. He waited until the children had opened all their presents, until he had thanked Eleanor for *Fortune* and a new signet ring, until she had exclaimed over the giant topaz that formed the body of an exotic insect that would climb on her lapel. Then he disappeared and came back with a tremendous white box.

"Gosh, it's a house and lot! Open it, Mother."

"Here, I'll help you with the ribbon."

The soft brown-black fur glowed in the Christmas lights. She put her hand on it, felt its luxuriant depth, marveled at its sleek rippling.

"A mink scarf!" Alice breathed.

"Mink, nothing! That's sable, young lady, genuine Russian sable, and from what I had to pay for it I know I've been in the wrong business all along. There must be a fortune to be made in animal skins!"

Alice lifted it from the box. "Oh, isn't it beautiful! When can I have one, Daddy? I've got to try it on!"

He took it from her. "Let your mother try it on first. Like it, Eleanor?"

"It's the most gorgeous thing I've ever seen. I—I don't know how to say thank you for anything as grand as this."

"Don't try. Makes her look like a queen, doesn't it, kids?"

She saw herself in the foreground of the mirror, tall and pale with the varicolored lights behind her. John's face beamed over her shoulder and on the other side Alice clasped her hands in wonder. Even Sonny's face was lit with reluctant approval.

A sob rose in her throat so suddenly that she must put a hand up to still it. Why did such a lovely thing have to happen on the very last Christmas they would all be together? Why must they make it so hard for her? This was not Christ's birthday. This was Gethsemane.

It was better when the children had gone to bed and he began to lament over the party she had arranged to give them on Christmas Day as their special holiday treat.

"We'd better get to bed, Christmas Eve or not. Need all the strength we can get for tomorrow when the house'll be full of howling youngsters. How many are coming? Lord, as many as that? There aren't that many in town!"

"Some of them are coming from out of town. Their friends from school, you know."

"We'll have a regular bus service from here to the station all day, no doubt. What's the earliest any of 'em can possibly get here?"

"I believe there's one train that gets in at seven."

"In the morning? Great Scott! Have you told Jackson he's going to have to work tomorrow for a change and not sit around all day polishing fenders?"

"I've made all the arrangements, and you're getting off easy. They'll have a buffet lunch here, and then they're going sleighing and skiing and tobogganing all afternoon. Then Alice and Sonny and our house guests—there are only ten of them—will come here for dinner, and you can come down or not, as you choose. The dance starts at nine, and I do think it would be nice of you to attend, at least for a little while."

"And when are these house guests going to leave?"

"The next morning, most of them. I believe that four are staying for the week end, the children's special friends."

"And they'll stay up till all hours and put all sorts of horrible concoctions in their stomachs and yawp and scream and sit around on the middle of their spines and act sophisticated! I wouldn't be sixteen again if you paid me. Nor fourteen either. Though I wasn't nearly as silly at that age as youngsters are nowadays."

She patted his hand. "Try to bear it, dear. It's only once a year."

He blew a ring of cigar smoke at the ceiling. "You know, Eleanor, there's one thing your worst enemy would have to say about you. You always do the right thing, no matter how much it puts you out. Yes sir. I don't believe you've ever short-changed a soul." He looked at the clock and stubbed out the cigar. "Bedtime. Merry Christmas, Eleanor."

"Merry Christmas, John."

They came back from the South in time for Easter week. Jackson was sent to the station on Good Friday evening to meet Sonny's train. His sister had arrived a day earlier.

Eleanor was out on the porch peering through the rain when the big black car came up the drive and Jackson got out, rain glistening on his head and shoulders.

"He wasn't on it, ma'am. I saw everybody that got off and he wasn't there. Then, when it started to pull out, I ran alongside it, trying to see in the windows, in case he'd fallen asleep or something, but I never saw him."

"Oh dear, he must have missed it at the other end. I'll call the school and see when the next train will be."

Sonny was not at the school. He had left the grounds with his suitcase in hand in plenty of time to catch the proper train home.

"Then he must have ridden past the station. We'll wire ahead and see where he is."

"I tell you," said John, "kids' brains nowadays are in their feet! Imagine getting yourself carried forty miles or so past where you live on a rainy night with gas rationing. Hope he has to stay in some rotten hotel till morning. May teach him a lesson."

By nine o'clock they had ascertained that Sonny had not been on that particular train at all.

John was brick-red with temper. "Where's the young idiot got to? What's he up to? He must know he's got you worried to death. Why doesn't he wire or telephone? He has money, hasn't he?"

"I mailed him his month's allowance Monday."

"I'll thrash him for this, damned if I won't!"

"He couldn't have been kidnaped, could he? They don't kidnap sixteen-year-old boys, do they?"

"Of course not!" He turned white around the mouth and went to the telephone. "Long distance. Cleveland." He put a hand over the mouthpiece. "I know a firm of private detectives up there. Might as well send them on this wild-goose chase. He'll probably be home before they get started though."

They waited all night, Eleanor with tensely folded hands, John alternately dozing and fretting at the inaction. At five in the morning he called the headmaster again.

"No, he isn't home. What kind of a place are you running down there to let a kid get lost like that? No, I wouldn't have the faintest idea where he was. I don't live with him. You do."

A bell rang in her mind. "Dixie Baker," she said. "Ask them to check up on a girl named Dixie Baker."

"My wife seems to think that a girl named Dixie Baker might be mixed up in this. Is Mr. Sheridan down there yet? Well, tell him about her. He's investigating this thing for me."

Mr. Sheridan did not call back until twenty-four horrible hours later. John said, past the telephone, "It's all right. He's found him!" With the wonderful sensation of air rushing into her lungs, she knew she had hardly dared to breathe for almost two days.

"Is he—married?"

"No, thank God. He started out to be, but there was a bottle in the car and he and Dixie must have been hitting it pretty hard. Anyway, he wrecked the car in a culvert—no, he wasn't hurt, just scratched up a little—and because it was raining and she was sore, she left him there and hitched a ride back home. Kept her mouth shut about it too; Mr. Sheridan couldn't get a word out of her. Her parents are pretty strict and she didn't want them to know what she'd been up to."

"Then where is he?"

"In jail."

"Jail! What for?"

"Well, he went staggering into this little town near the state line, looking a mess, with liquor on his breath, and they ran him in. Found

270

a lot of money on him, and he wouldn't say where he'd got it, so they were suspicious."

"But when they found out who he was——"

"They didn't find out. He gave them a phony name, threw away all his identification. He had sense enough to do that or there'd have been a fine mess in the papers by this time. Find out what's the quickest transportation I can get down that way, will you? He won't come home with Sheridan, so I guess I'm elected."

"Don't—don't be hard on him."

"I'm so damned thankful things aren't any worse that I can't be hard on anybody. But I intend to try!"

His voice on the telephone next morning was gentle. "Listen, Eleanor, we're not coming home right away. The kid doesn't want to face you yet, I guess. Anyway, he and I are going on a little two-week trip together. I've called Frank Harrison and asked him for the use of his lodge in the Upper Peninsula. He must have thought I was out of my mind in this weather, but he said O.K., and he's going to call his caretaker to have it ready for us. So here's the address. Pack some clothes for us and ship 'em up there right away. Anything that'll keep out the cold and damp. And tell——"

She felt weak and relieved and grateful. She wandered around the house happily, smiling at the majolica vase, looking out the windows at the green spears that the bulbs were sending up, admiring the pair of cardinals at the feeding station. All was well, her little world was again serene and beautiful.

Those two weeks were a wonderful opportunity for the spring cleaning. She engaged two extra women in the town and they and the maids turned the place out thoroughly, airing, scrubbing, beating. Slipcovers and rugs went to the cleaners, the house was aromatic with ammonia and with starch meeting a hot iron. She washed the precious pieces herself, the Wedgwood, the Lenox, the best crystal. Meals were eaten standing and bedtime was at dusk.

Most women hated spring cleaning, but she loved it. It was the best excuse she knew to become reacquainted with her treasures, even those long disused and stored in remote cupboards. And to see the house emerge, smiling and splendid, out of the suds, all its parts reassembled and in order, was to meet an old friend at his gracious best.

"Mrs. Kendrick is sure particular about things," she heard Mrs. Abbott, one of the town domestics, say to Hilda.

Hilda made excuses for her mistress. "She's a real homebody, Mrs. Kendrick is. A real homebody."

It amused her to reflect how tightly the description fitted. A person whose life centered around a home. A homebody.

John and Sonny stamped in one evening, demanding supper.

"We had dinner on the train," John said, "but this kid never gets filled up. And I haven't found anything fit to eat since I left here. What can you rustle up for us?"

She brought milk and sandwiches and watched them as they ate. John's face was tired and a little pinched, but Sonny had never looked better. His cheeks were pink, his eyes clear, his manner gay. If he had been repentant he was so no longer. She didn't care, she would have hated to have him sullen and hating.

"House looks fine, Eleanor. Bet you did the spring cleaning while we were away. Good! Now I won't have to run from room to room, pursued by muscular females with angry brooms. Listen, son, you run along to bed. I've had about all of you that I can stand without a little separation."

Sonny laughed and bent to kiss her. "Good night, Mother. It's nice to be home."

"Thank you, dear. Good night."

"It'll be a treat not to have to listen to Dad's snoring. I'm that much to the good anyway."

He went up the stairs three at a time and John lit a cigar.

"That's all the apology you'll ever get," he said.

"I don't mind."

"He was pretty broken up at first, but I guess it was mostly his vanity. Couldn't understand how Dixie could ditch him like that. He's got the wildest set of values, the most upside-down idea of the universe that I've ever listened to. We're going to have a lot of trouble with him before we're through, we might as well make up our minds to it."

"He's been a lot of trouble already."

"So I understand, though I wasn't allowed to be in on it."

"You were so busy. I tried to keep you from being bothered by it."

"Well, you were probably right. I'd have yelled my head off if I'd heard that he was expelled even once, much less six times, and I

272

wouldn't have thanked you for the news. And now that I can appreciate the problem, it may be too late to solve it, but I'm going to give it a try. He's not going back to school."

"Oh, John, he has only one more year before he enters college!"

"Don't make me laugh. Enter college with his grades? Anyway, one of the services may have him by that time. So he's going into the plant tomorrow morning. Don't ask me what he's going to do there, I don't know. And don't expect him to start working his way up like an Alger boy, because he hasn't got the stuff. We might as well face it, Eleanor, he isn't going to amount to much. If we can keep him at home and out of trouble till he's twenty-one we'll be doing well."

Hard as that knowledge was to bear, his sharing it made the worry lighter. "I know," she said.

"There's only one thing in his favor. He's not a fool. He acts like one a lot of times, but he isn't one. Beyond that I'm not prepared to go." He stretched. "Let's not talk about it any more tonight. What have you been doing with yourself?"

It was after eleven when they went up to their room. He sat down and began taking off his shoes.

"Can't wait to sleep in a decent bed again. Did Roy call from Dayton while I was away? Maybe I'll have to run down there next Monday. Let's see, what date'll that be?"

She poured herself a glass of ice water from the carafe on the bedside table. Her throat was dry; she hadn't talked so much in ages. When she was in bed she saw that he was standing by her desk with her calendar in his hand.

"Say, I've meant to ask you before," he said. "What's this circle around May first for? It's May sixth now. What happened on the first?"

She felt as though a hammer had crashed down on her skull. She lay there blinking at him.

Patiently he repeated, "What happened on May first? A bath in the dew, a fling around a Maypole, or the President to dinner?"

Laughter swept her, wildly, unreasonably. She turned her face to the pillows to stifle it, but she could not stop it. What a joke on her! What a tremendous joke!

"Stop it, Eleanor! Aren't you feeling well? What's the matter?"

273

"Nothing," she gasped. "Not a thing. And that's what happened on May first too. Nothing."

"I'm damned if I can see why that should be so funny."

She looked around at the room, the gray satin chairs, the kidney-shaped desk where she had spent so many hours, the familiar crystal bottles on her dressing table. She thought of her beautiful clean house and her treasures, and Sonny sleeping in his room down the hall. She watched John marching into the bathroom to take one of his vile iron mixtures.

"The only person I was fooling was myself," she said softly. "Nothing ever *could* have happened May first."

He was in bed and asleep when she began giggling again, in the dark. He woke and sighed, a man at the end of his rope.

"What now?"

" 'To forgive and forget is dearly bought experience thrown away,' " she said.

"If it's a game I don't get it."

"It's not a game. It's a philosophical gem. 'To forgive and for-get——' "

"I heard you."

He was silent so long that she thought he was asleep again.

"I suppose all women get a little queer around forty," he said.

"It isn't that." She reached for his hand. "I love you, darling."

"Well, don't sound so surprised, that's not news to me. Now for heaven's sake let's try to get some sleep. If you want to have a good laugh save it till tomorrow morning when you see Sonny starting out to be one of the great laboring class."

He kissed her briskly and fell asleep.

19.

The daily routine of the wife of a colonel in Army ordnance was not irksome. Home was a hotel or a furnished apartment. The colonel ate breakfast and lunch somewhere. Penny was vague about meals, but for dinner they went to one of the current town's smartest restaurants or a glossy bar. There were always other Army people about and they were sociable within their small clique. No, the life was wonderful. Only the colonel was difficult.

For the first three months of their marriage he couldn't let her alone. Hard as she tried to evade him, he would come upon her while she was doing her nails or creaming her face and his big hands would maul her and his heavy lips crawl upon her face and throat. Indiscreetly, she could not keep from showing that she hated it.

"Don't, Tom!"

If he were sober he would cajole. "Come now, what's a pretty woman for? Don't play hard to get, lambie. Cuddle down and let's be friendly."

"I have to hurry. We'll be late."

"Let's stay home then, and I'll mix us a few and we can have a wonderful time. Put on that thin pink robe you have and——"

"I will, but let's go to the Atkinsons' first."

With luck he would come along and she would encourage him—no heavy task—to drink himself drowsy. She did not mind bringing him home with the assistance of a sympathetic taxi driver and putting him to bed. There was almost nothing she would not have done to avoid his fantastic advances for an hour.

But there were times when he turned vicious.

"You're a hell of a wife! This kittenish stuff might be all right for a girl, but it's a joke in a woman who's over thirty and has been married twice before. No wonder your other husbands divorced you."

"I divorced *them.*"

"The minute they tried to explain to you that love was more than birds, bees, and flowers, I'll bet. Well, by God, you watch out, or you'll find yourself right back in Ashland!"

Once she found the temper to answer him, "If I do it'll be with alimony."

Eventually he left her alone. He no longer came home directly from his work. He would stagger into their apartment at two in the morning, reeking with alcohol, with rouge marks on his shirt. The next time they moved he flipped her a key.

"All yours," he said. "Your room is on three. Mine's on four."

She could scarcely believe her good fortune at being free again, her own mistress. But that had its drawbacks too. After she had eaten her dinner—in the hotel dining room, since other places did not welcome lonely ladies—there was nothing for her to do. Because she dared not give him any grounds for legal complaint she could not answer the salutations of strange men. There was only her room or the movies.

One good thing, he was not stingy. She had her own checking account, and she established charge accounts at all the better stores. He paid the bills without complaint, maybe because her looking well was important to his prestige, maybe because a colonel could not let his creditors down. She didn't care what the reason was as long as she could buy the things she wanted.

Infrequently he joined her at Sunday morning breakfast. "No use having any more talk about us than is necessary," he said. "We're shoving on next week. Be a good thing too. I'm sick of this place."

She spoke idly. "What did your first wife——"

He nearly leaped from his chair. "You leave my wife's name out of this!" he roared.

The heads of the other breakfasters turned. There were snickers. He looked abashed.

"Didn't mean to roar like that, but what I said still goes. I'm not going to have you throw Esther up to me, no matter what silly gossip you've been listening to. She was a fine woman, a lot better than I deserved, and I didn't have the sense to appreciate her till after she was dead. She followed me from one cracker-box place to another and brought up two kids while she was doing it, while I drank and caroused and had a good time. Well, I'm getting paid off for it now, all right!"

"Children?"

"Sure. Florence is twenty-five and married. Wally's a lieutenant in the Air Corps. Here are their pictures. See?"

"I didn't know. I've never seen any letters from them, and you've not mentioned them before."

"They don't write to me, except maybe once a year or so, and they do that because their mother taught them it was their duty. They haven't any use for me, but they're fine young people just the same."

They were more friendly after that. Their rooms were still apart, but they ate together three or four nights a week and once in a long while he took her to a party. She did not want a reconciliation on a bigger scale. She was better off this way. Still, it was her duty to be a good influence on his life. How could he do his work when he was drinking more and more heavily all the time? She spoke to Captain Atkinson about it.

"I don't know how Tom manages to get through a day at the office when he never goes to bed," she said with wifely disapproval.

"I'm glad you mentioned it, Mrs. Ashley. It's not my place to say anything, but we've all been worried about him. The pace he's going, he'll have a stroke one of these fine days. Can't we slow him down a little?"

She rubbed her forehead with a well-manicured hand, the one with Tony's diamond on it. "I do my best, but he's so much older that he thinks I'm a child. He won't listen to me."

"He ought to. Try to make him see a doctor."

"I have, and he gets mad. The way we talk to each other, you'd think that *I* was the fifty-two-year-old and *he* was the twenty-five."

"So you're only twenty-five? I've wondered. Of course you look awfully young, but I thought—it's hard to tell women's ages these days. What are you doing running around with us old fogies? Find yourself some young lieutenant's wife, make friends with the younger crowd!"

"I don't think Tom would like it. He's a bit stiff and formal, you know."

Actually Tom liked the younger set too well. It was ridiculous, the way he would corner some young man and pump him dry about his work, the number of children he had, the strength of his forehand drive. It was absurd to see him tweak the ear of a twenty-year-old girl and then sit down to give her an hour's information on how to make the best of whatever temporary living quarters she and her husband had found. And some of the girls were so very pretty! Though their clothes might be plain, though they did their hair any old way and slapped their make-up on carelessly, their very lack of years achieved the miracle for them. There was a glow to their cheeks, a luster to their hair, a lithe juvenile grace to their bodies that made them beautiful. She told herself that ten years ago, had she been in the same room with them, they would have been invisible. Even now a man with sense might well prefer Penny's finished perfection to their heathen naturalness. But she did not seek their company, she would not sit next to one of them if she could help it.

She said to Tom, "I should think you'd get yourself into a lot of trouble, playing around with these young married women."

"What do you mean 'playing around'? I'm friendly with them, that's all."

"As long as their husbands understand that."

He barked mirthfully, "Say, these are decent youngsters. They've got too much on their minds to think about any funny business. Sure, I'll admit that if a woman gives me a come-on I'll chase. I'm no saint, never was. But if a girl is disinterested and respectable she doesn't have to worry about me."

"I guess I'm the only one who has misunderstood."

He worried about that, she could see. The next time they ran across a group of young people at a dance he avoided them.

"Come on over, Colonel Ashley, you'll die when I tell you what Jim's doing to our three-by-six back yard!"

"Not right now, Sally. Some other time."

It wasn't long until they left him alone, accepting his indifference as an inexplicable but not too important fact.

Carefully she wove his friends into a conspiracy against him. She said tearfully to Major Klein, "Tom's killing himself, you know, and he won't listen to reason. If only he wouldn't drink so much, stay out so late. He ought to begin to take a little care of himself at his age."

Major Klein was Tom's bon vivant, his best elbow-bending company. "He hasn't been looking so good lately. I never thought about it till right now. Don't worry so, Mrs. Ashley. He's lived this kind of life for years, and he's strong as a horse."

"If he drops over dead someday I don't know what I'll do! I'm very fond of him, Major."

"Well, sure, I know how you must feel. I'll tell you. The next time he wants me to go out on the town with him I'll tell him that I've got another date. He's not so apt to go by himself. And I'll tell Berringer too. We don't want anything to happen to the Old Man."

"Oh, I knew you'd be sweet about it! Everybody said there was no use talking to you, that you were such a barfly——" She put her hand over her mouth. "You must forgive me, Major, I didn't mean to repeat unkind gossip."

Major Klein was annoyed. "They've got a lot of nerve, saying a thing like that. I don't spend any more time in bars than anyone else!"

He spent less after that. Army gossip was a perpetual-motion machine and once your name had been fed into the hopper you never heard the last of it.

More and more Tom was forced into her company. "I'm damned if I know what's wrong with everybody. All they want to do is get right straight home from the office and sit around on their fannies. There's not a bit of life in this burg!"

"I'm going window-shopping after dinner. Want to come along?"

She liked to be seen with him. They made a striking couple, and civilians always turned around to give his uniform a second look. They went to shows, took boat or motor rides, sat in the parks on warm nights. Best of all she liked to stroll through crowded streets with him.

"I'm tired walking, Penny. Let's stop in here and have a drink."

"Such a horrid little place, there won't be a soul in there. If you want to stop anywhere let's go to the Copper Mug."

In the Copper Mug the crowded tables would watch them as they followed the headwaiter to their chairs. She kept a look of shy animation on her face and listened for the whispers.

"Look at that Army officer over there. Good-looking, isn't he? Wish I could stand as straight as that. What's his rank? I never can tell from all those things on their collars."

"Colonel. Pretty girl with him. His daughter?"

"It can't be his wife, she's paying too much attention to him."

She exerted all her enchantments to keep Tom's eyes on her. It was important that these people should see that, with her beside him, he could look at no one else.

"Look, Tom, such funny glasses."

"Don't see anything funny about them. They're full."

"Only two now. I'm setting up your quota. You may not care anything about your big bad self, but I do!"

"Sometimes I think that you almost like me."

"Silly! I married you, didn't I?"

Sooner or later the waiter would bring a message from another table. "Mr. Henshaw wants to know if he can buy you a drink, Colonel."

"I don't know Mr. Henshaw. Which one is he?"

"Over there, sir. He owns the biggest department store in town, has three sons in the service."

"Well, say, guess I'll go over and meet him. Excuse me, Penny."

He would come back for her and they would join the Henshaws' party. It was a nice easy way of making acquaintances, of getting to dance with new people, of passing an evening pleasantly. The colonel had a way of drawing attention to himself without having to do anything about it, but she learned to divert that.

"Your husband's a mighty fine man, Mrs. Ashley. You must be pretty proud of him."

"Oh, I am. I—I wish he wouldn't order drinks so fast."

"No harm in it. He's just feeling a little gay."

"The doctor says he shouldn't drink at all. I try to take care of him, but he's so stubborn, so headstrong. Sometimes I think I'll die of worry."

"Well now, don't you fret. I'll give the waiter a signal to slow down." And later: "Not many women look after their husbands the way you do, Mrs. Ashley. The colonel's lucky to have you, take it from me."

"Thank you. That's very kind of you. I'm quite young, you see, ever so much younger than he is, and now and then the responsibility is too much for me."

There were men who carried their sympathy for her to more practical lengths. "What do you do with yourself all day, Mrs. Ashley? Can't I give you lunch once in a while? No harm in it, is there?"

"Oh, I don't—well, if it's just for once. Certainly there's nothing wrong with eating lunch in broad daylight with a man you find—interesting, is there?"

"I'll say there isn't."

She accepted these invitations freely. If the men got out of hand she hinted at Tom's knowledge and displeasure and they melted away like snow in the sun. She couldn't lose.

The only drawback to a gay evening of this kind was that Tom, not having drunk enough to be sleepy, would remain sociable after they got home.

"Come on into my room—Penny. I'm going to have some drinks sent up."

"I'm tired. I want to get to bed."

"I won't come within ten feet of you, I swear. Just come in and talk awhile."

"Really, Tom, you aren't very considerate. I'm tired, I tell you."

The words would wrench themselves out of him. "I'm lonesome, damn it! Don't know a soul any more, haven't anybody to talk to. Just for ten minutes. Please."

"Tomorrow night, maybe."

She always locked the door to her room though he never tried it. Once he pounded on the panel just at daybreak, and his voice was besotted and angry.

"Just thought I'd let you know that I think I can get to sleep now."

"Go away, Tom. You can't wake up the whole hotel."

"That'd be too damned bad, wouldn't it? Might make people wonder if you're the wonderful little wife you're supposed to be."

For a few days after, they did not see each other. Then, driven by lack of companionship, he came back.

"Sorry I made a fool of myself the other night. It won't happen again."

"I hope not. You can be very nice when you want to be."

"Never thought I'd turn into a tame cat, but—well, I'm not getting any younger."

The minute he showed he was co-operative she was ready to be pleasant to him. That's one thing about me, she thought, I never hold a grudge.

"Sit down and order your dinner, Tom, and then we'll go for a walk."

"Say, General Howitt said a funny thing today. He put a hand on my shoulder as if I were a long-lost brother and said, 'How are you feeling these days, Tom? Better have a checkup. The best of us have to look after our health.' I told him I'd never felt better, but he kept looking at me as if he could hear a death rattle. What do you suppose gave him an idea like that?"

"It's just what I've always said. You ought to be more careful."

He picked up the menu. "Maybe you're right," he said wearily. "Everybody else seems to think so."

She was dressing to go out to lunch with a Mr. Bates whom they had met in a bar some nights ago. Life was wonderful, she was riding high, she had never felt better. There was no use talking about it, you looked better when your spirits were good. Today the lines around her eyes hardly showed. She would wear the yellow dress with the plunging neckline. It was daring, as were most of her clothes these days, but she had found there was nothing that men found more fetching than revealing dresses plus a modest ladylike demeanor. That was one thing she had over these younger snips, anyway. They could not wear dresses like that, it would have been bad taste at their age, they couldn't carry them off.

The telephone rang. It was Tom.

"I'm a grandfather!" he shouted at her. "Just had a telegram from Florence. The baby was born last night. A boy. Weighed eight pounds!"

"How nice."

"You sound pretty lukewarm about it. Not many women get to be grandmothers after only two years of being married. That ought to be a record."

"Don't be hateful, Tom."

"Hey, I didn't mean to make you mad. I was just kidding. What do you say we take a trip this week end to see the kid?"

"I think you're out of your mind. Florence doesn't like you, you said so yourself. And hospitals don't like to have visitors these days, so even if she wanted to see you, which isn't likely, you couldn't get in."

There was a pause. When he spoke again his voice had lost its excitement. "Well, it was just an idea."

"Why should you put yourself out for Florence when she's never done a thing for you? Traipsing all over the country with your health as bad as it is. If she cared for you it would be different. Send her some flowers and forget about it."

She had had to scotch that. She wasn't going to get herself put in the position of a grandmother at her age. Besides, there was an estate involved. Not a large one, but considerable enough to make it worth while. If Florence and her brat thought they were going to get all of it they were mistaken. As a woman got older she had to think of these things. What a fool she had been not to get a penny out of Tony or Perry! All the best years of her life wasted and nothing to show for it. This time she was going to be sensible. Unless, of course, an attractive, generous man showed up who seemed to really appreciate her. Then she wouldn't have to worry no matter what Tom did.

In the lobby of the Statler she sat down across from a circular mirror to wait for Mr. Bates, deliberately early so that passers-by might see her and admire. Two young men were interested almost immediately. They walked past her twice, while she kept her eyes lowered beneath the small nose veil of her hat. They went into a conference at a distance. They were going to ask her to lunch with them, and she would refuse with dignity, but she put the veil up so that they might see her better. She crossed her nylon ankles and waited.

One of the young men started across toward her, and she pretended to be absorbed in a war poster by the door. When he was within four feet of her he seemed to have lost his direction. He stopped, looked vague, and retreated. She thought that her attitude had scared him off, but his remark to his companion was unfortunately clear.

"Say, that's no girl. When you get up close to her she looks old as the hills! She must be all of forty. Let's see who's in the lounge."

A bellboy stopped by her chair.

"Are you Mrs. Ashley? Mr. Bates is awful sorry, but he finds he can't get away. He says you're to have lunch anyway and sign his name to the check."

"Thank you, but I don't believe I'll wait." She looked at her watch, a woman in a hurry. "I must run. I really didn't have time to lunch anyway."

Back in her room she threw her purse on the bed in a temper. Tom and his being a grandfather had spoiled her whole day!

In St. Louis Tom stopped drinking. He would not take even one before-dinner cocktail.

"No, honestly, I don't want it. Do you mind eating dinner by yourself, Penny? I have to rush right back to the office."

He was sober, he was friendly, she saw him only ten minutes a day.

"If you're at the office these nights it's funny that there's no answer when I call your office."

"Not so funny. The girls at the switchboards go home at five o'clock."

She took to sorting through their mail before he saw it, and in two months she had the answer. She ripped open the light gray envelope that smelled, ever so slightly, of sachet powder, an expensive kind.

My dear:
I know it is not wise to write you at your hotel, but I have just found that I cannot have dinner with you tonight. My brother is here from out

of town and there is going to be a family roundup. If you would care to join us, come on out.

I tried to get you three times at the office, but you were out and I did not like to leave a message.

Affectionately,

DORIS

She looked up from the letterhead and spoke to the hotel clerk.

"Do you know a Doris Downing? She lives on Bryant Street."

"Oh yes. They used to entertain here quite a bit. Mrs. Downing is a widow; her husband died a few years ago, he was a doctor. A handsome woman. Don't see her around much these days."

"I just wondered. She's asked us to dinner."

"You'll have a very nice time. We think quite a bit of the Downings in this town. Lovely people."

She was sick with fright. That was the worst thing about Tom, any unprincipled sneak of a woman could attract him. Well, she wasn't going to let any woman steal her husband from under her nose. She was going to do something about it!

It was Tom's raving over the pictures of his grandson that gave her the idea. She would have a baby! That was it, that was the perfect solution. A baby would tie him to her, give her a claim on him he'd never shake off, make her status as his wife primary and solid. Moreover, it made a woman seem younger to have infants around. Nobody could guess you were over thirty when your first baby wasn't even a year old.

She'd better have a physical examination, make sure she was strong enough to go through with the ordeal. She didn't want a baby so much she was willing to die for one! Someone said that Dr. Timken was a good man.

"I know you're terribly busy and may not want to be bothered by me," she said, "but this is important to me. My husband and I have been married some years now, and I've never been—pregnant." Horrible word. She was glad to get it out of her mouth.

"There's usually no cause for worry, Mrs. Ashley. How old are you? Have you ever had any serious illnesses? And your husband is in his fifties. Hmn. Well, we'll soon see. The nurse will get you ready."

He was thorough in his examination and outspoken about what he had found, though he put it as mildly as he could. Mrs. Ashley would never bear a child. He did not say the word "abortion." He said "inefficient surgery and infection."

"But there must be something I can do. I *want* a baby!"

"You didn't always. I'm sorry, Mrs. Ashley. You can consult another physician, but he will tell you the same thing. It is always dangerous to interfere too much with nature's mechanisms."

Mrs. Downing had children, no doubt. Some women certainly had things dished up to them on a silver platter.

She followed him one evening to the Blender Café. Peering through a slat in the venetian blinds, she saw him sit down at a table where a tall dark woman was waiting for him. She gave them ten minutes before she went in.

"Why, Tom, how nice to find you here! I was about to eat my usual solitary dinner. Oh, you'd rather be alone, wouldn't you? I can take another table just as easily as not."

Tom was ill at ease, but Mrs. Downing was not disturbed. "We couldn't have you doing that, Mrs. Ashley. Sit down, please."

Her eyes implored him. "I didn't mean to run into you, dear. Really, I don't mean to inflict myself on you. Don't be angry with me."

Mrs. Downing was looking at Tom quite crossly. "Of course he won't be angry with you. What nonsense!"

"Oh, I didn't mean that. He has a marvelous disposition, really. It's just that I'm such a foolish creature that I annoy him sometimes, with my fussing and my little attentions."

"Penny, this is Mrs. Downing," Tom said. "What would you like for dinner?"

"Anything at all." She leaned over to put a solicitous hand over his. "Don't have anything to drink, dear, for my sake."

"I haven't had a drink for three months, and you know it!"

"How could I know it when I never see you?" she said reproachfully. "But if it's true I'm the happiest woman in the world. Does your husband drink, Mrs. Downing? It's an awful worry, the worst one a woman can have. I hope you've been spared it."

"I have no husband; I'm a widow."

"I'm so sorry. It's terrible to be alone, as well I know. But you have your family and friends here, haven't you, and mine are all miles away. I have only Tom."

The other two did not say much, but Penny laughed and chattered at them all through the meal. Their responses were polite and perfunctory. They seemed to be thinking of something else. She must make Mrs. Downing loosen up.

"It must be wonderful to live in a real home, a place you can fix up and fuss over, knowing that you won't have to leave it the next minute. I'm used to taking care of a house and I miss it. I tell Tom that I'll be glad when he retires so we can find a place in the country and never have to move again." She *had* said to Tom that she was tired of the constant packing, that it was hard to keep your clothes in shape when they were in a suitcase most of the time.

"Something Tom said made me think you weren't domestically inclined, Mrs. Ashley."

She smiled at him forgivingly. "Well, you know how men are. Just because a woman doesn't complain every minute they think she's satisfied with what she's doing And of course I knew what Tom's work was like before I married him. I have no right to object now."

"Most women aren't so reasonable."

"Perhaps they're more independent than I. I'm one of these silly creatures who isn't happy unless she's building her life around someone else. My sisters laugh at me. 'You should think of yourself once in a while, Penny,' they tell me. 'If you don't no one else will.' But I can't seem to help it. When Tom is contented, then I am too."

Mrs. Downing's eyes were not particularly friendly as she looked at the colonel. "There's such a thing as having too much faith in a man, showing him too much consideration."

"Oh, I know. I've spoiled him, I know it. If I could have had children—it's the greatest sorrow of my life that I've been deprived of them—I would have them to think about, I wouldn't be so lonely. Do you have children, Mrs. Downing?"

"Three. Two boys and a girl. They're almost grown up by now, at the age where all they ask of their mother is that she let them alone as much as possible."

"But you've had all the fun of watching them grow up. Tell me about them. What were they like when they were babies?"

They talked about Mrs. Downing's children, while Tom sat, red-faced and sullen, not looking at either of them. It was easier now that she had the Downing woman started. All she had to do was appear attentive and breathe, "Darling," and "Oh, cute!" in the right places.

Mrs. Downing refused a second cup of coffee. "I'm very glad to

286

have met you, Mrs. Ashley. I may say that Tom gave me quite the wrong impression of you. I'm happy that it's been corrected."

"You aren't leaving? But I'm the intruder. I'm the one who should leave."

"I think not, Mrs. Ashley. No, don't see me out, Colonel. My car's right outside."

"Then let Tom drive you home, Mrs. Downing. The hotel's only a block or so away. I can walk it easily."

Mrs. Downing smiled at her. "I wouldn't hear of it. I'm afraid we would have nothing to say to each other."

She was not out the door before Tom beckoned the waiter. "Bring me a double scotch and soda and make it quick."

She waited until he had had three before she asked him, "Can we go out for a little walk?"

"I guess so. Sure, I don't care."

Imagine! She had thought of having a baby when the whole thing could be solved as easily as this.

When they moved to Detroit he was abruptly crippled with rheumatism.

"He's going to have a long siege, Mrs. Ashley. If you could find a house where he'd be comfortable it would be better for him than the hospital. He's fretting his head off there."

She told Tom that he would have to be patient, that there weren't any houses to rent.

"Can't you find one to buy then? I'd like to get out of here."

"This is the best place for you, really. You have good care and the proper kind of food. If I could find a house I'd never be able to find anyone to do the work."

"There wouldn't be much with just the two of us, would there?"

"But if they're going to pull all your teeth you'll have to have a special diet, and until you can walk you'd have to be pushed around in a wheel chair and helped into bed and I'm just not strong enough for that kind of thing."

Nurse Cramer walked out to the main desk in the hall and slammed her charts down. "Honest to God, Sharpie, the longer I'm in this business the more I realize that it takes all kinds to make a world."

"The old glamor boy been giving you trouble again?"

"Today I'm almost sorry for him. Have you seen his wife? Paint

287

so thick you could scrape it off with a putty knife and a face as hard as nails. Well, he wants to get out of here—as who wouldn't?—and she's whining that it would be too much for her, she simply couldn't do it! If I were she I'd try to hang onto him, even if he is a broken-down old playboy. She's never going to be able to do any better."

"Good thing they're married to each other. Shame to spoil two families with them."

"You could never tell *them* that. They each have such a wonderful opinion of themselves. I'll bet he never guesses that if it weren't for his uniform nobody would give him a second look. And she still imagines she's the belle of Oakwood Ridge or wherever. Gosh, it must be nice never to have to grow up!"

Penny was glad she had procrastinated, because after they pulled his teeth he improved rapidly. In less than six months he was on his feet, and you'd never have known his teeth were false.

"Aren't you glad we didn't find a house now, Tom? It would just be something to get rid of. This way we won't have a load of stuff to move and everything will be easier."

"I'm glad because I'm going on a little trip for a few weeks."

"Where are we going?"

"Not 'we.' I'm going by myself. Florence has asked me to come down for a visit and Wally might be there on leave. The three of us will have a lot to talk over, and you wouldn't be interested."

"I suppose they'll try to get you to sign your life away for them. That's all they want, something out of you."

"They have a right to get something out of me if anyone has. I'm their father."

"And what do you expect me to do with myself while you're enjoying a nice vacation?"

"Why don't you go back to Ashland and visit your sister?"

"And be humiliated when you didn't write to me? Or forgot to send for me?" She wept. "But you don't care. You just want to get rid of me. You've never appreciated a single thing I've tried to do for you, not one. Well, let me tell you, if there's a divorce I'm the one who's going to get it, and I'm going to name your wonderful Mrs. Downing as corespondent!"

"There wasn't anything between me and Mrs. Downing, except that she was a fine woman and I admired her."

"If I hadn't stepped in and broken it up there'd have been something! We'll just see what the courts and the newspapers make of it."

He sighed. "Oh, I'm coming back, you don't have to worry. I'll spend a couple of months a year with the kids if I can. The rest of the time we'll be together. Frankly, I'm surprised that that's important to you. Since I haven't kissed you for more than two years now——"

"Oh, that's my fault too, is it? I'm supposed to encourage you to make an animal of yourself!"

"I overdid it a bit at first, but I'd have settled down. Now I don't care any more, so that part's all right."

"I'm glad to hear it. If you think you can behave like a human being I don't mind sharing a suite of rooms with you."

He looked serious and frighteningly old. "Sometime you must tell me the reason you want to stay married to me, Penny. It can't be to eat dinner with me and to talk a little. You could find other men to do that. And it can't be my money, because you're going to get one third of that whether you go or stay."

"I'll tell you the reason. I won't be ditched! I never have been and I'm not going to start now."

He smiled crookedly. "Then you'd better watch out. There may be other Mrs. Downings, you never know."

She tossed her head. There wasn't a woman in the world she'd ever been afraid of. And if Tom didn't appreciate her she could find some man who would any time she made up her mind to. She didn't have to worry about a thing.

While he was away she flew out to California. She had not been there before, and she had always been curious about it. The first hour she spent in Los Angeles she knew that she hated the place.

There were girls everywhere, young, luscious, dazzling, so beautiful that they could be indifferent to it. You saw them waiting at tables and working behind counters. Or they stepped out of cars in old slacks with rubies as big as Eleanor's fastened on a sweater. She could not take her eyes off them, and she loathed them. Silly, immature creatures, how could men possibly stand them!

In three days she was on a plane heading East. Lordy, if she'd stayed there much longer she would have had a complex! What she needed was some new clothes and a day in New York's beauty salons. That would put her right.

An attractive man was sitting across the aisle. She cleared her throat daintily, and he looked up from his magazine, looked down again.

He probably couldn't guess that a woman who looked as she did might occasionally be glad of a minute's conversation with a stranger. Perhaps she should have given him more of a hint, smiled a bit more graciously. Or maybe he was shy, a little dazzled by her beauty. Unfortunately he did not see her drop her purse. The stewardess picked it up for her.

She snapped open her compact. The lines weren't showing at all today, that new cream was a marvel. "Lovely," she whispered to her reflection. "Lovely!"

There might be an even better cream in New York.

20.

Martha ran a damp cloth over the linoleum counter top and looked out the kitchen window to see if Jay were still in his sandbox under the apple tree. Yes, there he was, shoveling sand into his wooden pail, his sturdy arms and legs going mightily, his hair, clipped as short as becomes a three-year-old, shining yellow in the afternoon sun. The baby book said that he should have playmates but neglected to give the formula for materializing playmates out of thin air. The other children in the neighborhood were too old for him.

"At first I thought they could play together anyway," she worried to Dr. O'Malley. "Well, they can't, and do you know why? It's because all older children are dead set on killing younger ones. They hit them with sticks and push them down and try to walk on their faces. And that's not bad older children, that's *any* older children. The six-year-olds push the five-year-olds off the swings and the four-year-olds kick the three-year-olds in the shins and the three-year-olds throw things at the heads of the two-year-olds. It's an infallible practice. Where did the idea come from that children are tender, gentle little souls? They're unprincipled little savages, the lot of them!"

"Nobody will push Jay around much longer. He's the biggest, healthiest boy for his age I've ever seen. You've done a fine job, Martha."

"It ought to be a good job. It's taken every minute of my time for three years, and the first year and a half of that I thought I'd lose my mind trying to keep up with the schedules in that book you gave me. Jay, don't ride that tricycle so fast, honey, you'll break your neck!"

"He's almost past the schedule stage. He'll be turning into a human being any time now."

"I'm going to say something that will shock you."

"I doubt it."

"I don't think there's any such thing as a maternal instinct. It's an idea men invented for women to save themselves trouble."

"Then why is it you won't let anyone else take care of Jay? You could find somebody if you tried, you know."

"For the same reason I wouldn't let anyone write my books for me. If my name's going to be on a thing I want to have done it myself so I'm sure I won't be misrepresented. Honestly, now, can you name me one person who *likes* taking care of children?"

"I've heard a good many women of fifty say that they'd like to live those years over again."

"But they've forgotten how it was—the bedlam, the anxiety, the upside-downness, the squalling, the coaxing, the terrible responsibility of having something helpless absolutely dependent on you. You've never taken care of a youngster for a whole day and tried to get some housework done besides, have you? Well, try it sometime."

"How about the women who have three and four and five children? How do they get along?"

"If they can keep that many clean and well fed and clothed and emotionally stable and happy they're the heroines of the world. They're the girls I take my hat off to. I'm in favor of having a medal struck off for them and awarded by Congress. Only I don't think there are many of them. In the large families I've seen the kids grow up any old way."

He laughed. "There are some women who seem to cope however."

"I wouldn't be one of them. I'd lose my sanity." ·

"You only think that. A woman who can bring up one child well would do just as good a job on two or three. Oh, they wouldn't know all that Jay does at his age—nursery rhymes, the alphabet, colors. But they'd be good kids nevertheless."

"Maybe. But I wouldn't like it while I was doing it. What's more,

I don't believe any woman likes it, except in retrospect. Only I'm frank about it, and they're not."

"As long as you do it——"

"It doesn't matter whether I like it or not. You're right there. Only I don't want anybody to butter me up with a maternal instinct and make me pretend I'm having a pink tea party."

Bill thought Jay was the wonder child of the century. "Look at the way he pounds those pegs! There's muscular co-ordination for you. And smart? Sometimes I worry about him. Is there such a thing as a mind developing too fast?"

She liked to hear him talk like that. But what she waited for him to say and what he never did say was, "I know you've arranged your whole life around Jay and me and you've given up a lot to do it. But he'll be in school pretty soon, and you'll have more time for yourself, and he'll be worth more than anything you've missed, you'll see." He took it for granted that she was a completely happy, completely fulfilled woman.

In her exhausted evenings she occasionally found time to write in her journal.

My life changed completely with Jay's coming, but Bill's is just the same. He did not have to make a single adjustment, other than to be willing to hear a baby cry once in a while without grumbling. I've worked at a profession, I put in my eight or ten hours a day, and I know what I'm talking about when I say that no outside employment is half as hard as taking care of a child. Why don't mothers say this? Why must they pretend that their day is one long sweet song and it's poor Daddy, coming home from eight hours at a desk, who should have the best chair and quiet in the evenings? There have been many days when Daddy nearly came home to find me flat on my face on the living-room rug!

I can't think what I used to do with my time. I must have had so much of it. When I look at the book shelf and see *Positive Answer* by Martha King Knight, I feel that it must have been written by a stranger. Certainly this woman, dumpy now that her waistline has expanded, who travels to market looking any old way, clutching a prancing youngster by the hand, who falls asleep at nine every evening, who reads only Mother Goose and the alphabet books, who runs to a window every ten minutes to see what a child may be doing outside, who ponders toys and elastic waistbands and proper sleeping garments, this woman could not have written a book that had excellent critical reviews from coast to coast and was translated into foreign languages besides.

She had not realized that the other women in Orchardia—Ellen Plover excepted—had regarded her with wary aloofness and polite restraint until, with Jay's arrival, they had become so much more friendly, so completely at ease with her. In the old days they had appeared at her door in carefully correct clothes at a regulation calling hour, pushing the bell briefly, looking away from the door until she answered.

"If we're disturbing you we'll run right along," they had said. And "Since we didn't hear the typewriter we thought we'd take a chance on coming in and trying to talk you into our Red Cross circle."

Now they walked in at any hour, looking any old way, calling directions to their children to play in the sand pile and to let Jay's tricycle alone.

"Say, they have lamb chops in the store today. Want me to pick up a couple for you?"

"Lamb chops! I'll come right along with you!"

Often she slipped a couple of extra potatoes into the oven before she left.

"Janie might as well stay and have lunch with Jay. No use wasting the oven with one potato. I have frozen peas for a vegetable and we can slip the chops in to broil when we get back."

"Now listen! We didn't come here to get a free lunch."

"It won't be free. I'll use one of your own chops for Janie. My red points have a bad way of expiring two weeks early. And while I'm looking after them you can make us some sandwiches. You don't know how nice it is to see a human, adult face in the middle of the day!"

She meant that, and they knew she did. They had felt the same way themselves. Taking care of children was a lonesome business. It was a godsend to find someone else who could share it with you. And "share" was the right word. The hostess-guest relationship was entirely suspended. While Martha arranged the children's plates, tied on bibs, and shoved the little chairs in closer to Jay's small table, the visiting woman would have located the coffeepot, invented a sandwich filling, and set the big table with a minimum of china and silver.

"We won't need knives. No use putting them on when we'd just have to wash 'em up afterward. I used the cream out of the front bottle. Was that all right?"

They came to be at home in her kitchen and she in theirs.

There was never much time for talking. The children needed too much attention. The mothers jumped up to retrieve dropped spoons, to wipe chins, to mop at spilled milk. If they had not had a hard-acquired adeptness at returning to an unfinished sentence and completing it, if they had not developed a conversational shorthand, they could not have talked to each other at all.

"Jackie Ziegler had a runny nose this morning. Esther's keeping him in bed. There's a lot of measles around."

"If he comes down with them, what'll she do about the baby?"

"Take him to get shots. Her mother'll have to come up and help out, I guess."

And from that you knew that Esther was having a worrisome time, that you had better keep Jay strictly at home until the measles scare was over, that Bill could run over to Zieglers' with a custard that evening—he'd had the measles, he couldn't bring them home—and that you'd watch for their upstairs lights across the orchard that night. If they stayed out all was well; if they stayed on you'd better call up in the morning to see how sick Jackie was and whether there was anything you could do for Esther at a distance.

Bill was happy that she liked the "girls."

"Even though I'm not away as much as I used to be," he said, "I'm away enough to worry about your being lonesome."

She had almost laughed at that. He had forgotten how well equipped she was to cope with loneliness. He didn't guess that her fingers itched for the feel of typewriter keys. Lonely indeed! She knew women who stood on the porch and cried the first day they waved their children off to school. Devoted to Jay as she was, she knew that she would be smiling as she watched him down the street on that far-off day, that she would rush back into the house—such a beautifully quiet house—and hunt through the desk for her notebooks in a tremble of joy at being left to her own devices again.

She said none of this. She was too tired. Sometimes it seemed to her that she would never be rested again, that the morning would never arrive when Jay would not wake her at six-thirty, nor the night when she could sleep, really sleep, without keeping an ear bent toward the nursery. Other women said that such a day would come. Right now she didn't believe them!

Bill saw her watching for him from the window as he came up the drive, and he didn't wait to put the car into the garage.

"What's the matter, Martha? What's happened?"

She could scarcely hold up her head. "I thought you'd never get here. I've caught something and I don't want Jay to get it."

"Why didn't you call me at the office? I'd have come home on the run. Here. Let's get you to bed."

"You'll have to get Jay to bed and find yourself something to eat. Maybe Dr. O'Malley will let you borrow Mrs. Martin if you need help."

"I'll get along. Here. Put on this flannel thing."

She crept into bed and dozed almost immediately. Far away she could hear Jay's voice and his splashings in the tub. There was the clink of china in a distant dishpan. People were tiptoeing in and out of the room. Something small and cool was thrust into her mouth. She opened her eyes. It was a thermometer and Dr. O'Malley and Bill were standing there.

"Strep throat, Martha. You'll have to stay in bed a week."

That made her laugh. "Don't be foolish. I can't possibly stay in bed a week."

"You have to. Mrs. Martin will look after things in the daytime and Bill can take over when he comes home from work."

She looked up at her husband's solicitous face. "Brother, what you have coming to you!" she murmured, and was asleep again.

Long after the doctor had left, Bill sat in a chair by the bed and watched her. Lord, she had a beautiful face! Pale and feverish as she was, the bones articulated the sweet lines more plainly than ever. And funny how such a little, round body could carry so sharp and indomitable a spirit. She'd be better in the morning, poor darling. Good Lord, it took a thing like this to make a fellow realize that she was the very rooftree of the place. Nothing was any good without her.

She stirred and he bent forward. "What do you want, sweet? Can I get you something?"

"Orange juice. The oranges are on the bottom shelf of the refrigerator and you'd better squeeze them by hand because you don't know how to put the juicer together and anyway the noise might wake Jay. There's a bowl——"

"Don't worry about it. I guess I can squeeze a few oranges all by myself."

"And turn on a light, please."

He pulled the chain of the lamp beside her bed. "Sure that won't get in your eyes?"

He was horrified to see her reach for a book on the table. "You can't read, Martha. You're sick!"

"I've been wanting to get at this for two weeks. I'll never have a better chance than now."

But she did not open it. She lay back and fell asleep again with it in her hand.

He went down to the kitchen soberly. He didn't like the way she had reached for that book. With a temperature of a hundred and four, she shouldn't be thinking about reading. It was almost as if she had said, "When I'm well I can't do what I want to, but now that I'm ill I don't have to do those things, I can do what I want."

Frowningly he found the oranges. Maybe Martha wasn't as happy as he was. True, she'd been accustomed to a life of peace and books and hours to herself. But she'd swapped that for a home and youngster and a husband who thought there was no one in the world like her.

It must be the writing that she missed, though she never said so and there was no reason why she shouldn't talk about it. He thought it was perfectly swell that she could write, even though he didn't always approve of the things she had written. She must know that he was proud of her for it. Pretty soon now, with Jay growing older, she'd be able to get back to it again. As far as that went she could get back to it now, evenings when she wasn't too tired.

She'd changed a lot in the past three years, now that he came to think of it. She'd been so honest, so outspoken, so animated when they were first married. She kept more to herself these days; it was hard to tell what she was thinking.

He went up the stairs carefully, so that the orange juice would not spill. The light was still on in her room and she was sitting up in bed. The look on her face made him reel back a step. She looked young and flushed and jubilant and alive. There was a tremulous rapture in her voice. "Grandmother?" she said, testing the glorious illusion. "Grandmother?"

"It's Bill, darling. Lie down and let me cover you."

She lay back obediently, and the look vanished. In its place was only pale patience and subtle bereavement.

He sat in the chair beside her until after midnight, remembering her face as he had seen it when he came in. That was the way she had looked in the old days, so vigorously alert, so vividly seeking. The transformation must have taken place right under his nose, and he had not noticed it until now. That was the way she had looked when she was happy and in love with him. Was she no longer happy or in love? Was it possible that her dead grandmother meant more to her than a living husband?

Watching her when she was back on her feet again, he was relieved to find that he had been wrong. She ate well and played with Jay and laughed. He must have been hysterical to imagine that she was wretched and concealing it. She was happy and contented, and he could stop worrying about her.

"How did you like looking after Jay?" she asked him.

"Well, he wasn't used to me and I didn't know how to do things for him. He gave me a pitched battle every step of the way. Couldn't even get a look at the evening paper until he was in bed. Shouldn't he be learning to let us alone more, when he sees we're sitting down or reading or busy?"

She laughed until tears came into her eyes. "That's the golden goal, all right. He's a little young for it yet."

"And even when he is playing by himself you don't dare take your eyes off him. You never know when he's going to take a notion to start climbing a tree or weeding up all the flowers in the borders. I was doing dishes one night and he came in with a delphinium in his hand. 'I was weeding, Daddy,' he said."

"And what did you do?"

"You can't punish a kid for trying to help. I had to take time to go outside with him and try to explain about weeds and flowers being different. That was an awful job, so we finally decided that until he knew the difference he'd let the dug-up places alone. By that time he had to have his bath and go to bed, so I was still washing dishes at ten o'clock!"

"I'm sorry to laugh so hard. It's the look on your face that does it. That gentle, injured surprise. I've felt that way so many times myself."

"It was one thing or another the whole damned time! I suppose mothers don't mind, but it sure had me running around in circles."

"Oh, I mind, all right. It's just that I'm used to it. I know what to expect. Still, he's a sweet child, isn't he, in spots?"

"None better!" he said stoutly.

She liked him for that. In the growing strength of their common bond she had only one reticence with him. Once, late at night, he came upon her writing in an old, bulky book.

"What are you doing? Starting a new opus?"

She shoved the book hastily into a drawer. "Oh no. I was checking my laundry list. No, I'm not doing anything."

Mr. Wayne, of the New York publishing firm of Wayne and Wister, arrived at the front door on a gentle September evening. Bill was obscurely embarrassed at having to say that Martha was just finishing up the dinner dishes.

"Figured he might be annoyed to find that I was keeping one of his writers in bondage," he said to Martha in the kitchen. "Go in and talk to him. I'll lurk."

She went in, wiping her hands on her apron. "I thought you were just a voice on the telephone," she said.

"It's an honor to meet you, Mrs. Knight. I've looked forward to it more than I can say."

"Can we give you a drink? Bill——"

"Really, I haven't time. My train leaves Laketown in less than an hour and I had to pay a fortune to bribe a cab to bring me out here and wait for me. I came to talk to you. Juggled trains all over the map to get here. Since you won't come to New York and since your answers to our letters haven't been satisfactory to us——"

"Come on into the study. Bill wants to get back to his catalogue and he'd be bored with our shoptalk anyway."

She smiled apologetically as she closed the study door. "Bill doesn't know about my having been asked to New York or all the rest of it. I knew I couldn't come because of Jay and there was no use talking about it."

"When are we to have your next book? That's the question I was sent to ask you." He was a tall, rangy man with white hair and quick dark eyes.

"I don't know. I have no time now. I told you that."

"It seems to us that you have no right to say that, you must make time. After all you are one of the most promising American essayists. You're represented in some of the new textbooks. You have a duty to the reading public."

"That's very nice to hear. I also have a duty to my family."

298

He offered her a cigarette. "It just isn't possible that you haven't written a line for three years!"

"Truly, though, I haven't. I'm lucky to find a chance to scribble in my journal now and then."

"Journal?"

"Here. It's in this drawer. It won't do you any good, but you can look at it if you want to. Scribbled opinions, eighteen years' worth, that's all it is. Formless, shapeless, not worked over."

He leafed through it, pausing now and again to read a page. "May I take this with me and give it a good reading?"

"Take it, by all means. You'll send it back soon enough."

He was careful to put it inside his brief case before they went out to talk generalities with Bill, and she was pleased by his perception. Mr. Wayne was a very clever man.

She was playing with Jay on the lawn on a blue October afternoon when Mr. Wayne came back. This time he dismissed his taxi and came purposefully crunching up the drive.

"Hello," she called. "We're over here. Did you have a good trip?"

He had no time for amenities. "We want to publish your journal, Mrs. Knight. I've made bold to bring the contract with me so we can get everything settled right away."

"Sit down. I'll go make us some lemonade."

"Lemonade for me too, Mama!"

"Lemonade for you too. Excuse me, Mr. Wayne."

By the time she came back she saw that he was aware of her opposition.

"Why don't you want us to have it? It's a good book, even a great book, maybe. Certainly just the book for times like these. It's clear and sane and concise and intelligent."

"And personal—very, very personal. Anyone who read it would know every least thing I'd ever thought or felt."

"That's what makes it exciting. You're original, clever, breath-taking sometimes. Why should you object to people seeing that you are?"

"Whatever I am, I'd rather keep it to myself for a while. I have two sisters and a husband to consider too. I've written too frankly about them for public consumption."

"You let me take the manuscript with me," he reminded her.

"Only to keep you quiet." She smiled at him. "Honestly I didn't

299

believe that you'd want it. After I'm dead you may have it if you still care to."

"Suppose we published it under a nom de plume, would you allow it then? Or we could fictionalize the title. Make it *The Life and Times of Jane Doe* by Martha King Knight. That might be better, because your name to a book means something."

"I'm hungry, Mama."

"Of course, it's suppertime. Bill's out of town, Mr. Wayne, and we're both having fruit and cereal and milk. Nursery diet. Join us and I'll concede some coffee."

For the next two hours she was safe from importunity behind the rampart of Jay's needs and wants. She was tempted to say that the book could be printed. Some of it wasn't so bad, though she wasn't sure, it had been a long time since she had read it all. Perhaps if she deleted some of the more personal passages it might be possible.

By ten o'clock she had made up her mind. "All right," she said. "We'll do it. Leave the thing here with me to put into shape and I'll see that you get it back soon."

He didn't want to part with it. "You'll cut its heart out, that's what you want to do! We'd better go over the cuts together."

"I promise not to. I won't hurt it, you'll see."

"And what'll we call it?"

"Why, *The Life and Times of Jane Doe* by Martha King Knight," she said, reaching for it.

It was exciting to have a book on the market again. It was fun to read the reviews that the clipping bureau sent in.

Surprisingly the book sold very well. It wasn't on the best-seller lists, but it came close. The size of the royalty checks astounded her.

Bill whistled. "This one's for three thousand dollars! Are you sure they haven't made a mistake? If this keeps up I'll be able to retire. What are you going to do with it all?"

"Put it in our bank account. Build us a new house after the war, maybe, or save it for Jay's education. Whatever you want."

He ruffled her hair. "Innocent little angel face, wasn't writing a thing, was she?"

"I'm glad you don't mind."

"Mind? Why on earth should I? Everybody says it's a knockout." He looked down at the check. "Though if many of these come in I might begin to wonder what you need me around for."

She pulled his arms around her for the first time in years, of her own initiative. "I'm so happy. So awfully happy!"

He said slowly, "I believe you've held it against me all this time, the way I shot off my mouth about that essay on women. You don't forgive easily, do you, Martha?"

"Whatever was wrong, it's all right now. Oh, I've missed you so!"

"Great Caesar, how could you have? I was only away for three days this time."

Mr. Brockway, scenario writer for United Studios, was calling. Mr. Brockway evidently neither knew nor cared that, whatever time it was in Hollywood, it was midnight in Laketown's suburbs.

"Mrs. Knight?" he bellowed. "Mrs. Martha King Knight?"

She pulled her robe tighter around her. They had shut the furnace down to sixty degrees and the room was cold.

"This is Steve Brockway in Hollywood. You may have heard of me. I wrote the scripts for *No More Laughter* and *Ebony Is the Night.*"

"Are you the Steve Brockway I've read about in *Time?*"

"That's me. Now listen. Before I became a screen hack I wrote plays. *Rain Comes Early*, remember that one? That was mine. And *The Other Mrs. Carey.* Ran a year and a half."

"That's very interesting, Mr. Brockway, but——"

"I'm not telling my life story. What I want to tell you is that there's a play in that *Jane Doe* thing of yours, and I want to write it."

"Go right ahead. Get in touch with my publishers for the rights to it." She was shivering with cold and excitement. *Jane Doe* might make a good play, she ought to have seen that for herself. The theater. Lights, grease paint, properties, lines. Right back where she had started.

"I need more than the rights. I'd like you to collaborate with me. Know anything about the drama?"

"Yes."

"Like to do it?"

"Yes, but——"

"Listen, you write me a letter and tell me when you can come out here. It'll only take us a couple of months to do it."

There was the catch. For a minute she debated hauling Jay out to the coast, finding a woman with whom she could leave him, rearranging his whole pleasant little life, risking germs and poor care and

301

strange food. And Bill would be miserable too, though these days he'd tell her to go ahead and not worry. She could picture him standing in the station, forcing a smile as her train pulled out, living at a hotel, wandering around like a lost pup. She could hear Jay's piping voice. "Where's Daddy, Mama? Where's my own tricycle? I don't like Mrs. Whosiz, Mama. I want to go home. Can't we go home?"

She grabbed a straw. "Can't you come out here? I think I might arrange to work with you for a few months if you could stay here. It wouldn't be easy; there's no help anywhere, and I have a youngster to look after."

He was indignant. "I can't come there. For one thing, I'm under contract."

"So am I, Mr. Brockway. I can't get away." A marriage license is a contract. So is a birth certificate.

He said, "Ridiculous!" He said, "As much as twenty-five grand, if we're lucky." He said, "Other women do it all the time."

"Then they are cleverer or more unfeeling than I. Perhaps in a year or two . . ."

Her feet were like ice when she went back to bed.

"Who was that?" Bill asked, half opening his eyes.

"The lady in the new house across the field. Thought she'd seen a burglar sneaking around. I told her where to reach the sheriff, and she's settling down."

"Trust a woman to get all excited about nothing at an inconvenient hour of the night!"

She turned out the light and stretched her cold feet against his warm ones. "Yes indeed," she said.

Bill always picked up their mail at the little post office a mile away. The evening of April second he came in and tossed a wide envelope on the dinner table.

"One for you from the old Alma Mater," he said. "Maybe they want you to come back for a class reunion."

She turned the envelope in her hands, smiling at the familiar seal. "I'd give a thousand dollars to go back for a day, wouldn't you? Do you know how long it's been since I was graduated? Seventeen years. It doesn't seem possible!"

"That's what you get for being a child prodigy. If you said that to anyone else they could figure out that you're five years older than you are. Now I was a good, solid twenty-four when I took my sheep-skin in hand, and——"

"Bill, look!"

"Don't tell me the new stadium has caved in!"

"No. They're offering me an honorary Doctor's degree! They want me to come down for Commencement in June."

"Doctor's degree!" He took the letter and read it. "'For literary achievement and integrity.' Well!"

"Mama, I want to go to the bathroom."

"Don't bother Mama right now, son. She's just been crowned queen of the May. I'll take you upstairs."

"No, Mama!"

"All right, honey. Come along."

By the time she came downstairs she had it all planned. "It's only three hundred miles. I could take a plane down in the morning and fly back at night. We could get Mrs. Martin to look after Jay, and you might try to get home from the office a little early."

"What in the world are you talking about? Jay and I are coming along with you. And let's ask your two sisters if they wouldn't like to come up for it."

"Or if they didn't we could stop off in Ashland on the way home to see them. No, we couldn't, we wouldn't be driving and there wouldn't be a plane to Ashland."

"Well, if we have to fly straight back we'll have a little party here in the evening. This is an occasion!" An awkward thought struck him. "Will people be supposed to call you 'Doctor' after that?"

"They can if they want to. Chances are I'd still be 'Mrs. Knight,' though. That's all right with me. Oh, Bill, I haven't seen the school in years! Do you think Keenan will still be there? And Rowell? And the theater?"

"Lord, Rowell must be dead by now. And I read in the papers a few years back that they built a new theater. It's in a building all by itself, very swank. Not the old rough-and-tumble wooden place we worked in."

"Seven years ago I went down there to see about some graduate work, just before I married you, you know. It looked a lot the same."

"Well, don't worry about getting there. I'll make all the arrangements."

"You're being wonderful about this," she said shyly.

303

"Oh, I'm not such a bad gent. I enjoy seeing you get the rewards for your work." He laughed wryly. "I resent only the time you have to spend on the work that gets you the rewards."

"Read your paper out on the lawn so you can keep an eye on Jay, will you? Dr. Knight is going to do the dishes."

She rinsed the plates dreamily, watching the red sunset through the window above the sink. In her mind's eye she saw another sunset, flaring over scholastic buildings, tinting the trees along the campus walks. The university was still there, really there, and it had reached out a long arm to tap one of its daughters on the shoulder. "Come back and let us tell you that you have done well," it said. "In those hoarded hours over a littered desk, in those scrambling moments that make up your day, you were not alone, for we were watching you. We have seen your work and we have found it good."

It was Grandmother who really deserved the degree. It was she who had paid for the schooling, who had encouraged and waited, who had made herself lonely for Martha's sake. Maybe, thought Martha, maybe it's always the wrong person who gets the degree. I wish she could be here to see it, she would be so happy for me. And Dad. The only two people in my life who have loved me deeply and unselfishly. Now I have Bill and Jay, and they love me too, but I am not free as I used to be in the old days. When I am old and alone, perhaps I shall be free again, not before.

She brought her thoughts up sharply. The worst sin in the world, the worst crime you could commit against yourself, was to wish time away. She had almost been guilty of it.

The telephone rang. It was Mr. Wayne calling from New York.

"Just wanted you to know we've issued the new edition," he said. "I'm sending you a few copies. We've changed the format, and I think you'll like it."

"My school is giving me an honorary degree this June. I just had the letter today." She could not help telling him. She would have had to tell anyone who had called just then.

"Congratulations. Though why they're giving a degree to a woman who's done only a tenth of the work she might have done is a mystery to me."

"You're so impatient. I'll do more. Later."

"Your most productive years should be now. Do you think you're going to live forever?"

"Don't be a carrion crow. Thirty-six is no great age."

"Thirty-seven next month, isn't it?"

"That's what I meant by hesitating about the journal. I haven't a secret in the world!"

"They can always look you up in Who's Who too, don't forget. Anyway, I think it's swell. Been writing anything lately?"

"There's a good nursery school near here now. If I send Jay there in the mornings, starting in September, I ought to be able to get going again."

She sat down at the desk to write to Eleanor and Penny. Let's see. Penny's new last name was Ashley and she was in Chicago now. Where was the paper with the address on it? And, by June, wouldn't Eleanor and John be down at the summer place? Well, she'd write and tell them anyway.

Pen poised in air, she caught sight of herself in the mirror above the fireplace. She'd have to get a new permanent the end of May. And you couldn't get up on a graduation platform in play shoes! Was there another ration stamp? A new dark sheer, that's what she'd buy for a dress, and this time she'd go downtown and try it on. There were some things a shopping service couldn't do for you. She hadn't been downtown in Laketown for two years, hadn't found time for it; good thing the war was an excuse for looking shabby. She must spend more time on her appearance from now on. Almost she could hear Mr. Wayne's dry voice: "The time that she does get to write she spends shopping." Well, a woman couldn't go around indefinitely looking like a scarecrow. If someone would invent a good forty-eight-hour day she might be able to get around to everything.

Howls and shrieks ripped the quiet of the house. Bill came in carrying Jay.

"He fell down on the drive and skinned his knee. Come and keep him quiet while I get a bandage on it."

They sat him up on the kitchen counter, and Martha stilled his sobs by pretending to be a tractor.

"Look, Jay. There's a plow I'm dragging behind me. Here I go." She coughed like a motor, made the motions of steering. "Oh, I'm an awfully big tractor and I'm painted red. First-aid kit's in the lower cupboard. Dat-dat-dat-dat. Watch me go!"

He smiled tremulously, tears glinting on his lashes. He concentrated on the tractor, his mouth a little open with absorption. Bill washed his knee, sterilized it, made a light bandage.

"Now then, darling, Mother'll carry you upstairs and we'll have a nice splashy bath, and——"

"Will you be a motorboat, Mama?"

"I'll be the fastest motorboat in the world!"

She kissed the curve of his neck, hugging him, feeling the soft arms on her shoulders and the sturdy legs that gripped her waist. "Angel baby," she crooned to him.

So completely had she forgotten the letter from the university that she was agreeably surprised to come upon it the next morning at six-thirty when she set the table for breakfast.

Three other people were being granted honorary degrees at the same time as she. The dean introduced them to each other in the president's office. There was a Mr. Kniffel, who had performed great engineering feats in certain war projects; Mr. Langston, the new superintendent of schools in Philadelphia; and Gretchen Breckner, a physicist.

"Here are your gowns," said the dean. "You'll walk at the head of the procession, immediately behind the faculty. When we reach the platform, follow us up. Your chairs are the four at the right side of the first row. When your names are called out you will stand and listen while the citation is read. Then you will come forward and stand by the president while your hood is slipped over your head. He will hand you the diploma and shake hands with you. You may then return to your chairs. Are there any questions? Then I'll come back for you when it's time to get in line."

Gretchen Breckner was a tall slender woman with graying hair and a warming smile.

"I didn't get your name," she said to Martha. "Knight, was it? Miss Knight?"

"Mrs. Knight."

"And literature's your field? What have you written? Oh, how stupid of me! Of course, you're *the* Martha King Knight and I've read your *Jane Doe*. I liked it very much."

"Thank you. And you're a physicist. I don't quite know what your work is."

"Laboratory. Experimental. It's fascinating work."

306

"It must be. How do you manage to combine your family and a full-time job?"

"I have no family. I'm not married. You must be one of those brave women who try to get something done with a horde of babies around your knees."

"Only one baby. And I don't get much done."

"The wonder of it is that you get anything done. Now I live at a women's club where the maid service and the food are good. I wouldn't know how to cook as much as a string bean. Fine wife I'd make."

"Keeping house isn't a God-given talent, I've found. I had to learn it, and I'm still not too good. I may say that I have no natural predilection for it."

"I thought that women—all but myself—could do those things as easily as breathing." She gathered her black folds around her and sat down. "What would be your answer to this? Here's a man and a woman, neither of whom have ever washed a dish or cooked a meal. Which one would learn to do it the more easily?"

"If they had the same intelligence they'd learn at exactly the same pace."

"Do you think that, really? Then the reason that most women do learn it is——"

"Because they have to, and men don't."

Miss Breckner laughed. "Then I'm going to stop feeling apologetic about my domestic shortcomings. I don't have to learn either."

"If you did it would take you about three years to get good at it. After that—well, you don't mind it so much any more. Parts of it are fun."

Miss Breckner said softly, "You're a happy woman, aren't you?"

She thought about it. "Yes, I am, I guess. If there weren't so many things I'd like to read and if the sight of my idle typewriter didn't nag at me I'd be completely happy. I console myself by thinking that I can get back to that later on."

"At least you're not lonely. You don't have to wonder what to do with yourself after seven-thirty at night."

They smiled at each other. Martha said, "That's the choice, isn't it? Work and loneliness or a family and no work. Only a man can have a family and a satisfactory career together."

"I know, and I find that depressing. For a long time I actively re-

307

sented it. As I grew older I calmed down and accepted it. But I'm keeping an eye on Russia to see what happens when men and women are put on the same basis."

"Russia isn't going to change biology."

"There are things that can be done to spring the biological trap. A great deal has happened in the last forty years. In the old days a woman had but one choice—to marry or not to marry—and that wasn't much of a choice because all the social pressure was for her getting married. Nowadays, thanks to medicine, she has a further choice—to have children or not to have them. And I think that, shortly, education supplied by the state will give her a third choice—whether she wants to look after her children herself or send them to an accredited nursery school at an early age. Oh, I know there are nursery schools now, but most of them are handled by people who haven't been prepared for such work, and the good ones are frightfully expensive. You wouldn't mind turning your child over to the care of someone who knew exactly what to do for him and was paid for doing it well, would you?"

"Theoretically, no. Actually——"

"It's not fair asking you that, because you're one of the women who has a right to feel that you could do as well by him as the very best school. But how many other women are there like that?"

"Thank you."

"But let's grant the nursery schools, and let's say that a mother's working-outside hours be short enough so that she could be home every minute her children are. That's not so unreasonable, is it?"

"No, that seems fair enough. And you'd have a community laundry and a trained housekeeping guild? Yes. Well, there's only one catch to it. Women wouldn't like it."

"Why not?"

"Because the way it is, a woman is her own boss. She can do her housework or not, as she prefers, and she can look after her children or turn them loose. She isn't obligated to anything but her own conscience and her husband's temper."

"She could be educated out of that attitude. If she were trained along some line or other, mathematics or nursery keeping or medicine, or ironing, according to her tastes and abilities——"

The dean came back before they were half through talking. Martha felt as though she had known Miss Breckner for years, that they had been hatched out of the same egg. It was hard to believe that such a brilliantly able woman should have to confess to being lonely. Martha smiled to herself. If Miss Breckner could take Martha's place for one week it might make solitude look more admirable when she got back to it.

Again the black line curved down the walk, again the stadium rose as the first bright faculty hood appeared. This time, though, she sat facing the crowd, trying to pick out Bill and Jay, or Eleanor or Penny, but they were lost in the rustling sea. To her horror she realized that she had forgotten to take off her reading glasses. Well, she had no place to put them now. She would have to leave them on. The president began to speak.

Penny pressed the colonel's arm. "That's Martha. The one on the end."

"She certainly doesn't look much like you. Younger, though, isn't she?"

"Heavens no! She's ages older."

"She doesn't look it. No lines or wrinkles. Still, it's hard to tell from this distance." He had lost interest in the proceedings. His eyes searched the crowd. Say, there was a pretty girl, the one over there in blue. She'd caught sight of him too, and was admiring his uniform. He sat up straighter, pulled his stomach tighter.

Penny saw the girl in blue too, and tried to recapture his attention. "I can't get over it, Tom, your thinking that I look older than Martha. In the first place she doesn't have a figure. Never did have. And she's never cared a nickel how she looked, never fussed over herself for a minute."

"That's something nobody could say about you."

"Well, I do try to take care of myself."

The girl in blue had turned her back, and Penny relaxed. It was nice to see Martha again after all these years. They'd stop by at the platform for a minute afterward and say hello. Then Tom could see that Martha wasn't anything to write home about. They'd meet John and Eleanor there, no doubt, and that would be even nicer. Tom was impressed by John and Eleanor; he'd be pleasant while they were around.

Good heavens, what long-winded speeches! Was it possible that Martha was enjoying them? She decided magnanimously that she hoped Martha was. Looking as dowdy as she did, the poor girl ought to be able to console herself with *something!*

Eleanor said to John, "There she is. Oh, poor dear, she looks so tired! Next year I'm going to *make* her come down to the Gables. She always says she can't get away."

"Well, I suppose she's got to look after her youngster. You have to be lucky to get a good nurse these days."

"I don't think she'd have a nurse even if she could find one."

"Oh, I know Martha! She's always thought that nobody could do things as well as she could. Stubborn as a mule, always was. I've never been able to figure out why Bill married her. I thought he was a good guy, the one time I met him."

"I think they get along very well together. I just wish she hadn't had to work so hard all her life."

"She can quit any time. Her books are all very fine, if you can understand 'em, but she doesn't have to write. She has a husband that's well able to support her. I have no sympathy for her. If she wanted to she could be as happy as you've always been." He missed the quick look she gave him. His eyes were on his watch.

"How long do you think this business is going to take?"

"Martha King Knight," called the president.

She stood up, catching the echo of his words across the field.

"For having created for herself a position in the field of the American essay, for——"

Heavens, could she have left one of the burners of the electric stove on? She tried to think. They had caught the seven o'clock plane and there had been a mad rush to get out of the house, and Jay had had to go to the bathroom at the very last minute. Well, Mrs. Martin would be in and out, and she'd take care of it. And the Laketown Dairy had promised to deliver the ice cream, and she'd look after that too.

If they got back home at eight she'd snap the oven on to let the beans finish baking while she got Jay to bed. Then all she'd have to do was make the salad—God send that the lettuce would not be rusty, you got such bad lettuce these days—and set the table while Bill made cocktails. How many people had he asked? He said ten or twelve, but

310

the chances were there'd be twice that many. She'd better fill both coffeepots. . . .

What silly, boring, necessary details was housework made of! She marveled at women who could interest themselves in it beyond the line of functional necessity.

". . . our honor and privilege to award her efforts the degree of Doctor of Philosophy."

She walked forward and stood, feeling the satin hood slide over her shoulders, hearing the applause ripple up to her.

As always, the minute she let her mind slip the leash of duty her home vanished, and her husband and son with it. She was Martha King again, scholar and essayist, and all she needed for absolute happiness was a desk and typewriter in an empty room and a large library across the way. The inward fretting for it grew stronger every day. Too many more years of her present routine and all her brain children would be dead of malnutrition! She must, she would, find a way to save them.

She was shaking hands with the president.

"Thank you," she said. "I'll try to show you that I've deserved this."

For a moment she smiled into the sun, blinking like a small, round, downy owl. Those people out there, they'd hear from her again somehow, that was a promise. As she went back and sat down her mind was spinning out the opening sentences she would put on paper tomorrow if she had to stay up until three o'clock to do it!